Chickamauga

A Novel of the American Civil War

By

Blair Howard

Chickamauga
A Novel of the American Civil War
By
Blair Howard

Copyright © 2014 Blair Howard

ISBN-13: 978-1500715823

The Cast:

Fictional Character:

Blake Winter: Lieutenant Colonel - Union

Gene Marshall: Union Doctor, Colonel - Union

Jesse Dixon: Sargent -.Union

Patrick McCann: Private - Union

Billy Cobb: Private, Confederate

Jimmy Morrisey: Private - Confederate

George Bradley: Southern farmer

Sarah Bradley: his daughter

Tom Bradley: his son

Corporal Isaac Williams, alias Captain Isaac Williams - Confederate

Non Fiction Characters:

Eliza Glenn - Widow

The Union Army of the Cumberland

William Rosecrans - Major General Commanding

XIV Corps

George H. Thomas - Major General Commanding

Absalom Baird - Brigadier General: First Division

James S. Negley - Major General: Second Division

John M. Brannan - Brigadier General : Third Division

    Colonel John M. Connell: 1st Brigade

    Colonel John T. Croxton: 2nd Brigade

        Sargent Jesse Dixon - 10th Indiana

        Private Patrick McCann - 10th Indiana

    Colonel Ferdinand Van Derveer: 3rd Brigade

Joseph J. Reynolds - Major General: Fourth Division

    Colonel John T. Wilder: 1st Brigade, Mounted

        Lt. Colonel Blake Winter

Artillery:

Captain Eli Lilly: 18th Battery, Indiana Light Artillery

XX Corps
Alexander McDowell McCook - Major General Commanding
Jefferson C. Davis - Brigadier General: 1st Division
Richard W. Johnson - Brigadier General: 2nd Division
Philip Sheridan - Major General: Third Division

XXI Corps
Thomas Leonidas Crittenden - Major General Commanding
Thomas J. Wood - Brigadier General: First Division
John M. Palmer - Major General: Second Division
Horatio P. Van Cleve - Brigadier General: Third Division

Reserve Corps
Gordon Grainger - Major General Commanding
James B. Steedman - Brigadier General: First Division
Daniel McCook: Colonel 2nd Brigade

Cavalry Corps
Robert B. Mitchell - Brigadier General Commanding
Edward M. McCook - Colonel: First Division
George Crook - Major General: Second Division
    Colonel Robert H. G. Minty: 1st Brigade

Confederate Army of Tennessee
Braxton Bragg - General Commanding

Polk's Corps
Leonidas Polk - Lieutenant General Commanding
    Cheatham's Division: Benjamin F. Cheatham - Major General Commanding
    Hindman's Division: Thomas C. Hindman - Major General Commanding

Hills Corps

Daniel H. Hill - Lieutenant General Commanding

Cleburne's Division: Patrick Cleburne - Major General Commanding

Breckinridge's Division: John C. Breckinridge - Major General Commanding

Buckner's Corps

Simon Bolivar Buckner - Major General Commanding

Stewart's Division: Alexander P. Stewart - Major General Commanding

Preston's Division: William Preston - Brigadier General Commanding

Reserve Corps

William H. T. Walker - Major General Commanding

Walker's Division: William H. T. Walker - Major General Commanding

Liddell's Division: St. John R. Liddell: Brigadier General Commanding

Longstreet's Corps

James Longstreet Lieutenant General Commanding

Johnson's Division: Bushrod R. Johnson: Brigadier General Commanding

Greggs Brigade: John Gregg - Brigadier General

Lt. Colonel James Turner - 30th Tennessee

Captain Charles Douglas - 30th Tennessee

Private Billy Cobb - 30th Tennessee

Private Jimmy Morrisey - 30th Tennessee

McNair's Brigade: Evander McNair - Brigadier General

Hood's Division: John Bell Hood - Major General Commanding

Evander M. Law - Major General

Forrest's Cavalry Corps

Nathan Bedford Forrest - Brigadier General Commanding

Artillery:
Captain John Morton - Chief of Artillery - Forrest's Cavalry Corps

Part 1
Chapter 1
Thursday, September 7, 1863, 4:15p.m. Lookout Mountain

It was already late afternoon when the two men reined in their horses on the lower slopes of Lookout Mountain. The day had been warm; fall was already in the air, heady with the sweet earthen smells of late summer. A hawk wheeled slowly overhead, drifting on widespread wings, its feathers fluttering as it searched for its evening meal. A dove cooed softly in the treetops. Other than that, the woodland on the mountainside was quiet, the wildlife gone to ground, unsure of the riders' intent. A dry twig snapped under the lead horse's hoof; the leaves rustled against the horse's flanks as the riders thrust the branches aside with gloved hands.

Slowly, the two horsemen edged forward through the trees and scrub, the horses edgy, nervous but sure-footed until at last they reached the edge of the dense undergrowth and were able to look out across the river. The sun was already casting long shadows when they entered a small clearing, a break in the undergrowth, little more than a thinning of the trees and scrub.

Both men were gaunt, their faces heavily lined and tanned; both wore beards in the fashionable Van Dyke-style favored by many military officers; both wore Confederate gray.

On the far side of the river, the sun's rays glittered among the stacked arms in the Federal encampment, casting bright shafts of light across the walls of the tents.

Together, the two riders reached for their field glasses. The taller of the two men looked back over his left shoulder and, shielding his eyes with one hand, took careful note of the position of the sun still visible just above the ridges away to the west. He turned in the saddle to place his body between the tree-filtered rays and the metal glasses, and then raised them to his eyes and surveyed the scene unfolding just a few hundred yards away across the water.

As far as the eye could see, from Friars Island just to the east and to the mountains four miles away beyond Williams Island to the west, the smoke of perhaps a hundred campfires spiraled upward from among the trees.

Out of the trees now, and in the clearing, they could hear the distant sounds of axes thumping on wood echoing faintly across the water; men were at work deep in the undergrowth. Directly in front of them the men in blue were already cooking the evening meal. Above the tents the banners of the Army of the Cumberland, fluttered proudly in the late afternoon breeze.

"It looks like General Reynolds, with Wilder, King, and Turchin," the smaller of the two men said in a whisper. He kept his glasses to his eyes, shaded by the wide brim of a soft, gray hat.

"Well... Wilder, for sure," his companion said, shifting slightly in the saddle. He was a tall man, gaunt; his skin burned dark by the summer sunshine. The beard added a somewhat arrogant look to the hard lines of his face. His immaculate gray uniform bore the insignia of a Confederate brigadier general.

"I can see him, there, in that group over to the right, shirt-sleeves, and suspenders. And I think the tall, thin one.... That's Robert Minty, on Wilder's left. Be still, George. They're looking our way. They'll see us."

For several minutes more, the two Confederate officers continued their surveillance. The hammering continued and, with the crash of falling trees, seemed to spread deeper into the woodlands beyond the river.

"I don't like it, George." Nathan Bedford Forrest lowered his glasses, tapped them thoughtfully against the pommel of his saddle, and turned to his companion. "There's too much going on over there; a lot of men at work yet they cain't be seen; and there's a great many fires.... Not enough men. Where they at, George? Either they're dug in among the trees or, by God, they ain't there at all. What do you think?"

Colonel George Dibrell continued to stare at the small gathering of officers in the clearing beyond the riverbank. He swept his glasses back and forth, trying to make sense of the seeming lack of the usual hustle and bustle of a great army bedding down for the night. Finally, he lowered his glasses, shook his head, and shrugged his shoulders.

"Damned if I know, General. The number of fires indicate a force of at least corps strength, twelve, maybe fifteen thousand men; look at the banners. My guess... they're building for a river crossing. If so, the terrain should be seething with men. But it's not."

Forrest nodded in agreement. "There're no infantrymen, George," he said thoughtfully. "Wilder's mounted infantry, I think, and Minty's cavalry brigade for sure, perhaps a few more, but there ain't no infantry, only horse soldiers. Perhaps two thousand, or so, but that's all." He paused for a moment, deep in thought, and then continued, "George, I think the wily General Rosecrans is putt'n on a show for us. They're making much noise with little effect, and I think you're right. They'd like us to b'lieve they're building pontoons for a crossing, here. I don't b'lieve it. I just don't b'lieve it."

The statement was punctuated by the distant boom of a Federal cannon high on the ridge to the north of Chattanooga and then, seconds later, by the dull crunch of the exploding shell. The two men took no notice. For almost a week, the city had been under steady fire from the ridge. The shells fell one every twenty minutes or so, more to annoy than with any real intent to do damage.

Just then, Forrest's stallion, a great blond beast, impatient from standing still, snorted, tossed his head, danced a few steps sideways, and turned as if to leave. At the same moment, on the opposite riverbank, there was a small puff of white smoke followed a second later by a sharp crack and the shrill whine of the bullet as it passed between the two Confederate officers.

Forrest pulled the startled horse back into line, grinned sideways at his brigade commander, took off his hat, waved it above his head, and bowed, a mocking salute to the group of Federal officers now watching them from the clearing across the river. Then, replacing the hat on his head, he leaned forward and affectionately slapped the horse's neck.

"Well now, George. That was close," he said, "and it seems they knows we're here. I guess it's time we was elsewhere."

The two men wheeled their horses and cantered away into the deeper cover of the wooded slopes on the mountain.

Across the river, Colonel John Wilder, a big, burly man with a full, heavy beard, turned to his companion and said, "Colonel, was that who I think it was?"

Colonel Robert Minty frowned, "Damned right it was; Forrest himself. Do you think he knows what we're up to, Colonel?"

Wilder shrugged. "Who can tell? Forrest always did have an uncanny knack for sniffing out the truth; blessed with second sight, so some believe. But no, I don't think so," he said with more confidence than he felt. "But even if he does, it may not matter. The river crossings at Stevenson and Bridgeport have already been completed. By daylight, all eight divisions will be ready to cross the valley and make their way through the mountain passes. Three more days and the roads south from Chattanooga will be in our hands. Retreat from the city will be impossible."

Wilder turned to go to his tent, but paused when he heard hoof beats approaching rapidly along the trail from the west. Seconds later, a dispatch rider burst from the trees, slowed his horse almost to a stop, spotted Wilder, and spurred the horse toward him.

"Yes, Captain, what is it?"

"Orders from General Reynolds, sir."

Holding his stamping horse in check with one hand, the rider unbuttoned his tunic, reached inside and pulled out a folded sheet of paper. Leaning forward over the horse's neck, he handed it to Wilder.

Wilder read the note quickly, then looked up at the rider. "Please assure General Reynolds that I understand and will move at first light."

The rider nodded his head, saluted, wheeled his horse, and rode away at the canter.

Wilder turned to one of his aides. "Lieutenant, go find Colonel Atkins, Monroe, Funkhouser, Winter, and Major Jones, and ask them to kindly join me in my tent." Then to Minty, "You, too, Colonel. Things are about to happen."

To another of his aides, he said, "Lieutenant Scott, please go to Captain Lilly on the ridge and ask him to please increase his rate of fire, ask him to double it."

Twenty minutes later, Lieutenant Colonel Blake Winter, hat in hand, ducked through the open flap of Wilder's tent to find the other officers already engaged in an animated discussion.

"Ah, Colonel Winter, good," Wilder said. "Sit down. Have a drink. Help yourself." Winter poured himself a generous measure from the already open bottle of malt Scotch whiskey and sat down.

"Here it is, gentlemen," Wilder said. "General Rosecrans with eight divisions has completed the river crossings to the south. General Crittenden with three more divisions is only a day's march from here to the northwest. Colonel Atkins, you are to head south along the riverbank and then cross the river. You are then to turn east, make your way around the head of Lookout Mountain, and move on Chattanooga."

Atkins grinned as he nodded.

Wilder continued, "The rest of us are to move onto the ridge north of the river at first light, engage the enemy with every piece of artillery we can lay hands on and make him believe that we are about to attempt a river crossing here, and to the north. We are to keep them busy, hold their attention, until General Rosecrans can cut Bragg's line of retreat to the south, and occupy the heights of Lookout Mountain and the surrounding ridges. Colonel," he said, turning again to Atkins, "General Crittenden will follow you across the river and into the city from the west.

"So, gentlemen, it begins." He raised his glass in salute, and then downed the contents with a single swallow. Together, his companions did the same.

4

Thursday, September 7, 1863, 7:00p.m. - Confederate Headquarters, Chattanooga.

They stood together around the map table talking softly: eight men in gray uniforms, their names already written into history. Major General Simon Buckner, the fair-haired hero of Fort Donelson, was engaged in a heated discussion with Lieutenant General Leonidas Polk, an overweight blustering man and one-time Episcopal Bishop of New Orleans. On the far side of the table, his shoulders flat against the heavy brocade that covered the walls, Nathan Bedford Forrest was talking to Major General John Breckinridge, the one-time vice president of the United States.

The burning logs in the fireplace crackled beneath the ornately carved mantelpiece, casting stark shadows that flickered in the dim light of the room. Major General Patrick Cleburne, a tall austere Irishman, late of the British Army, stood with his back to the fire enjoying its warmth and talking in a low voice to Major General A. P. Stewart, a silent, brooding man. Lieutenant General Daniel H. Hill was talking animatedly to Braxton Bragg, commanding general of the Army of Tennessee.

Bragg looked tired. His gaunt face was heavily lined; his hair and beard were almost entirely gray; the general had been rendered old beyond his fifty years by more than half a lifetime of military service, many months of ill health, the stress of high command and the concerted efforts of some of his subordinates to have him removed. The campaigns of Shiloh, Perryville, Stones River, and Tullahoma had taken a terrible toll on his frail body, and now he faced what he knew must be his most difficult task, the defense of Chattanooga. If he failed, the gateway to the Confederacy would come crashing down around his ears.

Bragg turned away from General Hill, walked to one of the great windows, pushed aside the drapes, and gazed out across the street. Outside, the early evening air was still and humid. High above the city, the top of Lookout Mountain was already shrouded in mist. The streets of the city were growing dark, but were still crowded with civilians heading out of town, carrying their goods on an assortment of outlandish vehicles. Anything that could be made to move, on hoof or wheel, had been piled high with impossible loads of furniture, pots, pans, and assorted bric-a-brac of doubtful use, and now all teetered southward through the great pall of dust that hung over the streets like a vast thunder cloud.

There was, however, no panic, only people in a hurry to leave before the battle for the city would begin in earnest. All evening long, the Federal bombardment from the ridge to the north of the river had been steadily increasing, and the shells now fell with deadly accuracy, one every few minutes. All along the waterfront, the buildings were in ruins. The steamboat *Paint Rock* now rested on the bottom of the river. A wisp of smoke from its stack, all that remained above water, spiraled upward through the dust. The burned out remains of a second steamboat, the *Dunbar*, was still moored at what once had been the city wharf, now a shattered pile of useless wood and iron. The rows of Confederate pontoons, which would soon have been thrown across the river, had been pounded to matchwood. The Tennessee River was in Federal hands.

Bragg sighed, shook his head, turned again to face the room, and walked over to the great dining table and the map that covered most of its surface.

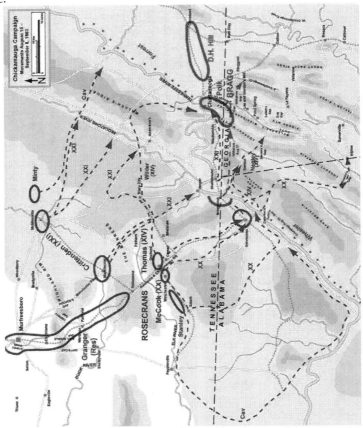

The generals gathered closer, restless, fidgeting, and uneasy; they all realized that events beyond their control were rapidly moving toward a climax. Forrest, ever confident and self-assured, a tight smile on his face, folded his arms across his chest and stared down at the map. Buckner twirled his mustachios, and Polk muttered inaudibly to himself, his lips moving rapidly and silently.

KABAM! Outside on the street, only yards from the front door of the house, a Federal shell exploded and caused dust and flakes of plaster to rain down from the ceiling upon the table. Startled, Bragg looked up at the heavy chandelier. It swung back and forth, its heavy glass baubles tinkling as the building shook under the impact. Then he shrugged, leaned forward, placed both hands on the edge of the table, and then gently thumped the center of the map with a clenched fist, shook his head and said, "They're coming, gentlemen. The bombardment, the demonstrations across the river, they are meant to divert our attention from what's happening to the south. General Forrest?" Bragg looked at Forrest, questioningly, and then said, "If you please, General."

Forrest, the "eyes" of Bragg's army, unfolded his arms, leaned forward, placed his right hand on the edge of the table and, with a pointing finger, began outlining the enemy positions on the map.

"General Rosecrans, with Thomas, Walker, McCook and eight divisions have already crossed the river and are heading over the ridge here, into the Lookout Valley," Forrest said, pointing as he concentrated on the map. "Their advance units are making for the mountain passes here, and here. Crittenden, with three more divisions is moving to reinforce Reynolds and Wilder to the north of the river, here." His hand swept back and forth over the map. "Palmer and Van Cleve seem to be heading for a river crossing, here, just to the southwest of the head of Lookout Mountain." He paused for a moment, and then continued, "And there's something strange going on here, across the river. To all intents, it seems General Reynolds is preparing for a river crossing there, but I don't b'lieve it. I think they're tryin' to trick us."

Forrest looked in turn at each of the assembled generals, and then said, quietly, "Gentlemen, if Palmer and Van Cleve make that crossing, they'll be here, in Chattanooga, pretty damn quick, no more'n a couple of hours. Then they'll be in control of the whole damn road south. We'll be trapped here with our backs to the river facing the entire damn Federal army." He paused, looked Bragg squarely in the eye, and said, "That, General, would not be good. We need to vacate this place pretty damn quick." He nodded for emphasis, then took a step backwards and clasped his hands behind his back.

Bragg was silent, thoughtful for a moment, and then he nodded his agreement and said with some resignation, "It makes no difference,

General Forrest, they will all be here within a matter of days, and we shall not be ready for them. We are but forty-two thousand compared to their one hundred thousand. We need reinforcements. You're right; we must leave this place; find something better."

"Your pardon, General Bragg," Hill said, his tone argumentative. "My scouts have been watching Rosecrans for weeks. They estimate his strength to be little more than sixty-five thousand, perhaps only forty thousand effectives. We can hold them here."

"I agree with General Hill," Polk said emphatically, waving his hands in the air. "We cannot keep running from Rosecrans. Let him come. God is with us, and we are well entrenched here. The river defends us on three sides. We can hold him indefinitely, and should he decide upon a major confrontation, his casualties will be significant."

Forrest snorted, shook his head, seemed about to speak, but changed his mind and remained silent.

"No!" Bragg sounded tired, resigned. With his hands clasped tightly behind his back, he turned from the table, walked slowly to the fireplace, placed both hands on the mantle, lowered his head, gazed into the flames and said, "If what General Forrest says is true, and Rosecrans makes it through the mountain passes, we'll be trapped here. Should he gain the high ground, he will command not only the river, but the approaches to the city as well. And, although I do agree with General Hill that we could hold this position if we had to, we could not withstand an extended siege. And I do not intend to go the way of General Pemberton at Vicksburg."

For a long moment, Bragg stood staring into the flames; then he turned again and moved back to the table. "I am expecting reinforcements from General Johnston in the west," he said. There was a fierce light in his eyes and a new fervor in his voice. "And President Davis informs me that General Lee is sending General Longstreet with three divisions, fifteen thousand men. The president also suggests that we bide our time until Longstreet arrives; then we will have the advantage of numbers, but that I will not do."

Bragg smiled, looked at each of his officers in turn, and then continued, an edge in his voice, "No, gentlemen, I do not intend to run from General Rosecrans. I intend to destroy him, and he, in his eagerness to destroy me, has, I think, provided us with the means by which we can do it.

"It would seem that he has divided his army into three sections, each section widely separated from the other two. Is this not so, General Forrest?"

Forrest merely nodded his head.

"Then our strategy will be to lead the enemy to believe that we are again on the run. We will move from here southward, leaving behind scouts who will pose as deserters to be captured and to tell the tale that we are heading for Atlanta, demoralized, disordered, and outnumbered. In reality, we will move with all speed to McLemore's Cove, here." He indicated a position on the map with his forefinger. "There we will lie in wait for General Thomas as he exits the mountain pass."

Bragg paused for effect, and then continued, "McCook is heading for Winston's Gap, here, twenty-five miles farther south; too far away to reach Thomas in time to save him. We will destroy Thomas, and then turn southward to meet with General Johnston's reinforcements, and then fall upon McCook and overwhelm him by sheer weight of numbers. Then we will turn again northward and drive Crittenden and Rosecrans from Chattanooga. Gentlemen," he smiled contemptuously, "we will have no need of General Lee's reinforcements. By the time they arrive, all will be over."

Bragg turned away from his officers and said, "That is all, gentlemen. Prepare your divisions. We move southward at first light. You are dismissed."

It seemed as if General Polk was about to speak again. Instead, he merely shrugged his shoulders, took Forrest by the elbow, and with heads together they followed the others out into the night, leaving Bragg alone with his thoughts.

Chapter 2

Friday September 18th, 1863, 7a.m. - Hazelwood

Blake Winter awoke as the first rays of early morning sunshine fell across his face. He blinked, squinted, shaded his eyes with one hand, then, with no little effort, pushed himself up onto one elbow, and looked around the tiny room. His head was splitting.

He was lying on one of two small beds in a corner of the room. The other bed was empty. The rest of the furniture, what little there was of it, was sturdy, and made from oak. The walls were rough-hewn logs laid one atop the other and hung here and there with quilts. Two small windows set into the far wall gave access to shafts of sunlight that shone like bars of pure gold across the room.

The smell of coffee and fresh-baked bread filtered up from below. He licked his cracked lips, lowered himself back onto the pillow, and closed his eyes. This cannot be real, he thought, not real....

And then it all came flooding back, the memories of the past ten days, the pursuit of the supposedly fleeing Confederate army, of endless skirmishes with enemy cavalry, of constantly moving from one confrontation to the next, of the Confederate cavalry officer pointing a pistol that seemed to be bigger than a twelve-pounder field piece. He remembered the cold gray eyes, the mocking smile, the three gold stars on the collar of the officer's uniform, and then the pain. After that, nothing, until he'd looked up into a pair of the bluest eyes he'd ever seen. It was then he'd known he must be dead and in heaven, but he was not; he was flat on his back in the long grass. Then the vision had spoken, "Lie still, Colonel, your wound is not severe. My father and brother have gone to fetch a board to carry you." The face had floated before his eyes, and he had lapsed again into unconsciousness.

He lay with his head on the pillow, eyes open now, but still no more than half awake, and stared upward into the timbers of the roof, still dark and shadowy.

As he dozed, images of the past floating before his mind's eye. He was a little boy again, back in Illinois, no more than ten years old, playing in the creek with his younger brother and sister, his mother and father sitting together, holding hands on the riverbank, the sun shimmering on the surface of the water. The images changed. He was older now, seated in the little one-room schoolhouse, Miss Trask intoning something he couldn't hear. The images changed again, and he was back at West Point, but only for a moment, so it seemed, before he was at Pittsburg Landing, Shiloh, where the air was filled with smoke and terrible noise: the roar of gunfire, and the screams of the wounded and the dying. The smoke cleared a little, and through it, he could see three men on horseback, some distance away on a low bluff. He recognized them. There, to the left, were his friends, John Wilder, Robert Minty, and General Grant, all three men reaching out a hand toward him. The noise of battle died away as Grant spoke, the words echoing, blowing on the wind, as if spoken from a long way away.

"Are you awake, Colonel?" The images swam in the dark reaches of the roof above, shimmered, and disappeared. "Colonel, are you awake?"

No, not General Grant, he thought, a woman's voice, and vaguely familiar.

"Cover yourself, Colonel; I'm bringing coffee."

Winter lifted his head and looked down at his body. He was naked but covered to the waist with a quilt; his lower chest and belly were swathed in white cotton.

"I'm covered," his voice was cracked, his throat dry. He put a hand to the bandage, pressed gently, and gasped aloud as the pain seared through his lower right side, just above the hip and all the way to his armpit.

"Gently, Colonel, the wound will be sore for a day or two, but you will live."

She was standing by an opening in the floor, looking at him. There was a low rail around it. He hadn't noticed it before, but now realized it must be the way up from the room or rooms below.

She held a small tray in her hands. There was food on it, and a china mug from which steam rose and shimmered in the shaft of sunlight. Suddenly he was hungry. Even so, he couldn't help staring at her.

She was petite, a little more than five feet five inches tall, perhaps twenty years old, maybe a little more. Her fair hair was tied back with a pale blue ribbon that matched the color of the simple cotton dress. Gathered at the waist by a dark blue cord, the dress accentuated her small but obviously well formed figure. But it was her eyes that held his gaze: twin pools of deep blue, sparkling, full of life. Eyes he'd seen before through the mists of pain.

Blake Winter, a lieutenant colonel in the Union Army of the Cumberland, was born in Jackson County, Illinois on May 10, 1831. He was not a big man, slim, standing just five feet ten inches tall in his bare feet. Like all battle-worn soldiers, his face was deeply tanned from long months in the wind and sun. There was a small, crescent-shaped scar under his right eye, the result of a wound received more than a year earlier at Stones River: a flying shard of wood torn loose from a fence rail by the impact of a 12-pound solid shot. He wore a small mustache, neatly trimmed; no beard, and his wavy, dark brown hair was long enough to touch his shoulders. He was not a particularly handsome man, but he was attractive in an offbeat sort of a way. And what he lacked in good looks he more than made up for with his easygoing and fun-loving personality.

"Well, Colonel." She placed the tray on a small nightstand beside the bed. "There seems to be little wrong with your vision, at least." Her voice was soft, low, and refined, with an almost imperceptible hint of a southern drawl.

She sat down beside him on the bed.

"Let's see if we can get you up and about." She took him by the arm on his good side and gently eased him into sitting position. "Sit still; I'll fetch a bolster to support you." She removed two large pillows from the other bed and arranged them at his back, then gently lowered him onto them.

"Who are you?" he asked, not a little breathless from his exertions. "Where am I? What day is this? How long have I been here?"

"All in good time, Colonel," she smiled at his impatience. "Here, drink this. It will make you feel better." She held the steaming cup to his lips. As the scalding, fiery liquid hit the back of his throat, he gasped and began to cough, holding his side as pain coursed through his upper body, but she was right; he did feel better.

"My God, woman, what's in that?" he asked, recovering slowly from the spasm.

She laughed softly, "Just a little of Daddy's finest grain whiskey. Now, try some of this." She spooned something white and mushy from a bowl on the tray and held it to his lips. He reached to take it from her, but she stopped him with a look and said, "No, let me."

He shrugged, winced at the pain it brought, then dutifully opened his mouth and took the spoonful, chewed it slowly, made a wry face and swallowed hard.

"Damn," he said. "That's disgusting."

She smiled, mocking him.

"Grits," she said. "It's about all we can get these days, but then, you'd know all about that. Wouldn't you, Colonel?"

He opened his mouth, but before he could answer, she fed him another spoonful, then another, and another, until the bowl was empty.

She rose from the bed, took the tray, crossed the room, and disappeared down the stairs, only to return a moment later with another tray, upon which was a bowl of steaming water, a towel, and some other objects he couldn't readily make out.

"You need a shave, Colonel. Will you do it yourself, or will I?"

"I'll do it, and please stop calling me Colonel." He smiled up at her, unsure if her formality hid a hint of sarcasm. My name's Blake. What's yours? Am I a prisoner?"

"My name, Colonel, is Sarah Bradley," she said, ignoring his request for informality. "And no, you are not a prisoner. In fact, you are lying in my brother's bed. His name is Tom. Fortunately, he is away, engaged, I fancy, in killing as many of your companions as he can. I only hope I can get you out of here before he returns. He's not overly fond of your kind."

Suddenly worried about his possibly dangerous situation, Winter reached forward, grabbed her by the arm, and said, "Where exactly am I, Miss Bradley? Where are my people? And, more to the point, where the hell is the enemy?"

The blue eyes blazed as she snatched her arm away from him and rose quickly from the bed

"The enemy is, as far as I'm concerned, all around us and, in fact, lying on the bed in front of me. You are a guest in my father's house, Hazelwood, on the Lafayette Road just south of Rossville, Georgia. I found you bleeding to death not a mile to the west of here, and I helped you, just as I would help anyone else that I might happen to find along the wayside." She paused, stared at him, her head cocked angrily to one side, eyes glinting, her hands on her hips.

"My home, Colonel," she continued, "is surrounded by Yankee soldiers, at least for the time being; a situation I think that's about to reverse itself. General Bragg and the Army of Tennessee are less than ten miles away to the east." She smiled grimly. "So, if you don't want to spend the rest of the war languishing in a Confederate prison, I suggest you get dressed and get out of here before you and yours are overrun."

She stooped, opened a small door in the bottom of the nightstand, and removed a pile of neatly folded clothes: his uniform freshly laundered and mended. She tossed the clothing onto the bed and turned to leave.

"Wait, please?" he said, quietly. "I'm sorry. You don't understand. This is all too confusing. One minute I'm about to die and the next I wake up in a strange bed...." He paused, lifted the quilt a few inches with his free hand, looked down at himself, grinned up at her, and said, "Naked."

The blue eyes softened, and she nodded. For a long moment, she looked at him, remembering the prone body, the pale face stark against the russet browns of the woodland floor. Now his dark brown eyes twinkled as he smiled up at her.

"You've taken a bullet in the fatty part of your side. It went all the way through," she said, matter-of-factly. "It's a relatively minor flesh wound compared to some I've seen, and it will be painful for a while, but I've cleaned and dressed it, and if you keep moving, the muscles shouldn't stiffen too much. You also hit your head when you fell. I imagine you must have something of a headache, but you should have no trouble riding a horse."

"Thank you," he said, "but why? I'm your enemy."

She shrugged. "My enemy, Colonel? Well, yes, and no." She smiled. "We're all Americans, aren't we?"

Just then, there was a noise downstairs, boot heels on the wooden floor.

"Miss Bradley, are you there?"

Blake looked at Sarah. "John Wilder?" he asked.

She nodded, "And Colonel Minty, I fancy. Come on up, Colonel Wilder." She rose from the bed. "He's awake."

Wilder rushed up the stairs and into the room, closely followed by Minty.

"Damn it, Blake." Wilder grabbed Winter's hand and pumped it. "We thought you were a goner. Right, Bob?"

Minty, ever a serious man, merely nodded.

Winter laughed, then winced as pain lanced through his body. "Yeah," he said, through his teeth. "I thought so too, and would have been, if it hadn't been for Miss Bradley." He looked at her, and smiled.

"We've a lot to thank you for, Ma'am. We've been friends a long time. It would be hard to do without him, and there's no doubt you saved his life."

"There's no need to thank me, Colonel Wilder. I have a brother out there somewhere, and I pray that should anything happen to him, someone would be there to do as much for him." She turned away, moved to one of the windows, and gazed out across the fields and forest.

Then, in the distance, the silence of the early morning was shattered by the crackle of musket fire, followed a moment later by a deeper booming as one cannon after another added its voice to the sounds of battle building to the east.

Wilder and Minty ran to the window and looked out across the Lafayette Road. Winter leaped from the bed, cursing as pain racked his body. He grabbed his uniform britches and, hopping from one foot to the other, not bothering to cover his otherwise naked body from the wide-eyed Sarah Bradley who'd turned in fright from the window and was staring at him, he dragged them up over his hips.

"What is it?" Winter asked, as he joined the others at the window.

To the northeast, a great pall of gray smoke was rising above the trees. The noise grew louder as blast after blast of cannon fire echoed across the woodland, and the crackle of rifle fire turned into a single, sustained roar.

"It's Captain Lilly." There was tension in Wilder's voice. "We have to go, Colonel Winter. Can you make it?"

"Of course, but I'll need a horse,"

"We've brought one for you. We'll wait, but a moment only." The two Federal officers turned and ran down the stairs.

Blake returned to the bed and struggled into the rest of his clothes.

"Wait," she said. "You can't. Your wound.... It's bleeding again."

He rose again from the bed, looked at the red stain at his side, and said, "It's all right, I'll have the field surgeon take a look at it. If I can, I'll return this evening."

She nodded, her hand to her mouth, and he turned and went quickly down the stairs and out into the open where Wilder and Minty were waiting for him. He mounted the horse with some difficulty, turned in the saddle and waived, and then the three men rode swiftly away, Winter doubled over the animal's neck, holding onto the reins with one hand and his injured side with the other.

Chapter 3

Friday September 18th, 7a.m. - Confederate Field Headquarters

Confederate General Braxton Bragg listened to the sounds of the gunfire to the west. He was agitated, angry.

Just an isolated action, he thought, not the combined effort he'd expected. The campaign was not going well; Johnson and Forrest were in position as planned, but the others....

He remembered the meeting only twelve hours before, in the early evening of September 17, at Leet's Tanyard some ten miles to the southeast of Chickamauga Creek. He'd spent hours explaining a complicated series of troop movements to his field commanders, movements designed to bring about a battle in which he would have a decided advantage.

The atmosphere in the sparsely furnished, half-timbered room had been tense. The conversation had been one-sided and terse. Bragg, never known for his sense of humor, had been in a no-nonsense mood. His generals, ever wary of their commander's ill temper, stood back from the table as if distance alone would shield them from his acid tongue.

"It is my contention, gentlemen," Bragg looked sharply at his assembled officers, "that we must move the entire army northwest from here at first light, move across the Chickamauga to the north of General Rosecrans and his army, thus separating him from his base at Chattanooga, and then bring him to battle." He looked around at the generals, challenging them, waiting for comments. There were none.

Brigadier General Forrest's gaunt face was impassive; the ice-blue eyes stared back at him without blinking. Buckner seemed not to be listening, to have much upon his mind as he stared thoughtfully out of the window. Bishop Polk, as ever, looked well fed, his complexion ruddy, but his usual jolly demeanor was now serious. Brigadier General Bushrod Johnson, however, seemed at ease, relaxed, his tunic unbuttoned all the way, thumbs hooked comfortably in his belt, feet crossed at the ankles, as he leaned casually against the wall next to Forrest. *And Hill,* Bragg thought, *if it hadn't been for him....*

He shook his head, brought himself back to the matter in hand, and continued, "General Johnson's division, supported by General Forrest's cavalry, will cross the Chickamauga here, at Reed's Bridge." He pointed with a gloved finger to a position on the large map in front of him. "Simultaneously, Generals Walker and Liddell will move their divisions across the creek here, at Alexander's Bridge.

General Johnson, when you have crossed the bridge you will turn south and join General Walker, and then all three divisions will move southward along the Chickamauga in a flanking movement, rolling up the enemy's left." He paused, head down, arms folded across his chest, frowning thoughtfully before continuing.

He looked up at his enigmatic corps commander. "General Buckner; if you please, sir," he said loudly. Buckner turned from the window, and Bragg continued, "On my command, you, General, will cross the creek with your entire force here, at Thedford's Ford." He indicated the position on the map. Buckner, his face stony and indifferent, merely nodded, said nothing, and then turned again to stare out of the window.

"And you, General Polk. You, too, will move your corps into position and hold yourself ready to move across the creek, here, at Lee and Gordon's Mill, where you will immediately move against the enemy's right in support of General Buckner."

Polk smiled, hitched his belt, looked around the table, stuck his thumbs into the lapels of his uniform coat, and said, an edge to his voice, "And what of General Hill? Will he not be engaged?"

Hill glared at Polk, his eyes hard, his lips set in a thin hard line.

"Of course," Bragg said, emphatically and without rancor. "General Hill, you will make your crossing here, three miles farther south at Glass's Mill. From there you will move north in support of Generals Polk and Buckner." Hill said nothing; his haughty expression remained unchanged.

Bragg looked at each of them through narrowed eyes, his brow furrowed. "Gentlemen, it is absolutely essential that all sections move across the Chickamauga precisely at the appointed time. If we can do so, we can assail the enemy on all fronts, the hammer-blow being delivered by Generals Johnson, Walker, and Liddell at the northern end of the field. You, gentlemen," he said to the three men concerned, "will drive the enemy's left flank into the waiting arms of Generals Polk and Buckner. Rosecrans' forces are still scattered from the Brotherton Farm to Crawfish Springs. Is that not so, General Forrest?"

The cavalry commander nodded his agreement, but said nothing.

"Then," Bragg said, as he hammered his fist into the center of the map, "he cannot withstand such a concentrated assault. Are there any questions, gentlemen?"

They looked at one another, then, in turn, shook their heads.

But can I rely on you? He thought. Will you move on my command? Or will we have a second McLemore's Cove? Whom among you can I trust? You, Nathan Bedford Forrest? Yes, I think so, upstart that you might be, and arrogant. You,

Bishop Polk? Well, only time will tell. And what about you, General Buckner? Yes, of course. You are too honorable a man to do anything other than your duty, but where are you now? What are you thinking? And you, General Hill, what of you? Why did you not carry out my orders a week ago? If you had done so, this would all have been over now.

He turned away from the table, cleared his head, and then turned again to face his generals, stared hard at them, then softened a little.

"General Johnson," his tone was crisp, terse, even, "tomorrow morning, you will move across Reed's Bridge at exactly seven o'clock." Again, he indicated the position on the map. "You will be well beyond the enemy's left flank, a position where you should find little resistance.

"General Forrest, you will support General Johnson, leaving behind two brigades to assist Generals Walker and Liddell with the crossing at Alexander's Bridge."

Forrest nodded to Walker, clapped Bushrod Johnson affectionately on the shoulder, and said, "It will be my pleasure, General, as always." Johnson dug Forrest gently in the ribs with his elbow.

Bragg looked at each of his officers in turn. "If you have questions, gentlemen, now is the time to ask them."

There was a general shuffling of feet; the generals were decidedly uneasy.

"Er," Bushrod Johnson hesitated. "I can assure you, General, that I will be at Reed's Bridge at the appointed time," he said, thoughtfully. "But it's a long march, for everyone concerned. What if the rest of our army is late to the field? What if the crossings are defended, as I'm sure they must be? General Forrest and I could find ourselves fighting the entire Army of the Cumberland on our own."

Braxton Bragg nodded his head in agreement. "I'm led to believe that there are no Union forces of any strength nearer than Crawfish Springs, well to the south of the designated crossings points. Is that no so, General Forrest?"

"That was the situation four hours ago, General," Forrest said, gazing down at the map. "There are, of course, all sorts of detached Federal units scattered from Chattanooga to Lafayette, but, as you say, General, no concentrated forces. Rosecrans, with the main body of his army, is still at McLemore's Cove."

"Good." Warming to his subject, Bragg continued. "Then I expect all of you to have your divisions ready and in position by the appointed time. By noon tomorrow, the way should be clear for the remainder of the army to cross the Chickamauga and drive southward, rolling up the Army of the Cumberland as we go, and thus we will destroy the invader."

"That," Forrest whispered in Polk's ear, but loud enough for Bragg to hear, "might be easier said than done."

Polk, his face impassive, merely nodded and moved away from the cavalry general, obviously disturbed about something left unsaid. Forrest smiled impassively as he watched Polk move to the wall and begin to study a large, uninteresting painting.

Bragg took a glass from a small side table, filled it to the brim with water from a crystal jug, raised it to his lips, and drank deeply before returning it to the table.

"General Longstreet, gentlemen," he said grimly through his teeth, "will arrive from Virginia with fifteen thousand men the day after tomorrow." He paused again, then continued, "I want this over with before he gets here. I do not want the arrogant Dutchman bragging throughout the Confederacy that he had to leave General Lee in order to come south and rescue us from Rosecrans and his army of farmers. Is that understood, gentlemen? Is that quite clear?" He looked at each officer in turn and received a terse nod from each.

"There will be no more mistakes," he said, looking directly at General Hill, who returned his gaze without blinking an eye.

"It is imperative, General Johnson, General Forrest," Bragg continued, "that you cross at Reed's Bridge no later than seven o'clock. You, General Walker, must be ready to make your way across Alexander's Bridge as soon as General Johnson has drawn Rosecrans' advance units away to the north. The rest of you will stand ready to move on my command.

"Get a good night's rest, gentlemen," he'd said, "we've a big day tomorrow."

But all that had taken place yesterday, and now.... *Why wasn't Walker at Alexander's Bridge? And Buckner? Why wasn't he at Thedford's Ford?*

Bragg stared into the distance at the clouds of smoke rising above the trees, listening to the distant thunder of the guns. *Too far*, he thought. *Far too far. Not enough time. Johnson had known, known the others all too well, and now he and Forrest were doing the unthinkable. On their own, facing... what? Where are you, General Walker? Where are you?*

Chapter 4

Friday September 18th, 6a.m. - Lee and Gordon's Mill

Sergeant Jesse Dixon woke early. The night had been long, and he'd slept only fitfully, plagued by insects from the creek and the steady creaking of the water wheel at the nearby mill. For endless hours, so it seemed, he'd tossed and turned until, finally, he'd given up, opened his eyes, stretched, then winced as a cramp seized the back of his right leg. Carefully he'd angled his toes backwards as his mother had taught him to do, easing the muscles until the cramp abated, leaving him with a nasty aching sensation at the back of his knee.

He turned on his side under the coarse blue blanket, rubbed his leg, then turned again onto his back and looked upward into the leafy branches of the oak tree under which he'd bedded down the night before. The first streaks of dawn were already filtering through the treetops.

For a long while he lay there, listening as the Federal encampment around him slowly began to stir, thinking about his family back home in Indiana and about the past several months spent, so it seemed, endlessly marching the trails, tracks, and dirt roads from Murfreesboro to Chattanooga in pursuit of the ever-fleeing Confederate army.

Jesse, slightly more than six feet tall, woefully skinny, with a straggly goatee beard and an even stragglier mustache, would be twenty next month, and he felt fifty. *Christ*, he thought, *will it never end?*

He heard someone poking the ashes of the fire, the sounds of metal clinking upon metal, and then he smelled the irresistible aroma of hot coffee.

Jesse rolled onto his side, struggled for a moment as he became tangled in the blanket, then managed to throw it off, staggered to his feet and looked around. Pat – Patrick - was lying next to the spot from which he'd just risen, still asleep, mouth wide open, snoring gently. *Only sixteen*, Jesse thought. *Christ, he's just a kid. Same age as Cathy.* He smiled at the thought of his baby sister, and stared down at the tousle-haired, pimply-faced young soldier at his feet. The boy, as yet still innocent of the horrors of war, looked even younger than his years.

Pat stirred in his sleep, coughed, spluttered, then clamped his mouth tight shut and breathed hard through his nose.

Jesse had bedded down for the night almost fully clothed, removing only his shirt beneath which he wore a dirty undershirt; the oversized uniform pants he had left on to ward against the cold of the night. Now, in the early light of morning, he stretched his arms upward, threw them down again, touched his toes, and then walked, stiff-legged, in a small circle, easing the stiffness brought on by a night on the damp, unforgiving ground. He paused for a moment, looked around the line of trees, picked a spot, hitched up his britches, and walked off into the woods to relieve himself. That done, he returned to his bed roll, rummaged for a moment inside his pack, retrieved a small, grimy cloth bundle that contained a small shard of mirror, a fragment of soap, and a well-worn razor. Then he turned and placed a well-aimed and none-too-gentle kick into the still sleeping Pat McCann's ribs.

McCann came to life with a start and a curse, looked round in wild-eyed terror, then, when he saw his grinning companion, realized where he was.

"By God, Dixon, you ever do that again, and I'll cut your goddamned throat."

"So you say," Jesse said, "so you say." Then he kicked him again. Pat howled in pain, leaped to his feet, and chased the laughing Jesse Dixon to the edge of the creek. With a great yell and a bound, he dived onto Jesse's back, locked his arms around his neck, and together they fell headlong into the muddy waters of the creek.

"Dammit, Pat," Jesse yelled, fighting to free himself from the choking grasp of his triumphant friend, "I've dropped my goddamned washing kit. Get off, you crazy bastard." He rammed an elbow into McCann's ribs, driving the air from his lungs, and for a moment, the two young men sat gasping on the creek bed, fighting to get their breath.

They looked at each other, heads tilted to one side. Then, with a yell and a laugh, they began the struggle all over again, each trying to push the other beneath the murky water. For several minutes, the two friends were able to forget their cares and the horrors they'd never grow used to.

At last they lay side by side in the shallow waters, heads resting on the muddy river bank, their energy spent, feeling good, enjoying the cool morning air, and gazing upward into the canopy of green leaves.

"Are we going to die, Jesse?" Pat asked thoughtfully, still staring upward into the trees.

"Christ, no, Pat." Jesse was emphatic, "We've come too far, done too much. We're smart, too damned smart." The words were right, but, even as he was saying them, Jesse didn't believe it. After two years in the field, he knew their chances of survival were slim at best, especially now.

"Look," Jesse raised himself onto one elbow, and struggling to steady himself as it sank slowly into the muddy creek bottom, he said, "we've got to look out for each other, see? That's all there is to it. I'll watch your back; you watch mine, all right? Here, give me your hand," he reached forward with his free hand and grasped Pat's left hand tightly. "We'll make a pact. The only way we can get hurt is if we take chances, so we won't. You swear?"

"All right, Jesse, I swear." Pat grinned as he said it, and went on, "You know I'll watch after your sorry ass." He threw a great handful of mud and water into Jesse's serious face, but it was only a half-hearted attempt to regain the carefree atmosphere of the earlier moment.

"Stop fooling around, Pat; this is serious." Jesse was angry now. "For Christ's sake, all it takes is one lax second, and you'll get your head blown clear offen your shoulders. Do you hear me?" he said, loudly. "I said do you hear me?"

"All right, all right. I hear you," Pat said, taken aback at his friend's sudden anger. "Take it easy. I'll be careful, all right?"

"All right then." Jesse said, somewhat mollified by his friend's reaction to his warnings, "When the fighting starts, there'll be no time for fooling around. You'll listen to me, and you'll listen to me good. Yes?"

"Yes." Pat nodded as he said it.

They looked at each other for a moment. "Come on," Jesse said, "let's go get coffee and something to eat. Christ; what's that?"

Far away in the distance, they could faintly hear the thunder of gunfire drifting in on the early morning breeze.

Chapter 5
Friday September 18th, 7:40a.m. - Reed's Bridge

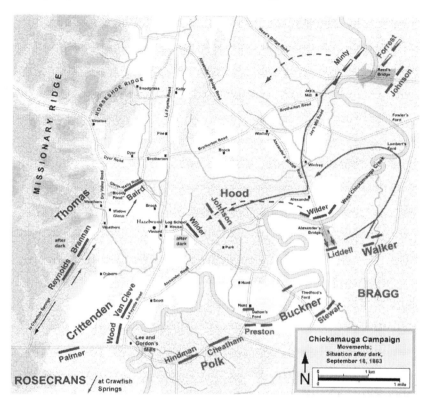

It was just past seven-thirty when Wilder, Minty, and Winter reached the position where Wilder's brigade was deployed in a forward position to the west of Alexander's Bridge on the Chickamauga Creek. It had taken the three men less than five minutes riding at full gallop to cover the more than two miles of open country from the Bradley home on the Lafayette Road. No sooner had they reined in their horses than Blake Winter, almost fainting with pain, slid to the ground and, holding his side with one hand and the reins with the other, leaned against the heaving beast, his brow against its neck. Wilder and Minty remained mounted.

Artillery Captain Eli Lilly was waiting for them. His six three-inch Parrott rifles, silent for the moment, were ranged to sweep a wide area to the east in front of the long wooden bridge. More than nine hundred of Wilder's men, two of his five regiments, were spread out behind a hastily

23

constructed, V-shaped log breastwork forward of Lilly's battery. Their Spencer repeating rifles were also silent. Two more of Wilder's regiments were just to the rear, being held in reserve, and a fifth was on detachment farther to the north. To the northeast, the sounds of battle seemed much closer.

"What's the situation, Captain Lilly?" Wilder asked.

"Colonel Minty's brigade is under attack to the east of Reed's Bridge, sir. It sounds pretty bad."

Wilder nodded, turned in the saddle, and said to Minty, "You'd better get over there, Colonel. Let me know what's going on as soon as possible. I'll send help if I can."

Without a word Minty, dug his spurs into his horse's flanks and headed out toward the sound of the gunfire. For several minutes, he rode at full gallop along the woodland footpath that ran parallel to Chickamauga Creek, oblivious of the overhanging limbs and branches that slashed at his face like so many rawhide whips. Soon he had reached a point where the trail joined a much wider dirt road leading east and west. Without slowing the horse's headlong gallop, he wrenched its head to the right and, without breaking stride, careened on at full speed in a cloud of dirt and flying debris.

A minute later, he was clattering at full speed across Reed's Bridge, the horse's hooves beating a hollow rhythm on the thick wooden boards, and then thumping once more on the hard-packed surface of the dirt road. On around a bend Minty charged, the horse snorting now with every stride, withers lathered white with sweat. The noise ahead was deafening. Then, suddenly, as he rounded another bend in the road, he saw his way was blocked. Almost two hundred of his mounted soldiers, each holding onto three more rider-less horses, were milling round and round in one solid mass beneath the overhanging trees.

"Let me through," Minty shouted, dragging hard on the reins. His horse slid to a stop in a cloud of dust, tried to spin, but Minty dug his heels into the heaving, snorting beast. It reared, almost throwing him beneath the hooves of the wheeling mass. Then he was pushing the horse forward again through the solid wall of flesh. For a moment, he thought he wasn't going to make it. Then, suddenly, he was through, bursting out of the trees into a clearing several hundred yards wide, almost a mile to the east of Reed's Bridge.

To his left and right, behind whatever cover they could find, the rest of his brigade - some six hundred men, - was spread out along the line of trees firing steadily across the clearing. To his left, set back deep inside the undergrowth, a section of the Chicago Board of Trade Battery - two twelve-pounder Napoleon guns - was firing load after load of canister at the gray-clad hoard he could barely see through the thickening clouds of white gun smoke. Heavy fire was being returned from the line of trees at the far side of the clearing some four hundred yards away.

Minty quickly turned the horse and headed back a few yards along the dirt road until he was hidden from view of the Confederate force. Swinging his right leg forward and over the horse's ears, he dropped to the ground.

The air was alive with the buzz of incoming Confederate Minnie bullets. All around him, Minty could hear the crackle of bullets tearing chunks of wood from the trunks of the trees in the forest. It seemed to be raining twigs, leaves, and wooden debris of all shapes and sizes. Under cover of the trees, he could see the bodies of his wounded soldiers, and he suddenly felt sick.

"Hey, soldier," he said, and holding onto his prancing horse, he reached forward and grabbed the collar of the private who was at that moment lying on his back stuffing a ramrod vigorously down the barrel of his rifled musket, and jerked him to his feet. "Where's Colonel Klein?" he shouted in the man's ear in an effort to be heard above the deafening roar of gunfire.

The private turned, eyes watering in the acrid smoke, and pointed toward the muzzle flash of one of the Napoleon guns a dozen yards away among the trees.

Minty stuffed the reins of his horse into the man's hand and shouted, "Take him back and join the others on the road." Then without waiting for a reply, he ran, head low, into the trees and came up between the two guns where Colonel Klein, commanding the 3rd Indiana Cavalry, was with Artillery Captain James Stokes, who was directing their fire.

Minty grabbed Klein by the sleeve and shouted over the shattering roar of the gunfire, "What the hell happened? That goddamned bridge back there is supposed to have been down by now. For Christ's sake, what happened?"

Klein pulled his sleeve from Minty's grasp and shouted, "They came out of nowhere, were on us like two dogs on a bitch in heat. We had no option but to try to defend our position here."

He turned back toward Stokes, who was at the right hand gun, cupped his hands over his ears, as the artilleryman shouted at the top of his voice, "FIRE!"

BAM! The great gun roared, its muzzle reared two feet in the air, and then the wheels crashed back to the ground.

"Canister! Double shot! Reload!" Like a well-oiled machine, the gun crew swung into action as Klein turned again to Minty, wiped his soot-covered brow with the back of his glove-covered hand, and shouted through cupped hands, "I don't know, Colonel. We were about to move back to the bridge when they came down the road out of nowhere."

Stokes turned, his head down, and shouted at the gun crew on the left side, "FIRE!" The gun roared, reared, and then settled back on its wheels. "RELOAD!

"FIRE!" Stokes yelled.

BAM!

"Swing it over, man. And lower it. I said lower it; depress the damn gun. You're shooting right over their heads." He turned again toward the other gun crew, "FIRE!"

BAM!

The second gun roared, reared, and crashed down again. "Sergeant, get that man out of the way," Stokes shouted, pointing at a man lying in front of the gun. "Reload that thing. Christ, man, get him out of it. I said get him out of it, god dammit, NOW!"

Two men ran forward and dragged the bleeding man away from the gun.

"All right, Captain, take it easy," Minty laid a calming hand on the Stokes' shoulder. Then he turned again to Klein.

"What's the situation, Colonel?"

"There are at least two brigades of cavalry over there, maybe more, and infantry, too. We're outnumbered at least three to one and we've taken heavy casualties. It's hard to say how many."

Minty shaded his eyes with both hands, flinched as a Minnie bullet whined past his right ear and another smacked into the trunk of a tree less than two feet away to the left, and looked with eyes squinted though the smoke toward the far side of the clearing. Faintly, through the haze, he could see a group of men, officers, on horseback down the road to the rear of the Confederate line of battle. Stokes' two guns thundered together, hurling their deadly loads of canister across the clearing into the gray-clad mass beyond.

Minty unhooked his field glasses from his belt, raised them to his eyes, and smiled grimly as, even through the smoke, he recognized the tall figure to the fore and center of the group. "No, Colonel, it's not just two brigades," he said, barely audible above the noise. "That's Forrest over there with what looks like his whole goddamned cavalry corps; four full brigades, more than three thousand men." He was silent for a moment as he surveyed the Confederate positions, "And I think that's Bushrod Johnson with him. If so, we're also facing a full division of veteran Confederate foot. Christ, look at that."

Across the clearing, some two dozen Confederate artillerymen were hastily unlimbering four cannon and turning them toward Minty and his beleaguered brigade.

Chapter 6

Friday September 18th, 7:30a.m. - Confederate Column East of Reed's Bridge

Billy Cobb felt as if he'd been marching all his life, and so he had been for more than five months, moving from one god-forsaken place to the next. This time, however, he knew it was different; he knew that this time the Army of Tennessee was going to fight. For almost four hours, since long before sun-up, the long column of Confederate infantry had been on the march from Ringgold, Georgia, westward, going who knows where. Only the officers knew that, and they weren't tellin'. All Billy knew was that the sooner they got to where they were going and off the dusty track, the better he'd like it, even though it would mean getting shot at again. Anything would be better than slogging from one rest stop to the next.

I joined to fight, by God, he thought, reaching for his canteen, but then images from the past rudely invaded his thoughts. He saw again, perhaps for the hundredth time, the face of the defenseless youngster, only a lad, not more than sixteen years old. The soft brown eyes had looked up at him, pleading, full of shock, pain, and despair as he'd rammed the twenty-one-inch bayonet into the boy's ribs. The memory sent him into a cold sweat. For a moment, his steady step faltered, and he almost stopped, but then he gathered himself together, thrust the unwanted memory from his mind, and drank deeply from the canteen.

Billy Cobb was a small man, but lean and strong. He wore his dark brown hair long, past his shoulders. Most of his face was covered by a thick bushy beard. His eyes small, black, and fierce, glittered beneath a ragged, wide-brimmed, floppy hat. What little of his face that was visible behind the great beard was burned almost black by a lifetime spent under the sun.

Born in the Cumberland Mountains of Tennessee, Billy prided himself that he was a mountain man born and bred. He was skilled in the arts of the land. A first class hunter and tracker, he could, with his beloved Springfield rifle, take down a raccoon at a hundred and fifty yards, provided the wind wasn't blowing. And he could bring down a man just as easily at five hundred yards, the impact of the huge, 58-caliber Minnie bullet inflicting a devastating wound no matter what part of the body it might hit.

At thirty-nine years of age, Billy Cobb had been soldiering with the 30th Tennessee for more than two years. And although he'd never even spoken to him, he regarded General Bushrod Johnson as his friend. Together they'd somehow survived the horrors of Shiloh, even though the general had been badly wounded there. Then there'd been the campaign in Kentucky and the hell on earth that had been Stones River. Billy had taken a Yankee bayonet in the thigh at Stones River and would have died if it hadn't been for his friend Jimmy Morrisey. Now? Well, who knew? He was tired, bone tired.

"Hey, Jimmy," he said to the pole bean marching - shuffling more like - along beside him. He replaced the cap on the canteen and wiped his mouth on the sleeve of his jacket. "How's about it? We gonna get to fight, or what?"

"Hell. Who knows?" Jimmy replied, shaking his head and spitting a wad of tobacco across Billy's front and onto the roadside. "I reckon we'll do just about what they tell us, though, and that's a fact," he added, nodding his head in agreement with himself.

"Damn, Jimmy, you really know your stuff," Billy said, sarcastically. "Hell, I don't know how they ain't spotted you already and raised you right on up there to corporal, or even sergeant, by God."

"Yeah, I was kinda wonderin' 'bout that myself." Jimmy Morrisey was serious, not catching the gentle ribbing from his friend. "Yeah," he said, "it's just about time. I might have a word with Captain Douglass when we get through where we're goin'."

Billy Cobb looked sideways at him, and grinned.

They'd been together a long time, him and Jimmy, even before the war. Raised next door to each other, they were both farmers. Then, when the trouble started, they'd joined up together. Close. Yes, they'd always been close; like brothers. Jimmy was two years older and scrawny, like an old gobbler turkey without its feathers. Long, straw-colored hair hung about his neck and over his eyebrows so that he had to squint through it to see, his brown eyes never quite visible. He wore a wide-brimmed planter's hat and an old brown jacket, too big for him by far, a souvenir from a lady friend.

He might not look like much, Billy thought, *but Jimmy, he was all right, a good friend, the best.*

For several minutes, they marched on in silence, close to the head of the column. The soft sounds of the marching feet made little noise on the dirt road, but raised clouds of dust that swirled around them, covering them with a fine coating of dark red clay, filling their noses and mouths with a clogging, cloying mess that choked them and brought tears streaming down their sun-tanned faces and leaving dirty trails from eye socket to chin.

"Christ," Jimmy said as he wiped his eyes, "ain't life grand?"

Billy looked at him and said grimly, "It ain't so bad, Jimmy. Could be a durned sight worse. We could be all shot up, crippled. Why, we could even be dead. And I for one am mighty glad to be here after all we bin through these last several months."

Not getting a response, Billy looked again at his friend. Jimmy was holding a dirty green bandanna to his nose and mouth. His head was down, and he seemed to be making heavy going of the march, which was unusual, because they'd all grown used to the long forced marches. Now, though they'd been on the move for almost four hours, the early morning air was cool and, but for the dust, the pace had been a comfortable one. But then, Jimmy was older than most. His heavily lined features and the stooped shoulders told a story all their own.

Perhaps things are gettin' to be too much for old Jim. To hell with that, it's gettin' to be too much for all of us, Billy thought, bitterly.

Billy Cobb marched stoically onward through the dust, trying not to breathe too deeply. The pace had quickened, and with it the clouds of dust had thickened to a point where it was difficult to see even the man in front. From front to rear, the column was more than three miles long. More than four thousand men marching in three brigades, along with more than a thousand of General Forrest's cavalry, and from front to rear the coughing and spluttering continued unabated.

"Hey, Jim," Billy said, "What's the time?"

With some difficulty, Morrisey undid the top buttons of his tunic, reached inside, unbuttoned his shirt pocket, and removed an ornate, silver pocket watch. Carefully, with a dirty fingernail, he prized open the front of the watchcase, gazed at the piece with some pride, and said, "It's exactly twenty six minutes after seven, Bill." Then he closed the watch, returned it to its pocket, carefully refastened his tunic, and said, "'Bout time we stopped for a while, ain't it?"

Almost as if he'd been heard by those who can make such decisions, the command to halt rolled back along the column, from company to company, regiment to regiment.

And then came a sound that filled them both with dread. Ahead, not more than five hundred yards, the early morning stillness was suddenly rent by the crackle of musketry, and then by the thunder of cannon fire. As one, the column broke ranks and dived for the trees on either side of the road.

Two minutes later, Captain Douglass, flustered and excited, came galloping back down the road toward them. "Companies A, D, and E. Move forward, at the double-quick."

Together the three companies, including Billy and Jimmy's Company A, reformed, and, with rifles held at the ready, moved quickly down the road toward Reed's Bridge.

Chapter 7

Friday September 18th, 8a.m. - Federal Positions at Alexander's Bridge

Colonel John Wilder and his chief of artillery, Captain Eli Lilly, were standing to the rear of the battery's six three-inch guns watching the road across the fields to the east of Alexander's Bridge, and listening to the gunfire raging away to the northeast when they heard the sounds of hoof beats. A single horse was galloping at full speed toward them along the woodland trail to the north; the same trail Robert Minty had taken some thirty minutes earlier. Both men lowered their glasses and turned toward the sounds; a lone rider burst from the trees and, in a long skidding turn and without slowing, came charging across the field toward them at full speed.

Wilder and Lilly looked at each other, questions unasked, and waited. Seconds later, a bareheaded Lieutenant Cross hauled his snorting horse to a stop, showering the two officers with dust and loose earth. The horse, covered with white foam, barely in check, reared, spun on its hind legs, staggered, almost fell, and then regained its feet.

"Colonel Wilder, sir," Cross shouted, over his shoulder, trying hard to regain control of his plunging mount. "Colonel Minty is under heavy fire and requests assistance." He managed to check the heaving horse, turned to face Wilder and Lilly, wiped the sweat and grime from his brow with the palm of his hand and, breathless, continued, "He asks, sir, that you send every available man with all speed to his position east of Reed's Bridge."

"What's the enemy's strength, Lieutenant?" Wilder asked, calmly.

"It's difficult to say, sir; perhaps a full division of cavalry, and at least that many infantry, and two batteries of artillery."

"All right, Lieutenant. Go to the rear. Find Colonel Winter and ask him to join me here. He should be with Doc Marshall." Cross saluted and headed off toward the tents beyond the line of trees to the west, with the sound of heavy gunfire echoing and rolling over the woodlands behind him.

Wilder turned to Lilly and said, "What's Colonel Minty's strength, Captain Lilly?"

"Just his own brigade and a section of the Chicago Board of Trade battery, two Napoleons under the command of Captain Stokes; about nine hundred and seventy in all."

"He has to hold that bridge, Captain." Wilder shook his head, worried. "And we have to hold our positions here." He looked around. The site was a good one, selected for its slight elevation and its wide field of fire toward Alexander's Bridge and the east. His men, all armed with the new seven-shot Spencer repeating carbines, were in well-protected defensive positions behind rocks and log breastworks. Eli Lilly's long-range rifled cannon commanded the road and the line of woods to the east of the bridge, a distance ranging from six hundred to twelve hundred yards with a clear field of fire. Between them, provided that Minty could hold on, he and Lilly could devastate any enemy advancing from the east.

"They're trying to cut us off, Captain. Trying to get between us and Chattanooga. We have to hold them here, buy time." He paused for a moment, deep in thought. "We have to reinforce Colonel Minty." His tone was hard, decisive. "Detach a section of your battery, Eli. I'll send it along with the 72nd and 123rd Illinois. The remaining four guns of your battery and our Spencers should be more than enough to hold out here until nightfall, if we have to."

Minutes later, Blake Winter arrived with Colonels James Monroe and Abram Miller. Winter looked better than he had a half an hour ago, though his skin still had a pallor about it. "What's happening, Colonel?" Monroe asked.

"Colonel Minty has requested aid. I'm sending you, Colonel Monroe, with Colonel Miller and a section of Captain Lilly's battery. How are you feeling, Colonel Winter? Are you fit enough to go with them?"

"Yeah," Winter smiled ruefully, "Doc Marshall strapped me up good and tight. It hurts, but I can handle it."

"Good. Lieutenant Cross will also return with you." Wilder looked at Winter and his two regimental commanders and said, "That bridge must be destroyed. If the enemy breaks through, they'll be between us and Chattanooga. I will hold this position here. If you cannot hold, and are driven back, I suggest you retire westward and join with General Granger and the Reserve Corps. I'll meet you there."

The three officers nodded their heads in agreement, and watched as the gun crews limbered their weapons. Eli Lilly moved the remaining four guns into position to cover the gaps left in his line of fire by the removal of the two guns. Five minutes later, Monroe, Miller, Winter, and Cross rode out at the gallop along the woodland trail at the head of the two regiments of mounted infantry, almost nine hundred men and two rifled cannon.

It took the Federal column almost fifteen minutes to reach Pea Vine Creek, where Robert Minty and his lone cavalry brigade were fighting a desperate action against the slowly advancing Confederate force. The area to the west of the clearing was heavily wooded with scrub oak, pine trees, dogwood, cedar, and undergrowth thick and dense with briar, honeysuckle, trumpet vine, and poison oak. Minty's horses had been withdrawn along the road, westward beyond Reed's Bridge, and the remainder of the brigade, now under heavy fire, was spread out, just inside the line of heavy undergrowth that bordered the clearing to the east, under cover of the brush and whatever fallen trees were available.

Four hundred yards, away, Forrest's cavalry had pulled back down the road, and Bushrod Johnson's infantry had deployed north and south along the line of trees and were pouring heavy fire at the beleaguered Federals.

Monroe halted the column just short of the action and rode forward to assess the situation. Quickly, he dismounted, tied his horse to the branches of a fallen tree, and ran forward, head down, to find Minty with Stokes and the two Napoleons, well back among the trees. All around, spread over a two hundred yard front, blue-clad soldiers were pouring a hail of fire across the clearing. The continuous crash of rifle fire, interspersed with the thunder of Stokes' cannon, deafened him. Clouds of acrid smoke swirled through the trees like a heavy winter fog and hung over the field of fire like a great gray blanket, obscuring the enemy line of battle to the east. The air was filled with the angry whine of thousands of Minnie bullets and iron canister balls. The sky seemed to be raining chunks of wood, branches, and debris torn from the trees by the enemy gunfire.

"Colonel Minty," Monroe shouted above the firestorm, and grabbed him by the arm. "I've brought help," he shouted as Minty turned to greet him. "Two regiments and a pair of Parrotts. Where do you want them?"

Minty grinned. Red-eyed, his face grimy, his beard matted with sweat and dust, he coughed as he grabbed Monroe by the elbow. "Thank God, you're here," he shouted. "Deploy your men over there, to the south," he pointed in the general direction beyond the road to the right. "Wait a minute; I'll come with you." He turned to Stokes and shouted something Monroe couldn't hear over the roar of battle. Stokes, head down, hands over both ears, nodded and turned again to his guns. Minty turned, grabbed Monroe by the arm, and together they ran through the trees to the road.

"Once already," Minty shouted as they ran, "they've tried to make it across the clearing; we drove them back, but I have a great many casualties. At least fifty dead and more than a hundred wounded. We gave them hell, though. Look out there." Minty pointed through the smoke as they burst from the trees onto the road in front of the waiting column; the field was littered with Confederate bodies, wounded and dead.

"Colonel Miller, Colonel Winter," Minty shouted at the mounted officers at the head of the column, "you're a welcome sight. If you would, please deploy your men in the line of trees to the right of the road. We'll give them quite a surprise, by God. Let's give them a taste of those Spencers of yours.

"Colonel Winter," he shouted in his ear. "Help me get those two guns into position alongside Stokes."

The two men ran toward the rear of the now dismounting column, where they found the gun crews hurriedly unlimbering the two Parrott rifles.

"Lieutenant," Winter ran to the battery commander, "you'll find Captain Stokes in the trees to the left of the road. Let's get those guns into action, quick as you can."

Within seconds, the gun crews were dragging the heavy field pieces down the road toward the clearing, the ammunition caissons following close behind. In less than five minutes, the two guns had added their terrible voices to those of Stokes' two Napoleons. The long-range rifled guns hurled load after load of lethal canister, each load containing forty, one-inch iron balls, with deadly accuracy across the clearing at the four Confederate gun crews beyond. Through the haze of smoke, Winter could see the Rebel gun crews pitch and fall as the murderous hail of iron decimated their ranks. For a moment, the Rebel cannon were silent. Then, as the fallen men were replaced, they spoke again, hurling exploding shells into the woods around the Federal battery in a desperate attempt to knock them out, but to no avail.

"Colonel," Winter shouted over the roar of battle, "we've got to knock out that artillery."

Minty nodded and pointed toward the caissons just to the rear of the guns. "Solid shot!" he shouted. "Captain Stokes." The battery commander turned from his task and looked in askance at Minty. "Depress and load solid shot," Minty shouted.

"Sir!" Stokes turned again to his crews and began shouting orders. Swiftly, the gun crews, seemingly oblivious of the firestorm around them, turned the elevating screws, lowered the barrels of their pieces, and loaded them with twelve-pound iron round shot. The hail of Confederate fire continued unabated. Then, after much careful sighting,

BAM. The Napoleon closest to Stokes thundered, reared, then settled heavily back upon its wheels.

The heavy iron ball flew across the clearing only four feet above the ground. Three hundred yards out, it clipped the ground, tore a furrow several yards long into the soft earth, skipped into the air again, clipped down again, and skittered across the remaining yards of the clearing like a pebble thrown across the smooth surface of a pond until, like a great black thunderbolt, it smashed into the wheel of the nearest Rebel gun, upending it and sending great chunks of wood flying into the air, and smashing into the attendant gun crew. One man was speared through the chest, another through the stomach, and yet another took a piece of wood in the eye. The carnage was insane.

A great cheer went up all along the Federal line of battle when they saw the Rebel cannon had been disabled. Stokes' second shot missed its target, but the speeding ball smashed into the crowded Rebel line with devastating effect, tearing away legs and inflicting massive wounds.

Still the battle raged on. The combined effect of the Federal repeating carbines and the two rifled cannon now added to the two Napoleons were holding the Rebel line at bay. Slowly, however, the overwhelming numbers on the Confederate side began to take their toll, and the tide began to turn. More and more Confederate troops were rushed forward to join the line of battle.

Billy Cobb, Jimmy Morrisey at his side, his highly-developed instincts for self-preservation guiding his every step, ran forward, head down, toward the edge of the line of trees, looking wildly around as he went. To his left, he could see the red and blue Confederate battle flags and his own blue and gold 30th Tennessee regimental colors, moving fast, flying bravely on the breeze. He grabbed Jimmy by the arm, and pointed first toward the flags, then in the other direction. "No time to be a hero," he shouted. "Over there. Let's go." Together they veered to the right, away from the banners they knew were a magnet for the iron and lead already howling in upon them.

I sure ain't the bravest man in the field, Billy thought, *never was, but I'm still alive, by God, still alive.*

Quickly, ever aware of the firestorm raging around him, he found what he was looking for, and, dragging Jimmy down with him, dropped to the ground behind a fallen tree at the edge of the clearing.

Four hundred yards away across the fields, he could see the heavy clouds of gun smoke rising above the trees. Overhead, the air was filled with the shriek of a thousand angry hornets: Minnie bullets, canister, and shrapnel that tore through the densely packed woodland, shattering the limbs of the trees above, smashing and tearing at the trunk of the downed tree in front of him, and showering him with sharp shards of wood. And all around him, the deafening roar of a thousand Confederate rifles grew to a crescendo as his companions opened a deadly hail of fire on the Federal positions to the west. For a long moment, he kept his head well down behind the trunk of the tree, trying to assess his situation, to get a feel for the deadly firestorm howling overhead from across the clearing, but it was impossible, since the hail of lead and iron didn't let up for a single second.

No time to get careless, he thought, *keep your head down, Billy boy; they can't hit you if they can't see you.*

Bill Cobb was no coward, just filled with an overwhelming desire for self-preservation born of two long years in the field and half a dozen battles. He was calm now, at ease, even under the deadly barrage, in control. This was what he did best. He glanced sideways; Jimmy, too, was taking the situation in his stride.

Good man, Jimmy.

Gingerly, keeping his head well below the edge of the fallen tree, he edged his way to the right where he found a fork in the thick branches of his fortress. Carefully, he positioned himself so that he could fire through the fork without exposing himself to the enemy sharpshooters.

There was no point trying to aim the heavy Springfield rifle. All he could see through the billowing clouds of smoke was the hazy outline of the trees four hundred yards away beyond the clearing.

Take your time now, Billy Boy. That's it, juuuust about neck high, good. Now.

He cursed aloud as the Springfield bucked and slammed back against his shoulder. "Damn! That hurt." Quickly, he pulled the rifle back from the fork in the fallen tree, rolled onto his back, reached into the pouch at his waist, tore at the paper cartridge with his teeth, reloaded the weapon, slipped the ramrod back beneath the barrel, then rolled again onto his belly and, with great care, fired again through the smoke at the unseen enemy beyond.

Suddenly, to his left and rear, horses, four teams of six, great heavy-footed draft animals, came crashing through the undergrowth, dragging behind them four twelve-pounder Napoleon guns.

Billy rolled onto his back and watched as the crews, shouting and screaming at one another, unlimbered the four guns and brought them quickly to bear on the Federal line across the clearing.

BAM,BAM,BAM,BAM! The FOUR guns roared, one after the other, and then again, and again.

For several minutes, the four Napoleons kept up a steady pattern of fire across the clearing. Then, so it seemed, as if caught in the funnel of a howling tornado, all four gun crews were torn apart, to shreds, bodies lifted from their feet, clothes ripped from their backs, limbs torn away, flesh stripped from their bones, as an entire broadside of double-shotted Federal canister swept them aside like so much corn in a hailstorm.

Open mouthed, Billy watched as more than two dozen men, bleeding, dying, screaming, dead were dragged to the rear, away from the silenced Napoleons, and were quickly replaced by two dozen more; men who seemed to care little for the firestorm of death and destruction that had decimated their companions. Within minutes, all four guns were back in action, hurling load after load at the Federal line.

Billy turned again to the fork in the tree and went steadily to work aiming, at what he couldn't tell, knowing only that he couldn't stop.

Then, for a moment, perhaps longer, the fire from the Federal cannon ceased. *They're pulling back.* He thought. The thought was a fleeting one, for, as he watched, his rifle at rest in the fork of the tree, one of the Federal cannon thundered, belched a cloud of blue-gray smoke, and fell silent again. In awe, he watched the ball as it flew above the ground. He could see it, like in a dream, flying barely three feet above the surface of the field, then it dipped, tore a furrow a dozen yards long, rose into the air again, spinning, then down, skipped forward, seemed to gather speed, then like a mighty hammer, smashed into the wheel of the cannon only yards away to his left. The wheel disintegrated into a dozen pieces of flying wood and iron, inflicting grievous, jagged wounds on two of the gun crew. The mighty gun was lifted off the ground, flung into the air as if dealt a blow by the heavy hand of God Himself. The heavy gun cartwheeled, turned over, landed on its back, and smashed two more of its crew beneath its great bronze barrel. And the ball, its message of death still not completely delivered, tore onward into the ranks of the riflemen beyond the gun, taking one man, at that moment in the act of rising into firing position, in the shoulder, tearing his arm from its socket and sending him spinning backwards, screaming and showering his companions with blood.

Again, as Billy Cobb watched, a second ball came skipping across the clearing to his left. It missed the battery and flew onward into the undergrowth, waist high, decapitating one man and shattering the leg of another, before downing a sapling, its wide spread branches landing on top of four panic-stricken riflemen.

"On your feet, men. Form line of battle. Front and, Agh!" Captain Douglass was cut off by a Yankee Minnie ball that smashed through the back of his neck, killing him instantly. He pitched forward and fell on his face on the thick carpet of fallen twigs and leaves.

By noon, with casualties steadily mounting, Minty, Monroe, and Winter were already thinking it was time to pull back and destroy the bridge when, to the north, Minty spotted red and blue battle flags flying over a cloud of dust. A second Confederate column was rapidly approaching the battlefield.

"Heaven forefend, will you look at that?" Minty shouted. "It's time we were out of here. We'll withdraw beyond the bridge and destroy it. The creek is more than ten feet deep, deep enough to stop them if we can strip the bridge of its planks. We'll regroup to the west of the creek. We should be able to hold them there till nightfall."

"It's too late, look." Winter pointed through the smoke toward the far side of the clearing. A long line of gray-clad Confederate soldiers, six or seven deep, flags and banners fluttering bravely, rifles at the ready with bayonets fixed, was moving resolutely across the open fields toward them. Over the noise of gunfire, the steady beat of the drums and the sound of bugles playing the charge echoed on the breeze. It was an awesome sight, terrible, yet thrilling, even to those watching in the Federal ranks toward which the advancing Confederate line moved like a great gray wave over an ocean of green grass.

"Hell," Minty shouted, at the sight of the charging Rebel infantry. "Canister, Captain Stokes," he turned toward the battery, "double shot, and fire at will."

BAM,BAM,BAM,BAM!

Almost before the words were out of his mouth, the four mighty guns roared, hurling their packages of iron death across the clearing, tearing great gaps in the advancing Confederate line. Men and officers fell before the firestorm of canister and the hail of Minnie bullets from the Federal repeaters only to be replaced by those in the ranks behind.

On and on they came; the fire from the Federal ranks increased to a crescendo, and still the Confederate line came on. Again and again, the Federal cannon fire tore their ranks to shreds, and still they came on, almost to the line of trees, and then, for a moment, they hesitated. Men stopped, half turned their backs in a vain effort to avoid the shattering Federal fire. Then they were moving again, back the way they'd came, slowly at first, then faster and faster, until they were in full retreat, their officers trying to turn them back toward the Federal line, but it was over. The entire Confederate line retreated, back beyond the cover of the trees, leaving the field littered with dead and wounded.

"No more, Colonel Monroe," Minty shouted, over the cheers of his victorious soldiers. "We can't withstand another charge like that one. Let's get out of here.

"Captain Stokes, there's a clearing to the west along the road, on the other side of the bridge. Let's try for that. Maybe if we can disable the bridge, we can find a way to hold them from there."

Stokes nodded, snapped a salute, and turned to the gun crews. "Cease firing! Reload those things and drag them out of here, at the double, now, back along the road."

To the remains of his brigade of cavalry, and Wilder's mounted infantry, still on the ground, Minty shouted, "Keep shooting. Cover the battery." He looked over his shoulder and saw that the guns were already on the move.

Across the clearing, a great yell arose from the throats of the men in gray as they leaped to their feet and began streaming over the fields toward Minty's abandoned positions. Billy Cobb, ever the cautious one, was in no hurry to join them.

Behind them, four men on horseback watched as the soldiers dropped to their knees and began taking up new firing positions.

"Good." Nathan Bedford Forrest sat like a statue astride the great blond stallion, his uniform covered by a white linen duster, his hands folded together and resting on the pommel of his saddle. He smiled, turned to General Johnson, and said in a quiet voice as the noise of battle subsided, "Not too bad, aye, General?" Then to Colonel Dibrell, "Let's go get 'em, Colonel. I want that bridge intact." He put spurs to his horse and moved off after the charging infantry.

Chapter 8

Friday September 18th, Noon - Hazelwood

The kitchen at Hazelwood was empty except for Charity, the cook. The four iron hangers over the great open fireplace were loaded with pots, which Charity stirred, each in turn, as she bustled about, preparing the mid-day meal.

It was a large room, built onto the rear of the main house, cluttered, busy, the walls hung with sides of salt pork. The high, smoky ceiling was hung with a dozen or more brass and copper pots, pans and utensils that gleamed in the sunlight that filtered in through the windows. There were long wooden benches to sit on, and a large, much-scrubbed table with room enough to seat a dozen or so. The floor was tiled with red clay squares, polished, and worn by the soles of a thousand slippered feet. It was a homely place, comfortable and warm, where family and friends could sit easily at the table and enjoy a warm cup of mulled cider. Today, however, was different.

With each new roll of gunfire, Charity started and turned to gaze out of the window toward the trees a mile away across the fields to the east. It made no difference that the fighting was far away on the other side of the house; Charity was scared.

"Are you all right, Charity?"

Startled, the cook spun on her slippered feet, then laughed aloud when she realized the voice belonged to her mistress.

"Oh yes, Miss Sarah," she said, "but the fightin', it's coming this way. I knows it is."

Sarah nodded. "So it would seem, Charity. Have you seen Mr. Bradley? I'm worried about him."

"Not since he left before daylight this morning with Master Tom. Miss Sarah, will we be safe here, in the house?"

"We have been so far. The Yankees have been very polite and considerate, and the boys across the creek are our own. So I don't think we are in any real danger, at least not yet."

She walked over to the iron stove, lifted the lid of one of the pots, inspected what was inside then, in a whisper, she said, "I wonder where Daddy is." Then she turned, walked quickly from the kitchen into the large family room, and went to one of the windows that looked eastward toward the thick clouds of gun smoke rising above the trees. She stared at the smoke; it was much closer now.

At that moment, the door on the other side of the room burst open and with it, the sounds of distant gunfire reverberated around the room.

41

Two men, one in his early forties, the other little more than twenty years old, came into the room. Both men looked tired. The older man's clothes were stained with sweat.

"Daddy, Tom, where have you been?" Sarah rushed to her father and flung her arms around his neck.

Her brother Tom grinned at the display of emotion as he walked farther into the room. "My God, Sarah," he said, throwing himself down into a large, well-upholstered chair and draping a leg over its arm, "we've been gone no more than an hour, or two. You worry too much."

She turned angrily from her father, tight-lipped, eyes blazing, and said, "For heaven's sake, Tom. This is not a game. Grow up. You're a Confederate spy. There are Yankee soldiers everywhere. You both could have been killed."

"Spy? No, just a loyal scout, and yes, dear sister, they are everywhere, even in my bed," he said, without humor. His voice was soft, with only the barest hint of a Georgia accent. "How is the good colonel, by the way?"

Sarah looked at her brother, a tall, handsome young man. His fair hair hung to the collar of the white cotton shirt, which contrasted, starkly with the deep golden tan of his clean-shaven face and his butter-soft, form-fitting buckskin britches.

"He's gone. He left with his friends when the fighting started. He seemed... quite fit, I think."

Tom gazed up at her from the depths of the great chair, and said, "I hope he went westward. If not, I fear he's in for quite a surprise. General Bragg's army is on the move and is now less than five miles away to the east. By this evening, we will have more than sixty thousand men on this side of the Chickamauga." He paused seeing the look of horror on his sister's face. Then, with a small, tight smile, he said, "Why, Sarah, I do believe you've been smitten by the good colonel." His face hardened. "Be careful, sister; be very careful."

"Why, I'm sure I don't know what you mean." She turned and flounced angrily out of the kitchen, leaving the two men staring thoughtfully after her.

"I have to leave," Tom said to his father, rising from the chair and moving toward the door. "General Bragg has to know the enemy strength and positions. If he can move the army across the creek by nightfall, he will have the advantage at first light."

George Bradley nodded, "Be careful, son. Scout or not, things will not go well for you if the Yankees get their hands on you."

Tom turned at the door, embraced his father, took a step backwards and, with a mocking smile, snapped a salute, and said, lightly, "Have no fear, sir. I'll be back after dark." He turned and left, closing the door gently behind him.

Chapter 9

Friday September 18th, 12:15p.m. - Federal Positions at Alexander's Bridge

Captain Eli Lilly stared through his field glasses and pointed with his free hand. "Look! Over there, just to the right of the bridge, back in the trees; they're here, Colonel."

John Wilder looked in the direction his artillery officer was pointing. Deep among the trees, he could see movement. Men were gathering in great numbers, taking advantage of the cover. Wilder lowered his glasses and looked up at the sun high overhead.

"It's still six or seven hours until sunset, Captain. We have a great deal of work to do. Ready your guns, if you please."

"They're ready, sir. Just give the word."

"Good. We'll wait. It's about six hundred yards to the bridge, and fifty more to the line of trees. With the planks removed from the bridge, they will have to cross slowly, one at a time. We'll wait until they try."

Wilder turned for a moment and looked toward the column of smoke rising above the trees to the north. It was much closer now. Minty obviously had retreated toward Reed's Bridge. The sounds of battle continued unabated.

Worried, Wilder shook his head and turned again to Lilly. "I wonder how they're doing. They seem to be heavily engaged."

The two men turned at the sounds of a galloping horse approaching from the rear.

"Colonel Wilder, sir," the rider dragged hard on the reins and the horse skidded to a stop.

"Yes, Sergeant, what is it?"

"Orders from General Rosecrans, Sir." He handed the folded paper to Wilder and waited.

Wilder nodded as he read, then looked up at the waiting rider, and said, "Tell the general I understand."

The two men saluted each other, and the rider wheeled his horse and headed at full speed back in the direction from which he had come.

"General Rosecrans orders are quite specific," Wilder said, to Lily. We have to hold this position until nightfall. He didn't say so, but I believe he intends to move the army from Crawfish Springs."

Lilly looked up at the sun, high overhead, and then nodded his head. The two officers saluted each other, and Lilly went to his guns. Wilder turned and walked the length of his breastworks, offering a word or two of encouragement to his men along the way before returning to join his artillery officer at the center of his defensive line.

"Here they come, Captain."

Chapter 10

Friday September 18th, 12:15p.m. - Confederate Positions East of Alexander's Bridge

Almost seven hundred yards away, to the east of the Chickamauga, beyond the line of trees facing Alexander's Bridge, Confederate General William Henry Talbot Walker, commanding the Confederate Reserve Corps, and Generals Gist, Ector, and St. John Liddell surveyed the Federal defensive positions on the high ground to the west.

"This is not going to be easy," Walker said, his field glasses still at his eyes, "and the good General Bragg, I know, is already hopping up and down with rage because we are not yet on the other side of the creek. What do you make of it, General?" he said to Liddell. "Eight, nine hundred men and artillery, I think. And they've stripped the bridge, too. Not very considerate of them, was it? Not very considerate at all."

"Four field pieces that I can see, General," Liddell said.

Major General William Henry Talbot Walker, with his gaunt face, full beard and moustache, might, from a distance, easily have been mistaken for Nathan Bedford Forrest; both were slim, tall men; Forrest, though, had little sense of humor where Walker was a more light-hearted sort of individual. A career soldier having graduated from West Point in 1836, Walker had served with distinction in the Mexican war, during which he fought at the Battles of Contreras, Churubusco, and Molino del Rey.

After the war with Mexico, Walker did a stint at recruiting from 1849 to 1852, and then served as commandant of the cadets at West Point; he was promoted to major in the 10th U.S. Infantry in 1855. At the outbreak of the Civil War, Walker, a Georgian by birth, resigned his commission in the U.S. army and returned to his homeland.

"Well, there's no point in dallying here among the trees. Forrest and Johnson have been engaged all morning, so I suppose we can do no more than try to take some of the pressure off of them. Let's get things moving. God only knows what's happened to Polk and Buckner.

"General Liddell, please move Colonel Govan's brigade out across the clearing to try the bridge. In the meantime, let's see if we can find a fordable spot in the creek, either to the north or to the south. I see no point in giving ourselves a difficult time, or the enemy an advantage, if it can be avoided."

General Liddell saluted, turned in the saddle, called for his brigade commander, gave the necessary instructions, and then watched as the long lines of gray-clad infantry began forming in front of him. The first regiment had barely cleared the line of trees when the long-range Federal canister began to tear gaps in the lines.

"Bring forward Mr. Fowler's battery, General Liddell. Let's see if we can buy our boys a little time."

Chapter 11

Friday September 18th, 12:15p.m. - Federal Positions at Reed's Bridge

Meanwhile, a little more than a mile away to the north, Minty, Monroe, Miller, Winter, and their combined forces were steadily being driven back toward Reed's Bridge. Fighting hard for every yard, soon it would be every plank, it soon became clear that unless they could cross quickly and hold Bushrod Johnson's division in check, they would be unable to destroy the bridge, and would have to hold it.

Winter looked up at the sky through the trees and smoke, then east toward the advancing Confederate lines, turned, looked back at Minty, and shook his head to signal his assessment of the situation. It was barely noon, and the bridge was still at their backs. Everywhere, the trees swayed and bent in the wind of thousands of screaming Minnie bullets that tore, shredded, and stripped the trunks bare of bark, branches, twigs, and leaves. One minute the road was in deep shade, the sun no more than a few rays filtering through the leaves onto the hard-packed dirt, the next it was a boiling, sunlit cauldron of dust and gun smoke.

Winter turned to run back toward the bridge, shoved his heavy Colt navy revolver into his belt, and gasped as the chamber hit the wound in his side, sending spears of pain searing through his body. He dropped to one knee, took a deep breath, and started as he felt a hand on his shoulder.

"You all right, Colonel?" Lieutenant Cross yelled in his ear.

Winter nodded. "Yeah. Just give me a minute." He shook his head to clear away the pain.

"Keep those Spencer's hot, Lieutenant," he shouted up at him through cupped hands. "We've got to hold them. I'm going back to talk with Colonel Minty."

"Yes, sir. Oh hell!" A Minnie ball had torn through the cuff of Cross's jacket, flinging his arm upward with its force, leaving him shocked but unharmed, and diving for the dirt.

Winter watched him half run, half crawl, back to the front. He glanced down at the spreading stain on his own tunic, then he, too, scrambled up and ran, head down, zigzagging, more than a hundred yards, back down the road to where Minty was desperately trying to organize the tail end of his retreating brigade and the four heavy guns and their caissons.

"Colonel," Winter shouted at Minty, barely audible above the roar of gunfire. "I don't think we can hold them long enough to get the bridge down. We must get that artillery back into action. You'd better get as many of the men across as you can, and quickly; start stripping the planks.

Leave a few in place so I can get my men across. I'll do what I can to buy you some time, but they're too many for us, even with the Spencers. We'll pull the rest of the planks off as we come across. All right?"

Minty merely nodded. His face, streaked with sweat and grime, was drawn and haggard. He turned and headed for the bridge leaving Winter to face the Confederate advance alone.

Slowly, but surely, through the woods to the north and south of the road, and along the road itself, Bushrod Johnson's entire Confederate division, more than three thousand six hundred men, surged relentlessly forward, pushing Winter's defiant few back toward the bridge.

Suddenly, to the rear, beyond the bridge: BAM,BAM,BAM,BAM, a series of four terrific bangs; then the shrill scream of the Hotchkiss shells passing only feet above their heads, followed by dull, crunching explosions as the shells landed amid the forward ranks of the gray lines down the road to the east. Stokes had brought his heavy guns back into action.

Winter jumped to his feet, taking advantage of the surprise in the Confederate ranks. "On your feet, men. Back to the bridge. Move out. Now!

"Not you, Sergeant Hendricks." The big, red-bearded man stopped short. Winter grabbed his arm and pulled him into the shelter of the trees. "You and your squad will stay with me," he shouted. "As soon as everyone's across, we'll go too. We'll pull the planks as we cross."

"Sir!" The sergeant and his men dropped to the ground, Winter at their side with a Spencer, and began firing through the gaps in the trees. Behind them, the big guns continued their barrage, and the last of the Federal force cleared the bridge.

Winter looked back across the creek; Minty was frantically waving for him to move. "All right. Sergeant. Let's go." Then, heads down, the ten men ran, zigzagging, back to the bridge under a hail of covering fire; everything Minty could point in the direction of the advancing Confederate army was hurling a hurricane of death toward the advancing enemy.

Only a single row of planks remained on the crossties of the bridge. Below, the water drifted quietly by as Winter and his men grabbed the discarded planks and iron bars left behind by Minty's men and began levering the few remaining planks from the bridge. Oblivious of the firestorm raging around them, slowly, they moved backwards, flinging the uprooted timbers into the water as they went.

"SMACK." Winter was barely aware of the Minnie bullet that plowed wetly into the side of the head of the man at his side, cartwheeling him backwards and downward through the open slats of the bridge into the deep, dark waters below. Winter looked up; the enemy were close now. He looked down again at the bridge. They'd barely had time to strip away the first few yards; it would have to be enough.

"That's it. Let's get out of here. Move!" He watched as Hendricks and his men ran, teetering, arms flailing like windmills, along the single row of planks, cleared the end of the bridge, and then dived into the cover of the surrounding trees; then he, too, ran toward the wildly gesturing Minty. He'd barely cleared the end of the bridge when a terrific explosion, just yards away on the compacted surface of the road, sent him spinning sideways and forward into the bushes.

Within seconds, Minty was at his side, lifting him, pulling, and dragging him into the shelter of a nearby tree. Then, seeing Winter sit up, grin, and then shake the dust from his hair, he lost it.

"Jesus Christ, Colonel," Minty shouted above the firestorm. "What the hell did you think you were doing?" Minty was almost stuttering with anger. "You should've gotten off that damned bridge. Didn't you see me waving, god damn it?"

Winter looked up at him still a little dazed, wondering why Minty was so upset.

"We had to get the bridge down. You knew that."

"Damn it Colonel. How many Rebs do you think could cross that thing over a single plank, for god's sake? One at a time, no more than that. That's why we left it that way. You keep your damned head down from now on or, by god, I'll take it from your shoulders myself." He paused, shook his head, then looked at the stain on Winter's tunic and said, "Christ, look at you. What a mess. You're bleeding like a stuck pig. How's that wound?"

"Sore, but I'll live. I think," Winter said, with a grin.

"Jesus," Minty said, looking down the road beyond the bridge. "What a mess. What time is it, Colonel?"

Winter, now sitting up in the shelter of the tree, unbuttoned his tunic pocket and took out a pocket watch. Hands shaking slightly, he opened it, and then gazed at it in disbelief. They had been holding Reed's Bridge Road for more than five hours.

"It's twelve-thirty."

Minty looked up at the sky through the pall of smoke, shook his head resignedly, and then shouted, "Six, maybe seven more hours yet. Can we do it?"

"We can sure as hell can give it our best try," Winter shouted. "Here they come. Let's go."

And so they did, but by three o'clock, it was obvious that they could hold the position no longer, and Colonel Minty ordered the retreat. Slowly, fighting as they went, the Federal brigades moved westward along Reed's Bridge Road toward the Kelly farm.

Chapter 12

Friday September 18th, 12:30p.m. - Confederate Positions Reed's Bridge to Fowler's Ford

"General Johnson," Forrest leaned sideways in the saddle and shouted in Bushrod Johnson's ear above the roar of gunfire, "I don't b'lieve you'll have no trouble taking the bridge, now. I'll leave two brigades of cavalry with you and take the rest of my folks an' try to cross the river at Fowler's Ford, south of here. We'll join forces again on the other side."

Johnson pulled hard on the reins to steady his stamping stallion, saluted Forrest, wheeled, and galloped off toward the front where his men were moving quickly in pursuit of the Federals now conducting their desperate fighting withdrawal along the dirt road toward Reed's Bridge.

Nathan Bedford Forrest turned again in the saddle and began issuing orders. "Colonel," he shouted at Dibrell, "tell General Davidson to reform his brigade and join with us for Fowler's Ford. Mr. Morton, you'll bring your battery. Captain James, go to Generals Pegram and Armstrong and tell them to stay here in close support of General Johnson's infantry. Move it, gentlemen. Move it." Forrest put spurs to his horse, wheeled and, followed by a retinue of his officers, galloped at full speed back down the road in a great cloud of dust.

It was after two o'clock when Nathan Bedford Forrest's two cavalry brigades approached Fowler's Ford. To the north, clouds of blue-gray smoke were rising above the trees, and the constant din of musketry and cannon fire rolled and echoed across the woodland, evidence of the fierce fighting still continuing around Reed's Bridge.

To the south, a second pall of smoke was rising from the bluff and the lower ground beyond, accompanied by roll after roll of earth shaking gunfire.

Forrest, his white duster now covered with a thick coating of red grime, surrounded by a dozen of his officers, reined in his horse just short of the river crossing. He unslung his field glasses from his saddle, raised them to his eyes, and, from the cover of the trees, surveyed the ground to the west of the creek. Apart from the gunfire to the north and south, everything around them was quiet, the air still, not a leaf moving in the trees.

"It look's clear," he said to his brigade commander. "Better send a squad over to take a look around. Don't want no surprises, do we? Organize it, will you, please, Colonel?"

Colonel George Dibrell did as he was asked and together the officers watched as the patrol moved out of the cover of the trees toward the ford. Slowly, they walked their horses forward, alert for the first sign of movement that would betray the presence of an enemy on the other side. The water splashed, churned, and swirled around the horse's hooves as they entered the creek; and then they were across, and inside the line of trees beyond.

Forrest, his face an expressionless mask, waited. Behind him, more than fifteen hundred of his troopers also waited, quietly, in the gloom beneath the overhanging foliage. Only the occasional snort, or the stamp of an impatient hoof, betrayed their presence.

"Eee hah." The lieutenant on the other side of the creek called and waved a bandanna in the air to signal the all clear.

In column of twos, Forrest's small army, with Captain John Morton's Tennessee Battery at its head, closely followed by Forrest's own brigade with George Dibrell in command, moved out of the trees and across the creek toward the sounds of gunfire, and the fight that was already raging across the creek at Alexander's Bridge more than a mile away to the south.

Twenty minutes later, Forrest again reined in his horse to a stop, turned and faced his officers, and pulled a folded piece of paper from a pocket in his duster. He unfolded it, and gazed down at the hand-drawn map, then looked up, half turned in the saddle to look behind him, pointed, and said, "Over there, Mr. Morton, on the bluff, if you please, suh. Bring your guns into battery and wait on my command. Move out."

"Yes, sir, General." The young captain of artillery - he would be twenty-one years old tomorrow - wheeled his horse, gave his orders quietly to his gun crews, and then led the battery — two three-inch, steel, rifled Rodman guns and two bronze mountain howitzers - through the trees toward the rising ground to the right.

"General Davidson," Forrest said, looking down at the map, then pointing south, "take your brigade that way and work your way down to the river bank and follow it to Alexander's Bridge. George, you leave twenty men with me and continue along the road toward the smoke. We're now less than a thousand yards from the bridge. Go carefully, gentlemen. Don't engage the enemy until your hear Mr. Morton's guns open fire, and then give 'em all you've got. Move out, and good luck."

Forrest wheeled his horse and galloped off in the direction of the bluff with his escort trailing behind in single file. Less than two minutes later he was on the high ground, glasses to his eyes, surveying the terrain to the south. A grim, tight smile on his face, he watched the Federals on the bluff some six hundred yards away, blazing away with cannon and rifle at the gray-clad ranks in the forest on the east side of the creek. Some of

General Walker's men were returning, under withering fire, from the hill after an ineffective charge against the bridge; things were not going well for General Walker's Confederate forces at Alexander's Bridge.

"All right, Mr. Morton, let's see if we can ease the pressure some for General Walker. Place your two Rodmans in the center, twenty yards apart, with the howitzers one on either side. Load the Rodmans with Hotchkiss and have your gun crews aim for the Federal battery. Likewise the howitzers, but load 'em with case and use 'em against the riflemen. Quickly, now."

"Yes, sir, General."

Morton gave the orders and the more than sixty men in his battery, gun crews and drivers, swung into action, repositioning, realigning, and loading their weapons.

"Fire when ready, Mr. Morton."

Forrest, as always, considering himself virtually indestructible, remained astride his horse, out in the open where he could see what was happening around him. The Federals to the south were, as yet, unaware of his presence, but not for much longer.

"Ready your guns," Morton paused and looked from one gun to the other, then, "Fire."

BAM... BAM... BAM, BAM!

The four guns crashed almost together, then, but for the scream of the Hotchkiss shells as they arced skyward and then down again toward the surprised Federals, complete silence as Forrest, his officers, escort, and all four gun crews watched and waited. The hang time at six hundred yards for the two rifled guns was a little more than three seconds, for the two smoothbore mountain howitzers, four seconds. The two shells fired from the Rodmans landed first, one missed the target completely, the other hit the log breastwork sending great chunks of wood and a thousand shards flying into the air like a bursting rocket. The one-inch iron balls from the case shot fired from the bronze howitzers tore into the log breastworks a second later, right and left; chaos reigned in the Federal defenses.

"Wheehoo, Gen'l, lookee they rascals jump," yelled an excited gunner who could not have been more than seventeen years old. His enthusiasm was infectious. Soon every man in the battery was yelling and shouting along with him. Even Forrest, whose face was normally austere and without humor, couldn't help but smile.

The gaiety among the men of Morton's Tennessee Battery, however, didn't last long. Six hundred yards away on the bluff, the Federal positions were a hive of activity. Even without his field glasses, Forrest could see positions changing, heavy guns were being repositioned, and officers were waving their arms and yelling commands.

"Hit 'em again Mr. Morton." Forrest said, his voice barely raised, his glasses still to his eyes. "Before they can get those field pieces ranged on us. Fire when ready. Our two brigades should be getting close by now. Let's warm things up a bit."

Down by the riverbank and on the road through the woods, Dibrell and Davidson were nearing the point where the bluff and the Federal positions would be in plain view. The air among the Confederate infantry brigades on the east side of Alexander's Bridge was one of expectancy. General Walker, having learned that Forrest was now on the other side of the creek, had just received word that Lambert's Ford, a little more than a mile away downstream to the north, was clear of enemy troops and easily fordable. St. John Liddell's division, with Brigadier General Walthall's brigade in the lead, closely followed by that of Colonel Govan, was already on the move. The lead elements of General Gist's division were keeping the Federals on the bluff busy.

Unfortunately, for many of the men of General Liddell's division, the news of the crossing place to the north, and Forrest's appearance on the other side of the creek, came too late. In two desperate charges against the bridge, Liddell has suffered one hundred and seven men killed and double that number wounded.

General Walthall's men began crossing the creek at Lambert's Ford at three-thirty in the afternoon, just as Bushrod Johnson, having cleared the area to the west of Reeds Bridge began crossing the Chickamauga there.

Across the river, on the high ground to the north of the Federal positions on the rise, Nathan Bedford Forrest, still astride his horse and oblivious of the firestorm now raging around him, continued to direct the fire from Morton's battery. The entire battery, and Forrest, too, was open to the Federal gunners and riflemen alike. Two of the enemy rifled cannon were now directed toward his position and were firing double-loaded, long-range canister with deadly effect, the other two were still ranged across the river at the gray lines beyond the bridge.

"Where the hell are George and Henry?" Forrest muttered to himself as he fought to control his surging mount. "They should have bin here by now." The horse reared, twisted, almost fell as Forrest fought the reins to remain in the saddle. He wrenched the horse's head to the right, dug his spurs into its sweat-covered flanks, and galloped the few yards to where John Morton was realigning one of his Rodman guns.

The great horse, at first moving swiftly, suddenly faltered, staggered, and tried to continue, but its knees buckled and it plunged headlong to the ground, its muzzle hitting hard, rolling, withers crashing into the dirt, throwing Forrest forward in a long diving fall that ended only with his rolling headlong into the wheel of one of Morton's guns. The breath was smashed from his body by his first, bone shattering contact with the ground, his left arm and side throbbing with pain from his contact with the heavy gun, and he lay gasping for breath as Morton and a half-dozen of his men rushed to his side. Sweeping them away with his good arm, he scrambled, still gasping, onto his knees and made his way painfully to where his horse was lying flat out, sides heaving, blood spurting from one great gash in its neck and another in its lower chest, both were shrapnel wounds, and Forrest knew immediately that the animal was dying.

Holding his left side and gasping for breath, Forrest collapsed across the great beast's neck and tried to cradle its head; it was too late. With a single shuddering groan, the horse lifted its head, rolled its eyes, and died. For a long minute, Forrest lay across the dead animal's neck, trying to gather himself. Morton was again at his side with two of his men. Together, they pulled him away from the dead horse and into what little shelter there was behind a fallen tree, but Forrest brushed them aside, tried to stand, but fell heavily back again.

"It's all right, Captain," he said to Morton. "I ain't hurt bad; winded is all." He paused, gulped, gasped for air, then said, "Get me up, Captain, and find me another horse. We gotta get them Yankees off the rise." He rolled over and Morton helped him to his knees, and then his feet. He swayed, head down, still gasping, but managed to remain upright; staggered backwards a step, then turned and leaned heavily against the side of one of the caissons, both arms dangling over the wooden sides for support.

A few yards away, one of Morton's gunnery sergeants looked sideways at the corporal at his left, spat a wad of tobacco onto the ground at his feet, shook his head and shouted, "I guess ole Nate's not as bullet-proof as he thought."

"Ah, the old devil will survive, he always does," the corporal shouted back. "That's not the first time he's hadden a horse shot out from under him, and I truly doubt it'll be the last."

"All right, men," Morton yelled. "Let's blast them off the ridge. First Section. Hotchkiss. Load!" The crews at the two Rodman guns swung quickly into action: swab, load, ram, prick, friction primer, lanyard, cover, "Ready!"

"FIRE!

BAM, BAM!

RELOAD!"

Morton turned, uncovered his ears and shouted, "Second section. Case shot. Load!"

"FIRE"

BAM... BAM!

Suddenly, from the lower ground between Morton's battery and the creek four hundred yards away to the east, there was a great yell as a long line of dismounted cavalry from Davidson's and Dibrell's brigades surged out of the trees toward the Federal positions on the high ground.

Morton, seeing the charging men, moved quickly and efficiently into action. "Both sections. Canister, Double shot and fire at will. Quickly! Quickly! Cover the charge! Cover the charge!"

"General Forrest, sir."

Forrest, watching the action, still leaning heavily over the side of the caisson, turned and looked at the courier.

"Well, what is it, Lieutenant?

"Message from General Johnson at Reed's Bridge, sir."

"Well? Get on with it, man. Get on with it."

"Sir, General Johnson wishes to inform you that he has taken the bridge and is proceeding with all speed to your support. He should be with you within the hour."

Forrest nodded wearily, looked darkly at the body of his dead horse, and then said, "Tell the good general that I'll be mighty pleased to receive him."

The lieutenant wheeled his horse and rode quickly away. Meanwhile, Dibrell's and Davidson's men were already backing away down the slope, retreating in good order, from the storm of Federal fire emanating from the crest of the ridge in front of them.

For a moment more, Forrest leaned on the wagon, head hanging between his arms that were hooked over the sideboards to support his aching body, and then he turned, took the reins a trooper was offering, and, with no little effort, swung himself into the saddle. Once astride the horse, Forrest seemed to gather new strength. He put spurs to its flanks, slapped the withers with the tail end of the reins, and galloped the few yards to where John Morton was blasting away at the Federal positions with everything he had.

"Mr. Morton," Forrest shouted in an effort to be heard over the roar of gunfire, "Take command here. Keep 'em busy. I'm headin' down to see what's happening on the river bank."

Morton merely nodded, saluted, and turned again to his guns.

Forrest rode away at full gallop, down the hill toward the trees on the riverbank where the two Confederate dismounted cavalry brigades were regrouping for another assault on the bluff. Before he could reach them, however, the forest to his left seemed to come alive.

All along the line of trees, from a point on the riverbank six hundred yards to the north of the Federal positions on the high ground, almost to Morton's battery on the bluff some four hundred yard west of the riverbank, thousands of gray-clad soldiers burst into the open, banners, guidons and battle flags fluttering bravely in the afternoon breeze. The sounds of the drums and bugles echoing and rolling across the woodlands and fields above the gunfire; thousands of men, rank after rank of infantry, officers out in front, shouting and screaming their encouragement, all streaming at the double-quick, bayonets glistening in the afternoon sunshine, past Forrest's regrouping brigades, across the open ground toward the Federal positions.

Forrest reined in his horse at the edge of the line of trees, out of sight from the bluff, and watched. Even for him, a full-blown Confederate charge was an awesome sight. It was at that moment a small group of Confederate officers came riding along the line of trees toward him.

"Well, well, General Forrest," Major General William H. T. Walker said with a smile. "I see you are none the worse for your little fall. Shame about the horse, though. A gift wasn't he? From a grateful populace in Georgia after you rescued them from the bumbling Colonel Streight and his.... Well, I'd hardly call them "Raider's." Would you?

"Now then, Forrest," Walker continued, smiling over his shoulder at his officers. "We'll soon have you out of trouble. How many of them are there? Do you have any idea?"

Forrest glared at the smiling corps commander, looked around at Walker's companions, Generals Liddell, Gist, Ector, Walthall and Colonel Govan, along with an assorted retinue of captains and lieutenants, and then he, too, smiled, though somewhat tight-lipped, and said, quietly "Well, General Walker, so you've finally gotten yourself here. Linger a little too long over breakfast and lunch, did you?" And with that, he put spurs to horse and wheeled away in search of General Davidson and Colonel Dibrell, leaving General Walker and his officers gaping after him

Chapter 13

Friday September 18th, 2:30p.m. - Federal Headquarters at Crawfish Springs

Five miles away to the southwest at Crawfish Springs, Union General William Rosecrans was discussing the situation with his field commanders. It was obvious to all that Rosecrans felt the fighting to the northeast of Chickamauga Creek, although still isolated, was rapidly turning into a very uncomfortable situation.

Rosecrans, a stocky dour man with a full beard and a hot temper, was dressed in a spotless uniform beneath which he wore his signature white vest. Together with his corps commanders, Generals George Thomas, Alexander McCook, Thomas Crittenden, his cavalry commander General Robert Mitchell, and his chief of staff, Brigadier General James Garfield, he was desperately trying to outguess Braxton Bragg and his Army of Tennessee.

The six men were gathered around a small table on the center of which was a crude, hand-drawn map, and for once Rosecrans was indecisive, a situation he was unused to. Although the outcome of his bloody confrontation with Braxton Bragg at Stones River during the first days of the year was a matter of interpretation, his subsequent campaign, a series of brilliant maneuvers through Tennessee from Nashville to Chattanooga, had been fought with great skill and success. Rosecrans and his exploits had, for the past several months, been the toast of Washington. But now, although he thought he still might hold a slight advantage in numbers, he knew he was being out-maneuvered. His situation was growing ever more precarious.

"What in the name of all that's holy is he up to?" Rosecrans mused, more to himself than to the rest of the gathering. "He has us at a disadvantage, but seems unwilling to press it to its logical conclusion," he continued, thoughtfully. "What would I do if I were he?"

"Sir, I have no doubt that he is trying to place his army between us and Chattanooga," Thomas said quietly. "If he manages do that, we will be in serious trouble. There's no way out of here but to the west, and even that is a poor option."

Thomas was not a tall man - just five feet ten inches - but he was a big man, heavy-set, tough, his bearing strengthened by years of military service. His deep blue eyes sparkled, set in a genial face more than half-covered by a heavy, but neatly trimmed beard, above which peeped chubby cheeks burned dark red by the summer sunshine. It was a face that belied an authoritarian disposition and a strong sense of duty.

"General," Thomas continued, "I would strengthen the left flank as quickly as possible. Bragg has no option, if he is not already moving in that direction, he must, and soon."

"I agree," the thin-faced, goatee-bearded Tom Crittenden said. "He has no other choice. This cat and mouse game will go on forever if he decides otherwise."

"Yes." Rosecrans nodded his head in agreement. "You're right. It's what I would do, were I in his position." He looked up from the map and said, "General Mitchell, what's the present situation to the north? What of Minty and Wilder?"

Mitchell cleared his throat and said, "Colonel Minty is engaged at Pea Vine Creek, here," indicating the position on the map with his finger, "about a mile east of Reed's Bridge. He is facing perhaps two divisions of combined cavalry and infantry. According to the last report I received less than twenty minutes ago, he was holding his ground. A second Confederate force of at least two more divisions is moving toward Alexander's Bridge, here." Again, he pointed to a position on the map. "And they should arrive there sometime during the next hour. Colonel Wilder is in position just to the west of the bridge, guarding the crossing, here."

Mitchell leaned forward and turned the crude map so he could see it better, then continued, "Two more Confederate corps, commanded by Generals Polk and Buckner," he looked up at General Crittenden, "are approaching your positions here, General, and here."

Crittenden smiled, tight-lipped.

"My scouts, however," Mitchell continued, "assure me that Polk and Buckner will not arrive much before nightfall. I estimate the combined Confederate force to number some sixty thousand effectives."

Rosecrans was stunned. He looked hard at his cavalry commander and asked, "Sixty thousand. Are you sure?"

Mitchell, his eyes half-closed, nodded.

"And you are sure that Polk and Buckner will not reach the Chickamauga before nightfall?"

Again, Mitchell nodded.

"What of the four divisions to the north? Can Wilder and Minty hold the crossings until we get there?"

Mitchell merely shrugged his shoulders.

Rosecrans looked at Thomas, "What do you think, General? Can they hold?"

"If anyone can, they can."

Rosecrans nodded, then seemed to change his mind, shook his head, then changed it once more and nodded again, "They have to," he said, quietly, to himself, turning away from the others. "They have to.

"General Mitchell," he said, as he looked out of the window across the fields, "send couriers again to Colonel Wilder and Colonel Minty. General Garfield, write new orders; they must continue to hold the enemy to the east side of the Chickamauga at all costs. I must have time to move the army.

"General Crittenden, you will maintain your position at Lee and Gordon's Mill, and make ready to face Polk and Buckner. General Thomas, George, you must move your corps northward, and quickly. Establish a new position to the west of the Chickamauga, between Bragg and Chattanooga here... at the Kelly farm," he pointed to a spot on the map, then asked: How soon can you be ready?"

George Thomas looked thoughtfully at Rosecrans, and then said, quietly, "General, we will move with all speed, but I fear it will be at least two hours before we are ready to leave."

"Good, George. That's good, very good, as soon as you can. It will be a long trek. You must march through the night if you have to. We cannot afford to let Bragg take the initiative."

Rosecrans turned again to the window, his left elbow clasped in his right hand as he nervously stroked his beard with his left. Then he seemed to gather his thoughts, turned back to the map table, and said with new authority, "Yes, General Thomas." He tapped the crude map with his forefinger, "I think you might find this position at the farm will give you the advantage, should Bragg break through and cross the creek.

"General," he said, turning to face General McCook, "you and I, we'll follow with the main force as soon as we can make ready. General Mitchell, your cavalry must be deployed to support all three corps.

"General Thomas," Rosecrans turned again to Thomas, his tone earnest, persuasive, "should the worst happen, you'll have to stem the tide until we get there.

"James," he turned to General Garfield, write the order for me, will you? I'll sign it as soon as you're ready."

Rosecrans took each man's hand in turn, shook it vigorously and, at the same time, clapped each of them on the shoulder with his free hand, wishing them good luck and God's speed.

Chapter 14.

"So far, so good, Captain Lilly," Wilder said, looking down the slope after Forrest's retreating brigades. It was quieter now, and even though the Confederate battery to the north was still hurling load after load of case shot and shells against the log breastworks, Lilly was keeping his men down and conserving his ammunition for the second assault that must surely come at any minute.

"How much longer can we keep this up, though?" Wilder continued thoughtfully, "I hesitate to guess. Have you noticed how quiet it's gotten on the other side of the bridge?"

Eli Lilly nodded and said, "If I were a betting man, Colonel, which I'm not, I'd say they were looking for somewhere else to cross."

"Jesus," Wilder said. "I think you're right. Will you look at that? Here they come, Captain. Swing the second section round and double load. That's an entire division of infantry down there. Move it, Captain, and quickly.

"You men," Wilder ran forward and joined his men on the ground behind the breastworks, "make sure those Spencers are fully loaded, conserve your ammunition, pick your targets and fire slowly. Don't panic. Wait for my command to open fire, and then fire at will."

Six hundred yards away, all along the line of trees across a four hundred yard front, rank after rank of gray-clad infantry were moving resolutely forward at the double. Dozens of battle flags and banners waved and bobbed as their color bearers advanced them forward of the charging regiments.

Wilder, now lying prone behind the breastworks, scanned the long lines of men through his field glasses. *Oh my God*, he thought. *One... two, no four, four brigades. That's Walker's own division, and where they are, the other division can't be far behind.* Suddenly, he was more worried than he'd ever been. "Steady men, steady.

"Now, Mr. Lilly. Fire at will." *Now*, he thought, *just a few yards more.*

BAM... BAM... BAM... BAM.... Behind him, all four guns of Eli Lilly's battery roared, hurling a deadly hail of double-loaded canister into the advancing Confederate ranks.

Captain Lilly screaming commands, seemingly oblivious of the hail of canister and Minnie bullets that tore and shredded the logs, gun carriages, and caissons around him, ripping away great chunks of wood and hurling them skyward, to fall in a rain of razor-sharp shards that did almost as much damage as the iron and lead that had torn them loose.

"Now. FIRE," Wilder shouted, and some nine hundred men, to his right and left, opened fire with their Spencer rifles and delivered a devastating volley. The noise of the combined rifle and cannon fire was shattering. Wilder leaped to his feet cranking the lever of his Spencer and taking careful aim at a Confederate officer in full dress uniform, plumed hat, saber and all. Taking a deep breath, he squeezed the trigger. The rifle bucked, and slammed back against his shoulder. The Confederate officer, without breaking stride, pitched headlong to the ground on his face, saber and pistol flying right and left. The man lay still as the men following behind charged past and over him. In the middle of it all, Wilder saw one of the gray-clad soldiers stop at the fallen officer's side, stoop, just for a second, and then, with a yell he could hear above the din of battle, rose again, and charged onward, rifle and bayonet at the ready, and then, he, too, pitched forward and fell.

Banners fell from lifeless hands, only to be seized and carried forward again. On they came, yelling like banshees, firing their rifles as they ran, stopping, reloading, and then charging on, bayonets glittering in the sunlight against the thick pall of smoke rolling over the fields behind them. And, above it all, even, over the crash of gunfire, the Confederate drums rolling, beating out the charge, bugles playing, echoing across the fields.

Now they were less than two hundred yards from Wilder's breastworks, and still they came on, flags flying, bobbing, falling, rising again. Men falling, twisting, pitching, clutching at great gaping wounds, weapons falling from hands that were dead even before they hit the ground. Gaps in the long lines opened and then closed again, and still they came on. Two hundred yards, one-seventy-five, one hundred. Then, on command, they halted. All along the front, they kneeled, took careful aim and fired, quickly reloaded and jumped to their feet running forward again toward Wilder's positions.

Then, slowly at first, under withering fire from Wilder's Spencers and Lily's guns, they began to falter. They were now less than fifty yards from the breastworks, but slowing, then turning away from the hail of death. And then they were running back the way they'd came, falling over comrades still charging forward from the rear. In minutes the ground in front of the Federal positions was clear, except for the bodies of the Confederate dead, and the twisting, twitching, rolling, groaning wounded, some so grievously torn that life ebbed away even as the men in the ranks behind the Federal defenses watched.

On the high ground to the north, the Confederate battery had ceased fire. In the woods, new Confederate brigades were grouping for another charge. Bugles played and drums rolled as the long lines began to form.

"Continue firing, Captain Lilly," Wilder shouted. "Concentrate on the infantry at the edge of the woods. We've got to get out of here. We can't withstand another charge like the last one.

"Keep your heads down, men, and start falling back beyond the battery," Wilder shouted at his men on the breastworks. Behind him, on the high ground, Eli Lilly's battery was already hurling load after load of case shot at the Confederate brigades.

Wilder watched as his men began to pull back. He looked upward. The sun was still quite high in the western sky. He pulled his pocket watch from his tunic. It was a little after five o'clock.

Chapter 15

Friday September 18th, 5:30p.m. - Hazelwood

Sarah Bradley looked at the clock on the mantelpiece. It was already after five-thirty. It had been a long day.

She turned again to the window and looked out at the blue-clad soldiers milling around beyond the gate. To the east, the noise of the heavy guns had ceased. Only the rattle of musket fire, somewhere off in the distance, and the last wisps of smoke still drifting across the fields told of the fighting that had continued for most of the day.

She sighed, turned away from the window and wandered, distracted, into the kitchen where her father was seated at the table, drink in hand. He was lost in thought.

"Where, do you think, is Tom?" she asked, sitting opposite him.

"Probably with General Bragg," George Bradley said. "At least, that's where he said he was going. I don't think we'll see him again today. There must be thousands of Yankees out there. He'd never get through."

Sarah nodded, and sat down.

"Do you think the fighting is over?" she asked.

"Not likely, girl." He was silent for a moment and then said, "It's not even begun. That was no real battle today. Just a couple of isolated incidents. The real fighting will come tomorrow." He stared down into the depths of the cup he was holding and shook his head.

"Sarah, young lady, I think you'd better pack some things and get out of here while you still can. The Yankees won't bother you. No," he said, as she was about to interrupt, "I mean it. Take Nestor and the buggy and go on down to Lafayette, to your Aunt Elizabeth. You'll be safe there."

She bristled, set her shoulders, and said grimly, "I'm not leaving, Father. You'll have to bind and tie me and throw me into the buggy before I'll leave you and Tom here alone. Besides, if what you say is true, there'll be plenty for me to do here when the fighting begins again."

"By God, Sarah, you'll do as you're told."

She tilted her head, gave him a tight smile, and stared him in the eye. She didn't speak. She didn't have to.

George Bradley, looked fondly at her, shook his head, exasperated, and then smiled. He knew it was useless.

"Well then," he said, nodding. "But you'll stay out of the way and, by God, when I say so, you'll go to the cellar without a word of argument, not one word. Do you hear, girl?"

She nodded gravely, smiled cheekily at him, then rose, kissed him lightly on the cheek, smoothed her skirts, poured another drink, gave it to him, then turned and, without saying a word, walked out of the room and up the stairs to her own room above the kitchen, leaving him shaking his head, but smiling after her.

Sarah's room, on the upper floor at the rear of the house, was a small treasure house of feminine bits and pieces, the reminders of a childhood that had been happy and carefree, but now seemed so long in the past she could barely remember it.

She walked over to the dressing table beside the window, looked at the tintype of her mother and father, and smiled. There was another one beside it. This one pictured two smiling boys, both in uniform. When the picture had been made, one had been twenty years old, the other a year younger. They were her brothers Tom and Edwin. She picked up the picture and looked at it. A tear rolled down her cheek. Edwin had died more than a year ago, fighting the Yankees near Murfreesboro, a lieutenant in General Forrest's cavalry. Tom, her remaining brother, was the younger of the two.

She replaced the picture beside that of her parents, then reached downward and opened a drawer at the bottom of the dressing table, took out a small object, rolled it around in her fingers, and looked at it. It was a button: yellow brass with the image of an eagle, its wings spread, in sharp relief on the surface. It had come loose from Blake Winter's uniform jacket and she'd not had time to sew it back on.

She raised it to her cheek and, for a moment, held it there. Then she sighed, looked at it once more, and then dropped it back into the drawer.

Chapter 16

Friday September 18th, 6:30p.m. - Reed's Bridge Road

Federal Colonel Daniel McCook looked warily about him as he led his brigade of infantry eastward from Rossville along Reed's Bridge Road, past the McDonald farm on the right, and onward toward the bridge still more than three miles away. It was now well past six o'clock and the fighting that had caused General Granger commanding the Federal Reserve corps stationed two and a half miles away to the north at McAfee's Church to send him in support of Wilder and Minty had long since died away. Except for the sounds of sporadic gunfire seemingly far to the south, all was quiet along the dirt road. Silently, the long file of infantry, more than seventeen hundred officers and men, tramped onward through the dust in column of fours.

McCook, closely followed by his escort, reined in his horse, held up a hand to signal for the column to halt, then turned and faced his officers.

"I don't like it," he said worriedly. "Where the hell is everyone? These woods should be seething. Colonel," he said to Colonel Dilworth, his second in command, "Better send scouts on ahead. See to it, will you?"

Dilworth nodded, turned, and spurred his horse back a few yards to where six men dressed in a variety of grubby civilian clothes were waiting at the front of the column of foot soldiers; two of them were dismounted and working their horse's girths.

"You men get mounted," Dillworth said when he reached the group. "John, Seth, you two go on ahead. Stay on the road and report back as soon as you find anything. Jed, Mitch, you take the woods to the left of the road. Mica, you and Harley take the right. Stay sharp. Our leader," he said, "appears to be a little nervous." Dilworth then turned and rode back to rejoin the head of the column. Like ghosts in the night, the six scouts disappeared into the trees.

For thirty minutes more, McCook's brigade marched onward toward Reed's Bridge, never once did they see a single soul. Then, ahead, among the trees to the left of the road, voices shouting, dead wood cracking and breaking, leaves rustling. Suddenly, three men, unarmed, on foot and dressed in gray, hands in the air, stumbled out of the trees and onto the road, closely followed by two men on horseback, carbines at the ready.

McCook, pistol in hand, halted the column and, recognizing the two scouts, heaved a silent sigh of relief.

"What do we have here, men?" McCook said as the two scouts prodded their prisoners forward.

"Reb pickets, Colonel," the scout called Jed said, taking a pouch from his pocket and stuffing a wad of greasy tobacco into the corner of his mouth. "Picked 'em off just down the way apiece. Dint see any signs of more'n a few. These three was kinda preoccupied, wouldn't you say, Mitch?" he said, leaning on his saddle and turning to his companion. Mitch, grinned, chewed rapidly, nodded several times, but said nothing.

"Where are you men from? What unit?" McCook said, looking down at the three men. Their uniforms were ragged, their shoes decidedly the worse for wear, but they were fit and seemingly healthy. All three looked sheepish. One of them, a tall man badly in need of a shave, wore corporal's stripes on his sleeves.

Why, Colonel," the corporal said, "we was just mindin' our own business, so we was. Not harmin' no one. When here comes these two big fellers outa nowheres. I hardly had time to pull up m'britches before they was a shovin' an' a pokin' with them there carbines. Well, Colonel" he continued with a grin, "we just figured it would be only right to do just exactly whatever them ole boys asked of us. Yes sir."

The officers in McCook's escort grinned at the southerner's amiable attitude. McCook, however, was not amused.

"That's not what I asked," he said tersely. What is your outfit and where are they now?"

"Cain't rightly say, Colonel," the corporal said, still smiling up at him. "I knowed where they was. They was on the move south, to the west of the creek back a ways. We just kinda gotten left behind," he grinned slyly, "after we whupped up on them boys in blue back there at the bridge. Never did see anyone run quite as fast as they did when they seed what we had to offer. Why, they just upped an raaaan. Yippee! Yessir! Them good ole boys hotfooted it outa there just as fast as they could go. Sight for sore eyes, so it was, Colonel."

"Your outfit, man. What outfit?"

"Let me talk to him, sir," the scout called Jed made as to dismount.

"Whoa, man. Whoa," the corporal said, taking a step backwards. "I'll tell. No need to get upiddy. We's with the 39th Nowth Carolina, Colonel David Coleman commandin', of Brigadier General Evander McNair's brigade. Best Goddamn outfit in the entire Army of Tennessee, an' that's no lie." The corporal drew himself to attention and saluted the thoughtful Federal colonel.

"What's your strength, corporal?'

"Why, sir, I can tote a piece about as well as the next man, I spec'. Could do with a bite to eat, though," he said, looking hopefully up at the officers.

The Federal officers grinned at one another. One sniggered out loud.

"I don't want to know how strong you are, you idiot," McCook shouted, his face crimson with rage. "How many men are there in your brigade? What other units are close at hand?" He turned to the scout called Jed and said, "Liven him up a little, will you?"

"Now, now, Colonel. Call off your dog," the corporal said, a subtle change in his attitude and in the tone of his voice. He drew himself up to his full height, proud in his tattered uniform, all traces of the southern stereotype gone. "As far as I knows, Colonel, ours is the only outfit this side of the bridge. General McNair is preparing to bed down for the night just south of the woods at a place called Jay's Mill." The accent changed again, the lilting tone returning once more.

"You cain't be able to surprise him, sir. He has scouts and pickets spread out ever'where, each one within sight of the other. Be best you turn and head back the way you come, before you gets into something you cain't handle...." the corporal said, and then paused before continuing.. "Just as them good ole boys in blue did, back there on the bridge."

"Colonel Dilworth," McCook said, turning to face his field officers. Send messengers to General Grainger and General Thomas and inform them of our position. Tell them that there's a single Confederate brigade under the command of General McNair operating in the woods close by, and ask him for instructions. Tell them also that we'll bed down for the night here on Reed's Bridge Road."

McCook turned again and faced the three Confederate prisoners, looked contemptuously down at them, then at the two scouts and said, "Take them to the rear of the column and put them under guard."

No one saw the Confederate corporal wink and smile slyly at his companions as they were being hustled off at gunpoint. Corporal Isaac Williams, alias Captain Isaac Williams of Confederate General Bushrod Johnson's general staff, was very pleased with the outcome of his conversation with Colonel McCook. An hour later, the three men escaped their bonds, and disappeared swiftly and silently into the night.

Chapter 17

Friday Evening, September 18th, 9p.m. - Federal Campfire

The night air was quickly turning cold. The flames of the campfire flickered as the hardwood burned brightly, crackled, and cast a warm glow over the blue uniforms of the Federal officers sitting around it in a circle in front of the tents. A strange stillness seemed to have settled over the fields and forests. Occasionally, the silence was disturbed by the isolated rattle of musket fire somewhere off in the distance as a nervous sentry fired at ghosts in the shadows, setting off a chain reaction among his fellows. Then it would settle down again, the silence descending over the woodlands like a great soft blanket. Men stirred the embers of a thousand campfires, sipped scalding coffee, chewed upon some unmentionable morsel, and whispered among themselves of the conflict they knew must surely come at first light in the morning.

Somewhere, off in the distance among the trees, a harmonica was playing and a soldier was singing; the plaintive sounds wafted faintly in on the gentle breeze that now and then rustled the leaves in the treetops. Whether it was a Yank or a Johnny Reb, it was hard to tell, but the words of the popular song stirred deep feelings, memories, and brought tears to the eyes of many a strong man:

> A hundred months have passed, Lorena,
> Since last I held your hand in mine,
> And felt the pulse beat fast, Lorena,
> Though mine beats faster far than thine.
> A hundred months, 'twas flowery May,
> When up the hilly slope we climbed,
> To watch the dying of the day,
> And hear the distant church bells chime.
> We loved each other then, Lorena,
> It matters little now, Lorena,
> The past is in the eternal past;
> Our heads will soon lie low, Lorena,
> Life's tide is ebbing out so fast.
> There is a Future! O, thank God!
> Of life this is so small a part!
> 'Tis dust to dust beneath the sod;
> But there, up there, 'tis heart to heart.

Blake Winter, sore from his wound, worn out from the day's fighting, nursed a tin cup a third full of Irish whiskey and listened with some detachment as the others replayed the day's events for Colonel George Dick and his regimental commanders.

There were a dozen of them, a somewhat motley assortment of bearded men: colonels, majors and captains, the veterans of a dozen battles and skirmishes. Some carried the scars of battle on their faces and limbs; all were weary, relaxed now in the soothing light of the flickering fire, but attentive nonetheless.

They were camped some five hundred yards east of the Lafayette Road and about half that distance west of the Chickamauga in the fields of the Viniard farm. Minty's brigade, what was left of it, was bedded down for the night just to the east of the Kelly farm. Wilder's brigade, including Blake Winter's regiment, of which he was second in command, was bedding down for the night in a long line just to the north of the Viniard farm. Colonel George Dick's brigade, a part of General Van Cleve's division of Crittenden's XXI Corps, which had been sent to support Wilder in his frantic withdrawal from Alexander's Bridge, was bivouacked all around them. The weary officers had been relaxing thus for the past several hours.

The conversation between them had, at first, been animated as Minty described the early fighting around Reed's Bridge and their subsequent withdrawal in the mid-afternoon. Wilder, somewhat less verbose than Minty, had quietly described his delaying action at Alexander's' Bridge, Nathan Bedford Forrest's entry into the battle, and his own hasty retreat under heavy fire just prior to the arrival of George Dick's brigade.

Throughout the conversation, Blake Winter had been distant and withdrawn. At times, he seemed to gather his thoughts and pay attention, but soon wandered off again into a private world all his own. Now, he lay back in the improvised canvas chair he'd carted from one war-torn theater to another, sipped absentmindedly at the fiery liquid, coughed as the heavy cigar smoke whirled around him, and gazed absently up into the trees, alone with his thoughts.

Captain James Stokes was sitting just inside the flap of his tent at a small, rickety wooden table, pen and ink at hand, a couple of sheets of crumpled paper on the flat surface in front of him. He was writing a letter to his mother. For the moment, however, he seemed at a loss as to what to write, and so he listened to the conversation at the fire.

A dozen yards or so, away among the trees, the tethered horses stamped and snorted. One snuffled forlornly around at the bottom of its leather feed bag in search of a forgotten morsel. He lifted his head, shook it as if disgusted at the lack of food, and then dipped again to try once more.

As the night drew in and the temperature dropped, the conversation around the campfire took on a more serious note. As the officers discussed the unknown promise of the day ahead, guessing, theorizing, fantasizing, all with a deep sense of foreboding that no amount of half-hearted joking could dispel.

Then, at the sound of horses approaching through the trees, several of them started and reached for weapons. When they saw the blue uniforms, however, and the stars on the shoulder flashes of the approaching Federal officers, they relaxed again, heaved a combined sigh of relief, and started to rise to their feet.

"Good Evening, gentlemen, Colonel Dick. How are you all? No, no." Major General Thomas Crittenden held up a hand and motioned for them to remain seated. "Stay where you are. No need for formality," he said as he and his companion dismounted and gave their horses into the care of the escort. General Van Cleve and I are here to wish you all a pleasant evening and to make sure you have everything you need."

George Dick stood and offered the general his hand. "We're all fine, thank you, General," he said. "Just taking it easy and enjoying a cigar and a drop of whiskey. Would you care to join us?"

"Good. Good, but no thank you." Crittenden smiled, the heavy lines of his gaunt face accentuated in the firelight. He nodded, looked around the assembled officers, and said, "Well, Colonel, why don't you introduce the other officers?"

"Er... certainly, General." Dick turned and looked pointedly at Wilder, Minty, and Winter who rose quickly to their feet. "Colonels John Wilder and Robert Minty you already know. Colonel Winter; kindly allow me to introduce Major General Thomas Crittenden, commanding the Twenty-first Corps, and Brigadier General Van Cleve, commanding the third division, my own."

"Glad to meet you, sir." Winter said to Crittenden, shaking the general's hand.

"The pleasure's mine, Colonel Winter," Crittenden said. "I've heard good things about you.

"Colonel Wilder. Colonel Minty. I understand you were heavily engaged today."

"Yes, sir," Wilder said. "Please allow me to introduce my artillery officer, Captain Eli Lilly, Captain James Stokes, and Lieutenant Cross."

The three officers also rose and shook hands with both generals. Crittenden seemed genuinely pleased to meet them.

"I hear that if it hadn't been for all your good efforts today, we might well have been overrun. Good work, Cross," Crittenden said, as he laid a gentle hand on the young officer's shoulder.

The nineteen-year-old lieutenant blushed, turned beet red in the flickering firelight and said, "It was nothing, sir."

"Nonsense, m'boy. I don't know what you may have heard, but General Mitchell tells me that between you, you held back almost half of Bragg's entire army. We were vulnerable, gentlemen, extremely vulnerable, and would have been in a very dire predicament but for you men. General Mitchell's scouts, this afternoon, confirmed that Bragg's effective strength is now more than sixty thousand. Most of his army, however, is still beyond the Chickamauga, thanks to you.

"General Thomas is on the move," Crittenden continued, "and will pass through here sometime after midnight." He paused, and looked around the group of officers in front of him.

"General Rosecrans believes that we will take the full brunt of a combined Confederate attack by both Polk's and Buckner's Corps, right here, sometime after first light in the morning. Are you ready for them, gentlemen?"

The assembled officers answered as one, all nodding and speaking at the same time.

"Sixty thousand, General?" Wilder asked. "Is General Mitchell sure?"

"He is, Colonel. Apparently, Bragg has been receiving reinforcements from General Johnston in the west. Moreover, units of Mitchell's cavalry have taken Reb prisoners from four different Corps: Hill's Polk's, Buckner's and Walker's, as well as from Forrest's cavalry corps

"Hill is further south, near Crawfish Springs. General Negley will take care of him. Polk and Buckner are still on the other side of the creek, but less than a mile from the crossing. Walker and Forrest, as well you know, Colonel Wilder, crossed the Chickamauga this afternoon and are presently located somewhere between the creek and the Lafayette Road to the north of here. Bushrod Johnson's division is but a few hundred yards to the east of your position. General Thomas is moving quickly to contain them."

Crittenden paused again, and then continued. "Gentlemen," he said with some emotion, "all hell will break loose in the morning and we'd better be ready for it. I suggest you have a quiet evening and get some rest; you'll need it." Then he saluted, nodded once, turned, and together the two generals mounted and rode off into the night, leaving the officers at the campfire silent and thoughtful.

"John," Winter said to Wilder, "I'll be back later. I promised I'd go by the Bradley place and thank them. Don't wait up for me." He stooped, gathered up his belt and pistol, strapped them on, walked over to his horse, which was tethered with the others in the trees some distance from the tents, mounted bareback, and then he, too, disappeared into the trees.

Chapter 18

Friday Evening, September 18th, 9p.m. - The Road from Crawfish Springs

Hey, Pat," Sergeant Jesse Dixon said, slowing his pace to allow his friend to catch up. "How you doing?"

"Doin' good, Jess. How about you?"

"Could be better, I guess. We'll be making a rest stop soon. Make sure you fill both your canteens. Never can tell when you'll get another chance."

The column moved on. It was going to be a long night.

The leading elements of Major General George Thomas's XIV Corps had started the long march northward from McLemore's Cove at a little after four o'clock that afternoon. By nine o'clock, the three divisions of Absalom Baird, John Brannan, and Joseph Reynolds, more than 18,000 officers and men, were on the move in a column of fours more than three miles long, the tail end of which was only now able to get onto the road. Thomas's fourth division, James Negley's, had been left behind to deal with the threat from General Daniel H. Hill's Confederate division, still on the east side of Chickamauga.

Jesse Dixon and Pat McCann were in the leading regiment, the 10th Indiana, of Colonel Croxton's brigade of Brannan's division. They had joined the march more than two hours after the leading elements had set off, and were more than a mile and a half from the head of the column.

For the first two hours, or so, the soldiers had marched with a spring in their step, happy to be on the move again, though going God only knew where, and for what. As the evening wore on, however, and the temperature dropped toward freezing, they got down to the serious business of what was certain to be a long march.

By nine o'clock, Dixon, McCann, and the 10th Indiana had been on the march for more than three hours. All along the road, fires were burning brightly in the darkness. Everything that could be moved, easily cut down or pulled up, fence posts, rails, dead limbs and trees, had been piled along the roadside and burned to provide light and warmth for the marching column of men, and still the temperature dropped.

For as long as Jesse Dixon could remember, he and Pat had been the best of friends. More than two years ago, Pat had run alongside the train as it pulled out from the station taking Jesse off to war. Those had been tough days, lonely days, for them both. Pat hadn't yet turned fourteen when Jesse had donned his blue uniform. The boy had almost cried when he'd been left behind, and had sworn to join his friend just a soon as he was old enough for the army to take him.

Jesse had smiled at the thought, secure in the knowledge that the war would long be over before Pat ever reached that fateful age. He was wrong. Pat turned sixteen on January 7, 1863, only five days after the hell that had been the battle of Stones River. He'd turned up on the doorstep of the Indiana recruiting office the next day, his weeping mother at his side begging him not to go, to no avail.

Pat, after only three weeks of boot camp, had arrived in Murfreesboro, Tennessee, with several hundred other replacements in early March. Jesse, torn by his pleasure at seeing his friend again, and his dread at what he knew might happen to the boy, took him immediately under his wing. The two had seldom been apart since.

Battle, and all the horrors it brought, was nothing new to Jesse Dixon. He'd arrived at Shiloh just in time to help bury the bodies that were the result of the bloodiest two days of the war up until that time, but hadn't actually gotten involved in the fighting. Then he'd campaigned without receiving a scratch through the thick of a half-dozen minor engagements and skirmishes from Shiloh to Perryville.

All this had changed at Stones River. There he'd been initiated into the depths of bloodlust and destruction of human life on a grand scale. And it had been there, after the bloody action in what became known as the "Slaughter Pens," that he'd won his sergeant's stripes; a replacement for the man whose bleeding head he'd cradled in his arms until he died, choking to death on his own blood. How he'd managed to escape unscathed, he'd never been able to figure out. He had, however, prayed his thanks to the Lord for his deliverance every day thereafter.

Now, so it seemed, it was about to happen again. For days, rumors had been running riot around the Federal encampments that a major confrontation was at hand. All through the day, couriers had been seen arriving and leaving General Thomas's tent. Then Thomas had ridden off at the gallop to confer with General Rosecrans. He'd returned, hours later, red-faced, shouting orders, and began packing his things. From that moment, the several square miles around McLemore's Cove had become a seething mass of men, horses and equipment, all moving this way and that, officers trying to bring some semblance of order to the thousands upon thousands of soldiers all preparing to move at once. Then, miraculously, just as it always did, order came to the milling hoards. Rank by rank, company by company, regiment by regiment, and division by division, the great army had moved out and on toward their date with destiny.

Mile after mile they trudged on through the night, stopping, as Army Regulations demanded, for ten minutes in every hour for rest and refreshment. Of rest, they got little. Of refreshment, they got less, some none at all.

At nine-thirty in the evening, the long column came to a halt Unknown to Pat McCann and Jesse Dixon, the leading elements, having halted some ten minutes earlier, were already on the march again; it took that long for the order to work its way down the column.

Side by side, the two boys, men now, sat with their feet toward a pile of burning fence rails that crackled and sent sparks shooting high into the night sky. They lay back upon their knapsacks, lightened after they'd discarded everything they thought they wouldn't need during the battle they were sure was about to begin.

Now, they rested quietly together, sharing a strip of jealously guarded jerky, and sipping sparingly from one of the four canteens they shared. Jesse knew, that above all else, and in spite of arguments to the contrary from Pat, that water would be their most precious commodity in the long days and nights that lay ahead.

"Jess," Pat said wistfully.

"Yeah. What?"

"What's it like?"

"What's what like?"

"You know..." Pat paused for a moment, "battle."

"Well.... It's... it's like... battle," Jesse said. For a moment, he was quiet, and then he continued, "First it's quiet, see? Everyone seems to know what's about to happen and they're all scared, even the officers. Then you hear, in the distance, a single officer, a general most often, shout an order. At first nothing happens, then, maybe, there's a bugle call; doesn't matter which side it's on. It's all the same. Then," Jesse continued, gazing into the crackling fire, "you hear it, not much at first, just a faint yelling way off in the distance. Then it grows louder, and before long, the rifles join in, then the big guns; sometimes it's the big guns you hear first, and then the rifles. Makes no matter. It's all one when it comes right down to it. And then it rolls in, right on top of you." There was a fire in Jesse's eyes, and he sat up straight in the firelight, hands to his ears.

"And then all hell breaks loose. You move forward, slowly at first. Then, before you know it, you're running, and then you're up to your ankles in mud, blood, body parts, dead horses, dying horses, smoke and dust. You can't hear; your eyes are full of dirt and smoke, and you can't see, but you go on. And there's men dying, lying around all over the place: men with broken arms and legs, men running, screaming, falling, bleeding, crying, struggling, fumbling with their guns, dropping them, pushing load after load down the barrel without ever pulling the trigger, jamming them up, the stupid... silly... blessed... sons o' bitches." Jesse Dixon, quiet now, slumped back down again on the knapsack, and took a drink from the canteen.

Pat looked at him, his mouth open, eyes wide.

"Tell me about Stones River, Jess."

"I just did."

For a moment, the two were quiet, both staring fixedly into the flames.

"Jesse?"

"Yeah. What?"

"What's it like to kill a man?" Pat asked quietly. Dixon didn't answer.

"Jesse?"

"Yeah. Yeah... look, Pat, it's kinda hard to tell. It ain't like nothin'. At least, nothin' I can explain," Dixon said. "At a distance, down the barrel of a gun, ain't nothing to it. Bang, and it's done, see? But up close, it's different, real different." He stared into the fire, unblinking, eyes watering.

"You get to look 'em in the eye, Pat. Up close and personal. And they know, Pat. God damn it, they know. You can see it in their eyes. The pain. It's there even before it hits. I never killed a man up close it wasn't there. Like they've had some sort of premonition or something. It's always there...." He paused, hesitated, but said no more.

"Jess?"

"Quit it, Pat. Enough's enough. You hear? You'll learn quicker than's good for you."

But Pat McCann couldn't stop.

"Did you kill many men, Jess?"

"Too many, Pat. Too damn many."

They were silent for a moment, and then Jesse Dixon looked at his friend and said, "I had a real bad time at Stones, Pat. I saw more of my friends die in the space of two hours than I could count." He put a hand in his tunic pocket, took out something small, rolled it around in his fingers for a moment, and then held it up between finger and thumb. It was a Minnie bullet. Small, about as big around as a man's ring finger.

"See this?" he said, handing it to Pat McCann. "That's death you're holding, right there in the palm of your hand.

McCann looked at the small, conical object, hefted it. The paper charge was missing, only the lead projectile, innocent, seemingly harmless, remained.

"When that hits a man, Pat," Jesse said, "it's usually all over, no matter where it hits, unless it just grazes by. The damage that little jewel does to a man's insides is too great to bear. It smashes through flesh and bone, spreading out, tearing, gouging, and busting loose all sorts of bits and pieces inside. It hits you in the arm, and your bone's shattered; your arm has to come off. Same with a leg. Get hit in the chest and it's over, right there and then; your innards are turned to mush. Get gut-shot; it's the same. I found this one at Shiloh; keep it in my pocket for good luck. I figure if I've already gotten one, I won't get another. A bit like lightning. They say it never strikes the same place twice."

Pat McCann looked at him, eyes watering.

"I don't know if I can do it, Jess," he said. "I'm scared. Real scared."

"We're all scared, Pat. Wouldn't be human if we wasn't."

"Not scared like me, Jesse. I don't want to die."

Jesse Dixon smiled at his friend and said, "You're not going to die, Pat. We made a pact. Remember? You stick with me. Real close like. We'll be all right."

Pat McCann nodded, but even in the flickering light from the fire, Jesse could see his face was white, and his hands trembling.

"Come on, Pat," he said, rising to his feet. "On your feet. It's time to move. We'll be all right. Trust me."

Together, they joined the rest of the regiment already assembling on the road. Two minutes later the long column was moving slowly onward into the night.

Chapter 19

Friday Evening, September 18th, 9:30 p.m. - Hazelwood

It was a little after nine-thirty when Blake Winter rode his horse slowly through the campfires and tents that appeared to grow in the darkness like outlandish monsters. They seemed to bend and sway, constantly moving this way and that in the light of a hundred flickering fires. Many glowed from the inside, lit by lamps that cast fantastic shadows of their occupants and belongings onto the walls of the tents; others were dark, black shapes set against a dull red night sky to the west.

Each fire was a tiny community of ill-clad men who sat together and talked in the warm glow; faces burnished and shadowed, turned ghoul-like by the light of the flickering flames. Some were writing letters; others sat alone with their thoughts. Further on a man was singing. What it was, Winter couldn't tell. The words were of a language he'd never heard before.

Beyond the tents, in a clearing just to the west of the Lafayette Road, he could see Hazelwood, a stark black shape silhouetted against the sky to the east. Upstairs a light was shining in a window. Downstairs, there was another, the kitchen, so he thought.

Winter walked the horse slowly into the clearing, to the kitchen door at the rear of the house, dismounted, and flipped the reins over a hitching post. For a moment, he stood by the horse, wondering what, if anything, he should do next. Then, he took a deep breath, walked to the door, and knocked.

He heard the sound of a chair scraping on a stone floor from within, then a rattling on the door itself, followed by the sound of bolts being drawn. The door opened an inch or two, and a thin black face with wide staring eyes peeped out at him. Then the face lit up, beamed, flashed him a wide, toothy smile, and the door opened wider to reveal Charity's ample frame.

"Why, it's Colonel Winter, how you doin' sir? How's that wound comin' along? Never did see a man as lucky as you. No sir. I's Charity. You never did see me before, but I sure saw plenty of you, and that's a fact. Yessuh," and then she giggled, having said it all without pausing for breath.

"What you want? Want to see Miss Sarah, I'll be bound," Charity said, looking sideways at him. "You hold on right here, Colonel. I'll go get the girl," then she turned and closed the door, leaving Winter feeling slightly breathless, even though he'd not said a word.

Winter turned away from the door and walked over to where his horse was nibbling at the worn timber of the hitching rail. For want of something better to do, he checked the horse's bridle, and then scratched its nose. The horse nuzzled his hand with its lips, then swung his head sideways and gave him a gentle bunt in the ribs, causing fire to sear through his body.

"So, you came back."

He turned from the horse to face the door, startled. He'd not heard it open. She was standing there in the dark, arms folded across her chest, slim and trim in a pale lemon dress he could see by the faint light of the campfires fifty yards or so to the west. *God, she's beautiful*, he thought.

"Well... yes," he said, walking toward her. "You said I could. Remember?"

She nodded. "How's your wound?"

"It hurts, of course, but it's not so bad. I've seen worse."

"So have I. Better have a look at it. Let's go inside."

"No! It's fine. And anyway, what about your brother and father?"

"Father is in the kitchen taking a little refreshment. He'll be pleased of the company," she said. "Tom's off on the other side of the river, with General Bragg, I shouldn't wonder. Now. Do as I say, come on in and take off your shirt."

She opened the door, and the light spilled out onto her face. He hesitated.

"Now, Colonel! I won't be trifled with."

"Yes, Mam," he hesitated no more, and took a step forward into the room. Inside, sitting at a long wooden table, was an older man, perhaps in his early forties. He was cradling a crystal glass filled with a clear golden liquid in both hands.

"Well, Colonel Winter, you seem to have recovered," the man said, rising to his feet and extending a hand. He was tall, taller than Winter, and dressed in the garb of a southern gentleman farmer, tan trousers, crisp white shirt open at the neck, a leather vest and tan leather knee-length boots that shone in the light of the overhead lamp. His fair hair and finely pointed beard were already turning gray. His eyes were the same deep blue as his daughter's.

"Sorry I wasn't here to see you leave this morning. No offense intended. The name's George, George Bradley."

"Pleased to meet you, sir, and thank you," Winter said, shaking Bradley's hand, but somewhat bewildered by the man's affable attitude toward him.

81

"Oh don't worry," Bradley said, reading his thoughts. You're not the first Yankee soldier to set foot in this kitchen, and you probably won't be the last. We're all one under the skin, after all. You'll receive no military aid from me, nor do I expect to receive any from you. Hospitality and medical attention? Of course. Sit down. Have a drink. Made it myself. At least, Charity did."

"Not before he takes off his shirt and I check his dressing," Sarah said, stepping between them.

The two men laughed, and Winter obliged, pulling the shirttail from his britches and gasping as spears of pain seared through his side. The shirt was stuck to the bloody bandage beneath it.

"I thought so," Sarah said, shaking her head. "We'd better change the dressing. We don't want it to fester, do we, Colonel?" she asked, pointedly calling him by his rank, rather than by his name.

Winter didn't answer. Instead, he sat down on the bench with his back to the table, accepted the drink Bradley offered, took a strong pull on it, gasped as the fiery liquid hit the back of his throat, then settled back to watch as Sarah gently began to remove first the shirt, and then the blood-sodden bandage.

She hadn't removed many of the layers before she gave up, looked up at him, and said, "I'm going to have to cut and soak it off. It's glued together, and to your skin. If I pull it, it will cause you great pain."

Winter nodded, took another large swallow from the glass, and she began. The knife was small and very sharp. First she split the bandage vertically at the back, asked her father to hold the loose end in place so that it wouldn't fall and pull against the wound, then she did the same at the front. The bulk of the dressing fell away, leaving a large section stuck to his body.

"Charity, I'll need some warm water, please," Sarah said.

"Already comin', Miss Sarah. Already comin'. The woman turned from the fire, holding a large black pan by its iron handle, and placed it beside Sarah on the table.

"Soakin' cloth's a comin' too. Just got to get them from the closet." Charity left the room and returned a moment later with an armful of white linen.

Sarah took one of the strips, dipped it in the warm water, and, without squeezing it, held it to the remaining patch of dressing at Winter's side. His body went ridged as he reacted to the heat against the wound, then gritted his teeth and settled back again, to suffer in silence.

"So sorry, Colonel. Better me than a field surgeon, though. Don't you think?" she asked, smiling down at him.

He looked up at her, his face only inches from hers, and, for a moment, he remembered the sarcastic looks she had given him earlier that morning, but no, her face was soft, and her eyes were full of sympathy. Suddenly, he had an almost uncontrollable urge to kiss her. Instead, he looked away, raised the glass to his lips, emptied it, and handed it to George Bradley, who filled it again to the brim and handed it back.

"Please, Colonel," Sarah said, smiling, and returning the linen cloth to the water. "Take it easy with that. I don't need you falling down before we've done. It's not that bad, is it?" She returned the warm wet cloth to the wound.

"No, Mam, not bad at all," he said through tightly clenched teeth.

George Bradley laughed at his discomfort. "Well, Colonel," he said. "I suppose it was you kicking up all that racket over to the east today."

"Some, not all. Robert Minty and John Wilder were involved, too."

"Was it very bad?" Sarah asked.

He looked up into her eyes. They were wide, and full of concern.

"Yes, quite bad. I lost eleven men killed, eighteen wounded. Robert lost more than triple that number. John did better, though. He lost six killed and only nine wounded."

Sarah and her father stared at him.

"How about our boys?" George Bradley asked in a low voice.

"Not so good, sir," Winter said, twisting, trying to look at him, but thinking better of it as pain seared through his side.

"We ran up against Generals Johnson and Forrest at Reed's Bridge. That was the smoke we saw early this morning, Miss Sarah. We held them there until after three o'clock this afternoon. They lost a lot of men.

"John held out against most of General Forrest's cavalry corps at Alexander's Bridge, and then General Walker's, until after five. He estimates the Rebs, sorry, the enemy lost more than three hundred men killed and wounded."

Winter looked up at Sarah, shook his head, and whispered, "I'm sorry...."

The four people in the room were silent for a moment. Then George Bradley said, more to himself than to anyone else, "God alone knows what will happen tomorrow. May it please him to protect us all."

"Amen," all four said the word together.

For a moment, they were silent as Sarah worked gently at the dressing. Slowly she eased the sticky fabric from the wound. Each tiny progress brought a gasp of pain from Winter. By the time the sodden patch finally broke loose, he was sweating freely.

Charity brought fresh water and a pot of salve to clean and dress the wound. His arms in the air above his head he looked down at the double injury to his side. At the front, there was not much to see, just a small round hole that oozed bright red. Three inches to the rear, however, it was a different story. The exit wound was more than an inch in diameter; a bloody, sticky lacerated hole, torn and ragged at the edges, that now bled freely.

"Hell. Uh... sorry, Miss Sarah," he said, through tight lips. "I'm glad it was a pistol bullet and not a Minnie. I hate to think where I'd be right now if it had been any bigger."

George Bradley nodded and sipped his drink. Sarah said nothing, and continued cleaning the wound. She worked quickly, with swift strokes of the cloth, now soaked in some sort of clear ointment that smelled bad, but seemed to soothe.

"Charity. The salve, please," she said, without looking up.

She took the pot from the waiting Charity, who'd already opened it, and smeared the thick, green greasy concoction liberally over both wounds. Miraculously, the bleeding slowed. Whether it was the healing properties of the salve, or just its thick consistency, Winter didn't know. Sarah wiped the bulk of the salve from the wound, threw the sticky cloth down onto the table, and quickly applied a fresh coating of the salve. The bleeding stopped.

Satisfied, Sarah stood back, looked at the wound, nodded, first to Winter, and then her father and Charity. Then she sat down on the bench beside Winter, took the whiskey glass from her father's hand, and took a deep swallow. Winter watched in amazement as she handed the glass back to its owner without even the hint of a grimace from the effects of the fiery liquid.

"Now!" she said, standing up again. "Bandages, Charity."

The slim black woman smiled and handed her a square of heavy, folded material liberally smeared with salve on one side. Sarah gently placed the patch over the two wounds and, without turning, held it in place and reached behind her to take a large roll of white linen, six inches in width, from the waiting Charity.

"Now, Colonel," she said, still holding the patch in place. "Please stand, if you don't mind. And raise your arms high above your head." Winter did as he was asked.

"Thank you. Move away from the table please. Charity, I'll need you to help."

Together, the two women wrapped the bandage round and around his mid-section, until it was all used up. Sarah pinned the loose end to the rest of the bandage in front, just below his ribs.

"There," she said. "Good as new. Now, please try to take it easy. Don't twist, and don't bump it. It should hold you for a while, at least." She helped him on with his shirt, and then walked around the table and sat down opposite the two men. Charity removed the water and the dirty linen from the table and then returned to wipe it clean.

"How can I thank you?" Winter said. "You didn't have to...."

"I know. Be quiet."

"Better do as she says, Colonel," George Bradley said, handing him his drink. "She'll abide no thanks, nor arguments either."

"True, father," she said. "What can we give the Colonel to eat, Charity? Do we have any turkey left?"

"No. Really. You've...."

Sarah silenced him with a look that would have frozen pump water.

"We sure do, Miss Sarah," Charity said, ambling over to the larder.

"Here it is," she said, placing a large wooden platter on the table. "Brought some good crusty bread, too, and butter and honey. You'll eat, too. Yessir, Mr. Bradley, sir," Bradley nodded. "And you, too, Miss Sarah. Yes mam, you will. You's the one who's going to do as they's told. If'n I says you'll eat... so you'll eat. Yes mam."

Sarah smiled, but did as she was told, as Charity served all three of them generous portions of turkey breast, bread, butter, and honey.

For a while, they ate in silence, Charity pottering back and forth between the table and the larder, pouring drinks of cold tea or lemonade.

The meal ended and Charity cleared away the dishes.

"Smoke?" Bradley said, offering Winter a cigar.

"Er... no thank you, sir. I don't dare. Might cough. That would hurt."

Bradley nodded sympathetically, and lit up.

For a while, the three sat together talking, discussing the war, how it had effected their lives, how it would continue to do so. And then the conversation turned to times past. It was an altogether pleasant evening.

"Tell me, sir," Winter said, rising to leave. "How is it that you are so amiable toward me? After all, I am one of your enemies."

"That's true, Colonel, but I feel much the same as my daughter does. I've already lost one son to this infernal war. I've another out there, somewhere. But this war is not the doing of men such as you or I. We've the politicians to thank for that. You, like me, are an American, and whatever the outcome, we'll both remain so. I'll make no enemy that I don't have to. Treat me and mine as you would expect to be treated, and we'll get along. Do any one of us harm, and you'll find me a foe to be reckoned with."

"Fine thoughts, sir," Winter said, nodding. "I hope they never cause you pain. Thank you for your help and hospitality. With your permission, I'll leave now."

"Wait for me, outside, a moment," Sarah said, "I'll be with you directly."

Winter said he would do so and, with a nod to her father, and smile for Charity, he left the kitchen and walked out to his horse.

He'd not been there but a moment when he turned to find her standing next to him, head tilted upward, looking into his eyes. The shadows cast upon her face by the light from the campfires across the clearing seemed softer now; her hair was the color of burnished copper in the red glow of the firelight.

For a moment, they stood together, neither one saying a word to the other. Then, on a sudden impulse, he leaned forward and kissed her gently on the lips. Her hands rose to grip his upper arms as she responded.

Then, as suddenly as it had begun, it was over. He pushed her gently away, stepped back, and stammered, "Sarah... Miss Bradley, I... I'm sorry."

"Hush," she whispered, stepping toward him and placing her fingers on his lips. "It was as I'd dreamed."

She put her arms around his neck and laid her cheek upon his chest. "I knew the first time I saw you lying there, wounded in the forest," she said. "I couldn't understand the feelings. Then, when you rode away toward the sounds of the guns this morning, I knew. I thought I would die."

He put his arms around her and held her tightly, his chin in her hair, unable to believe what was happening; and then he realized she was crying.

"Hey," he leaned back, put a finger under her chin and lifted her face; her cheeks were wet, the tears glistening in the firelight. "It will be all right.... It will be all right."

She smiled up at him, sniffed, unable to meet his gaze, wiped her eyes with the back of her hand, and said, "You don't understand. I'm so happy, but so scared. I never believed for a moment that you could feel as I do, but you do. I can tell. But I'm going to lose you. If you're not killed tomorrow, you'll be gone from here and I'll never see you again. I know it," and then she burst into tears.

Winter held her face in both of his hands, wiped the tears from her eyes with his thumbs, and said, "No, Sarah. I'll be here. I promise. God willing, I'll be here tomorrow, after dark," and then he kissed her. She wrapped her arms around his neck and held him tightly. For a long moment, they stood locked together, neither one wanting to let go of the other. Then he pushed her gently away, just a little, and she put her cheek against his chest once more.

"Well, now. Don't that beat all?" The voice came from the shadows.

Startled, Winter stepped backwards away from Sarah as Tom Bradley emerged from the covering darkness of the trees on the far side of Winter's horse. The soft leather of his britches and jacket gleamed like molten gold in the glow of the fires, his face a mask of cold fury. He stood beside Winter's horse's head, stroking it, pulling his fingers gently through its forelock, rubbing the wide, bony area between its eyes, and then the soft silky skin of its muzzle. The horse nodded its head, and pushed its nose into Bradley's armpit. Absently, staring into Winter's eyes, he repeated the petting.

"My dear little sister," he said, barely loud enough to be heard. "My little sister and a goddamn blue belly Yankee, and a colonel, too, no less. At least you've picked a gentleman."

"Tom, I...."

"Quiet, little sister," he said, stepping around the horse and moving toward Winter, who took a step backwards and reached for his revolver.

"Tom Bradley, Colonel; scout, Army of Tennessee, and you won't be needing that," Bradley said, nodding at the pistol. "I don't believe I've had the pleasure." He extended a hand. The light from the fires glinted in his half-closed eyes.

"Winter, Blake Winter," Blake said, releasing the butt of the revolver, and reluctantly taking the offered hand.

"Oh, I know only too well who *you* are, Colonel. After all, we've shared a bed. Haven't we?" The words were humorous. The voice was hard, and with an edge that could have felled trees.

"Now, Tom," Sarah said. "We weren't doing anything wrong. Blake, Colonel Winter, that is, just came by to pay his respects and to thank us for our help." It wasn't really a lie, but it wasn't altogether the truth, either.

"Now, now, dear sister. From where I was standing, it seemed to me you two were becoming mighty friendly, mighty friendly indeed."

Sarah blushed and said, "And just how long were you spying on me, brother?"

"Long enough, my love, long enough." Then Bradley turned and addressed Winter directly, "I suggest you leave now, Colonel. I will forget what I've seen here tonight; at least I'll say nothing of it to my father. But go, and stay away from my sister, or, by God, I'll.... Well, I'll kill you." Bradley smiled as he said it, but his eyes were like flint, glittering. "I suggest you say your goodbye's. Oh, and if I see you on the field tomorrow, Colonel, I won't be quite so forgiving."

Bradley turned, and without another word, walked into the house and closed the door behind him without a backward look.

Sarah looked up into Winter's eyes. She was scared, he could tell.

"It's all right, my sweet," he said. "He'll get over it."

"No," she said. "He won't. He's not like father."

He pulled her to him, tilted her chin upward, looked into her worried blue eyes, and kissed her.

"I'll see you tomorrow, about this time. I promise. And I'll think of you all day long. I must go. It's late."

"Wait." She rose on tiptoe, wrapped her arms around his neck, kissed him hard, then stepped away and said, "Here, keep this with you." It was a thin golden pin, of a type used by a lady to secure a silk scarf at her throat. "And be careful, Blake Winter. I'll die if anything happens to you." Then she turned and ran into the house leaving him alone in the darkness.

Chapter 20

Friday Evening, September 18th, 9 p.m. - Confederate Campfire

It was dark. No, not dark; the tiny blaze in the depths of the forest cast stark shadows over the faces of the two men sitting beside it. Billy Cobb and Jimmy Morrisey preferred their own company to that of others. New friends meant new graves to dig, and new sorrows. After more than two years of losing first one old buddy and then another, and another, they wanted no more.

There'd been six of them when the war began. Then, during the first months of inaction, the group had grown to eight. At Shiloh, they'd lost George Morgan and Hubert Cole. Haggarty had lost an arm at Perryville, and young Doug Ramsey had taken a Minnie ball in the groin at Stones River; he'd died three days later. Frank Nicholls had died of the consumption; he'd coughed for days, slowly deteriorating, wasting away to nothing. The medicine they'd given him was no good. Either that or he'd lost his will to live.

Joe Kilpatrick had died only three weeks ago, of blood poisoning, the after effects of a knife wound to his left hand, sustained during a stupid fight with a corporal from the 10th, over nothing, at least nothing anyone could remember, least of all the corporal from the 10th, and he was under guard awaiting courts martial for murder.

Tempers that were short even in the best of times were lost real quick these days, Billy thought, *especially with supplies as low as they were, and what with being constantly on the move, and all. Damn, I could use a pair of boots. Well, maybe tomorrow.* He grinned at the thought.

Kilpatrick's death left just the two of them, now Captain Douglass was gone. Not that Douglass had been much of a friend, more an old acquaintance they'd both gotten used to having around. *Good man, Douglass,* Billy thought. *Damn shame.* The old man's death had left a gap that would be hard to fill.

Of the six friends who'd died, four of them had been childhood buddies. Billy had known Haggarty, as he'd also known Jimmy Morrisey, since before he was old enough to remember, since his own mother had met Haggarty's in the birthing room at the hospital just outside Pikeville, Tennessee.

At least Haggarty'd live to see the end of it, Billy thought. *One arm, though. Hell, better'n dead, by God. And who's going take over from Captain Douglass, I wonder? Not another kid, I hope. Had about all I can stand of snot-nosed youngsters who think they know all the answers. Shame of it is, every last one of them means real well, and then they die, mostly because they don't know. Hell, ain't one of them knows enough to keep them alive for more'n a week.*

He gazed up through the trees at the sky. His thoughts wandering back and forth, sometimes to his home in the hills on the Cumberland Plateau, sometimes to the horrors of a dozen mortal conflicts, Shiloh, Tullahoma, Perryville, and then, inevitably, to the white-faced youngster lying unarmed on the ground, who stared up at him with eyes wide and filled with fear. Again, he felt the scrape of steel against bone as he rammed the bayonet into the boy's ribs. The kid hadn't screamed or yelled. He'd just grabbed hold of the bayonet with both hands, coughed once, looked up into Billy's eyes, seemed about to smile, and then he just closed his eyes and fell back, dead.

"God dammit, why?" Billy said, leaping to his feet, distraught, unable to contain his emotions. *Why did I do it?* He thought agitatedly, walking back and forth around the fire as Jimmy gazed up at him. *The boy couldn't have done any harm. Why did I have to go and kill him?* He gazed, unseeing, into the night sky, his eyes watering at the memory; it was a memory he was sure would follow him to his grave.

"You're thinkin' about that boy agin. Ain't ya?" Jimmy asked, breaking in on his thoughts.

Cobb shook his head in denial, then looked his friend in the eye, nodded once, and then looked away.

"You got to quit obsessin' about it, Billy," Morrisey said quietly. "It'll kill you if'n you don't."

"Yeah, I guess so." Cobb heaved a sigh, sat down again, reached out, picked up a stick, and poked at the fire so that it flamed brightly in the night, crackled and sparked. Then he threw the stick down and stared dejectedly into the embers.

"Better get some more wood, I suppose," he said.

Morrisey nodded his agreement, but neither man made a move to fetch it.

Together they sat there, warm in the heat of the fire, arms wrapped around their knees, thinking, but not speaking. Billy Cobb stared off into the forest. The blackness beyond the circle of flickering light of the campfire was punctuated here and there by the glow of other campfires. The forest was silent, but they were not alone.

All around them, the scene was the same. In a hundred clearings throughout the woods between Chickamauga Creek to the east and the Viniard farm to the west, thousands of men of Bushrod Johnson's and John Hood's Confederate divisions - Hood's division was newly arrived from Virginia - were bedding down for the night. A short distance away to the north, fifteen thousand men of the three divisions of General Walker's corps were doing the same. To the south and to the east of the Chickamauga, thirty thousand more men of Polk's, Hill's and Buckner's Corps, were either asleep or talking softly. Almost sixty thousand soldiers of General Braxton Bragg's Confederate Army of Tennessee were poised to smash the Federal forces to the west of the Chickamauga. And more divisions were hurrying to join them.

Jimmy Morrisey took out his pocket watch and, by the light of the fire, stared at it. It was now almost eleven o'clock. He closed the watch, replaced it in the pocket, stood, stretched, and looked through a gap in the dark outline of the trees toward the southwest. Far away in the distance, on the Dry Valley Road from Crawfish Springs, the sky, lit by the flames of a hundred or more much larger fires, glowed red. An omen, perhaps?

The night air was cold, almost freezing. Everywhere, men huddled beneath thin blankets, gathered closer to the fires, and whispered of things they were sure would come to pass the following day.

"Better get some sleep, Jimmy," Cobb said, looking up at his friend.

Morrisey didn't look around, or reply. He merely nodded, and then sat down upon the ground, wrapped his blanket tightly around him, and stared into the embers of the fire.

Billy, shrugged, reached behind him, picked up his own blanket, draped it around his shoulders, and then laid himself down again. He squirmed, tried to get comfortable on the hard ground, rolled over onto his side to face the fire, wrapped the blanket more closely around him, and closed his eyes. All was quiet.

For several moments more, Morrisey sat staring into the glowing cinders. Then he shook his head, looked at Billy for a moment, and then said, "How much longer, Billy?"

"Huh," Billy opened his eyes, startled by the question. "What? Till when?"

"Not till anytime, I guess," Jimmy said. "What with Captain Douglass, and all, I just was wonderin' how much longer we can keep it up. How long before we get ours? They're all gone, Billy. Just you and me now. Just you and me."

Billy said nothing for a moment. He just stared off into the darkness. Then he turned, rolled onto his side with his back to the fire, looked at his friend and said, "It ain't gonna happen, Jimmy. We bin at it too long; gotten too damn smart.

"That's horseshit, Billy, and you know it. We ain't...."

"Hush, Jimmy," Cobb said, interrupting him and putting a hand on his arm. "Listen.... Do you hear it?"

"Hear what?" Morrisey screwed up his eyes and concentrated.

"There. Listen.... There it is again."

"Yeah, I hear it," Morrisey said sadly. "I hear it."

Far away in the distance, rising and falling with the changes of the gentle breeze, almost too faint to be heard, they could hear the sound of drums. It was a sound that filled them with a sense of foreboding.

"They're on the move, Jimmy. They's marchin' drums."

Morrisey said nothing.

Cobb looked up at his friend and saw, even in the red glow of the fire, that his face had turned white, and that his hands shook as they grasped the edges of his blanket.

Chapter 21

Friday September 18th, 11p.m. - Confederate Field Headquarters

The generals looked at one another, each unwilling to be first to take the plunge.

Forrest shrugged his shoulders, looked around at the assembled officers, and began, "Suh, my cavalry corps is now camped on the west side of the Chickamauga at Jay's Mill on our army's right flank. General Walker's corps is to my left...." He paused for a moment. Bragg remained standing with his back to his generals.

"Suh," Forrest continued. "I've been receiving reports all through the evening that a large enemy force, at least a full corps, is on the move, and quickly, from McLemore's Cove along the Dry Valley Road toward our right flank. My scouts have confirmed that the enemy force is three divisions of Thomas's XIV Corps. By morning they'll be between us and Chattanooga...."

Bragg said nothing.

"General Bragg, suh" Forrest said, looking around the group, a question in his eyes, "Crittenden's corps is camped to the south and west of the Viniard farm. Their position is weak. General Hood's and General Johnson's divisions are between them and the Chickamauga. If Thomas does as we think he will, General Hood can drive forward at first light, supported by General Walker on his right, and General Polk on his left...."

"Not good enough, General Forrest!" Bragg said, loudly, and spun around to face them. He was livid, his face red, eyes popping.

"Today's effort was a shambles; a travesty of military bungling and inaction. I know where you all are better than you do.

"General Polk: you were supposed to cross the creek this morning. You are still... STILL on the wrong side of the river."

"Sir...."

"ENOUGH," Bragg shouted, cutting Polk off, almost before he could get the first word out of his mouth. "I don't want to hear your puny excuses.

"And you, General Walker. You... you... you," Bragg was beside himself with anger, spittle flying from his lips as he tried to put angry words into sentences. "You dithered and stewed and danced back and forth on the banks of the river with no more than two regiments of dismounted cavalry to deal with on the other side. Pathetic, sir. PATHETIC!

"Look at you," he said quietly, looking slowly from one to the other.

"PATHETIC!"

General Polk jumped as Bragg shouted at them.

The atmosphere in Bragg's tent was charged. Outside, the officers of his general staff looked at one another and grinned as Bragg's voice echoed loudly through the trees, each one glad to be outside, away from the commanding general's wrath.

"Today," Bragg continued ominously, "the plan was to move to the northwest and insert this army between Rosecrans and Chattanooga and turn his left flank, and that's exactly what I still intend to do. Do you understand, gentlemen? Do you understand?"

They all nodded, not a one dared open his mouth to speak.

"Good. General Polk, you will move your corps across the river at first light and move to the right, then, together with General Walker's corps, you will press forward against all hazards. Do you both understand?"

Both men nodded.

"I didn't hear you, gentlemen.

"Yes, General," they said together.

"Good. Now then, General Buckner, it seems that you, too, lost all contact with reality this morning," Bragg said, turning his attention to the proud, mustachioed man. Buckner said nothing.

"At first light, General Buckner, you will move quickly across the river here at Thedford's Ford. Most of your corps is here at hand, so there should be no reason for delay. General Hill...." Bragg redirected his words from one general to the other without a break in continuity." The two men looked hard at each other. Lieutenant General Daniel Hill glared back at his commanding general without flinching. Bragg was the first to look away.

You, General Hill; your corps is more than four miles away to the south. At first light you will move it quickly northward and cross the river here, in support of General Buckner's Corps."

Bragg looked down at the map table between him and his corps commanders. In silence, he reached forward and traced lines on the great map, muttering to himself as he did so. The generals looked at one another, eyebrows raised.

Then, without looking up from the map, Bragg said, "General Forrest. My apologies, sir; as always, your conduct was exemplary; had you had the support you were promised, we would have carried the day. You are a credit to the Confederacy, sir. Thank you for your outstanding efforts....

"BUT NO MORE!" He slammed his fist down on the flimsy map table, collapsing it, sending it clattering to the floor, papers flying in all directions. Then he looked at them, each in turn, one after the other, and said quietly, "There will be no more of this, gentlemen, no more delays, no more of my orders ignored. From now on, you will carry them out to the letter. Any general not in full compliance will be removed from command and courts martialed at the first opportune moment. Now. Get out. General Hood, a moment of your time, if you please."

While the advance elements of General Longstreet's Corps had begun arriving in Ringgold from Virginia by railroad at noon that day, General John Bell Hood himself had not arrived until late in the afternoon. There, he found General Bragg's orders waiting for him. He was to take command of his own division and that of General Bushrod Johnson now in place east of the Viniard farm and await further orders. Longstreet himself was expected to arrive at Ringgold, momentarily.

Bragg and Hood watched as the five generals made their exits from the tent. When the flap dropped back into place behind them, Bragg turned to Hood, looked at the injured arm hanging limp at his side, then into his eyes, and said, "You don't look well, General."

Hood shrugged, glanced down at his wounded arm, and said, "A hazard of war, General Bragg."

"True. True. Tell me, General. How is General Lee? Gettysburg must have been a great disappointment to him."

Hood nodded. "He did not take his defeat well. For the past three months he has been subdued; spends much of his time alone."

Bragg turned and pulled up two small chairs, sat down on one, and indicated for Hood to take the other. He did so.

"Tell me General," Bragg said. "What happened? What went wrong?"

Hood sadly shook his head and looked pensive. "It's difficult to say, even now. As you know, after I received my wound," he looked down at his useless arm, "I spent the rest of the battle, and many days thereafter, in a field hospital...."

He paused for a moment, and then continued, "From the beginning, General Lee did not seem to be his usual self. He misses Thomas Jackson more than he cares to say. But it was much more than that. He seemed hell bent on destruction. He held a strong position on Seminary Ridge. Pete Longstreet wanted him to dig in, stay on the defensive, draw Meade to him. Had he done so, things might have gone well for us. Nevertheless, Lee insisted on taking the offensive, even though we were outnumbered almost two to one. Longstreet tried to persuade him to take a different course of action, but to no avail. The first day had been an outstanding victory, and Lee was sure that our good fortune would continue. Alas, it was not to be.

"On the morning of the second day, the 3rd of July, he insisted that I attack the slopes of the small hill through what has come to be known as the Devil's Den. This, even though the enemy's left flank was weak and ill defended. Had I been allowed to make my attack against Meade there, I might well have prevailed. As it was, I lost more than half of my division and the use of my arm...."

"Go on, General, "Bragg said, leaning forward in his chair.

"And from the beginning, Lee had problems with communication. Orders went ignored, or were misinterpreted. Ewell missed a God-given opportunity to take Culp's Hill on Meade's right flank. That was on the evening of the first day. It was not defended. Had we taken it, Meade's positions would have been untenable. As it was... "Hood paused, shook his head, and then continued. "Jeb Stuart was missing for almost the entire three days. Where he was is still anybody's guess. Off looking for glory, many believe. So, we fought with little or no idea of the enemy's disposition. Longstreet wanted Stuart courts martialed, but Lee would hear none of it; just slapped Jeb's wrist. The second day also ended in stalemate; nothing gained, nothing lost by either side. We had assailed them to the left and to the right, but both Federal flanks held firm. Then, on the third day: Pickett's fiasco. Poor George...."

"How is General Pickett?"

"Oh, you know George. He never was one for showing his true feelings. But he's a bitter man, and perhaps he should be. Lee was convinced that because Meade had been compelled continuously to strengthen his left and right during the second day, his center must have been dangerously weakened, and that a single mass attack there must punch through the Federal line.

"He was, of course, wrong. In less than twenty minutes, George lost more than six thousand men, killed or wounded: all three of his brigade commanders, and all thirteen of his regimental commanders. All those good men.... Dick Garnett, gone. They never found his body. Kemper... who knows? Poor old Trimble lost a leg." Hood sighed, looked up at Bragg, and said, "You know Lew Armistead died two days after the battle in a Federal field hospital?"

Bragg nodded, but said nothing. Hood was silent for a moment.

"Lee apologized to Pickett on the field," Hood continued, "but George couldn't look him in the eye. It should never have happened, General." Hood looked up at Bragg. "Time and again, Pete Longstreet begged Lee not to send George against the Federal center, but he would brook no argument; Pickett's charge cost Lee the battle."

For several long moments, the two men sat and stared at the dirt floor, each man alone with his thoughts. The candles flickered, guttering, almost spent. When Bragg looked up at last at the bearded face, there was a tear in Hood's eye.

"And you, John. How are you feeling? Does the wound still pain you?"

"It's not so bad. Inconvenient, that's all. Difficult to cope on horseback, but one learns to manage."

"Of course," Bragg nodded his agreement. "And what of General Longstreet? Does he fare well?"

"Old Pete doesn't change much, General. He says little, always reliable, even quieter now, though. So one wonders.... He should be here by late evening tomorrow. Transportation has been a real problem these last months; railroad lines are up everywhere. What are your plans for him, General?"

"That will depend largely upon what happens tomorrow," Bragg said. "If what Forrest says is true, and it usually is, we are on the eve of a major battle. How it will go is in the lap of God. I, too, am beset with incompetence. We should not even be here today. Had it not been for Hill, all would have been done with three weeks ago at McLemore's Cove. I shall have him courts martialed when this is over."

Hood raised his eyebrows at the statement, but Bragg continued, "I fear we shall lose this contest, General. I truly fear we shall lose." Bragg rose unsteadily to his feet and said, "Well, General, the hour grows late. We should get some sleep, if we can. Tomorrow will be a difficult day, I think.

To the west, the divisions of General Thomas's XIV Corps marched onward through the night. By two o'clock in the morning, the head of the column was approaching the Widow Glenn's cabin on the Dry Valley Road above Hazelwood. Eighteen thousand men, mostly silent now, stepped out quietly; only the occasional soft sounds of one piece of equipment clinking against another, and the tramp of marching feet on the dirt road betrayed their presence. Behind them, the dying embers of the fires along the roadside crackled and flared as the soft night breezes stirred them into new life.

97

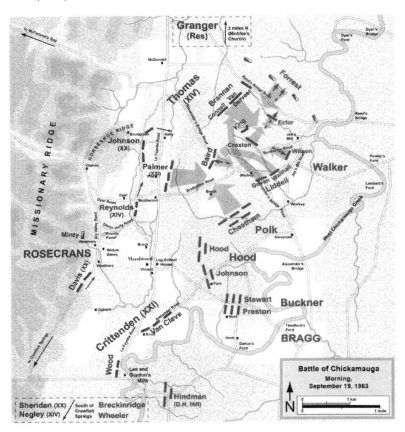

Major General George Thomas's XIV Corps, after marching through the night, was nearing the end of its march to the Kelly farm. The farm was just to the north and west of Reed's Bridge, off the Lafayette Road. General Absalom Baird's division was taking up a position around the Kelly house, and the first elements of General John Brannan's division had already crossed the field to the east of the farm and were making toward Reed's Bridge in response to Thomas's order to pursue and capture General McNair's "lone and isolated Confederate brigade," which had been reported to be in the vicinity of the bridge the previous evening by Colonel Daniel McCook. McCook having been recalled back to McAfee's Church to rejoin Grainger's Federal Reserve Corps

Thomas, never the one to pass up an opportunity, had, immediately upon his arrival at the Kelly farm, ordered Brannan's division forward to engage and capture it, thus putting what had been a defensive Federal army on the offensive.

At seven thirty, the 10th Indiana, the leading regiment of Colonel John Croxton's brigade, which was leading Brannan's division in the hunt for McNair, was moving silently through the dense forest toward Jay's Mill. Sergeant Jesse Dixon's squad, a part of the skirmish line, was in a forward position leading the regiment. To his left, trailing slightly behind some fifteen feet away, Pat McCann, white-faced, gripping his rifle so tightly his fingers hurt, moved forward with more caution than was good for an efficient advance.

"Hey, Pat," Dixon whispered as loudly as he dared. "Come on. Keep up," he said, waving him forward.

McCann gritted his teeth and did as he was asked. Every nerve in his body was strung as taught as a bowstring. His jaw ached from clamping his teeth together. He could barely see ahead through the trees, and was scared stiff even at the thought of what might lie waiting for him in the dense undergrowth.

Dixon looked across at him as he picked his way silently and sure-footedly through the trees. He shook his head, worried about what he knew was going on in his young friend's head. There was nothing he could do for the youngster. Both had known that this moment must surely come, and both knew that Pat would have to handle it on his own.

The early morning sunshine was just beginning to filter through the soft mist that hung in the treetops. The ground underfoot was wet with dew that soaked through shoe leather and turned uniforms into icy, sodden rags that clung to the skin, causing much discomfort to their owners.

The forest was a wild, dense tangle of scrub oak, pine trees, cedars, dogwood, honeysuckle, trumpet vine, poison oak, briar, and blackthorn that clung to and tore at the soldier's clothing. It was a struggle just to put one foot in front of the other, let alone maintain a silent advance. Somehow, though, the skirmishers managed to forge a path through the woods that the main body of the brigade could follow.

"Shush," Dixon hissed, and made signals for his squad to halt and get down. As one, they dropped to the ground on a carpet of sodden, half-rotten leaves and dead twigs, and they shivered as the cold bit deep into their bones. Only yards away to the front, they could see the heavy undergrowth was beginning to thin, to give way to a clearing some thirty yards or so beyond.

Through the mist that shrouded the clearing, they could see the darker shapes of tents, the shadowy images of people moving about. And, to their right, beyond the line of trees, they could hear the sounds of horses stamping and snorting. The soft breeze that blew through the forest brought new sensations; the smell of fresh coffee, and bacon cooking made Dixon realize, after his long night on the march, just how hungry he was.

Slowly, as his men watched the goings on in the Confederate camp, Dixon inched his way over to where Pat was lying wide-eyed and white-faced.

"Hey, Pat," he whispered. "Looks like we've found them. I want you to go back and tell Colonel Carroll; tell him what we've found, where we are, and ask him to send someone forward to assess the situation. Go now. Be careful, keep your head down, and for God's sake don't make a noise."

Pat McCann, his teeth chattering as much from fear as from the cold, nodded and crawled backwards a few yards, then rose to his feet and moved quickly toward the rear, head down, rifle hanging from his right hand.

For what seemed like an hour, but could only have been a matter of minutes, Dixon and his men lay, too cold to do anything but grit their teeth and wait. Then he heard sounds of men moving quickly through the trees to the rear. Unsure of who they might be, he rolled over onto his back and brought his rifle into firing position. Then he saw them. Pat was returning leading a group of officers that not only included Colonel William Carroll, his regimental commander, but also Colonel John Croxton, his brigade commander, several other colonels, and General Brannan himself.

"What do you have, Sergeant?" Brannan said, as he and the other officers dropped to their knees beside him.

"Well, Sir. It looks like a large Reb camp. Can barely see 'em through the trees. Haven't been able to get close enough to see for sure, but the camp extends way back that-a-way to the east," Dixon said pointing, "and quite a ways over to the west, and for sure it goes back further than we can see from here. I estimate there's at least a thousand men, maybe more."

Brannan nodded. "Good work, Sergeant, he said, and turned to Croxton. "What do you think, Colonel? Is it McNair?"

"I don't see who else it could be, General. If Colonel McCook's information is correct, as I'm sure it is, I'd have to say it was him. There certainly seems to be a goodly number of them."

Brannan nodded. "I agree. Well then, Colonel Croxton, you will advance your brigade and go into line of battle about a hundred yards back there in the trees where you can't be seen or heard from here. Have your men move with the utmost caution. Lieutenant Gary, you will bring forward your battery and place it at the center of Colonel Croxton's brigade and you will, on my command, open fire with canister. We still have the element of surprise. I would like to retain it," he said, pulling a large gold watch from his pocket. "If all goes well, you'll make your attack at seven o'clock, about thirty minutes from now. If you are discovered before that time, you will have to do the best you can and move forward against all hazards. Colonel Van Derveer's brigade will support your left flank with Colonel Connell's brigade to the rear in reserve. Let me know when you are in position and ready to attack. You can move out, sir."

Croxton saluted, and, together with his five regimental commanders, headed back through the trees leaving General Brannan with his two remaining brigade commanders, his staff officers, and Sergeant Jesse Dixon all on their knees peering through the trees like a band of fugitives.

"Colonel Van Derveer, how long before your men are in a position to support Colonel Croxton's brigade?" Brannan said, without turning away from the view through the trees before him.

"We are in position now, General. Just to the left on Reed's Bridge Road, less than a quarter mile away."

"Good. Good. Move out, gentlemen. Let's get this show on the road, as they say. If you need me, I'll be here with... what's your name, Sergeant?"

"Dixon, Sir. Jesse Dixon. 10th Indiana."

"Dixon. Good. I'll be here with my staff and Sergeant Dixon until Colonel Croxton comes up," he said, turning back to Dixon.

"Great work, Sergeant. Good unit, the 10th. Let's give them a taste, eh. What do you say, Sergeant? What do you say?"

"I say let's give 'em hell, General. Let's give 'em hell."

Brannan grinned at the young sergeant, nodded, and said, "A great sentiment, Sergeant. Let's do it."

Chapter 23

Saturday, September 19th, 6:30a.m. - Jay's Mill, Forrest's Camp

Nathan Bedford Forrest awoke to the sound of his orderly pouring water into the basin on the table at the side of his cot. The orderly left, and Forrest stretched, threw back the covers, and reached for his pocket watch; it was a few minutes after six o'clock. For a moment he lay on the cot, relaxed, rested, listening to the sounds of the camp already busy with the business of the day ahead. As always, he'd slept well. Very little ever bothered him enough to cause him loss of sleep. His officers joked among themselves that he could sleep on the barrel of a Napoleon gun during a barrage, and perhaps he could.

He stretched once more, rubbed his eyes, and rose from the cot. He washed, as he always did, with a certain amount of care. He cleaned his teeth on a piece of damp cloth, combed his hair and beard, and then began to dress. First, a clean white shirt, a black ribbon tie, gray britches and suspenders and black, knee-length leather boots. He'd barely pulled them on when his orderly returned with a heaping plate of bacon, eggs and fried bread, and a tin cup full of steaming coffee.

"Why'd you let me sleep so late, Corporal?"

"Seemed the right thing to do, General. I asked Colonel Dibrell, and he said he had things in hand, and after your fall yesterday, and all...."

Forrest nodded and dug into the eggs and bacon. "Is the patrol back yet?" Forrest said with his mouth full. He was referring to the first patrol of the day.

"Yes, sir. Captain Cole has just returned. The men are eating breakfast."

"Good. Have the captain report here to me as soon as he's finished eating," Forrest said, swallowing and taking another bite, "and ask my field officers to report here in thirty minutes."

The orderly nodded and ducked out through the flap, leaving Forrest eating hungrily. He finished the meal quickly, put the plate aside, downed a swallow of the coffee, rose from the cot on which he'd been sitting, pulled back the flap and looked out.

It would be a fine day. The air was crisp and cold, the dew glittered on the deep green grass, and a slight mist hung in the trees beyond the clearing. The sun was already visible as a watery yellow sphere in the eastern sky just above the line of the trees.

A good day for a fight, Forrest thought.

He turned and went back into the tent, letting the flap fall back into place behind him. He raised the mug to his lips and drained the last of the coffee, grounds and all. Then he took his knee-length, uniform frock coat from its hangar, put it on, and buttoned it almost to the throat. He turned down the collar, fingered the embroidered gold stars and wreath that were the symbols of his rank, then turned and reached for his leather sword belt. He strapped it around his waist, adjusted the position of the revolver at his right side, and then the sword itself to his left. He shrugged his shoulders to pull the heavy uniform coat into a more comfortable fit, raised his arms above his head to ease it still further, then, satisfied, looked once more at his reflection in the mirror that hung on the tent pole. He teased the beard, nodded to himself, slipped into a clean white linen duster, and sat down again on the cot.

"Captain Cole, General," Forrest's orderly said sticking his head through the flap.

"Good. Send him in, Corporal," Forrest said, rising from the cot. "Oh, and more coffee, and a cup for Captain Cole."

"Yes, sir, General," the orderly said, holding back the flap for the captain to enter.

"Good morning, Captain. Sit down," Forrest said, indicating toward a small canvas stool in the corner of the tent. "I hope your patrol was productive," he said, as he sat down once more on the cot. "It's a fine morning, so I declare, an' we must be ready for anything. What're the enemy doin' Captain?"

"Indeed it is, General, and, as we expected, there are large enemy troop movements to the west, in the vicinity of Kelly's Field. It would seem that General Thomas is moving his entire corps. His first division is already there, and two more are still on the road but making good speed. Negley's division is still way off to the south, but making ready to march."

Forrest nodded, unperturbed. "An' what of Crittenden and McCook?"

Crittenden's corps is still in position to the west of the Lafayette Road south of the Viniard farm. General McCook's corps is also on the march, but not yet in the area."

"And what about our own troops, Captain?"

Before Cole could answer, Forrest's orderly returned with the coffee. Cole took his gratefully, and swallowed deeply.

"That's quite a thirst you got there, Captain," Forrest said, smiling. "Please continue."

"Yes, sir. General Walker's corps is in position just to the south of here facing Crittenden's corps across the Lafayette Road. His right flank is less than five hundred yards from the edge of our camp here."

"Ah, yes," Forrest said, with a tight smile. "The good General Walker. What's his strength?"

"He is at full strength, General. Both divisions; five brigades in all."

"Hum, and I have two brigades. What of General Johnson's division, and that of General Hood? Where they at?"

"Generals Johnson and Hood are still in position on General Walker's left, also facing Crittenden's corps."

"And Generals Polk, Hill and Buckner, Captain Cole? Where are their corps?"

"Still east of the Chickamauga I'm afraid, sir. But they are on the move, and General Cheatham should arrive on the field quite soon, followed by the bulk of General Buckner's Corps."

"Yes," Forrest said, shaking his head. "Quite soon. That's quite wonderful, an' real good of 'em. All right, Captain. Thank your for your good offices. You can go back to your men, but have them make ready. We'll be moving out as soon as I've briefed my field officers...."

It was at that moment that the quiet of the early morning was suddenly shattered by the roar of gunfire and a hail of canister balls and Minnie bullets that tore through the camp, ripping through canvas and flesh, and turning the once quiet encampment into a shattered aggregation of utter chaos and confusion.

Chapter 24

Saturday, September 19th, 7a.m. - Confederate General Walker's Camp

Five hundred yards away to the west of Forrest's camp, Confederate General W.H.T. Walker was already preparing his corps to move to attack the Federal positions across the Lafayette Road, south of the Viniard farm to the west. His division and brigade commanders had already moved their units into position and were making ready to move off when the roar of gunfire to the right suddenly crashed and reverberated through the trees, shattering the stillness of the forest around them. So close did it seem that Walker at first thought it was he that was under attack.

It soon became apparent, however, that this was not the case, and knowing that Forrest was encamped on his right flank, and thus represented the extreme right flank of the entire Confederate army, Walker abandoned his plans for an attack on Crittenden's corps and sent his aids running in search of his staff officers.

For what seemed like an hour, Walker waited, pacing back and forth while an orderly held his horses, ducking every now and then as a stray bullet found its way through the densely packed trees and whined overhead. It was only minutes, however, before his generals and field officers came galloping into the clearing, one after another. From the high state of tension they were in it was obvious that all knew that a battle of momentous proportions was about to begin.

Walker, an impeccably dressed, bearded man with piercing black eyes, was not unlike Nathan Bedford Forest in appearance. His usually complacent attitude, now replaced by one of cold, hard efficiency that only came to the fore when he was faced with conditions that were dire enough to demand his full attention and respect, Walker swung quickly into action as the first of his officers began arriving.

Camped nearest to Walker's field headquarters, and thus the first to arrive, was Brigadier General States Rights Gist, along with his three brigade commanders, Brigadier General Matthew Ector and Colonels Colquitt and Wilson. The four officers didn't even have time to dismount before Walker sent them charging back through the trees with orders to wheel their brigades to the right and advance with all haste toward the sounds of gunfire. Brigadier General St. John Liddell passed them on his way in, just as they were heading back across the clearing at full gallop.

Liddell was accompanied by his two brigade commanders, Brigadier General Edward Walthall and Colonel Daniel Govan. They, too, were quickly sent back the way they'd came, with orders to follow in close support of General Gist's division.

Walker, happy now to be in action, rubbed his hands together, called for his horse, mounted and, with a string of staff officers in close pursuit, spurred to a gallop and headed off through woods toward the sounds of gunfire now building to a crescendo only yards away to the north.

Walker and his officers crashed through the trees and out into the clearing where the first thing he saw was Forrest, a pistol in either hand, blasting away at the unseen enemy deep in the woods while his cavalrymen were making a slow and orderly withdrawal southward in the direction from which Walker had just arrived.

Forrest, as ever, presented a magnificent spectacle. Proud, austere, beard combed precisely, face gaunt, and set, blue eyes glittering. His dress was immaculate. His uniform was covered, as it always was, by a white linen duster coat. His hat was positioned precisely upon his head. Like some heroic figure from Greek mythology, he was knelt on one knee, behind a dead horse, left shoulder leading the right, firing alternately, first with one revolver and then the other. He was, as he intended to be, an inspiring sight for his troops; he was an even more inspiring target. As always, however, he seemed to be leading a charmed life.

"For god's sake, General, get down," Walker yelled over the roar of the gunfire, his horse sliding to a stop close to Forrest as he jumped from the saddle and rolled to the ground at his side. Forrest's only concession to Walker's urgent request was to drop onto both knees and lean across the body of the dead horse, from which position he maintained a slow and well-aimed rate of fire at what few of the enemy he could see beyond the line of trees to the north.

"We must fall back, General," Walker shouted in Forrest's ear. "My corps will be here momentarily, but you are about to be overrun. Look," Walker pointed toward the long blue lines of infantry emerging resolutely from the trees, smoke, dust, and debris.

Forrest nodded. "Good to see you, General," he shouted as he reloaded his revolvers. "A more timely arrival, today, if I might say so, suh." He looked at Walker and grinned.

Walker, too, smiled. "Come, General. Now is not the time for such pleasantries," he shouted, and then grabbed Forrest by the arm.

The two generals rose to their feet and ran backwards, firing at the enemy as they went, Forrest signaling to his men to pull back beyond the trees on the far side of the clearing. That he and his men had been surprised by Brannan's approach there was no doubt. The evidence was lying all across the clearing. Bodies in various states of dress were lying everywhere. Horses, cut down by the first withering volley of fire from the 10th Indiana, were lying in heaps, some badly wounded and thrashing feebly, the rest had either run off into the trees or had been dragged away by their owners. Chaos reigned across the Confederate cavalry camp. Captain Cole's two companies had taken the brunt of the first Federal volley. Only a dozen or so of his men remained on their feet, and they were conducting what could only be called a hasty retreat. Of the rest of Forrest's division, more than fifteen hundred men were now in a state of retreat, and try as he might, he was unable, for the time being at least, to halt their headlong withdrawal into the woods.

But Forrest's untenable situation was not to last for long. Before his men had withdrawn under heavy fire, they had met with the lead elements of Walker's five brigades. Generals Gist, Ector, and Colonel Wilson soon joined with Forrest and Walker, and together they began to turn the situation around.

Ector and Wilson's brigades, closely followed by Gist's, surged past Forrest's badly mauled cavalry brigades that were even now regrouping.

"General Forrest," Walker shouted through cupped hands, "I suggest you gather your forces and move them to support my flanks. General Liddell will be through here in support of General Gist at any moment. We must protect the flanks. If we fail, we'll be overrun."

Forrest agreed, and immediately began issuing orders for the movement of his brigades. General Davidson's brigade, with George Dibrell's on his right, moved quickly northward to the right of General Ector's brigade.

Minutes later Gist's three Confederate brigades had smashed through the woods and were engaged at close quarters with Croxton's Federal brigade. The sounds of battle began to spread as more and more troops on both sides rushed in to support their own. Soon more of the singular sounds of cannon fire were added to the roar of massed rifle fire. The thunder of the great guns rippled back and forth along a half-mile-wide front as artillery on both sides, often with little more than a few yards visibility inside the close packed trees, opened fire against an almost unseen enemy.

The battle that had been expected for so long had begun in earnest.

Chapter 25

Saturday, September 19, 7a.m. - Federal Positions at Jay's Mill

On the Federal side, things at first had gone well. Colonel Croxton's brigade had come up and formed a line of battle to the left and right of where General John Brannan was still observing the scene in the awakening Confederate camp. Then, with the 10th Indiana leading, the entire brigade had moved forward to a point where they were still under cover of the trees and undergrowth at the edge of the clearing. There they halted and lay flat on the ground facing the enemy camp.

While the brigade waited patiently in line, Colonel William Carroll, in command of the 10th Indiana, ordered his colors forward and then quietly for his men to take aim. An expectant hush fell over the blue lines, and then the order to fire rang out loud and clear.

In response, Lieutenant Gary's six guns and more than nineteen hundred rifles let loose a withering volley of fire across the Confederate camp that stripped the trees on the far side of the clearing and swept aside many of the soldiers that were still cooking or eating breakfast, or otherwise engaged in the Confederate camp.

Unfortunately, probably because of the nervous state of the men in the ranks, the volley wasn't quite as effective as Carroll had hoped. Many of his men fired too high, some didn't fire at all. Even so, the once quiet enemy camp was turned into a chaotic caucus of men and horses, some dead, some wounded, most confused and disoriented.

The 10th fired a second volley, and then another. The Confederate camp was littered with bodies, the tents torn to shreds by the hurricane of Minnie bullets and canister balls. Wounded men and horses screamed, while those that could, ran back and forth in total confusion, until the stalwart figure of an impeccably dressed officer, a heavy revolver in each hand, seemed to gather them together by the sheer force of his own personality. And, try as they might, the officer seemed impervious to the efforts of the Federal riflemen that tried to bring him down.

Then, Colonel Croxton ordered the charge, and, to the beat of drums and the shrill call of the bugles, every man rose to his feet and, step by step, firing as they went, the entire brigade began to move out of the woods and across the clearing, driving the confused Confederate cavalry before it.

At the center of Croxton's brigade, Jesse Dixon's company was leading the 10th Indiana in the advance, and he was worried. Try as he might, he couldn't locate Pat McCann. And it was no wonder, for Pat McCann was no longer with the regiment. For the moment, however, Dixon was unable to do anything but handle his squad and his weapon.

Dixon, side by side with his regimental commander, Colonel Carroll, rallied his men and pressed forward. They hadn't advanced but a few yards into the clearing when he heard a terrific smack just to his left, and was immediately hurled to the ground by a spinning, falling body. The breath knocked from his own body, Jesse lay there for a second or two gathering his wits, the still body of the fallen soldier lying across his chest in a dead weight. Gasping for breath, he tried to sit up; he couldn't; he pushed at the body, moved it only slightly, and was suddenly aghast to see who it was. Colonel Carroll had taken a bullet in the eye and was dead; killed instantly. He could not have known what hit him.

In vain, Jesse shouted for help, but no one could hear him over the sounds of battle. Unable to move the big man from his chest he had no other option but to lie and wait. The regiment moved on forward and away from him.

It wasn't long, however, before he heard the sounds of battle now some distance away to the south, begin to grow louder again. Soon, there were men running past him in confusion, back toward the rear. Unable to get anyone's attention, in desperation, he grabbed the leg of a private who was running to the rear as fast as he could go, sending him rolling and tumbling to the ground.

"God damn. Whadaya do that for?" the private shouted, rising quickly to his feet and preparing to continue his headlong flight.

"Get me out from under here, for God's sake, will you?" Jesse yelled.

The man hesitated for a moment, unsure of what to do. Then he dropped his rifle, grabbed Carroll's lifeless arm, and hauled him roughly off Dixon's chest.

"Thanks...."

"Yeah, yeah," the private said, grabbing up his weapon and disappearing into the trees at the run.

Jesse sat still for a moment watching as the ever-increasing numbers of blue-clad soldiers ran past him into the cover of the undergrowth from which, only moments earlier, they had emerged at the charge. Rising to his feet, he looked around for his own weapon. He found it lying with the muzzle and half the barrel under the body of his regimental commander, and tried to pull it clear. Colonel Carroll, however, had been a big man, and it was only after an effort that left him more than a little breathless that he was able to retrieve it.

Breathing hard, he stood for a moment, and then grabbed at the arm of a sergeant, wounded and unarmed, that was half running, half stumbling toward him.

"What in God's name is going on?" he shouted in the man's ear.

The man, wide-eyed, tried to shake him off, but Dixon held on tight.

"I said, what happened?" he shouted in the man's ear.

"Ran slap dab into an ambush. Thousands of 'em. Thousands, by God. Took one in the side; hurts real bad. Let me go, dammit. Let me go."

But Dixon grabbed him by the shoulders and shook him, hard.

"Get it together, man," he shouted. "What outfit are you with? Where are they?"

The man calmed down a little, shook his head, and looked down at his left hip and the wound he was holding tight with both hands. Blood was pulsing through his fingers, coursing down his britches, and was already gathering on the ground at his feet. One look at it told Jesse the man had only minutes left to live. The look in the man's eyes told him that he knew it too.

"Let me go, will you?" the man gasped, hardly loud enough for Jesse to hear. "Got to find me a doctor." He pulled his arm free of Jesse's grasp and stumbled onward through the trees.

By now the stream of men moving toward the rear had grown in numbers, but had also slowed. Instead of running, the men were now backing slowly across the clearing, firing as they went. Jesse recognized a number of men from his own regiment, and, twenty or thirty yards away, a member of his own squad. With a last look down at his dead colonel, he took his rifle in both hands and ran across the clearing to join his comrade.

"Hey, Larkin," he shouted, as the man stopped to reload his rifle. "What the hell happened?"

"Sarge," Larkin shouted. "Hell, man. You're covered in blood. You hurt? Thought you was a goner. Where you bin?"

"Never mind," Dixon yelled in his ear. "Tell me what happened."

"Well, one minute you was there, right beside me, the next you was gone. Anyway, we moved right on across the clearing and into the woods, chasing them Rebs just as fast as they could run. Must have gone a quarter mile or more and we runs right slap dab into Reb infantry. Hell, Sarge, there was thousands of them. I mean thousands. Must have been a full division at least, and maybe more, and they's heading right this way. Better get moving, Jesse. Things is going to get right messy here."

"Where are Colonel Croxton, and General Brannan?"

"Hell, Jesse. How would I know?" he shouted, "I don't have no truck with the likes of them. Back there in the trees, I should say. And there they'll stay if they don't move out right quick," Larkin said, shoving the rifle's ramrod back into place beneath the barrel. "Let's get the hell out of here, Jesse, while we still can."

"Just a minute, man. Just a minute," Dixon shouted, holding Larkin's wrist, and barely avoiding a private who, after firing his weapon blindly into the trees, spun round and almost crashed into him. "Where's Pat, Larkin?"

"You're guess is as good as mine, Jesse. Christ, Jesse; let me go, will you?" he shouted, and tried to pull free. "The last I saw of him was over there in the woods," he said, nodding his head to indicate the direction, and tried again to pull clear of Jesse's grasp. "He was reloading. All right, all right. Let's go, Jesse. Dammit. Let's go."

Larkin, Jesse could tell, was on the edge of panic, so he released his grip on the man's arm and together they ran for the cover of the trees. Then, angling toward the right, he headed toward the spot where he'd last seen Pat McCann.

Jesse Dixon found his friend just beyond the line of trees in deep undergrowth. He was on his knees behind a large oak tree, rifle on the ground at his side. He was shaking violently, his eyes clamped shut, teeth bared, hands grasping either side of the trunk, grasping it so hard his knuckles showed white. His forehead was pressed hard against the bark, and he was moaning softly through his teeth; Pat McCann was petrified with fear.

Jesse dropped his rifle and grabbed the boy's shoulders. "Pat. It's me," he said, turning him from the tree and pulling him to his feet. "Come on, Pat. Let's get out of here." He picked up his rifle, and Pat's, put his free arm around the boy's shoulder, and led him slowly back toward the rear, both of them oblivious of the storm now gathering around them.

111

Chapter 26

Saturday, September 19, 9a.m. - Federal Field Headquarters at the Kelly Farm

By sun-up, General George Thomas had established his field headquarters in the Kelly house between the Lafayette and Alexander's Bridge Roads. By nine o'clock, his divisions were pouring into the area, down the Glenn Kelly Road and, as each brigade arrived, he deployed it immediately. Slowly, his defensive line was building. Baird's division, which had arrived first, was deployed in the fields around the farm. Brannan's division, following on behind Baird, had moved to the right and marched on by and was soon heavily engaged with Forrest's cavalry corps and Walker's corps of infantry.

As soon as Thomas realized that Brannan was not engaged with a single, isolated Confederate brigade, he sent a courier to General Rosecrans who, in turn, issued orders to General Crittenden to abandon his positions to the south, move northward and put his divisions into line of battle along the Lafayette Road in front of Hazelwood, the Viniard fields and beyond the Brotherton house almost as far north as the boundaries of the Kelly farm to the left of Thomas's headquarters there.

As intelligence reports began to come in from all around the battlefield, Thomas became aware of a fact that his commanding general was, as yet, unaware of: the Federal Army was outnumbered. Bragg's Confederate army now was more than sixty thousand strong; Rosecrans could field no more than fifty-five thousand.

For hour after hour, Thomas ranged back and forth on horseback between the Kelly house and the Lafayette Road, watching impatiently as regiment after regiment filed by, and then east to the edge of the woods beyond which Brannan's division was now fighting for its very existence. But in that direction, he could see nothing for the dense woodland that obscured his view. Only the shattering roar of gunfire that rolled and reverberated across the battlefield gave any indication of what was going on, and where. Only the scouts and couriers that dashed constantly back and forth from the front with news of one regiment and then another, offered any real clue as how the battle might be going. And already he knew that it wasn't going well.

Silently, Thomas watched as the long columns of soldiers marched in from the south. Repeatedly he conferred with his officers as to what might be the best disposition for his troops as they became available. Decisions were made, and then unmade, orders were given and then countermanded as he rushed brigades and regiments this way and that to answer one new Confederate threat after another. And the battle continued to escalate.

Thomas's aides wore new tracks in the dirt road as they galloped back and forth between the Kelly house and General Rosecrans, now on the road to join him on the field. So fluid was the battle that no sooner had Thomas sent one courier galloping off to the south, than he had to send another with an up-date. By mid-morning, he was frustrated and impatient. It was obvious that Brannan's division was in difficulties but, as yet, he had been able to do little to help him. And, try as he might, he couldn't keep abreast of the progress of the battle now raging like a gathering hurricane.

At last, at around ten-thirty, realizing that if he didn't do something to help Brannan, and quickly, the division would be lost. He ordered Baird's division to move quickly eastward along Alexander's Bridge Road and then turn north to join Brannan on his right flank.

Then, accepting the inevitable, Thomas began to form a new line of battle that would run from the Kelly house more than two and a half miles southward almost to the Scott house beyond the Viniard farm and Hazelwood to the south. It wasn't much of a plan, but it was the only one he had, considering the still essentially unknown enemy dispositions to the east.

Chapter 27

Saturday September 19th, 9a.m. - Confederate Campfire

As the quiet of the early morning exploded to the north, Billy Cobb and Jimmy Morrisey had already finished the remains of a sparse breakfast of beans and bread burned black over the rekindled embers of the previous evening's fire. For more than two hours, since long before sun-up, the two men had been sitting quietly beneath the crowded branches of an age-old cedar, talking together, and, between swallows of thick black coffee, cleaning their weapons. The tree was at the edge of the Confederate camp, far enough away from their comrades for them to be alone, but close enough to hear if anything untoward should happen.

Exactly where they were, they didn't know. For most of the night however, they had lay under the tree, wrapped in tattered blankets that had seen even more service than they had, and they had listened to the sounds of the Federal army preparing breastworks and defensive lines just across the fields and the Lafayette Road to the west. Early on, they heard the sounds of voices, some laughing, some singing, and then, as it began to grow lighter, the sounds of marching feet.

As the watery sun came up behind the trees to the east, the Confederate camp began to come alive. Fires were stirred once more into crackling blazes, and those that had the makings cooked the first meal of the day; those that didn't begged what they could from a friend; no one went hungry.

A little after six-thirty the officers had ridden by on their morning inspection. Bushrod Johnson, as he ever was, seemed cheerful and upbeat. General Hood, a man the two privates had only heard about, was quieter. While Johnson had an encouraging word for everyone Hood, impeccably dressed, as most Confederate general officers always were, had nothing to say. He simply sat at Johnson's side, watched, listened, and contemplated, and then the two generals and their aids moved on through the trees and, for a while at least, out of their lives.

Then, just to the north, it seemed as if the gates of hell had fallen. For a moment, there was panic in the camp as men ran here and there, stumbling and crashing into one another in their search for weapons laid aside the previous evening, but it soon subsided when they realized that it was not they that were under attack. Through it all Billy and Jimmy sat unmoving, unperturbed, beneath the tree and watched, too experienced to be affected by the general confusion in the camp. Then, as the officers began calling their regiments and brigades into line, they got leisurely to their feet, dusted off their rifles, swallowed the last dregs of coffee from their tin cups, and packed away their blankets and few precious belongings.

"So," Jimmy Morrisey said, "it begins. I wonder where we'll all be by dark; how many will we lose today."

"Who knows, Jim?" Billy Cobb said, shouldering his gleaming Springfield. "Who knows?"

"You know, Bill, I had a dream last night; bad dream. Dreamed you got hit, Bill; got hit bad. Hope it's not a preemen... a pree... aw hell, Bill, what's that dang word?"

"Premonition, you mean?"

"Yeah, that's it. Premonition."

"Well now, Jim. Y'all ought to know me better'n that. When did you ever see me put myself in the way of a bullet? Never did. And, by God, you never will. And you stick close to me. Y'hear? We bin together a lot of years, you and me, and we've got to make it through. Ain't goin' to lose no more friends. You're all I got left, Jim...."

Morrisey said nothing, but continued to gather his stuff together and ram it into the war-worn knapsack.

"You hear, Jim?"

"Yeah, I hear you. Not like we can do much about it, though is it? Just have to go where we're told; do what they tell us."

"Ain't true, Jim. We didn't make it this far to die now. Just follow me and do as I do and we'll make it. This is the big one, Jim. Chicken Shit Bragg wins this one, and we make it through in once piece, we can all go home, I bet. Don't crap out on me now, all right?"

"Yeah, I hear you. Let's move, before we get our assess kicked," Morrisey said, pulling on his knapsack. Then, head down, he pushed past his friend to join the line already forming in the center of the clearing.

Billy stood for a moment, looking after him. Then he, too, shouldered his knapsack and walked quickly after him. For the first time in his life, Billy Cobb was scared.

Chapter 28
Saturday September 19ᵗʰ 8:30a.m. - Federal Position at Jay's Mill

As Jesse Dixon and Pat McCann headed for the rear, Colonel Croxton and General Brannan were doing their best to rally the brigade. The surprise advance that had run into General Gist's Confederate division, which had by now been joined by that of General Liddell, had at first slowed, then turned and been flung back in disorder. Now, from what had a moment earlier been a headlong rout toward the rear, the brigade had slowed, regrouped and was now conducting a fighting withdrawal.

All along the front, the regiments of Croxton's brigade were slowing their rearward plunge, were turning, digging in and stubbornly yielding ground now only foot by bloody foot.

Federal Colonel Van Derveer, on hearing the roar of gunfire to his right and forward, moved his brigade quickly to support Croxton's left; Colonel Connell's brigade was following in close support of Van Derveer. Within an hour of the initial attack by the 10th Indiana, General Brannan's entire division was engaged, and outnumbered almost three to one.

At eight-thirty, General Brannan, having pulled his division back more than three quarters of a mile, was holding a clearing just a few yards to the north of Jays Mill where the fighting had begun. He called in his staff officers to evaluate his situation, which he already knew was grim.

Colonel Croxton, making his way through the trees toward the clearing on foot, was almost beside himself with rage.

"Damn McCook," he said to anyone who might be close enough to listen. "One brigade. One God damn brigade was what he said. We must be facing two divisions, at least, maybe even a whole damn corps. Captain Jackson," he said angrily. "Take a message to General Thomas. Ask the good general which of the five or six isolated enemy brigades now in front of me am I supposed to capture."

"Sir...?" Jackson hesitated, unsure if Croxton was serious. He was soon in no doubt that he was.

"Well? Go on, Captain," Croxton shouted. "Go and ask General Thomas which one. And while you're there, let him know that I said Dan McCook's a fool, a God damn fool; the man needs to wake up and join the living. Then, maybe, someone will realize that misinformation is dangerous, dammit."

"Yes, sir." The captain saluted, and left the colonel without a backward look.

"Damn incompetence," Croxton said, calming a little as he walked into the clearing to join Brannan, Connell, and Van Derveer.

"Not much time, gentlemen," Brannan said briskly. "Got to get back to the men as soon as possible. There's a lot of enemy out there...."

"Huh!" Croxton looked at him incredulously.

"What's your situation?" General Brannan continued, giving Croxton a sharp-eyed look.

"I've lost Carroll, and God knows how many men," Croxton said impatiently. "Lieutenant Colonel Taylor has taken over command of the 10th. What went wrong, General?" he continued without pausing. "One brigade.... One Goddamn brigade. That's what McCook said. God damn it, General, there must be a whole Rebel corps out there, not to mention Forrest. Look, sir, I don't have time for this. If you've finished, I'd like to get back to my men. We're, even now, in great danger of being overrun."

"A moment, if you please, Colonel." Brannan said. "No more than that, I promise you. Help is on the way. General Thomas has reached the field and is not unaware of our situation. He has sent General Baird's division to our support, and he is already on the move toward us along Alexander's Bridge Road; he will be here within the half-hour," he said, looking thoughtful.

"We must, if we can, gentlemen, maintain our positions," Brannan continued. "Can we hold?"

One by one, he looked at his three field commanders, and one by one, Croxton, last, they nodded that they could.

"Good. Then I suggest we get to it. Colonel Croxton, kindly allow me to accompany you back to your brigade."

Chapter 29

Saturday Morning September 19th, 8a.m. - Hazelwood

Sarah Bradley and her father were already up and about, and the house was bustling with activity when the thunder of guns to the northeast caused everyone to stop what they were doing and listen. Along with several of the servants, including Charity and Nestor, they were in the kitchen eating breakfast. Sarah had just risen from the table and was about to take her plate to the sink when the battle exploded more than two miles away to the north. Her brother Tom had left the house sometime around midnight the previous evening and hadn't returned, so Sarah and her father were eating alone.

Sarah, startled at the ferocity of the sudden outburst, dropped her plate on the floor, ran around the large wooden table, threw herself onto her father's lap and wrapped her arms around him. For a moment, they huddled together. Then, realizing that they were in no immediate danger, they went to the windows and looked out.

Outside, all around the house, and across the fields to the north and south of the Bradley home, the Federal camps had suddenly become a hive of activity. Several thousand men, who had at first stood and watched the huge clouds of smoke rising above the trees to the northeast, began gathering their equipment. Junior officers and regimental sergeants were running back and forth, screaming orders, and then, everywhere, tents were coming down, horses were being fitted into their harnesses in front of the great guns, and fires were being put out.

Further to the south, they could just see the leading regiments of Major General John Palmer's division of Crittenden's Federal infantry corps gathering themselves together in response to the sounds of battle, and General Thomas's orders to move to the north.

As quickly as they were moving, it still took time to organize more than eighteen thousand men. Slowly, however, General Crittenden's XXI Corps began to come together. By ten o'clock, it was moving northward along the Lafayette Road toward the Brotherton house in response to General Rosecrans' order. In awe, they watched as column after column marched by. Then, more than two hours after the leading elements had passed by the house, the marching ranks began to slow. The leading regiment of what they supposed must have been an entire division came to a stop some five hundred yards to the north. One by one, section by section, the long column came to a complete halt. When it did, it extended for more than a mile along the road from north to south. Then they turned, and, like a great river of blue, moved to the east, off the road beyond Hazelwood and began forming into a line of battle.

Sarah and George Bradley, along with five of their servants that had gathered with them at the windows at the front of the house, watched the activity building in the fields just beyond the Lafayette Road. For as far as they could see, thousands upon thousands of Federal soldiers were gathering in long lines, one behind the other. Company after company, regiment after regiment, banners aloft, fluttering bravely in the morning breeze. Behind them came the artillery, battery after battery, caisson after caisson, more than twenty cannon, each gun with its team of six horses and three riders, lined up by section behind the infantry. Behind the artillery were the ambulances: strange-looking four-wheeled carts with one horse and two drivers; there were dozens of them.

Never had the occupants of Hazelwood seen so many men or so much equipment. The fields to the east of the road were a heaving, rolling sea of blue that moved and undulated as the long lines formed and stepped forward. Sarah, even though she was used to the crowded streets of Chattanooga, and even Atlanta, could hardly believe that there were so many people alive in the world, let alone right there on her own front porch.

To the west of the road on a small hill, less than a hundred yards from the house, they could see a small group of officers on horseback, motionless, watching the long lines as they slowly formed. Even from there, they could see the gaunt man, General Crittenden, slightly forward of his companions, hands folded together on the pommel of his saddle.

Suddenly they were startled by a loud and persistent knocking on the back kitchen door. Before they could move, however, they heard it open and the sound of boots and spurs crossing the stone floor of the kitchen. Then a Federal captain of artillery, followed by a lieutenant and a sergeant, walked through the door leading from the kitchen into the living room.

"Good morning, sir, Captain Williams, at your service, sir," he said, saluting casually, and looking around the room. "I hope I find you well." He slapped his heavy leather gloves against his thigh. "I'm afraid I'm going to have to ask you to leave," he said, looking at George Bradley."

"That's very considerate of you, Captain, but we'll be fine right here. I don't intend to leave my home."

"I'm afraid you don't understand, sir. It's not a suggestion; it's an order. I'm taking over the house to use as an artillery observation post. Therefore, the chances are it will become a target for enemy guns. I suggest you gather together whatever possessions you might need, and take your slaves and go while you still can."

"First, captain, I suggest you take your men and get the hell out of my home. Second," George Bradley said, taking a LeMat revolver from an open drawer in a sideboard next to which he was standing, "you may be sure that I will defend it and my family with my life, if need be." And, with practiced ease, he casually cocked the weapon and pointed it at the captain, "Now, raise your hands and move back into the kitchen, slowly. If any of you so much as twitch a finger I will kill you, Captain."

The captain stared down the barrel of the .42-caliber revolver and slowly raised his hands.

"Do as he says," he said, without looking round at his men. They, too, raised their hands and began backing slowly into the kitchen. It was at that moment that Blake Winter and John Wilder, followed by Eli Lilly, Lieutenant Cross, and Lieutenant Scott of Lilly's battery walked in through the already open back kitchen door.

"What's going on Captain?" Wilder said, holding out an arm to keep the others behind him.

"I'll tell you what the hell's going on," George Bradley said, before the captain could answer. "This buffoon thinks he's going to use my home as a target. I'll kill him first."

"Captain?" Wilder said.

"Sir, the house is at a strategic location and I thought...."

"Yes, Captain. What did you think?"

"Well, sir. I was going to place my battery around the house and direct fire from an upstairs window. I'm sure you'll agree with me sir, that with the terrain and all, we need every advantage we can get."

Wilder nodded. "I do agree, Captain, most definitely so," he said, shaking his head at George Bradley, who was already raising his revolver. "But this is not the place. My own staff," he indicated the officers to his rear, "have already appropriated the house for our own use. I suggest you find somewhere else."

For a moment, the captain looked hard at the heavily bearded colonel, then at Winter, then at the Bradleys, and then he inclined his head, smiled, saluted, and walked quickly past the officers, through the kitchen and out the back door. George Bradley, however, did not lower his weapon. Instead, he leveled it at Wilder's chest.

I appreciate your help, Colonel Wilder," he said in a hard voice, "but I meant what I said. I will not allow my home to be used by my country's enemies, and that means you, too."

"Wilder laughed, "I have no intention of using your home, Mr. Bradley. We merely dropped by to see if there was anything we could do to ensure your safety... and," he raised his eyebrows, "perhaps beg a cup of fresh coffee?"

"Of course, Colonel," Sarah said, brushing past her father to stand between him and the Federal officers. "You're welcome to coffee and something to eat if you wish. Charity...?"

"Thank you, ma'am," Wilder bowed slightly. "Coffee will be fine, if it's no trouble."

"No trouble at all, Colonel," she said, averting her eyes from Winter's unabashed gaze. "If you will take a seat at the table in the kitchen."

Wilder nodded to his men to follow her into the kitchen, and then turned again to George Bradley who had replaced the LeMat in the drawer from whence it came.

"Mr. Bradley, sir," he said, taking the farmer's elbow and walking with him to the kitchen. "I don't think you and your people should stay here. It's not safe. We have a major battle brewing here and this house is going to be slap bang in the middle of it. We'll do what we can to protect your property but...."

"I thank you, Colonel. But we'll be just fine. We have the cellars to go to if things get too bad," he pointed to the already open trap in the corner of the kitchen and the stone steps leading downward. "They are deep and well-constructed with stone walls. There's a table and chairs down there, a fireplace, and enough food to see us through if need be."

Wilder nodded. "Even so, sir, I think the lady should leave while she still can."

"I agree, Colonel, and I've tried to persuade her to go, but she won't hear of it, won't leave me. But there's little to fear I think. Those are our boy's after all. It's your people I'm worried about."

Wilder sighed, shook his head, sat down with Bradley and the others at the table, gathered the large stoneware mug of steaming coffee Charity offered into both hands, sniffed the steam, and stared silently at the wall above the iron stove.

"So, Colonel," Sarah said, to Winter. "What are we to expect? What is the situation? And how is your wound?"

Winter looked at Wilder who shrugged and nodded.

"The wound is a little painful, but otherwise I'm fine. The situation, however, is far from good, Sarah. As far as we can tell, several of our divisions are already fighting a mile or so to the north, and we know several more Confederate divisions are gathering less than a half-mile to

121

the east of this house, with more on the way. Our men are deployed north and south of here along the road for more than four miles, and we also have more on the way," he said, looking at her and then at Bradley.

"Sarah. You have to get out of here. Now!"

"'I' won't leave my father, and he won't leave the house. So...." She shrugged, tilted her head to one side, and smiled.

"Oh don't worry," she said, seeing the frown on Winter's face. "We'll be all right. It's as father says, the cellar is deep and strong, though a little damp and not the place I would choose to spend a Saturday. But it will keep us safe, and we are in no danger from our own boys."

"Well," Wilder said. "I think it's time we moved out and made ready to receive our guests. My brigade, along with that of Colonel Dick's, is deployed in the fields on the hillside just to the south of your property. You should be able to see us from an upstairs window. And, of course, we'll keep an eye on you, but I can promise you nothing, I'm afraid."

"I thank you, Colonel, for your consideration," Bradley said, extending a hand. Wilder shook it, nodded, then took a step backwards, saluted, turned, and walked quickly from the house followed by everyone except Blake Winter.

"If you don't mind, sir," he said to Bradley, "I'd like a word with your daughter."

Bradley nodded and then jerked his head at Charity who followed him from the room leaving Sarah and Winter alone together.

"So," Blake said, taking both her hands in his.

"So," she said, looking up into his eyes. "You must go?"

"Yes."

"Well, then," she said, "we'd better say goodbye."

For a moment there was an awkward silence between them, neither one knowing what to say to the other. Then she leaned forward, rested her brow against his chest.

"Hey," he said, letting go of her hands and putting his arms around her. "I'll not be far away. My regiment is with John's, dug in behind some mighty strong breastworks. They can't get me. I'll be safe.

"You fool," she whispered. "You stupid fool. You have no idea how many of our boys are about to fall upon you? General Bragg has you outnumbered almost two to one. I know. Tom is one of his scouts."

"Well, now," Blake said, making light of it. "Haven't we always claimed that one Yankee is worth four Johnny Rebs?"

"Hah," she said, pushing away and looking up at him, a wry smile on her lips. "You've got that the wrong way round, which means you truly are outnumbered."

He smiled down at her, caressed the curve of her cheek with the back of his hand, pinched her chin gently between his thumb and forefinger, then leaned forward and kissed her forehead, each now tear-filled eye, the tip of her nose, and, finally, her lips.

She shuddered, put her arms around his neck, buried her face deep in his chest, and sobbed gently. He was at a loss as to what to do or say to console her.

"Sarah," he said, lifting her chin with his finger. "What is it?"

"I don't know," she whispered. "I can't seem to get it out of my head that this will be the last time that I'll see you. I know...," she said, before he could speak to reassure her. "I know. Just hold me, for a minute longer, then go."

For a long moment they stood, arms around each other, her cheek next to his chest, his cheek lying gently against the top of her head, his hand stroking her hair. Each, so it seemed, was lost in thought. The air in the kitchen was still, warm and heavy. Only the sounds of distant gunfire disturbed the silence of the moment, and then it was over.

"You must go." She said, abruptly pushing him away. Your friends will be wondering where you are."

"Sarah...."

"Hush," she said, putting her fingers to his lips. "I know. But you'll come back, won't you?" Will you promise?"

"I will," he said taking her fingers from his lips and holding them between both of his hands. "You know I will. And you? Will you take great care of yourself? Will you take good heed of your father? Do what he asks? Will you promise?"

She nodded, blinked up at him through her tears, then threw her arms once more around his neck and pressed her lips to his. Then she pushed him away, took hold of his arm, and pushed him toward the door.

"Please. Go, now," she said. "If you don't go now, I don't know what I'll do. I.... I...."

He turned, took her face gently between his hands, and kissed her.

"I'll be back just as soon as I can."

He turned and walked out through the door, closing it behind him. Never in his life had he felt so many mixed emotions as he did at that moment.

Chapter 30

Saturday Morning September 19th, 10a.m. - Confederate Positions West of Reed's Bridge

As quickly as Federal Major General George Thomas had moved, so the Confederate army was moving to contain him. While Brannan's division was holding its ground, Baird had fallen foul of Confederate General Liddell's division that had closed the gap to Gist's left. Forrest's cavalry corps, now dismounted and fighting as infantry, was also heavily engaged to the north of Reed's Bridge Road and was pressing Van Derveer's brigade hard.

Forrest had chosen his position well; he had deployed his artillery to the north of the road and was laying into Brannan's division with everything he had.

Just to the south of Reed's Bridge Road, General Matthew Ector, whose Confederate brigade was under heavy pressure from Van Derveer was worried; he sent his adjutant, Captain C.B. Kilgore to Forrest to let him know that he was uneasy about his right flank.

Forrest's reply was typical. "Tell General Ector that he needn't bother about his right flank; I'll take care of it."

Ector, however, was not at all happy with Forrest's reply. "Did the general say how he would take care of my right flank?" he asked, when Kilgore delivered the message.

"No, sir, not at all."

Ector frowned, ducked in reaction to a shell exploding only yards away from where the small group of officers was standing under cover of a clump of hardwoods, and shook his head. Then he turned away, muttering to himself, something his staff could neither hear nor understand.

But that was not the end of it. By ten o'clock, Colonel Wilson's Confederate brigade, heavily engaged with Connell's Federal brigade, had been driven back under a devastating firestorm, leaving Ector's brigade in a forward and, so Ector thought, thoroughly exposed position. And so, Ector, now concerned about his left flank as well as his right, sent Kilgore again to Forrest.

Kilgore found Forrest on foot with two of his artillery officers, Captains John Morton and Gustave Huwald, directing fire from their batteries. It was immediately obvious to Kilgore that Forrest was in no mood to be trifled with. The white linen duster coat had been abandoned, his hat was covered with a thick coating of dark red dust, his face was streaked with grime, and the once trim beard was thick with sweat, dirt, and soot. He had a revolver in one hand and a red bandanna in the other with which he constantly wiped the sweat from his brow. All around him, his men were firing across the road at the Federal lines beyond; the trees, now stripped bare of leaves, twigs and branches, offered no impediment to visibility, on either side. The twelve guns in the two Tennessee batteries were almost too hot to touch. The gun crews were bathed in sweat and grime, their hands raw from the constant handling of corrosive materials and hot metal. But they were handling their pieces with determined efficiency, each gun maintaining a devastating rate of fire of almost three rounds per minute.

"Sir," Kilgore shouted over the roar of gunfire, and ducking behind the cover of a caisson. "Message from General Ector."

"Well? Get on with it, man. What does General Ector want this time?"

"He says to tell you, General, that he's worried about his left flank."

"He's what?" Forrest shouted, incredulous. "He's worried about what?"

"His left flank, sir."

Forrest turned away from the guns, stepped behind the caisson where Kilgore was sheltering, and with hands on hips, yelled in his ear, ""Tell General Ector that, by God, I'll take care of his left flank, and his right damn flank as well. Is that clear enough, Captain?"

"Yes, sir, quite clear," Kilgore shouted, flinching as a piece of shrapnel half the size of a man's fist slammed into the side of the caisson just above his head. Forrest neither flinched nor moved. He stood with his hands still on his hips and watched as Kilgore ran, head down, back through the trees to convey his reply to General Ector. Then he shook his head in disgust, turned again to his guns, and went back to work.

Chapter 31

All through the morning the battle raged, first this way and then that. More and more troops on both sides entered the field and slowly the battle grew in proportion and ferocity. It soon became clear to both army commanders that this was no isolated engagement like that of yesterday; a major confrontation was under way.

By ten-thirty, Colonel Croxton, his ammunition all but gone, had been forced to withdraw his brigade in order to replenish it. His place had been taken in the Federal line of battle by Brigadier General John Starkweather's brigade.

At eleven o'clock Baird had hurled his entire division, three full brigades, against those of Ector and Wilson, forcing them to retire, but Baird couldn't pursue them because of a new threat to his own right flank from the direction of Alexander's Bridge, and he had been forced to send Brigadier General John King's brigade to meet it. It was a mistake that would cost him dearly.

Confederate General Walker, anticipating King's movement, with all the sagacity of the seasoned battlefield commander that he was, sent Liddell's division crashing through the woods and dealt King a devastating blow. Colonel Govan's veteran brigade of Arkansans tore into King's now badly exposed right flank, while Brigadier General Walthall's Mississippians smashed into Scribner's brigade.

King's brigade collapsed. All six guns of the 5th U.S. Field Artillery fell to Govan's screaming troops, along with more than five hundred prisoners of the 1st Battalion of the 6th U.S. infantry. What few of King's brigade that weren't captured or killed, ran from the field in blind panic. And, just to Govan's left, Walthall's brigade was enjoying a similar success. Colonel Scribner's Federal brigade broke at the same time as did King's, and his men also turned and ran from the field.

Having smashed Scribner's brigade, Liddell turned his attention to Connell and Starkweather. Starkweather didn't fare much better than King and Scribner; in a matter of minutes he'd lost ground and five guns. Connell, however, was better prepared. He had been in the path of King's fleeing brigade, and had ordered his men to lie down and wait. They and Captain Josiah Church's six guns, each double-loaded with canister, and six more of the 4th U.S. Battery, tore the Confederate front line to shreds. And, for a moment, Liddell's advance was checked.

For a while, Liddell's division held their ground under a withering hail of Federal fire from cannon and infantry, but soon was forced to retire, even though Brannan's division and King's brigade were still, as yet, in no condition to counter attack.

As mid-day approached, for Bragg's Army of Tennessee things were going well, even though he still didn't have all his troops across the Chickamauga. Forrest was still fighting like a mad dog to the north of Reed's Bridge Road, and General Walker's corps had regrouped and was mounting another attack. Buckner's Corps had made it across the river at Dalton's Ford and were in position to the south of Hood and Bushrod Johnson facing Crittenden. Daniel Hill's Confederate corps of which Major General Pat Cleburne's was the leading division, was moving quickly toward the creek, but was still more than two miles away. Of Lieutenant General Leonidas Polk's Confederate Corps, only Major General Cheatham's division was within sight of the field and wouldn't cross the creek until around one o'clock in the afternoon.

Unfortunately, what Bragg, Forrest and Walker didn't know was that Brannan and Baird were about to receive reinforcements. Major General Alexander McDowell McCook's XX Federal Corps was already arriving on the field after its long march from McLemore's Cove. General Reynolds's division was only a mile away to the southwest at the Tan Yard near Dyer's farm and would be on the field almost within the hour.

All through the long morning, General Thomas had been following the progress of the battle and, a little after eleven-thirty, realizing that Brannan and Baird were under extreme pressure, he moved Brigadier General Richard Johnson's division of McCook's corps straight on down Reed's Bridge Road to reinforce them; by noon they were less than a mile away and moving quickly. The battle of Chickamauga was about to enter its next phase.

Chapter 32

Saturday September 19th, Noon - Federal Field HQ at the Widow
Glenn's House

General Rosecrans, commanding the Federal Army of the Cumberland,
had slept little that night. He'd tossed and turned in his canvas cot, half
dreaming, half awake, plagued by thoughts that he couldn't shift from his
head; thoughts that maybe he'd been out-maneuvered, was badly
outnumbered, had the disadvantage of position on the battlefield.

Before first light, unable to sleep further, he and his general staff, along
with the members of his escort, had taken to horse and moved quickly
from McLemore's Cove northward after General Thomas. By noon, he'd
arrived on the field and had set up a field headquarters in a small log
house on a hill overlooking the battlefield.

Eliza Glenn, fondly known to the local farmers as The Widow Glenn,
and whose house General Rosecrans now occupied, was a cheerful and
personable young countrywoman aged twenty two.

She had awoken early that morning, as she did most mornings, in
response to the needs of her two young sons, and was already preparing
the mid-day meal when the general and his entourage came galloping up
the road in a cloud of dust. To say that she wasn't pleased to see them
would be something of an understatement. Her dark eyes flashed as the
men came to a halt at the rear of the cabin, dismounted and, without a
word or by-your-leave, tromped into the house and proceeded to take it
over with little consideration either for her or her sons.

Eliza Glenn was a tall young woman, almost as tall as Rosecrans
himself. Her dark brown hair was tied together at the back with a length
of wide black ribbon, accentuating her small, heart-shaped face and her
large, dark brown eyes. She wore a simple dress of pale yellow gingham.
Pretty, most people thought she was, and worldly beyond her years. She
was also a southerner through and through. The more so since her young
husband, John, had died so far away from home. True he'd not died in
battle, but had fallen victim to some unmentionable disease, but still....

Furthermore, she did not take kindly to being inducted into the Federal
army, even if it was only by association. Even so, she found herself
strangely attracted to this handsome Yankee general who, obviously the
life and soul of his large staff, had paid her little attention. For,
immediately upon entering her home, he had looked quickly around, and
then set about commandeering her only ground-floor room and turning it
into a battlefield operations center.

While the work was progressing inside the house, Rosecrans went out onto the porch at the front of the small log house, sat down in a rocking chair, and gazed out over the terrain to the east. The location of the Glenn home provided him with a magnificent view over the battlefield.

Knowing Rosecrans' edgy disposition only too well, his officers left him alone on the porch, and there he sat, quietly rocking, elbows on the arms of the chair, fingers steepled together at his lips, and for a while he seemed lost in thought.

"Your thoughts; not worth much more than a penny, one would think, General," a small voice said from the doorway.

Rosecrans looked round to see Eliza Glenn standing there watching him. Other than a slight nod of the head, he took no notice of her, turning instead to gaze once more out over the battlefield.

"May I join you, General?" she asked, and, without waiting for an answer, walked in front of him and sat down in a chair next to his. Rosecrans said nothing, didn't look at her, pursed his lips, and seemed to kiss the tips of his still steepled fingers.

Eliza smiled, placed her hands together in her lap, and then set the rocking chair in motion.

For several minutes the two of them sat without speaking, staring at the clouds of smoke rising over the trees to the northwest.

"What's your name?" Rosecrans said without moving or looking at her.

"Eliza. Eliza Glenn."

"Where's your husband?"

"Dead, General. Dead at Mobile."

He turned his head and looked at her. "Mobile?"

She nodded, but didn't answer.

"I'm sorry," he said.

"She looked at him. He looked at her, their eyes locked; he was the first to break. He dropped his eyes, then his chin and turned again to stare out into space.

Grand as the view from the widow's house might be, a vista of rolling fields and woodlands, Rosecrans could see very little of the great conflict that was rapidly developing to the north and east. Much of the area over which the two armies were now fighting was a tangle of thickets and undergrowth. Here and there, the underbrush gave way to cathedral-like stands of hardwoods: maple, black gum, hickory, and oak, while everywhere great cedars and short-leaf pine towered above the woodland. And dotted around the landscape there were clearings - cultivated farmlands and pastures - dotted with small log houses.

From the widow's home the ground dropped quickly away to the east. Two miles away across the fields to the northeast they could see that the battle was beginning to build, and even now seemed to cover an area of at least two square miles, and its boundaries were fluid and still moving ever outward.

Below the house, across the open fields to the south he could see the breastworks behind which John Wilder's brigade was preparing defensive positions. In the distance beyond lay Hazelwood and the Lafayette Road, and beyond the road the massed divisions of Generals McCook's and Crittenden's Federal corps. Farther out, however, only the trees and the billowing clouds of blue-gray smoke, and the rolling thunder of gunfire.

"Why?" Rosecrans said in a low voice, more to himself than to Eliza Glenn. "Why did this have to happen? All those men down there, I wonder how many of them will survive this day. How many will walk away unharmed?" he said, then shook his head as if to rid himself of some unwanted thought, rose to his feet, and walked back into the house leaving Eliza looking after him.

Minutes later, Rosecrans had had his aids move the widow's large kitchen table out onto the porch and unroll a large, but somewhat tattered map. Then he looked round at the widow still rocking gently in the chair next to the one he had so recently vacated.

"If you don't mind, Mistress Glenn," he said, pointing down at the map. "I could use a little assistance. Would you?"

She looked at him, steely-eyed, then with a small sigh, rose to her feet and joined him at the table. The officers of Rosecrans' general staff crowded in behind her.

"Not much of a map is it, General?" the widow said, looking over his shoulder at the hand-drawn chart. "Why, old Farmer Brotherton, just down the road has a better one than that."

"Indeed," said Rosecrans dryly. "Unfortunately, the good farmer is elsewhere, so we'll have to make do with this one."

"Yes, sir," she said with a curtsey, "and whereabouts are we on your map?"

"Here," Rosecrans said, pointing."

"Oh yes... I see. Well then, that there must be the Brotherton place, and that's the Bradley farm, Hazelwood, so it is," she said, pointing them out. "Well, I do declare."

She looked up, first over one shoulder, and then the other, at the faces of Rosecrans' staff officers crowded around the small table, craning their necks for a look at the map.

"Oh my," she said, giggling softly and putting a delicate hand to her mouth. "So many strong men, and oh those nice blue uniforms...."

"Enough," Rosecrans said, seeing through her coquettishness and cutting her off. "We have work to do. Tell me, young lady. That cloud of smoke over there to the north. Where is that?"

"Well, sir," Eliza said, with a wry look around at the officers and a twinkle in her eye. "That would be.... Now let me see.... Perhaps that's Reed's Bridge. No, more likely it's Jay's Mill, I should say. But then, I would have thought the mill was farther away than that. Perhaps it's the McAbee place, or even the McDonald farm. Might even be the Kelly farm. Why, General, it's so confusing, It's difficult to say for sure," she said, holding out both hands, palms up, and fluttering her eyelids.

Rosecrans' staff officers grinned at one another, looked away, and did their best to hide their mirth. Rosecrans, however, was not amused.

"Oh, come now, General," Eliza said with a smile. "There's no need to take on so. There, see?" she said pointing directly to the east. "Alexander's Bridge is directly beyond the small hill, about two miles." Rosecrans nodded and adjusted his map slightly. "And there, that large field just down there to the left where all those boys in blue are running back and forth, that's the Viniard farm. Beyond that, well, that's where our boys are, General, but I'm sure you'll find that out soon enough. And the smoke? Well, sir, that runs from here, Mr. Youngblood's farm," she said, looking down and pointing to a spot on the map, "all the way over here, beyond the McAbee place, just about as far as the McDonald farm.

"There now, sir," she said, taking a step backwards, forcing Rosecrans' staff to do the same. "Now you know almost as much as I do."

"And where do you think the bulk of Bragg's army is located?" Rosecrans said, turning his head to look at her.

She smiled, a little grimly, and stepped forward again. "Here," she said, pointing to a spot on the map. "And here, here, here, here, here, here, and here." She stepped back again put her head on one side, smiled and said, "Why, sir, General Bragg's army is all around you."

Rosecrans didn't look up from the map. Instead, he leaned forward, placed both hands on the table, one on either side of the map, and concentrated. His staff stood silently by and watched. Eliza Glenn turned and went back into the house and sat down in a rocking chair. To the east, the thunder of guns rolled across the battlefield, growing in fury and intensity, like the gathering storm that it was.

Chapter 33

Saturday September 19th, Noon - Confederate HQ at Thedford's Ford

Confederate General Braxton Bragg, after a night of dreamless sleep, woke refreshed and ready for battle just before daybreak. His staff, however, had slept little.

All through the long night, his lookouts had kept a vigil, watching as the glow of the Federal campfires burning way off to the west increased. By dawn, they were able to tell Bragg what he already knew, that the Federal army was building in strength across the creek.

He washed, dressed, combed his graying hair and beard, and then called for his adjutant. An orderly poked his head inside the tent and inquired what he would like for breakfast. He took nothing, only coffee served in a china cup, complete with saucer and spoon.

When his adjutant arrived, only seconds after the coffee, he requested a meeting with his general staff.

Bragg, easy in his mind that at last he was on at least even terms with his old enemy, smiled a little, said less, nodded in response to one staff officer after another as they filed into his tent and gave their reports. The news they gave would, at any other time have chilled him to the bone. This time, however, nothing could dampen his optimism.

After the last of his officers had left the tent, he sent for his orderly and ate a small breakfast, one fried egg and a small piece of ham, in the company of his adjutant. Then he gave orders to move his headquarters nearer to where he felt the action would begin. By noon, he was establishing a new field headquarters at Thedford's Ford, just to the east of the Chickamauga, at around the same time as General Rosecrans was moving into the Widow Glenn's cabin.

By noon, the Confederate divisions of Bushrod Johnson and John Bell Hood had been standing in line of battle for several hours. The long lines of gray-clad infantry were beyond the woods just to the east of the Lafayette Road facing the unseen ranks of Crittenden's Federal corps and, behind them, the semi-fortified positions of John Wilder's mounted infantry and Colonel George Dick's brigade.

All morning long, they had suffered first the cold, damp early hours, and then, as the sun rose steadily into the cloudless sky, the heat and humidity as the temperature rose into the eighties, they had sat or stood listening to the gunfire less than a mile away to the north. And all morning long, they wondered when it would be their turn.

Side by side, the two divisions waited; Johnson on the left, Hood on the right, and in the middle of it all Billy Cobb, Jimmy Morrisey and the

30th Tennessee sat together on the ground in the center of two long lines, one behind the other. For the most part the men were quiet. Some, however, talked among themselves of things unrelated to the events going on around them, more to hide feelings of uneasiness than to pass the time. And, as always, the two veterans kept themselves to themselves, sitting together in the open, backs turned to their comrades, whispering.

"I've had it, Bill," Morrisey said. "I can't do this anymore. I want to go home."

"Huh. You and me both."

"No, Bill. You don't understand. I want to go home now. Today."

Cobb looked at his friend, and then said, "What you tryin' to say?"

"I'm not tryin' to say it. I am sayin' it; I'm sayin' we just get up and leave, now, while we've still got the chance. Hell, Billy," he continued, "you heard 'em last night, and this morning. There's gotta be thousands and thousands of them out there. And listen to that mess goin' on over there," he jerked his head to indicate the direction. "By God, Billy, this ain't goin' to be no damned skirmish, and I know I cain't handle another Murfreesboro.... Billy, that ain't all. I ain't told you this, but I got a real strong feelin' I'm not goin' to make it this time; had it for days now, so I have. Strong, real strong. So come on, Billy. Let's go. Yeah?" He started to get to his feet, but Cobb grabbed his arm and pulled him down.

"You're nuts, Jimmy," he whispered loudly, looking around to make sure his friend hadn't been heard. "How far d'you think we'd get, by God? You said it yourself; there's thousands of Yankees beyond the trees, and even if we could make it through our own lines, we'd never make it through theirs. Just look around. There's officers every goddamned where. We wouldn't get ten damn yards before someone asked us what we was about, and you know it. An' I'd rather get shot by a Yankee than our folks. Now settle down. All right? Just settle down and relax. Ain't nothing going to happen to you, nor to me neither."

Jimmy Morrisey sadly shook his head and said nothing. There was a tear in his eye when he looked at Billy.

"It appears we are about to receive new orders, General," John Bell Hood said to Bushrod Johnson, twisting in the saddle as they heard the sounds of hooves fast approaching over the hard-packed dirt road to the east.

Seconds later, a captain of General Bragg's staff came tearing around the bend at full gallop. On seeing the long lines of gray-clad soldiers stretching across the fields and into the woods on either side of the road, he slowed his horse momentarily, then, spotting the group of mounted officers, put spurs to its flanks, galloped across the field to where they were waiting, skidded to a halt in a flurry of dust, saluted, reached inside his tunic, and took out a folded sheet of paper.

"Sir, begging the general's pardon," the courier said. "Orders for Major General Hood from General Bragg."

"Thank you, Captain." Hood nodded, took the paper from him with his good hand, held it against his chest to open it, then read its content without expression.

A dozen yards away, in the rear rank of the 30th Tennessee, Billy Cobb and Jimmy Morrisey watched the proceedings with interest.

"Better get ready, Jim," Cobb said. "Looks like we're in for it now." They continued to watch as the officers talked among themselves.

"Well, General," Hood said, turning slightly in the saddle to face Bushrod Johnson. "It would seem that we are to advance our position westward."

"About time," Johnson said. "The men have been in line for more than four hours now. We'll be beaten before we begin if we have to wait any longer."

Hood nodded, then turned again and addressed Bragg's courier.

"My compliments to General Bragg," he said, to the captain. "Tell him that we are in position and will move against the enemy forthwith."

"Yes, sir."

The captain saluted, wheeled his horse, and galloped away at full speed back the way he'd came.

"Are you ready, General Johnson?"

"I am, General."

"Then I suggest you look to your division and I'll look to mine. We'll move forward on my command. Please indicate when your brigades are ready to advance."

Bushrod Johnson walked his horse a few yards to the left with Brigadier General John Gregg and joined Lieutenant Colonel James Turner forward of the first rank of the 30th Tennessee, and only yards ahead of Billy Cobb and Jimmy Morrisey.

"Look, Jim," Cobb said. "We've got to put as much distance between us and those dad-blamed colors as we can. When we move forward, we take whatever chance comes up, and we move to the right, together. Those fools carryin' the flag never make it more than five minutes or so, and I sure as hell don't want to have to pick the durned thing up when it goes down; and go down it surely will; it always does. So stay right there beside me, and do what I do."

For a moment, Cobb had a twinge of conscience. Thoughts of cowardice flashed through his mind, but he put them away. Billy Cobb was no coward. Careful? Yes, but Billy was afraid of nothing and no one. When the time came to fight, he would do his share, and more. But medals and glorious deeds were for fools, and fools always ended up on their backs, torn apart, and for no good reason that he could see. *By God,* he thought. *I've come this far without hardly a scratch, and by God, I'll make it the rest of the way.*

"On your feet, men," Colonel James Turner shouted, as he walked his horse the length of the front rank. "Time to earn your keep. Get moving, now. Form ranks in company order, sergeants to the rear." Then, his sword in one hand, the other on the reins, he turned, took up a position at the front and center of the regiment at the side of Bushrod Johnson.

Billy Cobb looked sideways at his friend. Jimmy Morrisey's face was a mask of determination, the lines on his brow sharply defined, his jaw set, lips apart, teeth clamped firmly together. His old, sweat-stained planter's hat was pulled forward, shielding his eyes against the harsh sunlight, his heavy coat discarded. He stared ahead, unblinking, then reached behind his back, unclipped the bayonet from his belt and snapped it into position on the muzzle of his Springfield rifle. Then he turned, looked Billy square in the eye, nodded once, bared his teeth in a wild grin, turned to look forward once more, and spat a large stream of dark brown juice onto the grass at his feet.

"Reckon this is it, then," he said. "Good luck, Billy."

Billy nodded, then he, too, fixed his bayonet.

To the front, Bushrod Johnson dismounted and turned his horse over to an orderly; General Gregg and Colonel Turner did the same. A hundred and fifty yards away to the right, General Hood remained mounted, watching, and waiting.

Johnson took two steps forward, raised his sword above his head, looked at Hood and nodded his head, then looked left and right along the ranks of his division.

"Oh shit," Jimmy said. "Here we go."

"READY?" Johnson shouted.

All along the line of battle on either side, company and regimental commanders raised their swords aloft in answer. Johnson looked down the line to where Hood also had his sword raised above his head. For a moment the long lines of gray-clad soldiers were silent, only the sounds of gunfire to the north disturbed the peace of early afternoon, then Hood swept his sword downward, giving the command to advance.

"ADVANCE THE COLORS," Johnson shouted.

To the left and right the regimental color guards stepped forward, flags unfurling in the breeze, flapping, snapping, blue and gold regimental banners, red and blue battle flags. Then, to the rear, the drums began to roll.

"GUIDE CENTER! FORWAAARD!"

Bushrod Johnson lowered his sword to point the way and stepped forward.

Billy Cobb took a deep breath; it never failed to stir him. Time and again, he'd advanced into battle, just as they were doing now, and time and again the magic of the moment took over as the colors fluttered and snapped in the breeze, the drums thundering at the rear, the bugles calling the advance.

Step by step, in good order, the long gray lines moved forward toward the trees at the edge of the field. More than seven thousand men in the two Confederate divisions, arms at the ready, moved as one across the no-man's land toward the smoke spiraling upward from the kitchen chimney at Hazelwood, a half-mile or more away to the west.

At that same moment, the courier arrived at General Bragg's field headquarters at Thedford's Ford, with the news that Johnson and Hood were moving forward to engage the enemy. Bragg nodded and looked at his watch. It was just after one o'clock in the afternoon.

Almost at the same time, Brigadier General Richard Johnson's Federal division arrived at Alexander's Bridge Road north of the Brock farm, a mile west of Reed's Bridge, and Major General Benjamin Cheatham's Confederate division crossed the Chickamauga at Dalton's Ford.

Within minutes, St. John Liddell's Confederate division had fallen under Richard Johnson's hammer and was being pushed steadily back toward Reed's Bridge.

Without stopping, Cheatham ordered three of his five veteran brigades into battle on Liddell's left and caught Johnson completely unawares. For the next several hours, the Confederate brigades of Cheatham and Liddell, and the Federal brigades of Richard Johnson and Absalom Baird fought like furies, and the battle rolled back and forth from east to west as first one side held the advantage and then the other. And the battle continued to escalate.

Cheatham's division was followed across the river by Stewart's division, which moved into position on Cheatham's left and Hood's right. Stewart was followed by Preston's division, which crossed the river, turned west, and fell into line of battle on the left of Hood and Johnston.

On the Federal side, Thomas was receiving heavy reinforcements in the form of Palmer's division of General Crittenden's corps and Reynolds's division of his own XIV Corps. These he sent quickly to the aid of Richard Johnson and Absalom Baird, already under heavy pressure from the combined Confederate forces of Walker's corps on the right, Cheatham's division in the center, with Stewart's division poised to the left and rear of Bushrod Johnson. By one-thirty in the afternoon, more than fifty thousand soldiers of both sides were fighting across a front more than two miles wide. And the battle continued to grow.

Chapter 34

Saturday September 19th, 1p.m. - The Widow Glenn's Field

"Listen," John Wilder said. "Can you hear it?"

They were sitting together behind a pile of large tree trunks that formed Wilder's breastworks on the rise some two hundred yards to the north of Hazelwood on the hillside just to the south of the Widow Glenn's house.

There were six of them: Wilder, Blake Winter, Colonel John Funkhouser of the 98th Illinois, Colonel Smith Atkins of the 92nd Illinois, Colonel James Monroe of the 123rd Illinois and Captain Eli Lilly. Wilder's two other regimental commanders, Colonel Abram Miller of the 72nd Indiana and William Jones' of the 17th Indiana, were with their men some three hundred yards away to the north. All had been in line behind their defenses for most of the morning, listening to the sounds of battle raging away to the northeast, waiting, knowing that only the thin blue line of infantry they could see just to the east of Hazelwood and the Lafayette Road stood between them and the fury that was surely building just beyond.

"What?" Winter said, straining. "It's growing louder, we know, but what?"

"There. Listen."

The six men sat still on the logs and listened. Then, faintly at first, but growing in intensity, they heard the rhythm of drums and the sounds of bugles echoing faintly over the trees to the east.

"Oh my God," Lilly said, quietly. "Here they come."

"Sure enough, Captain," Wilder said. "Better look to your guns."

"Yes, sir."

Lilly jumped to his feet and ran the few yards to the rear of Wilder's breastworks where his battery was deployed in a line, north to south, some one hundred yards long; six three-inch Parrott rifles, fifteen yards between each gun. He went from gun to gun, said a few encouraging words to each crew, defined the loads he might require, and then returned to the group of officers still watching the skyline to the east.

Four hundred yards away, just beyond the Lafayette Road, Federal Brigadier General Jefferson Davis had also heard the martial sounds of the Confederate drums and bugles, and was calling his division into line.

Wilder and his men watched from their vantage point on the hill as the blue lines readied themselves to receive the Confederate attack.

Then, as they watched, the forest to the west in front of the Federal division seemed to explode. It started at the north end of the line, and spread southward in a long rippling eruption of Confederate rifle and cannon fire that grew in strength and intensity as regiment after regiment, still hidden in the trees opened fire. From one side to the other, over a front more than a half-mile wide, the fields and trees were suddenly hidden beneath a blanket of thick white smoke, and the air was rent asunder by the crash of volley after volley of fire, now from both sides, as the Federal infantry hunkered down to defend its positions.

"What's the range, Captain," Wilder asked.

"About three fourths of a mile to the edge of the woods, I would estimate," Lily said.

"Good," Wilder said, nodding. "Load with case shot and let's give our boys some help."

Lilly turned and ran to the first of his guns and began shouting orders, it was difficult now the roar of battle was so close. From the first gun he ran to the second, then the third, fourth, fifth and sixth. By the time he'd returned to take up a position at the center of the battery, between the third and fourth gun, each crew had loaded their weapon and was standing ready to fire.

For a moment, Lilly stood calculating the range. He used a small metal device of his own invention. Then he looked to the left, signaled for the number two gun to raise its elevation slightly, then he looked to the right and raised his arm.

"FIRE," he yelled at the top of his lungs.

BAM, BAM, BAM, BAM, BAM... BAM.

Almost as one, the six guns of Lilly's battery crashed, belched forth great clouds of thick blue-white smoke that billowed, swirled, and lifted quickly skyward on the freshening breeze, reared, then thudded back down upon the ground; the crews were already in position with sponge, ammunition, ram, friction primer and lanyard for a second volley. Lilly's men were the best at what they did. On a good day they could easily maintain a rate of fire of more than two rounds per minute, and they now were going to work with a will.

Wilder, Winter and the others watched through their glasses as the first salvo from Lilly's battery arched across the field in front of them, and then the road, and the Federal divisions beyond, to explode in the air midway through the downward side of their trajectory, sending showers of one-inch iron balls flying into the forest, tearing, ripping, limbs and leaves from the trees.

"Well done, Captain," Wilder shouted. "Now give them hell.

Chapter 35

Saturday September 19th, 1p.m. - Confederate Positions West of the Lafayette Road

They covered the open ground to the trees at the run. Then, they were suddenly confronted by a jungle of tangled undergrowth and scrub, so thick it was barely possible for a man to force his way through it without injury. But force their way through it they did. For more than two hundred yards, the long lines of Bushrod Johnson's and John Bell Hood's Confederate divisions smashed their way through the woods, men pausing only to climb over the dead and fallen trees that lay in their way everywhere, or to disentangle themselves from the blackberry and blackthorn that tore at their clothing and skin.

At the center of each division, the two commanding generals, one on foot, the other on horseback, pressed forward at the run. Johnson, sometimes turning and running backwards, sometimes stumbling, almost falling, waving his sword and pistol in the air, his face bloody from the thorns, was only yards ahead of Billy Cobb and Jimmy Morrisey.

Breathless and sweating profusely as the temperature rose into the mid-eighties, the adrenaline coursing through their bodies, screaming, cursing, and howling the Rebel yell, the two men followed Johnson in the headlong rush through the undergrowth.

Suddenly, to the right, the air was split asunder as more than four thousand soldiers of Hood's division opened fire. And then, the more than three and a half thousand men of Johnson's division stopped dead, almost at the edge of the trees, beyond which they could see the massed lines of Federal infantry. The entire division took what cover it could find, and, without orders it, too, opened up a deadly hail of fire.

The noise of almost eight thousand rifles was like nothing they'd ever experienced before: ear shattering, the more so because of the dense undergrowth that contained it, and amplified it to a point where it was more than unbearable. The noise grew and reached a crescendo as volley after volley blended one with another until it became a single sustained roar that hammered against the skull, concussed the eyeballs, and induced mass disorientation and confusion. And everywhere, a blanket of acrid, choking smoke that burned into the eye sockets, and was thick enough to grasp, reduced visibility to zero. So thick was the forest that the breeze couldn't penetrate it, and so the smoke gathered and thickened and choked and blinded. Within minutes, Johnson's men were firing by instinct alone.

Then the forest turned into an inferno as exploding shells and Minnie bullets howled inward from the Federal positions to the west, and case shot from the battery on the hill. The trees overhead, once thick with greenery, in a second were stripped of their leaves, branches, and even limbs. The debris rained down upon the Confederate battle line causing almost as much damage as the enemy gunfire.

At the first sign of incoming fire, Billy Cobb and Jimmy Morrisey had dropped to the ground behind a fallen tree, and all along the line of battle, the rest of Johnson's division had done the same. The light, once dim under the canopy of greenery, suddenly grew brighter, and then they could feel the heat of the afternoon sun on their backs. If they could have looked upward through the smoke, they would have seen a clear blue sky where once there was only a dense covering of leaves.

Slowly, as the smoke began to lift, the Confederate divisions began to organize themselves. Men threw off the covering of twigs and debris, looked around, got their bearings, and then settled down to the task in hand. Fifty yards, or so, to the rear, the five Confederate batteries of Johnson's division had gone into action and all twenty guns were already hurling load after load of case shot and shell over their heads into the blue lines beyond the trees. The huge bangs of the guns echoed through the forest like great claps of thunder, but, as the rate of fire increased and maintained they drew together until the cannon fire became a single, sustained roar that shook the ground and trembled the trees.

Bushrod Johnson, still unharmed at the head of his division, had found cover behind the roots of a fallen tree. Colonel Turner and another officer had joined him. Together they sat with their backs to the stump, and they waited.

The 30th Tennessee's colors had gone down under the first volley of Federal fire, but had been taken up again, and now waved bravely over another fallen tree some dozen or so yards to the left of where Billy and Jimmy, under cover of their own, were working a steady rate of fire.

They kept it up for some ten minutes, or so, and then Billy rolled over and lay flat on his back, looked up through the trees, wiped his eyes and took a deep breath. For a moment, he listened to the howl of the Minnie bullets and canister flying by only inches above his head, to the earth shaking explosions of incoming shells, and the sharp crack followed by the whirring sounds of iron balls launched onward from exploding case shot. Then he looked to his side where Jimmy was mindlessly going through the motions of loading and firing his Springfield.

"HEY, JIMMY," he yelled.

141

Morrisey looked round.

"WHAT?"

Cobb just shook his head, but said nothing. Morrisey turned away and resumed firing.

Billy lifted his head a little and looked around. The once lush forest had been turned into a desolate wasteland of shattered and broken trees. The ground behind him was covered with a carpet of fallen twigs, leaves, and branches that was at least afoot thick. Shattered tree trunks stood in groups, stark and bare, broken off or sheared away. Some were twenty of thirty feet tall, others less than the height of a man. And everywhere, the bodies of the wounded, the dying, and the dead littered the ground around him. And still the Federal fire shrieked and howled through the air just above his head.

To his left, as far as he could see through the haze of smoke, men were pinned down, but returning fire steadily. A dozen or so yards away three bodies lay crisscrossed, one lay half on top of another, which was itself draped across the one below. Two more bodies lay next to them, a little further back lay two more, and only feet away from where he was lying was another. Next to that, a sergeant lay on his back, still alive, but barely, with eyes wide and staring upwards, his life pumping slowly away through the stump of his shattered arm.

Billy looked to his right. The scene was the same, more bodies, more wounded, some crying quietly, some screaming in pain, some already gone beyond the point where they could feel anything.

"Oh Jesus," Billy said out loud. "Oh Jesus.... Oh Jesus." He clamped his eyes shut, screwed up his face, and clapped his hands over his ears, trying to shut out the screams and the shattering, mind-rending cacophony of the battlefield.

Then he shook his head, gritted his teeth, rolled back onto his belly, picked up his Springfield, loaded it, took careful aim, and fired. Jimmy turned and looked at him, his face now covered with filth and grime, grinned at him, winked, and then went back to firing steadily at the enemy lines now easily seen as a stiff breeze blew the smoke quickly away.

Billy shook his head. "Oh Jesus. You crazy son of a...." he said quietly under his breath.

For more than an hour, the two Confederate divisions remained pinned down just inside the line of trees. Jefferson Davis' division, with Wilder's brigade supporting with artillery fire from the rear, heavily outnumbered by the two Confederate divisions, hung on for dear life. The sheer weight of numbers, however, soon began to tell. Hood and Johnson bided their time, waiting for the steadily mounting numbers of Federal casualties to weaken their defensive positions.

At two o'clock Hood sent a courier to Johnson, who was still waiting patiently in the shelter of the great tree stump, with orders to ready his division for a charge against the Federal line. At five minutes after two, a great yell rose from more than seven thousand Confederate throats as they burst from the trees like a great, gray tidal wave. The minute they left the shelter of the trees they came under a hail of deadly fire from the Federal ranks less than three hundred yards away.

Dozens of gray-clad soldiers fell at the first volley of fire; great gaps were torn in the line by a hurricane of canister from Wilder's Federal battery on the hill beyond the enemy lines, and enfilading fire from a second battery of six guns some five hundred yards to the south on the edge of the Lafayette Road.

Each yard of the Confederate charge was bought and paid for with the lives of a dozen soldiers, each yard of the Confederate charge cost Jefferson Davis' Federal division just as dearly.

A hundred yards out, the charge slowed as men stopped, raised their weapons and fired at the Federals at almost point-blank range. With men dropping all around, they reloaded, charged onward, then stopped and fired again. The volume of fire from the more than seven thousand Confederate rifles and twenty cannon was devastating; the hailstorm of canister and Minnie bullets was so heavy that nothing could stand in its path. The Federal positions in front of the Lafayette Road became untenable, and the line collapsed. Soon Davis's two brigades were falling back in disorder, only the combined fire of the two Federal batteries and the fire from the Spencer repeating rifles of Wilder's brigade on the hill, saved Davis from a complete disaster. As it was, he fell quickly back to a new defensive line south of and beyond Hazelwood, leaving the ground in front of the house and the Lafayette Road itself in Confederate hands.

The two triumphant Confederate divisions swept onward to take up new positions behind the breastworks that were only moments earlier occupied by their now retreating enemy.

Billy Cobb and Jimmy Morrisey, much to their astonishment, emerged from the firestorm unscathed, and, together with several thousands of their comrades, they flung themselves down on the ground under the protection of the piled high line of logs. Just as they did so, a strange lull fell over the battlefield, slowly, all across a five-mile front, the gunfire began to slacken and die away, and as it did, so silence descended. Soon, the sobbing and gasping of breathless men and the screams of wounded soldiers and horses were the only sounds to be heard; that and the ringing, roaring noise inside ears deafened and abused by incomprehensible noise of a volume far beyond the tolerance of normal men.

Billy Cobb and Jimmy Morrisey, safe now, lay with their backs against the log breastworks, indifferent to the shattered bark, sharp shards, spikes and splinters of wood, torn into the logs by many thousands of canister and Minnie bullets, and that now poked and stabbed through tunic and britches like so many nails. And they looked back across the fields over which they had so lately charged. As far as they could see, from where they were lying, all the way back to the line of trees, the ground was littered with the bodies of the dead, the dying, and the wounded. That single charge had cost Hood and Johnson almost a thousand casualties, and it was still not yet two-thirty in the afternoon.

Chapter 36

Blake Winter and John Wilder watched in awe as thousands upon thousands of Confederate troops poured from the cover of the trees three hundred yards to the west of Jefferson Davis's division beyond the Lafayette Road. For an hour, they'd watched the carnage wrought by the unseen enemy in the forest, and for an hour, Eli Lilly's battery had done its best to ease the pressure on Davis's division. Now, so it seemed, all their efforts had been for naught; there was no way that the decimated Federal division could stand against the gray-clad hordes charging toward it across the open field.

They stood for a moment, entranced, and watched as the Confederate regiments came on, firing volley after volley at the beleaguered Federals behind the log breastworks. Then, somehow, they jerked themselves back to reality, realizing that unless they did something, and quickly, the Confederate advance would sweep Davis from the face of the battlefield and then continue on up the hill and treat them in a like manner.

"What in God's name has happened to Van Cleve's division?" Winter yelled in Wilder's ear. "I thought he was on Davis's left flank. Where the hell is he?"

"I don't know," Wilder shouted through cupped hands. "He must have been hit, too."

Little did Wilder know that what he said was true. Confederate Major General A.P. Stewart's division had also been waiting in full battle order several hundred yards to the left and rear of Hood's division. And, when Johnson and Hood moved out, General Buckner, under orders from General Bragg, ordered Stewart northward across the rear of Johnson and Hood to the extreme right flank of the Confederate army.

Stewart, however, had not been happy with his orders. He suspected there was a weakness in the Federal line just to the north of Hood's divisions and, moving his own division just far enough to the north to comply with Buckner's orders, swung to the left, entered the battle on Hood's right flank, and advanced in column of brigade, one brigade behind the other.

Stewart's intuition had been correct. He found and then fell on Van Cleve's Federal division like a thunderbolt. By the time Hood and Johnson had cleared away Jefferson Davis, Stewart had already smashed into Van Cleve's division and thrown it back across the Lafayette Road, almost to the Dyer farm. Thomas's whole line of battle, from the Kelly farm, southward for more than two miles beyond the Brotherton farm and Hazelwood was in imminent danger of collapse.

Wilder quickly organized his brigade, now at full strength, with all five regiments in line behind the log breastworks some several hundred yards to the front and south of General Rosecrans' headquarters at the Widow Glenn's farm.

Lilly's battery hadn't stopped firing for more than an hour. Now his heavy guns were joined by the rapid fire of Wilder's infantry, almost eighteen hundred men, all armed with repeating rifles. They opened up a deadly barrage of fire on the advancing Confederate battle line. Effective as it was, it did little more than slow the enemy advance for more than a second or two before it seemed to gather strength and speed as it hurled itself onward.

Federal General Jefferson Davis, now realizing his precarious situation, began to withdraw his two battered brigades away to the southwest. Brigadier General Blake Carlin's was the first to go, quickly followed by Colonel Hans Heg's. As they pulled back, the Confederate divisions fell into cover on the outside of the now abandoned Federal breastworks; Davis pulled back beyond Hazelwood and the Lafayette Road to regroup and reform. In the meantime, with a supreme effort, Wilder's brigade was holding its own; the rapid fire of the Spencers and the heroic efforts of Lilly's gun crews had effectively tripled the strength of the brigade, almost to division strength.

In the minutes following Jefferson Davis's retreat, the pace of the battle seemed to slow. Then, unexplainably, the roar of battle died, and a strange quiet settled over the battlefield. It seemed as if everyone, every single unit had decided to take time out to regroup, to rest for a moment, to gather new strength.

Blake Winter had never experienced anything quite like it before. He sat on the ground behind the log breastworks and peered out through a gap between the logs: nothing. Beyond the one-time Federal positions, the Confederate colors fluttered in the breeze and the last wisps of white smoke rose skyward to dissipate and disappear. It was eerie, the lull before the storm.

"Sir," Lieutenant Cross said, scrambling along toward him behind the logs. "Prisoners."

A sergeant and a corporal were prodding two men in gray toward him at gunpoint.

"So? Why bring them to me?"

"You ain't going to believe it, Colonel," Cross said. "They say they belong to John Bell Hood's division of Longstreet's Corps."

"What?" Winter was incredulous.

"That's right, sir. Longstreet."

"But that's impossible. Longstreet's in Virginia."

"Not according to these two." Cross looked back over his shoulder at the two prisoners: a private aged about sixteen, and a captain of infantry. The captain grinned at Winter and then winked at him.

"Go and fetch Colonel Wilder, Cross. I don't like the sounds of this."

Wilder arrived minutes later, and together he and Winter tried to question the prisoners. At first, they thought the young private might be willing to talk, but he seemed scared to open his mouth for fear of the captain who now was lounging languidly on the ground with his back against the logs.

"We've got no time to fool around like this, Colonel," Wilder said. "If they are Longstreet's men.... Well, General Rosecrans needs to know. Take them on up the hill and see what he wants to do."

Winter looked back up the hill toward the Widow Glenn's cabin some three hundred yards away, and the group of officers gathered on the porch. He nodded, and scrambled to his feet.

"Get them on their feet, Cross," he said, "and let's go."

"Colonel Winter, General, with Rebel prisoners," Brigadier General James Garfield said to Rosecrans from the open door of the Widow Glenn's single ground-floor room.

"Show them in please, General."

"Good afternoon, General," Winter said saluting."

"What do you have, Colonel?" Rosecrans had never been one for pleasantries with his junior officers.

"Two prisoners, sir."

"Well? Why bring them to me?"

"They say they belong to General Longstreet's Corps, General."

"*What* did you say?" Rosecrans looked dumfounded.

"Longstreet, sir."

"Utter rubbish. Come here, boy," Rosecrans said, turning toward the young private who cowered away, overwhelmed by the exalted company of officers.

"Come, come, boy. Don't be afraid. There's no one here to hurt you. You'll answer one or two questions and be sent to the rear out of harm's way.

"Good," he continued as the boy took a halting step forward. "Now, what is your unit?"

The boy looked round at the Confederate captain who winked conspiratorially and made a slight nod of his head.

"Sir, Private Michael Jessop," the boy said quietly, "44th Alabama, Colonel Daniel Perry commanding, General Law's brigade, Hood's...."

"NONSENSE!" Rosecrans shouted, interrupting the boy who flinched and turned his head. "Hood is in Virginia. Now. Tell me the truth. What is your unit?"

But the boy was so frightened by the General's outburst he couldn't speak, and no amount of bullying or cajoling could persuade him to open his mouth again. In exasperation, Rosecrans turned to the broadly smiling Confederate captain.

"And what about you, Captain?" he snarled, barely able to contain his temper. "Where did you come from? Are you from Virginia, too?"

"Why, General Rosecrans; you *are* General Rosecrans I presume?" The captain said smiling benignly. "Captain Rice at your service, Suh. 1st Texas, General Robertson's brigade, Hood's division, late of the Army of Northern Virginia, and mighty pleased I am to make yo'quaintance." He offered Rosecrans his hand; Rosecrans ignored it. The captain took it back, not in the least bit abashed at the rebuff.

Rosecrans stood and stared at the affable Confederate captain, for the first time in his long military career he was unsure of what to believe. He was, however, sure of the empty, hollow feeling beginning to grow deep within the bowels of his stomach.

"So," Rosecrans said quietly, "you're a part of Longstreet's Corps, you say. When did you arrive?"

"Mmmmm.... Right around four o'clock in the afternoon of yesterday, I think it was. Yes, Suh. Four o'clock it was."

"And is Longstreet with you?"

"Why, General Rosecrans. Of course he is."

"And where are your lines, and where is General Longstreet, Captain?"

"Well now, General. I have no idea where General Longstreet might be at this precise moment, but I am certain that he knows exactly where you are."

Rosecrans shook his head in disbelief, and then said, "How.... How many has he brought with him?"

"About forty-five thousand," the captain said without blinking an eye.

"Is General Longstreet in command?"

"Oh no, suh! General Bragg is in command."

"Captain," Rosecrans said exasperated, "you don't seem to know much, for a man whose appearance seems to indicate so much intelligence."

"Well General," Rice said looking Rosecrans squarely in the eye, "I can understand why you might not be satisfied with my information, so I will say this to you, suh: We are going to destroy you; destroy your army and send you running from this field with your tail between your legs."

"Get him out of here," Rosecrans said.

"Thank you, suh," Rice said, bowing slightly from the waist. "I will not wish you, good day."

Rosecrans didn't reply. He simply shook his head, turned away, and stared out of the window.

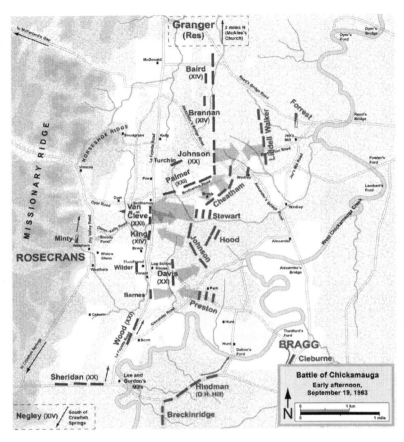

By two-thirty, Brannan's Federal division, out of ammunition and having suffered heavy casualties throughout the morning, had pulled back almost to the Kelly farm where General Thomas had his field headquarters, leaving the divisions of Absalom Baird and Richard Johnson to handle Forrest, Walker, and Cheatham. At first, it seemed that Baird's line might collapse, but the timely arrival of General Palmer's division had enabled the beleaguered Federals to fight the battle to the north to a stalemate.

By three o'clock in the afternoon, the Federal line was still intact and stretched southward from the Kelly farm along the Lafayette Road, more than four miles to Lee and Gordon's Mill, although Van Cleve's shattered division had been hurled back beyond the road, and Jefferson Davis, thanks to Wilder's brigade and Lilly's guns, was still hanging only tenuously onto his new position south of Hazelwood.

But Thomas was undaunted. Reinforcements were pouring in. Major General Joseph Reynolds's division was now on the field and moving quickly to Van Cleve's aid. General Brannan's division had re-armed and regrouped, and it, too, was now moving southward to engage Stewart's victorious division, and Major General Philip Sheridan's division was less than an hour south of Jefferson Davis, and also moving quickly toward the battlefield. Major General James Negley's division was on the Glenn Kelly Road to the southwest of Rosecrans' headquarters, and it too was nearing the battlefield. By late afternoon the entire Federal Army of the Cumberland, all sixty thousand of them, would be on the field.

On the Confederate side, things were also moving quickly. Units of General Longstreet's second division, although Longstreet himself had not yet arrived, were already beginning to trickle into the Chickamauga area from Ringgold. The tail end of General Polk's corps was approaching the river from the south, General Buckner's Corps was already across the creek, and Hill's corps was less than two hour's march away. By late afternoon the entire Army of Tennessee, plus Longstreet's Virginians, would be poised to hurl themselves against the smaller Federal army. General Bragg was, for the first time, facing his enemy with superior numbers and the advantage of position. For some strange reason, however, he couldn't or wouldn't believe it. He was still committed to his plan to move his forces to the north, smash the Federal left flank, and thus insert his army between Rosecrans' and Chattanooga. With Thomas now in position well to the north, it was a plan that would cost Bragg dearly.

Chapter 38

Saturday September 19th, to 2:30p.m. - Chickamauga Creek

For more than an hour after the initial attack on Forrest's camp, Jesse Dixon had been obliged to take care of his friend, Pat McCann. The boy had retreated deep into some lost world of his own, far away from the noise and the horrors that surrounded him. He could still walk, with help, but wouldn't speak, or even open his eyes. It wasn't until sometime after ten o'clock in the morning that Jesse managed to pull him away to one side and sit him down under the cover of a large tree, that Pat began to come out of his state of torpor. And when he did, Jesse wasn't too sure that he was happy about it; the boy began to shake uncontrollably, his teeth chattered, and try as he might he couldn't speak so that he could be understood. But Jesse knew that the situation couldn't continue. Either Pat had to snap out of it, or he would have to be taken to the rear. And that meant he would be branded a coward.

"Well, now, Pat," he said. "Looks like there's only one way to break you out of this."

He unslung his knapsack, fumbled around inside it, and removed a small silver flask. Quickly he unscrewed the cap and put it to Pat's lips.

"Here, drink some of this. It's good strong brandy. I was saving it for an emergency. I guess this is it."

He held the boy's head back, put the flask to his lips, and tipped it. A small amount of the fiery liquid trickled into Pat's mouth and down his throat. Pat swallowed, gasped, then coughed, then choked, then threw up. For several minutes, he lay with his head against the trunk of the tree, retching and coughing as his stomach fought, so it seemed, to reject everything he'd ever eaten. Slowly, as Jesse watched, Pat's spasms began to subside. Soon the boy was coughing intermittently, then he looked round at his friend, his eyes streaming, his face red, and his lips wet with bile. He sat up, laid his head back against the tree, eyes closed, mouth open, breathless. Then he opened his eyes, looked up at Dixon, and wiped his mouth on the sleeve of his tunic.

"Jesus Christ, Jesse," he whispered. "I can't take no more."

"Sure you can." Dixon said, his voice hard. "You ain't hurt. Nor will you be. Now for Christ's sake pull yourself together before someone sees you. Here. Take another pull on this." He handed the flask to his friend. Pat took it, looked at it, then put it to his lips and swallowed deeply. Slowly the color began to return to his face and the shaking stopped. He looked at Jesse and then turned and looked away.

"I'm sorry, Jess," he said. "I don't know what came over me. The noise; I was just in front of the cannon; didn't expect it; the noise shattered my head; deaf; couldn't hear; couldn't see; smoke; panicked...."

"Yeah, well, don't worry. You ain't the first, nor will you be the last. You got to pull out of it, though, Pat. We've got to find the regiment," Jesse said, looking around, trying to fix his position in the dense undergrowth. "Over that way, I think," he said, rising to his feet.

"Come on." He took the flask from Pat's fingers, looked at it, shrugged his shoulder, raised it to his lips and drank deeply, shook it, grinned, then screwed on the cap and put it away. Then he shouldered the knapsack, gathered up his weapon, and grabbed Pat by the shoulder of his tunic, hauled him to his feet and stood with his face close to his.

"Snap out of it, now!"

"All right. I'll be all right. Leave me alone."

"Leave you alone? After what's happened already? Huh."

He bent down and picked up Pat's rifle.

"Here," he said, ramming it into the boy's chest. "Take it."

Pat looked down at the rifle, shuddered, then took it in both hands and looked up into Jesse's eyes. "I'll be all right."

"Yeah, sure. Come on let's move."

"Give me a minute, will you, Jesse? Just a minute to get myself together."

Jesse looked at him, saw the pale face, the wide, scared look in his eyes, hesitated for a moment, then nodded, turned and sat down with his back against the trunk of the tree. For a moment Pat stood, head down, looking at his feet, saying nothing, breathing deeply. Then he seemed to make up his mind about something, turned and faced his friend, and said, "I can't do it, Jess. I'm just not cut out for it." Then he turned again and made as if to walk away, but before he could do so, Jesse had jumped to his feet and grabbed his arm.

"God damn it, Pat," He shouted. "You can't just up and quit. Where the hell do you think you are? You're in the middle of a goddamned battlefield for Christ's sake. Where the hell could you go? They don't kill you, our people will shoot you for desertion under fire."

"I don't care, Jess," Pat said with a tear in his eye. "The blood, the noise, the screams; the horses are the worst. I love horses, Jess. I can't stand to hear them screaming. Got to go; get out of here." He tried to pull his arm away, but Jesse held on tight.

"Look at me, Pat. I said look at me, goddamn it," he shouted, not knowing what to do or say to drive some sense into the boy's head.

"You've got to pull through this. You ain't the only one to come over like this. It happens all the time when a body comes under fire for the first time, but you can handle it Pat. You can handle it."

The boy said nothing. He simply shook his head, looked down at his feet, and tried again to pull his arm free from Jesse's grasp.

And then Jesse lost control. He took a swing at Pat's head with his free hand, connected with the boy's jaw, and spun him off his feet. For a moment he stood there, aghast at what he'd done, then he dropped to one knee beside the boy, put his arm around his shoulder, and pulled him into sitting position.

"I'm sorry, Pat," he said. "I guess I can't handle it any more'n you can. But we've got to go on. We can't quit. You hear? We've got to go on."

Pat sat up and rubbed his jaw, which was already turning blue where Jesse's fist had connected. "All right, Jesse," he said. "I'll try." And with that, he scrambled to his feet, picked up his rifle, and stood looking down at his friend.

"Jesse," he said. "I hear what you say, but I know I can't do it. I'll try to make it through this battle, but then, if I do, it's over. I'm going home, and hang the consequences."

Jesse got unsteadily to his feet, nodded and said quietly, "Sorry I hit you, Pat. I guess I lost my temper. Won't happen again."

"No. It won't," Pat said. "Which way do we go?"

They left the old tree, heading through the forest toward the west and what they thought must be their own lines. For more than an hour they trudged onward, the sounds of the battle raging around them in every direction, the air among the trees and in the heavy undergrowth filled with thick, blinding, choking smoke, and everywhere, the ground was littered with the dead bodies of men and horses, Federal and Confederate. Here and there small fires burned, but everything was too wet or damp for a serious fire to take hold.

On and on they floundered through the dense undergrowth, stopping first here, and then there, to listen, only to find the movements they could see and hear up ahead were Confederate positions. Then they moved back again, only to stumble on yet another enemy stronghold. After more than two hours of stumbling around in the choking, clinging underbrush Jesse was forced to admit that they were hopelessly lost and were now well behind enemy lines.

It was close to three o'clock in the afternoon when, hot, sweating profusely, and filthy, they stumbled out of the woods onto the banks of the Chickamauga. For a while, they had thought the battle was over. The shattering noise of gunfire that had reverberated through the forest and woodland around them, had quieted down for a short while, but then it had resumed with a ferocity unlike anything Jesse had ever heard before, rivaling even his worst moments at Stones River. Then they were out of the woods and on the riverbank.

Together, they dropped their weapons, canteens and packs, and without looking to make sure they were unobserved, scrambled down the muddy bank and fell into the deep, cold water. For a moment, they clung to the overhanging branches of a shattered tree, fighting the current as the swollen river threatened to sweep them away. Jesse looked around. There was a wooden bridge that spanned the river only a dozen yards away downstream.

Then, in the distance, he heard it: the sound of singing voices. At first he thought he must be going mad, and then he realized what it was. A long column of gray-clad soldiers, four across, and stretching back down the road as far as the eye could see, was approaching the bridge, and they were singing as they marched:

"We are a band of brothers and native to the soil

Fighting for our Liberty, with treasure, blood and toil

And when our rights were threatened, the cry rose near and far

Hurrah for the Bonnie Blue Flag that bears a single star!

Hurrah! Hurrah!

For Southern rights, hurrah!

Hurrah for the Bonnie Blue Flag that bears a single star."

"Quick, Pat," he whispered loudly in the boy's ear. We've got to get out of sight. Let go the branch and follow me."

They drifted quietly the few yards to the bridge and grabbed hold of one of the wooden supports, and there they clung like a couple of half-drowned rats. Two minutes later the head of the Confederate column had marched onto the bridge. The supports shook, and dust, sand, filth, and dirt cascaded down upon them through the open planking above.

For more than an hour the two Federal soldiers clung to the wooden support, shivering, teeth chattering from the bone chilling cold of the icy water, as more than five thousand Confederate soldiers passed overhead. And every moment that passed, they expected to be discovered. But, somehow, their luck held, and then the Confederate column was gone, leaving them cold and stiff, but calm enough and well aware that they were deep in trouble.

For several minutes they stayed where they were as the terrible noise of the battle rolled, rumbled, and reverberated overhead like the mother of all thunderstorms. Then, tentatively at first, then scrambling to get out of the bone chilling cold, Jesse pulled himself around the wooden support and up through the mud of the riverbank at the side of the bridge onto firmer ground. He looked along the road after the marching column, and then back down the road the way they'd came, but he could see no movement.

"All right, Pat," he whispered. "Come on. Let's get out of here, and quick." Pat scrambled toward him, floundering clumsily as the mud clung, oozed, and sucked, then Jesse hauled him up and out of the water, and they ran, head down, along the riverbank to where they'd left their equipment. They grabbed up their rifles and packs and ran back into the tangled undergrowth, and didn't stop until they'd reached the cover of a heavy thicket. There they threw themselves down, shivering and shaking and chilled to the bone, behind a fallen tree.

"Jesus. Oh Jesusssss," Pat stuttered through chattering teeth. "I've never been so cold."

Jesse said nothing. Instead, with trembling hands, he reached into his pack and once more took out the small silver flask. He held it to his ear, shook it, then nodded his satisfaction.

"Here," he said, unscrewing the cap. "Drink some of this. It will help, but for Christ's sake save some for me."

Pat took a sip at the flask, screwed up his eyes, shuddered, took another, and then handed the flask to Jesse, who drank deeply, swilled the fiery liquid around his mouth, and then swallowed it. Gratefully he waited as the fire began to take hold inside his belly. Then, his muscles spasmed and he belched. Pat looked at him and, for the first time in several days, grinned. A moment later they were both coughing and grinning at each other, then laughing and slapping each other on the arm, barely able to believe their luck and their escape.

Overhead, the sun shone brightly down through the trees. The temperature was climbing. They were already beginning to warm up, and, although their course uniforms would chafe and scratch, they would soon be dry.

"Come on, Pat. We've got to find our boys; find our own lines, at least." And together, they scrambled to their feet, shouldered their equipment, and moved cautiously off through the forest, northward along the bank of Chickamauga Creek. It was exactly four-thirty in the afternoon.

Chapter 39

It was just after two o'clock in the afternoon when the train pulled into the tiny railway station at Catoosa, Georgia. And tiny it was; just a small wooden building and a short platform, no more than a refueling stop for locomotives, but it was the closest stop to Chickamauga. Thus it was that Confederate Lieutenant General James Longstreet, resplendent in a brand new uniform, accompanied by his chief of staff, Lieutenant Colonel Moxley Sorrel, and his chief of ordnance, Lieutenant Colonel P.T. Manning, stepped down from the train to hear the distant sounds of battle some nine miles to the west. Most of Longstreet's Corps had arrived earlier - Hood's Division yesterday and McLaws earlier today. Now, he would had to wait: most of his staff officers and all of the horses and equipment were following in later trains; the first was not expected to arrive for at least two hours.

Longstreet, flanked by the two officers, stood, legs akimbo, hands on hips, on the small platform and looked around; they were alone.

"Well, gentlemen," Longstreet said. "It seems the good General Bragg has forgotten us."

"Or," Sorrel said, with a sniff, "he just doesn't care."

"Maybe so; maybe so." Longstreet turned and looked down the railroad tracks in the direction from which they had just arrived. "We'll wait. Hah, we don't have a choice."

General Longstreet, second in command of General Robert E. Lee's Army of Northern Virginia, was a tall, pugnacious self-assured general officer, a man who did not suffer fools lightly, and his opinion of General Bragg was… well, now facing a long wait in the heat of the day, it was less than favorable. Not that Longstreet had ever been an admirer of his soon to be commanding general. Bragg had long been criticized throughout the Confederate hierarchy, and there had been multiple attempts to have him replaced as commander of the Army of Tennessee, especially by his subordinates, Generals Polk and Breckinridge. But commander he still was, and Longstreet would follow him, for better or for worse, to the very end. Even so, two hours of waiting, it was more than any man could bare, even for a patient man, and that, Longstreet certainly was not.

The train carrying the horses arrived at four o'clock, by which time, after walking endlessly back and forth along the small platform, Longstreet and his companions were hot, bothered, and in a particularly foul mood. Unfortunately, his troubles were not yet over; the lack of a proper platform meant there was no good way to get the horses out of the cars.

Longstreet, exasperated, climbed into the car where his horse was tethered, threw his saddle onto its back, secured it, mounted and then, with no little trouble, jumped the horse out of the car; Sorrel and Manning did likewise and all three galloped down the dirt road toward the distant sounds of battle.

At first the going was fairly easy; it was just after four-thirty when they left the station, but the road soon became blocked with the "wreckage" of the battle raging away to the west: hundreds of wagons and ambulances moving slowly in both directions; ammunition wagons, empty one way, full the other: Refugees, women, children, by the hundred. By six o'clock, it was already growing dark, and the Confederate officers had traveled less than two miles. Longstreet decided enough was enough, and took a turn toward the south, along a narrow dirt road; it was a decision he would soon regret. The quarter moon and the stars shone brightly in the cloudless sky; even so, it was dark among the trees, and the three officers became thoroughly confused as to what direction they were going, and hopelessly lost.

Around eight o'clock, they became aware of sounds up ahead, voices talking, and then....

"Who goes there?" a voice cried out ahead.

"Friends," Longstreet immediately replied.

But Longstreet, Sorrel and Manning were already backing their horses slowly away.

"What unit are you?" Sorrel asked the picket.

"Second Kentucky," was the answer, which confirmed what they already suspected. They had run into a Federal picket line. Confederate units were named for their commanders; Federal units were identified by numbers.

"Hold steady," Longstreet said in a low voice. "If we run, we'll die."

Sorrel agreed, and said in a voice loud enough to be heard by the Yankee picket, "Lets ride down the creek a little ways, and see if we can find a way across."

The three officers turned and rode quickly back down the road the way they had come. The Federal picket loosed off a hastily aimed shot in their direction, which fortunately, went wide, into the trees.

Some time later, around nine o'clock, they turned once again onto the main road from which General Longstreet had insisted they leave.

Moxley Sorrel questioned one of the passing wagon masters as to which direction they might find General Bragg's field headquarters. The man, fortunately, had only an hour or so earlier left Bragg's encampment. And so the three officers slowly made their way along the dirt road, twisting this way and that among the detritus of war, toward the battlefield.

Chapter 40

Saturday September 19th, 3p.m. - Confederate Line of Battle

By three o'clock in the afternoon, the situation on the Lafayette Road had escalated. The calm that had hung over the battlefield had lasted for almost two hours and had ended abruptly with an earsplitting, shattering cacophony of gunfire. Once again, the woods and fields were blanketed in a smothering, blinding cloud of white smoke. The breeze had dropped, almost to nothing, and the smoke hung over the battlefield, never more than treetop high, obscuring everything from view.

From Wilder's position on the hill above Hazelwood the view was spectacular. The tips of the tallest trees poked through the fog of war like tiny islands in the sunshine. And among it all, not more than five hundred yards from Wilder's vantage point, two Confederate privates, Billy Cobb and Jimmy Morrisey, prepared to meet what fate had to offer, once again.

To the south, just beyond the line of trees where the smoke was a little thinner, and in the shelter of a pile of fallen trees, they could see their generals, Bushrod Johnson, John Bell Hood, Evander McNair and John Gregg conferring with a number of lesser ranks. They looked like gray ghosts in the mist, but the action between the officers was animated, arms waving, heads shaking, nodding, mouths moving, so it seemed, all at once.

How the heck can they understand each other? Billy wondered. He shook his head, pushed his body a little closer to the pile of fallen tree trunks behind which he and Jimmy were huddled. He squinted through a chink between the great limbs, but could see little beyond the road because of the billowing smoke that swirled and boiled with each new explosion. He could hear yelling in the distance, looked south again, just in time to see a Confederate captain, on foot, scramble out of the woods, and join the assembled officers.

"Stay here, Jim," he shouted above the noise, and scrambled to his feet, "I'll be back."

"Hey, where you goin'?

"To see if I can find out what's happenin'. There's somethin' goin' on."

"No kiddin'? Damn, Billy; why don't you just stay put, for God's sake?" He grabbed Billy's arm and tried to pull him back, but Billy was set on going and shook himself free.

"Back in a minute," he shouted, and, head down, rifle trailing, ran off through the ever-thickening smoke toward the council of war.

He reached what he thought was a good position and threw himself to the ground behind a pile of brush just within earshot of the group, and just in time to hear a staggering piece of news. At Hood's request, the courier captain was repeating his message.

"Sir," the breathless captain, said. "General Stewart has broken through the enemy lines just to the north, and is requesting that you send reinforcements. At this very moment, he is pressing on through the Viniard fields sweeping all resistance before him. But his lines are extended, and he's concerned that the enemy will close in behind him and cut him off. He requests immediate reinforcements, sir?"

Hood turned to Johnson. "Can it be true?" he asked.

"Bushrod Johnson nodded, then said, "I'm sure if General Stewart says he's broken through, then that's exactly the situation. I suggest we move quickly to his aid."

"General Hood, Sir," one of the attending colonels shouted. "We can't evacuate this position now. If we do, we'll leave the way open for a Union counter attack. The effect could be disastrous."

"True," Johnson said, "but we can't leave Stewart with his flanks exposed. We have to take a chance. With any luck, we could, ourselves, flank the entire Yankee army. It's a chance that's too good to miss. And the alternative? We can't afford to lose Stewart and his entire division."

Hood nodded, thought for a moment, and then said, "gentlemen, we seem to be quite secure here for the moment, and I do believe we hold Stewart's left flank." He looked at courier captain. "But what is the situation to his right?"

"General Cheatham is in position on General Stewart's right, with General Forrest's cavalry holding the end of the line on General Cheatham's right flank."

Hood nodded again. "And the enemy?" he asked.

"It's difficult to say, sir. News from the line is scarce and the situation is changing so quickly it's inaccurate even before we get it, but it seems General Van Cleve's Federal division, which was facing General Stewart, has broken and is leaving the field in panic. General Stewart's forces have moved forward almost to the Dyer farm. From what we can tell, however, General Richard Johnson's Federal division is newly on the field and Thomas has put him in line facing General Cheatham. Last I heard General Cheatham was under heavy fire, but holding.

Hood was thoughtful; he stared at Bushrod Johnson, then at the gathered officers, seemed to make up his mind, then change it again. He shook his head, jammed his good hand into his tunic, turned away from the group, and walked off toward the rear, seemingly unheeding of the firestorm raging around him.

Billy also turned, but he ran back to where his friend was still huddled behind the makeshift log breastwork that had served them so well for more than two hours.

"All hell and then some's 'bout to break loose, Jim. We've broken through the Yankee lines just a bit away to the north an' Hood cain't make up his mind what to do next."

Morrisey simply nodded and continued to squint through the opening between the makeshift log breastworks in front of him. The fog of gun smoke lay even heavier across the road beyond. To the north, where General Stewart's Confederate division was fighting to retain its newly won position, the woods were on fire.

Chapter 41

Saturday September 19th, 3p.m. - Confederate Line at the Viniard Field

Confederate Major General Alexander Powell Stewart was not a big man; diminutive, some might say. But what he lacked in stature he more than made up for in tenacity.

He had crossed the Chickamauga River with his entire division at Thedford's Ford during the night. General Bragg, however, had held him in reserve all through the morning, a situation that was intolerable for a man such as Stewart, a man renowned for his lack of patience. He had been further frustrated when Bragg had finally ordered him northward behind the main Confederate line of battle with the intention of swinging westward around his own right flank to fall upon the enemy's left flank. From there he was to smash his way down the Union line, rolling it up as he went. It was the plan Bragg had clung to for more than a week, and he would continue to do so.

Stewart, however, was also renowned for his independent thinking. Unhappy as he was with his orders, he had reluctantly complied and started his three brigades under the commands of Brigadier Generals Brown, Bate, and Clayton, northward along the dirt road that ran almost parallel to the Confederate battle line.

At one o'clock in the afternoon, however, he sensed a weakness in the enemy's lines to the west. Maybe it was a slight reduction in noise, a slightly lesser rate of fire from beyond the trees; perhaps it was nothing that anyone but Stewart could put a finger on; perhaps it was just an excuse for him to abandon his march northward and join the fray. Whatever it was, he moved quickly upon it. He now felt he had moved far enough northward to have obeyed his commander's direct order, and so he turned his division westward into line of battle and, together, the three brigades moved quickly through the trees toward the Lafayette Road at a point between General Hood's division to the south and Cheatham's division to the north.

Whatever it had been that had caused Stewart to make his decision, he never told. It was, however, a momentous one. No sooner had he arrived at the Lafayette Road than he was fully engaged with Van Cleve's Federal division. He pressed forward with General Clayton's brigade ahead of that of General Brown, which was followed by that of General Bate.

Van Cleve was taken by surprise. By two o'clock, Stewart has smashed his way through the Federal line, sent most of Van Cleve's troops flying from the field in confusion, and was himself extended far out beyond the Lafayette Road all the way to the Dyer farm; he had, he soon realized, gone too far too quickly, and was in imminent peril of himself being overrun. It was at this point he had sent to General Bragg for reinforcements. Bragg, however, still fully committed to turning the enemy's left flank, sent word back that he had no reinforcements to send; Stewart now turned to Hood and Cheatham for help.

General Hood returned to the small group of staff officers assembled in the woods just to the east of the Lafayette Road, took a deep breath, then gave the orders for his field commanders to ready their brigades.

"General," he said to Bushrod Johnson. "We will go to General Stewart's aid. Be ready to move off in column of brigade in ten minutes."

Johnson nodded, saluted Hood, then turned and began issuing orders to his brigade commanders.

"General McNair, you will take the left flank; General Gregg will take the center; you, Colonel Fulton, will take the right flank. Ten minutes, gentlemen. Be ready on my orders."

Five minutes later, Brigadier General John Gregg, commanding the center of Johnson's division was pulling his brigade into line just inside the woods to the east of the Lafayette Road, less than five hundred yards from Eli Lilly's guns on the hill below the Widow Glenn's home.

At the center of Gregg's brigade was the 30th Tennessee; among them Billy Cobb and Jimmy Morrisey.

They stood together in the front rank, just to the right and behind the color bearers, quiet, watching Hood, Johnson, and Gregg mentally preparing for what might lie ahead. The three Confederate generals, other than their exalted rank, were no different from the two Confederate privates that were, by now, ready to follow all three generals to the grave.

The noise around them was incredible, insane. Wave after wave of cannon fire reverberated across the woodlands as General Johnson's five Confederate batteries opened up a withering curtain of shell and case shot toward the Federal batteries on the hill to the west.

General Hood, the only officer now on horseback, turned to Johnson, nodded his head, raised his sword in the air, and looked left and right along the lines of gray-clad troops.

Billy Cobb glanced sideways at his friend. Jimmy's face was white; he was chewing something; his jaws working hard; his eyes staring straight ahead. The battered old planter's hat was pulled well down on his head. The lines of his face, old lines, deep folds, were hard and sharply defined; his eyes mere slits. Billy nudged him. He looked round, quickly.

"You stick with me, Jim. You hear?"

Morrisey looked at him, nodded twice, and then looked ahead once more.

To the front, Generals Johnson and Gregg had also raised their swords; away to the left and right, so had General McNair, and Colonel Fulton.

Billy took a deep breath, and a sense of peace descended on him; for a moment, time seemed to stand still. He looked upward, trying to penetrate the haze that swirled through all that was left of the woodland canopy; here and there he glimpsed a ray of sunshine that turned the smoke into billowing clouds of gold. He smiled. It was a good sign. He looked down again, clasped his rifle in both hands, and relaxed; he was ready.

Hood looked again at Johnson, nodded his head and swung his sword downward. Johnson responded immediately.

"GUIDE FRONT AND CENTER. FORWAAARD."

General Johnson's voice rang out loud and clear over the roar of battle, and the more than thirty-five hundred gray-clad soldiers of Johnson's division moved forward through the tangled undergrowth, fallen trees, and clinging, clawing briars, and the now decimated woods toward the Lafayette Road.

Chapter 42

On the slopes of the hill to the west of the Lafayette Road and Hazelwood, John Wilder, Blake Winter, and Eli Lilly waited behind their log breastworks. As they looked eastward across the road, the fog of gun smoke swirled low among the trees. Only the tips of the tallest trees now poked through the fog, like stark ghosts in the sunshine. The road itself was invisible beneath the blue-white mist; but something, they knew, was happening. Already they were taking heavy fire from the Confederate batteries in the woods to the east.

"They're coming, I think," Wilder said, to himself, so it seemed. And he was right, for, even over the roar of battle, the drums and bugles could be heard echoing across the open fields in front of them.

"Prepare your guns, Captain Lilly. Double shot with canister. Oh my God!"

Suddenly, like phantoms in the mist they appeared line upon line of gray-clad soldiers. Out of the trees they came, one rank behind the other, and then another, and another, seemingly endless. As far to the right as they could see, and as far to the left, thousands of enemy soldiers were marching resolutely toward them; officers to the front, colors and battle flags flying bravely in the breeze, rifles held at the ready, bayonets glistening in the sunshine.

Wilder stared, then shouted:

"TAKE COVER. NOW!"

At first, the Confederate lines moved forward at the walk, then the pace quickened, then quickened again. Soon they were racing forward at a dead run, screaming and yelling as they came; the noise was incredible. Now they had closed the gap to less than four hundred yards, now three-fifty, and still they had not fired a shot. Suddenly, they stopped; the front ranks kneeled and more than three thousand rifled muskets were leveled, aimed, and fired. Behind them, beyond the trees to the east, the massed guns of all five Confederate batteries opened fire. The crash of cannon and gunfire rippled and rolled across the battlefield like huge bolts of thunder and lightning; the effect of the combined broadside was devastating.

The logs to the front of Wilder's breastworks were torn to shreds by that first shattering volley; great chucks of wood, and smaller, needle-like shards spun into the air tearing flesh from bone as they hurtled across the Federal positions. And behind the breastworks themselves, the hail of lead and iron seemed to find every chink and gap. Lilly's gun crews were decimated; one man alone went down with thirty-two separate wounds, every one of them received in a single terrible second. Men who had thought themselves safe behind the makeshift shelter soon found differently. That first deadly blast from the Confederate line of battle dealt Wilder some fifty casualties.

But Wilder's brigade was quickly back in action. Even though they were outnumbered by at least five-to-one, and Lilly's guns were virtually out of action, and while the Spencer repeating rifles did much to even the score, it not enough.

Wilder, head down, ran from one regimental commander to the next issuing orders for a withdrawal to higher, safer ground. Eli Lilly's guns were the first to move under cover of withering fire from the Spencers. Then, slowly, taking heavy fire from the Confederate ranks below, the main body of Wilder's brigade pulled back to establish new positions just beyond and under cover of the crest of the rise.

Chapter 43
Saturday September 19th, 3:30p.m. - Confederate Line of Battle

In the Confederate ranks, now strung out across the open fields beyond Hazelwood and the Lafayette Road, General Hood, seeing the movement toward the rear of the Federal troops on the rise, gave new orders. McNair's brigade was to maintain its westward advance upon the hill and the Widow Glenn's home, while Johnson, Gregg, and Fulton were to wheel to the right and move northward in support of General Stewart's now beleaguered division.

The mood in the ranks to the center of the Confederate line of battle behind General Johnson was exuberant. The flags and banners waved; soldiers yelled and waved their rifles above their heads; it was all the officers could do to restrain them from making a headlong charge up the rise in pursuit of the retreating Federals.

"All right, Jimmy," Billy Cobb yelled in his friend's ear. "So far, so good. If we can keep 'em on the run we might make it through this day. Keep your head down, and try to stay with me. We need to be in one of the rear ranks." He ducked as a Minnie bullet whirred like an angry hornet between them and found its mark, shattering the wrist of a company sergeant just behind.

"Jimmy. You hear?"

But his friend had a strange light in his eyes. He was excited, breathing hard, his nostrils flared, and yet, at the same time, he was steady and resolved.

"No, Billy, by God," he shouted. "I cain't do it no more. Cain't keep on dodgin' like this. I gotta stay with it. If my time's a comin' then it'll come no matter where we be. Might as well go with our heads held high."

"What'? You nuts?" Billy Cobb looked at his friend in amazement. "We can get killed out there, Jim, or hurt bad, which might be worse than bein' dead. An' I don't see any point in pushin' our luck, time to go or not. Now you stay by me, you hear?"

But Jimmy Morrisey merely looked at him, his face grim, teeth clenched tightly together, eyes watering from the sting of gunpowder and smoke, his faced streaked with grime.

"Naw," he shouted, shaking his head slowly. "Reckon I'll take my chances up front with Gen'l Johnson. You realize, Billy?" he paused, spat, and nodded his head toward where Bushrod Johnson was preparing his brigades to move to the north, "Johnson's the biggest goddamn target on the field; always has been, always will be. If he can do it; if he can make it through; so can we. Jeez, Billy, an' lookit Hood. He's banged up so bad he cain't get on an' off his horse. Makes a man ashamed to be in the rear, Billy. Gotta be a man, Billy; gotta be a man; yessir."

Billy, speechless, stared at his friend, shook his head in despair, gripped his rifle hard, spat on the ground between his feet, and resigned himself to what he knew must lie ahead.

Jimmy turned and looked at him and, for the first time in days, grinned at his friend, nudged him hard in the ribs with his elbow.

"Don't you worry none, Billy boy. I reckon it's my time that's up, not your'n. You'll make it through just fine."

Billy closed his eyes and turned his face to the sky, but said nothing.

To the front, Brigadier General Bushrod Johnson was calling the charge. Together, with more than a thousand screaming men on either side, the two privates moved off at the run toward the vast clouds of billowing smoke to the north; to the east, the woods from which they had so lately emerged were on fire.

They had not moved forward more than one hundred yards when they came under heavy fire from Federal batteries located far beyond the range of rifle fire. But, never for a moment, did the pace of the charge slacken. On they ran yelling and screaming at the top of their lungs.

The air around them was filled with flying lead and iron; men were pitching and falling, running as hard as they could go. And, at their head, ten, maybe fifteen, yards in front of the charging Confederate line of battle, General Bushrod Johnson, sword in one hand, pistol in the other, frock coat tails flying, hat long gone, was yelling like a demon.

Just behind Johnson, to his left and right, were Brigadier General John Gregg and Colonel Jim Turner. To his right rear was the color sergeant of the 30th Tennessee. The tattered blue and gold regimental banner was fluttering and snapping on the breeze. To his left rear, yet another color squad, this one bearing the red, white and blue Confederate battle flag at their head ran forward screaming and yelling. In the front rank, directly behind the regimental flag, Jimmy Morrisey was also yelling and screaming at the top of his voice. Billy Cobb, not quite as enthusiastic as his long-time friend, was running hard, coughing and choking as he gulped down the smoky air.

On across the open fields toward the Dyer farm they charged, running men pitching and falling to the left and right, but the two Confederate privates seemed to be living charmed lives. The Federal lines to the north that once were only distant clouds of gun smoke on the horizon took form as the charging lines drew nearer. The enemy fire from front and left began to build and intensify as they drew closer.

To the right, they were drawing level with the temporary positions taken up by General Stewart's three brigades, also under heavy cannon fire from the ridge to the left of the Dyer farm, along with intense infantry fire from ahead. On the rise, the Federal gun crews were maintaining a rate of fire of almost three rounds a minute, each great gun double-loaded with canister. The noise was insane. The very ground was shaking. Casualties in Stewart's ranks were heavy. The bodies of the dead and wounded lay like a brightly colored carpet across the green fields over which they had so lately charged.

And still Johnson's brigades charged onward. But now, the intensity of the enemy fire from three Federal infantry divisions - Reynolds, Brannan and Negley - and from the massed batteries on the ridge ahead - fourteen guns of Reynolds' division - had tripled, and they had also been joined by Eli Lilly's six guns to the west on the hill near the Widow Glenn's home. Into this veritable curtain of lead and iron, Johnson's men ran headlong. Then, they were wheeling to the right to join with Stewart's decimated brigades. The charge slowed as the two Confederate divisions merged and became one small army, pinned down under the weight of the Federal barrage.

Then, as the two divisions combined, it gained impetus as Stewart's men joined Johnson's at the run. At first, the weight of numbers began to tell, but Federal reinforcements were already arriving on the field. The First Division of McCook's Federal Corps under the command of Brigadier General Jefferson Davis had regrouped and now joined the three already holding their ground around the Dyer farm.

When Johnson and Stewart's blow fell, Brigadier General William Carlin's brigade of Davis's division was holding the center of the Federal line; it took the brunt of the Confederate charge, was overwhelmed and pushed to the west side of the Lafayette Road, leaving three guns of the 8th Indiana Battery and the flags and banners of the 21st Illinois behind. Brigadier General Henry Benning's Confederate brigade tore into Davis's Third Brigade commanded by Brigadier General Hans Heg, while McNair's Confederate brigade smashed into Davis's flank.

Heg's brigade faltered under the onslaught; within minutes he had lost almost half his brigade, but his men stood their ground, never giving up so much as an inch. Then Heg took a Confederate Minnie bullet in his stomach. The bullet did not kill him instantly and, with what little time he had left, he rode around his beleaguered brigade, slumped over the saddle, trying to rally his men. Finally, he collapsed from loss of blood. Heg died on the field just as the sun was going down. But his efforts had not been in vain. The combined might of the four Federal divisions began to tell on the lesser numbers in the Confederate line of battle.

Slowly, but surely, the Confederate charge began to slow. Billy Cobb and Jimmy Morrisey were close to the front center of General Gregg's brigade, close behind the regimental flag of the 30th Tennessee, which already had changed hands four times, its bearers going down in the hail of fire from the Federal forward positions.

Here and there, the Confederate line began to falter. Men began throwing themselves to the ground in an effort to avoid the hail of Federal fire. The line, some forty or fifty deep and more than a half-mile long, became ragged as more and more men took to the ground.

Generals Stewart, Johnson, Gregg, Bate, Brown and Clayton, along with Colonel Fulton, did their best to rally their forces, but the end was inevitable. The Federal forces, constantly receiving reinforcements from General Thomas, were growing ever stronger. The rate of fire from the long lines of blue-clad infantry and the more than thirty cannon ranged on the higher ground to the north and west had increased to unbelievable, insane proportions. General Hood, still on horseback and still unscathed, watched in horror as the grand Confederate effort began to look more and more like General Pickett's glorious, but ill-fated charge at Gettysburg only three months earlier.

At the center of the line, the color bearers had slowed almost to a walk. With heads down, as if they were advancing against a storm of rain, they struggled onward into the curtain of lead and iron. Men were falling, pitching, dropping all along the Confederate line. And still Billy and Jimmy managed to maintain their forward momentum. Ahead, the red, white and blue battle flag, and the blue and gold colors of the 30th Tennessee had been torn to shreds by the hail of fire, reduced to little more than rags but still flying bravely. Ten yards ahead of the two privates, General Gregg and Colonel Sugg had turned their backs to the storm, were walking backwards toward the enemy lines, arms waving, still trying to rally their faltering line. Then, only feet from the two Confederate privates, General Gregg went down.

Jimmy Morrisey got to him first, closely followed by Billy Cobb and Colonel Sugg. The general was on his back, still conscious, but bleeding profusely from a ragged wound in his neck. His eyes were wide and he tried to speak to the three men on their knees at his side, but all he could do was gurgle.

"God damn it, Billy. They've killed him," Jimmy shouted across the wounded general. But the general grabbed Sugg's arm and shook his head, tried to speak, grabbed the colonel's hand, gritted his teeth and nodded his head.

"You two men," Sugg shouted above the noise. "See what you can do to stop the bleeding, and take him back to the road. See if you can find a doctor and get him some help." He looked at the fallen general; his eyes were closed and his breathing was quick, but ragged. Sugg shook his head, stood up, grabbed Billy by the shoulder and pulled him away.

"I think he's dying," he yelled in his ear, "but do your best for him." And, with that, Sugg turned and ran toward the front of the stalled Confederate line.

Jimmy Morrisey pulled the old green bandanna from somewhere inside the depths of his tunic, rolled it into a pad, then inserted it between the high collar of Gregg's frock coat and his neck, covering the wound and slowing the flow of blood.

"It don't seem to have hit a big vein," Billy said. "Maybe he can make it. Let's get him out of here."

They grabbed the general by the arms and pulled him to his feet. He, the general, opened his eyes, then closed them again and would have fallen.

"Here, give me a hand," Billy said, moving in front of Gregg. "You hold him steady while I grab him." He bent down put his shoulder to the general's mid-section, wrapped his arms around the back of his knees, then lifted him bodily onto his shoulder, staggered a little, then turned and started to run toward the rear, Jimmy following close behind, carrying both his own and Billy's rifle.

For more than a half-mile, Billy carried the wounded general, dodging this way and that to avoid tripping over the fallen bodies of comrades. He was gasping, barely able to breathe, staggering under the dead weight on his shoulder. As they approached the crest of a gentle rise, his pace slowed, but he gritted his teeth, his breath hissed between them and his parted lips, and he staggered on. Every now and then a bullet would whirr close by, sometimes too close, but all three seemed to be living charmed lives, for none found their target. Then they crested the rise and Billy gained new momentum as they continued on down the slope toward the Lafayette Road, and a large log house beside it.

"Billy, stop," Jimmy grabbed his friend's arm in an effort to slow his headlong run. Let me take him for a while."

But Billy shrugged him off and ran onward.

"Jeeze, Billy. You're goin' to kill yourself. Let me take him, for God's sake."

Then they were at the back door of the house. There were dead bodies lying all around, some in blue, but most in gray. Jimmy hammered on the door while Billy leaned with his load against the door jam, barely able to stand. The door was opened immediately by a blue-clad soldier. Jimmy leaped backwards bringing his rifle forward.

"Hey, whoa, don't shoot," the man flung his arms upward."

Jimmy lowered the rifle as Billy staggered backwards under the weight of the Confederate general, then forward through the door, knocking both men sideways as he did so.

They were in a large kitchen. There were wounded men lying everywhere: on the floor, the table, benches. Around them, several men in blue uniforms, two more in gray, a civilian, a young white woman and a tall, thin black female. They all stopped what they were doing and stared at the two Confederate privates and their load.

"Clear a space on the table, now," Billy gasped. Nobody moved. "NOW, I said; Jimmy!"

Jimmy Morrisey leveled his rifle.

One of the blue-clad officers moved forward. His white duster coat bore the green shoulder patches of a medical officer, a colonel, along with the blood that cover most its front and sleeves; the man was a doctor.

"Steady boys," the doctor said. "We're doing the best we can. He'll have to wait his turn."

"No, Sir," Jimmy shouted. "He cain't wait. This here's General Gregg, an' he's bad wounded an' he'll die if he don't get no help, right now. Now you clear a space, like Billy said."

The colonel moved closer to Billy, lifted the Confederate general's head, parted the collar of his tunic, then turned and nodded his head for one of the privates to clear a space on the table.

Chapter 44

Saturday September 19th, 4p.m. - Federal Field Headquarters: Widow Glenn's Cabin

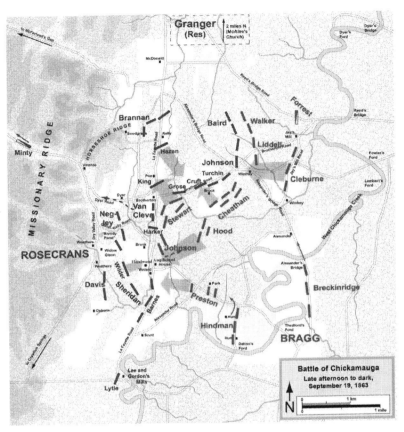

High on the crest of the ridge above Hazelwood, just a little to the south west of the Widow Glenn's home and General Rosecrans' field headquarters, Blake Winter, John Wilder and Smith Atkins watched the fighting in the fields below from behind hastily erected breastworks. Behind them, Eli Lilly's guns were hammering the Confederate positions to the northeast. The shells from the great guns screamed only feet over their heads and they could see each one as it reached the top of its arc, then fell in a long downward curve to explode among the Confederate lines.

They watched as the long gray lines continued to move toward the Federal positions to the north and, as they moved onward, the fields behind them were littered with the dead, dying and wounded. The carnage was mind numbing, beyond belief. Winter estimated that the Confederate divisions had already lost a fourth of their numbers.

But Wilder's brigade had, itself, not gone unscathed. That first terrible Confederate barrage had devastated his earlier positions. Then, as his men pulled back beyond the crest of the ridge, they had had to make a fighting withdrawal as General McNair's Confederate division had pressed forward up the rise toward the Widow Glenn's house where General Rosecrans was watching the battle from a rocker on the front porch.

Relaxed as he seemed, Rosecrans was in full command. All around him, his general staff bustled this way and that; General Garfield writing order after order as Rosecrans issued them, then sending couriers galloping to every position along the Federal line of battle.

Wilder's men, thanks in no small part to their Spencer repeating rifles, had wreaked havoc on McNair's brigade as it slowly covered the ground toward the crest of the ridge. They had laid down an almost impenetrable curtain of fire against the gray-clad lines on the lower slopes, but the Confederate batteries beyond the trees across the Lafayette Road had also taken their toll on Wilder's brigade. During the retreat to the crest of the rise he had left wounded and dying men strewn all over the slopes. His casualties now numbered more than two hundred, and his soldiers were still taking hits from shrapnel as Confederate shells continued to explode overhead.

But Wilder and Winter knew that, now McNair's division had been driven back beyond the Lafayette Road, the Federal forces had the upper hand. They could see that the two Confederate divisions ranged across the fields in front of the Federal positions, almost seven thousand soldiers could go no farther.

The Confederate generals, Hood, Johnson, and Stewart, recognizing the inevitable, were already giving orders for their brigades to withdraw. Slowly, the great gray line began to reverse itself and move back the way they had come. All along the Federal line to the north, men were shouting and cheering as they watched the reversal of fortunes in the fields in front of them.

Chapter 45

Saturday September 19th, 4:30p.m. - Confederate Line of Battle

With their divisions still under heavy fire, the Confederate commanders, under cover of a small wooded area just to the east of the Lafayette Road and the Viniard field, were gathering to discuss the situation. General Stewart was beside himself with rage; he was still on horseback when Hood arrived, closely followed by Johnson, Fulton and Sugg.

"We're done, General," Stewart shouted as Hood approached. "Betrayed, by God." Stewart's horse was bucking and stamping its feet, its rider controlling it only with difficulty.

"Look at them," Stewart screamed. "Almost half of my division gone; destroyed, and it's not over yet. What the hell is Bragg thinking? We had 'em; had 'em. Christ, General Hood. What a mess."

But Hood was in no mood for recriminations. He, too, was angry. And it showed in his red face, brought on as much by the overdose of laudanum he had taken earlier as by the exertions of the past hour.

"Get hold of yourself, General," Hood shouted as he reigned in his horse close to Stewart's; the two generals were still out of earshot of the other commanders approaching from the open fields at the run.

"We'll get no help from Bragg, and General Cheatham has all he can handle. Ranting will do us no good. We have to consider our options."

"Options? What options? We have to get our men the hell out of there. That's the only option we have. If not, we'll be wiped out, by God."

Hood, sour-faced, nodded his agreement and, reluctantly, Stewart made ready to return southward across the territory he had just won at a horrendous cost. Together with Hood and Johnson, he gathered what was left of his brigades and, under heavy fire from massed Federal artillery to the north, and from Eli Lilly's battery on the hill, he withdrew from the field; He was beside himself with rage.

It was four-thirty in the afternoon; the Confederate lines reestablished themselves, almost at the point where they had stepped off so lively an hour-and-half-earlier.

Needless to say, Confederate General Bragg was also beside himself with rage, and he had not yet given up for the day, nor had he given up the idea of hammering Rosecrans' left flank and pushing the Federal army southward. And so he ordered Major General Patrick Cleburne's division northward to meet with General Polk on his army's right flank, just to the south of Reed's Bridge Road. General Forrest was just to the rear, guarding Polk's right flank.

Chapter 46

Saturday September 19th, 4:30 to 7p.m. - Chickamauga Creek

"I think we need to head that way," Jesse said, pointing north along the riverbank. "We must be at least a mile behind the enemy lines," he continued. "Listen to it."

In the distance, away to the west, the sounds of gunfire was one sustained roar, but they could see nothing. The surrounding woods, scrub and trees were too dense. The sun shone brightly through the treetops, and glittered on the slow-moving waters of the creek. Pat shivered, but not just from the chill of his still-damp clothing.

"We can't get through, Pat, they're everywhere. We'll have to go around them." Jesse stood with his back to the river, listening to the sounds of battle to the west. "That way," he said, pointing. "We'll follow the river bank."

Pat rubbed his bruised chin and nodded. Together, they shouldered their rifles and moved off along the riverbank. It would not be an easy walk; the bank was overgrown. For an hour, they stumbled and fought the dense undergrowth. It was slow going, but they were making headway. By five-thirty, they had traveled a little more than a mile and had reached a place where the water was shallow enough to ford the river, and the light was failing quickly.

"We'll go across, Pat," Jesse said. "Maybe it will be easier on the other side." McCann merely nodded his head, and walked into the icy water. They followed the dirt track east for about fifty yards to the intersection with another dirt track. There, they turned to the left and walked on, keeping the sounds of battle on their left side. There was no one using the track, so they were able to walk quickly, making a good pace. As they did so, they warmed up, even though the early evening air was turning cold. For another forty-five minutes, they continued on, the track following the line of the river, until they arrived at what appeared to be a much wider dirt road. It was, in fact, Reed's Bridge Road, and it was busy. Wagons of every size and description were moving slowly in either direction, some carrying wounded soldiers, some ammunition; all of the travelers were wearing gray.

Together they dived off the road and dropped to the ground in the dense undergrowth. It was after six o'clock, and night was beginning to close in around them, too dark for the men on the wagons to see much of anything, except the road on which they were traveling; Jesse Dixon and Pat McCann lay in the shadows, watching, and waiting.

To the west they could just make out the bridge; fires were burning just beyond it; smoke and sparks billowing into the air, and they could see the silhouettes of men on the structure, stark shadows against the light of the fires burning in woods beyond.

By six-thirty, the darkness was almost complete, but the sounds of battle, and the flashes of gunfire had diminished not even a little as General Cleburne's division assaulted the Federal lines across the Winfrey field; but they knew nothing of what was happening beyond the bridge, only that the fighting was continuing in the darkness.

"What are we gonna do?" Pat whispered.

"We got to get across the road," Jesse replied. "We'll wait for a gap between the wagons, and then make a run for it."

"I dunno, Jesse."

"No choice, Pat. Either we make a run for it, or we stay here until someone sees us. Get ready."

Not more than a couple of minutes later, they spotted a gap of about twenty yards between the wagons heading east; the traffic heading west had dwindled almost to nothing.

"Get ready.... Now! Into the trees!" Together, they rose and, heads down, dashed across the road between the slow-moving wagons. As they did so, they heard a shout, then two shots rang out in the darkness, but they were safe, scrambling through the dense woodland, faces whipped and scratched by the flailing branches, tripping and stumbling, they didn't stop running until they could run no more. Finally, they fell, gasping for breath: Jesse, his back against a tree, Pat beside him on the ground, flat on his back. Breathing hard, they listened: nothing, just the sounds of gunfire reverberating through the woods away to the west.

Five minutes later, they were back on their feet, pushing northward through the dense undergrowth. For more than 20 minutes they fought the tangled blackthorn and briar until, at last, they stumbled out of the forest and onto a narrow, deserted dirt track that disappeared into the waters of the creek, and then reappeared on the other side.

For a moment, they stood together at the water's edge, trying to get their bearings.

"Come on. Let's get across," Jesse said. "If we head that way," he continued, pointing to the west, "and keep the noise to our left, we should do all right."

Pat, still breathing hard, just nodded his head and, together they moved quickly across the ford and on along the dirt track. It was seven o'clock in the evening.

Chapter 47

Saturday September 19th, 6:30p.m. - Confederate Positions East of the Lafayette Road

Meanwhile, a mile and a half away to the southwest, three hundred yards to the east of the Lafayette Road, the Confederate line was consolidating its new positions; Hazelwood was, once again, behind the Federal lines. John Wilder's brigade had withdrawn up the hill to the west and was settling in beyond the Dry Valley Road and the Widow Glenn's house.

To the front, right, and left of the Confederate line, the fighting had dwindled almost to nothing, just sporadic outburst of small arms fire from the pickets on either side. Away to the north, less than a mile, however, it was a different story: General Cleburne was fully involved in a frantic, mile-wide assault on the Federal line to the east of the Kelly farm.

The woodlands to the east of the Lafayette Road that marked the new Confederate positions were all but gone, cleared away, for the most part, by hours of cannon and rifle fire from both sides of the road. Where once stood stands of tall, old growth pine trees, only the shattered stumps now stood, stark silhouettes against the fire-red sky that boiled and rolled over the battlefield like a pyroclastic eruption. The once-dense tangle of briar, blackthorn, and scrub oak had been stripped away by the firestorm, and then flattened by the thousands of feet passing over it, first one way, and then the other. And everywhere, there lay the bodies of the dead, men and horses, and the wounded, some sobbing quietly, some screaming in pain, some begging for water, some silent, seemingly lost to this world as they stepped out along the road toward the next one. In the blackness of night, lit only by flames of the burning forest to the north, the landscape was a stark nightmare of unbelievable proportions.

And it was here, within that nightmare, that Billy Cob and Jimmy Morrisey threw themselves down on the blanket of scrub to wait, perhaps to rest, if only a little. They were still in roughly the same position as they had been all day, close to the center of General Gregg's brigade – now commanded by Colonel Cyrus Sugg. Johnson's division, now part of John Bell Hood's command, would soon be under the overall command of Lieutenant General James Longstreet, who had not yet arrived on the battlefield.

"What you got left in your canteen, Billy?" Jimmy said to his friend. "Mine's about empty. Not much chance of gettin' a refill, huh?"

"I got a little. You're welcome to a taste," Billy replied. "And I guess you'd be about right. There'll be no more, leastwise not 'till mornin'." He raised the canteen to his ear and shook it, then handed it over. Jimmy unscrewed the cap and raised it to his lips, took a small mouthful, then made to hand it back.

"Take another pull," Billy said. "Leave me a little. What bit there is ain't gonna make any big difference."

Jimmy nodded his head, took another small mouthful, and then handed the canteen back to his friend. They sat for a moment; Billy with his head down, chin on his chest, eyes closed. Jimmy just stared at the boiling sky to the north. "You wanna go get some?" He said, without turning his head.

"Get some what?" Billy asked.

"Water! You wanna go get some water? The creek cain't be that far away, over there," he said, as he pointed the way. "It cain't be more'n a few hundred yards. Ain't nothin' happenin' here. Leastwise, not for a while, and I could use a good drink."

Billy looked at him, for a long moment. "Might could," he said, looking toward the creek, unseen, more than a half-mile away to the east. "Let's go find Sergeant Corn and ask if we can do it. I'd hate to get caught gone without permission."

Jimmy nodded. "Let's do it." He said.

They found Corn lying on his back under the branches of a fallen tree; he appeared to be asleep.

"Er, Sarge?" Billy asked.

Corn's eyes blinked open, and he sat upright. "What?"

"We thought we might head over to the creek and get some water," Billy said, shaking his empty canteen.

"Nope! No leavin' camp, and no fires. Them's my orders." Corn looked up at the two men, and then shook his head. "Go ask Colonel Turner. We all need water." And with that, he picked up his own canteen, it was empty. He tossed it to Jimmy, laid back down among the twigs and branches, and closed his eyes.

They found Turner sitting with his back against a shattered tree just a dozen, or so, yards away. His once-pristine uniform was dirty and tattered, the sleeves torn and snagged by blackthorn and briar, the gold trim torn loose and hanging from the cuffs.

"Colonel, Sir? Billy asked, as he offered a somewhat sloppy salute to his regimental commander.

"What is it, Private?" Turner looked bone weary, and his voice did little to offer anything different.

"Well, Sir, Colonel. Me and Jimmy here was wonderin' if we might hightail it back to the creek an' get some water."

"Not a bad idea," Turner said, "I could use some myself. Here, I'll write you a scrip." Turner pulled on the leather strap that stretched diagonally over his chest from his left shoulder and a flat leather satchel appeared from behind him. He opened the flap, took out a small notebook and the stub of a pencil, scribbled a few lines on it, tore it loose and handed it to Billy, along with his canteen. "That should do it," he said. "Here's my canteen. See if you can round up a few more of the boys and extra canteens along the way. There's no telling when we'll get more."

Billy nodded, took the scrip and Turner's canteen — it also was empty - thanked the officer, and together, he and Jimmy turned and walked off into the darkness. It was almost seven o'clock.

Over the next twenty minutes, or so, they gathered together ten more men, making twelve in all, each carrying four canteens. Together the small group crept away from the camp and into the night.

It was quite dark, but the flashes of gunfire just to the north, and the quarter moon in a cloudless sky, provided light enough for them to pick their way through the flattened undergrowth and shattered tree trunks, stark silhouettes against the moonlit sky.

Away to the north, the battle continued unabated; the sky lit intermittently by bright red flashes, followed less than a second later by the rippling roar cannon fire.

It was an uneventful trip. The canteens were filled and by nine o'clock the soldiers were slowly making their way back to camp, stumbling, and falling over unseen obstacles: logs, branches... dead bodies.

To the north, the fighting had dwindled to little more than sporadic rifle shots in the dark as pickets shot at anything that moved, real or imaginary.

Back at camp, they doled out the canteens and then settled down in the dark, to sleep. But their discomfort was only beginning: the night was turning cold, very cold; a hoar frost already covered the ground, and the temperature was dropping fast.

Chapter 48

Saturday September 19th, - Hazelwood

Four-wheeled ambulances were lined up ten deep at the back door; the back yard of the house was now a small tent village. To the left and right of the back door, two piles of severed limbs - hands, arms, legs, and feet – were already more than four feet high, and continuing to grow. Wounded soldiers were being carried in and out in a constant stream; the dead were carried out and piled into carts to be taken away, when time and the battle would allow. The tents were crammed with the wounded, many with head wounds; many more had lost limbs, all were in various states of consciousness; some lay close to death, all were bandaged, though that did little to stop the bleeding; blood pooled on and soaked into the dirt floor, blankets, bandages and clothing. The coppery stench hung inside the tents, so thick you could almost taste it.

The great kitchen table, and a smaller one brought in from the dining room, served as operating tables; the pine top of the kitchen table was soaked, almost through with blood – stained beyond repair; arterial blood was splashed over the walls and ceiling, and the flag-stone floor was wet and slippery. One after another, wounded men were hauled out of the ambulances and loaded onto the tables, then back out to the tents... or to the waiting carts already loaded with the dead.

The three doctors were handling upward of thirty wounded per hour, but it was never enough. The doctors cut, sawed, and stitched swiftly. Medical assistants swabbed and bandaged. Limbs with compound fractures were quickly removed; those with simple fractures were set and splinted; there was no time for extended surgery. Bone saws were worn dull; the piles of amputated limbs continued to grow; the line of ambulances in the back yard grew longer.

Colonel Gene Marshal had graduated Geneva Medical College in New York at the age of 26 in 1849. At the outbreak of the war in 1861, he joined the Union army and was attached to the XIV Corps of the Army of the Ohio. Soon thereafter, it was renamed the Army of the Cumberland. Now, more than two years later, and seemingly 20 years older, Marshall was the chief surgeon of the Army of the Cumberland and it was weighing heavily upon his shoulders. He was forty years old, and felt every day of it. Over the past two years, he had performed more than two thousand procedures; he was tired, bone tired.

It was now past three o'clock in the afternoon. The fighting was raging just to the north of Hazelwood and west of the Lafayette Road. The house shook from the shockwaves from the combined cannon blasts from the Confederates to the east and the Federal breastworks on the hill to the west. But it all seemed to go unnoticed by those at work in the kitchen at Hazelwood, now a full-blown field hospital served by medical teams from both sides, Confederate and Union. Federal doctor Colonel Gene Marshall was working together with two Confederate doctors, majors Glen Marr and Michael Roark. Those three, along with a dozen or more soldiers drawn from both sides to serve as aids to the doctors, were attending the wounded.

Doc Marshall could amputate an arm or leg in less than ten minutes; his Confederate counterparts were no less skilled. First, Marshall would administer chloroform and put the patient out. He would then saw through the bone until it was severed, leaving a large flap of skin; an aid would toss the limb onto the growing pile. Marshall would then tie off the arteries with horsehair, file the ends and edges of the bones smooth, so that they would not work through the skin. Finally, he would pull the flap of skin all the way over the wound and sew it closed, leaving a drainage hole. One of his aids would then cover the stump with plaster, bandage it; and the wounded man would be carted outside to one of the tents where he would, or not, awake, eventually. Instruments were swilled off in a bucket full of bloody water. And so it went on, hour after hour, one poor soul after another was laid upon the table, operated on, and then moved quickly onward. By six o'clock that evening, Marshall had performed more than eighty procedures.

Sarah, her father, Charity and Nestor were working at the fireplace. Four great, open kettles of water bubbled and boiled over the flames, The beds in the upper rooms, and the linen closets, had been stripped, the sheets, pillow cases and blankets torn into strips to serve as bandages.

At six o'clock in the evening, it was already close to dark outside. Sarah was a mess; her hair hung in limp strands over her sweat-covered brow; her once trim, blue dress was covered in blood from neckline to hem. Her father was in no better shape; his clothing, too, was soaked with blood. Marshall looked like a monster; his hair and beard matted with blood; his cheeks streaked, his once white duster coat looked as if it might have been borrowed from a slaughterhouse; under the duster, his dark blue pants were soaked where he had pressed his thighs against the blood-soaked table. His two Confederate counterparts fared no better. Only Charity seemed able to maintain some semblance of cleanliness, aside from a few small smears of blood, her white apron was... still quite "spotless."

It was just after six o'clock that evening when a young Confederate lieutenant, not more than twenty years old, was carried into the kitchen and laid unconscious on the kitchen table. He had been wounded four times: twice in the upper right leg, once in the left ankle, and once more in the face; none of the wounds were immediately life threatening, but all four were bleeding profusely and needed immediate attention.

Both wounds to his leg were flesh wounds; that is to say the bullets had passed through flesh and muscle, from front to back, without hitting bone, but the exit wounds in the man's thigh were horrendous, two jagged holes about two and a half inches in diameter that pulsed blood with every beat of the man's heart. The wound to the left ankle was also not life threatening, but the foot would still have to come off; the ankle bone had been shattered by a .58 caliber Minnie bullet.

The face wound was light in comparison to the other three, but devastating just the same; the bullet had clipped his cheek, scouring out a deep trench that chipped the bone and took away the lower half of his ear. This young man would never look the same. Still, Marshall, Roark, and Marr, working together, did what they could for him.

Marshall quickly removed the left foot, about six inches above the joint, while Marr trimmed, cleaned, packed, and bandaged the leg wounds. There was little that could be done for the face wound. Marshall cleaned it as best he could, then applied some of Charity's salve and a thick pad of linen, and finished off by binding the man's head. Marshall beckoned to two of the waiting aids, motioned for them to take the lieutenant away, then motioned again for the next in line to be placed on the table in front of him. Marshall was exhausted, but....

The doctors were strained to the limit, but the stream of incoming did not let up, even for a minute. Long into the night the work continued. The tent village grew, and by nine o'clock in the evening, the number of tents had grown to seventy-two, each occupied by four or more wounded soldiers. Since mid-day more than three hundred casualties had passed through the kitchen at Hazelwood.

Confederate Brigadier General John Gregg, conscious, but deeply under the influence of morphine, lay in a tent together with a captain, a lieutenant, a sergeant and a private, all Confederates; it was not considered a good thing to mix sides within the tents. And still it continued, but Hazelwood was only one of four similar field hospitals.

Finally, around nine o'clock, the flow of wounded men became a trickle; it was too dark for the ambulances to operate. Sarah, exhausted, walked over to the fireplace, and sat down on a stone slab next to the hearth, exhausted, arms and face streaked with blood, her bloody dress clinging to her body. She put her head in her hands, took a deep breath, and fought back the tears that threatened to overwhelm her. Her father sat down beside her and put his arm around her shoulder.

It was just then that Blake Winter walked through the door and into the kitchen. Sarah jumped to her feet and ran over to him, throwing her arms around his neck and burying her face in his coat. For a moment, the two held each other, and Sarah cried quietly, his uniform coat muffling the sobs.

Chapter 49
Saturday September 19th, at 6:30p.m. - Cleburne's Night Attack

Major General Patrick Cleburne, an Irishman, late of her majesty's 44th Regiment of Foot, where he had risen to the exalted rank of corporal, was something of an anomaly. He was a tall man, well proportioned, thin-faced with the inevitable Van Dyke beard, cheeks bare, hair short and neatly trimmed; he was a somewhat sentimental man, fiercely proud and quick to anger, but he had a good sense of humor, too. He looked younger than his 35 years. Irish he might have been born, but no man was more fiercely patriotic to his adoptive country.

Cleburne's service to the Confederacy began even before the insurrection when he joined a local militia company in Arkansas as a private soldier. He was soon elected captain and, when Arkansas seceded from the Union, the militia became part of the 1st Arkansas Infantry, later to become the 15th Arkansas. Within a month, he was elected colonel of the regiment and, on March 4th, 1862, he was promoted to brigadier general – not bad for a one-time corporal in the British Army.

The right flank of Bragg's army had not seen much of the heavy fighting of the late afternoon. In fact, General Polk had had something of a quiet time, especially as the fighting to the west of the Lafayette Road moved progressively southward and back to the east.

Federal General George Thomas had, for several hours, been consolidating his lines, withdrawing a few hundred yards to the west and some five hundred yards east of the Lafayette Road, settling into what he considered a superior defensive position, with several more brigades at the rear covering the withdrawal.

Cleburne, with three brigades in line abreast, supported by General Cheatham's division, launched a ferocious attack against the Federal left flank at sunset.

Cleburne's line of battle extended more than a half-mile, with Wood's brigade at the center. The Confederate brigades paused in the dense woods to the east of the Winfrey field and readied themselves to push forward against Thomas's rearguard. It was now barely twilight; the woods to the rear were on fire, and smoke from burning underbrush reduced visibility almost to nothing.

Wood's brigade cleared the edge of the woods and entered the Winfrey field, a large pasture some two to three hundred yards deep. As the attack moved forward, darkness began to fall, but the Union line on the far edge of the field was visible, just. The field was quite flat with few obstacles to impede the advancing Confederate brigades.

Thomas's brigades, now under cover of hastily constructed breastworks on the western edge of the Winfrey field, unleashed a storm of rifle and artillery fire across the open space. The Confederates replied in like manner and the noise of gunfire grew and reverberated across the fields until it became a single, insane, ear-shattering roar.

Cleburne's infantry, now under extreme pressure, returned fire, and were soon heavily engaged along his right and center. As the light continued to fail, and the field was covered with a dense, swirling fog of smoke, visibility dropped to zero; both sides were now firing blind with only the muzzle flashes of the enemy to aim at.

As the Confederate line advanced, Cleburne's artillery also moved forward and opened fire on the Federal breastworks. Even under cover of darkness, the Confederate artillery and rifle fire was devastatingly effective and the Federal line began to give. And then Thomas's brigades were in full retreat, but not fast enough: Cleburne's forces were advancing faster than the Federals could retreat. They overran the Federal lines and the fighting became a vicious, hand-to-hand brawl, and in almost total darkness; soldiers on either side could neither see, nor had they time to reload, thus rifles became clubs and bayonets became lances. For almost thirty minutes, the fighting continued unabated; a savage brawl where men stabbed, clubbed, grasped and even bit each other in desperation. Cleburne's night attack was a nightmare, a desperate, confused tangle of insane proportions.

General Deshler of Cleburne's division was shot in the chest and had to be taken from the field; General Preston Smith of Cheatham's division was shot dead.

By nine o'clock, it was all over. Somehow, Cleburne had driven Thomas all the way back to the Kelly farm; Cleburne was now in possession of the Winfrey field. The woods to the east were still on fire, turning the sky and smoke into a boiling cauldron of red.

Chapter 50

By nine o'clock that evening, General Bragg was in a slightly better mood. He was, to all intents and purposes, pleased with the day's events, even though his specific orders for the commencement of the attacks in the early morning had largely been ignored. Instead of his planned series of coordinated movements, what actually happened was little more than a series of sporadic attacks culminating in Cleburne's night attack on General Thomas. These isolated actions that took place all across the battlefield had sapped Bragg's effective strength and enabled Rosecrans accurately to pinpoint the Confederate positions. Nevertheless, Bragg was effectively master of the field.

On hearing that Lieutenant General James Longstreet had arrived and was on his way from Ringgold, Bragg sent for Lieutenant General Polk. Polk arrived at Thedford's Ford a little after nine-thirty. Bragg was waiting for him in his tent.

"Good evening, General," Bragg said, in a not unfriendly tone. "Please sit," he said. Polk sat down on a folding canvas stool, leaned forward, placed his elbows on his knees, and clasped his hands together; He did not look comfortable.

"Your report, if you please, sir" Bragg said.

Polk did not immediately reply. For a moment he sat, head bowed, staring at his hands.

Bragg, not a patient man, tapped his fingers on the tabletop.

"Well?" He asked.

"General, it has been a long and arduous day," Polk said, still looking down at his hands. "Our casualties have been heavy. General Preston Smith is dead; General Gregg is sorely wounded and unfit for duty; General Deshler is also severely wounded; Colonel Baldwin is also dead...."

"Yes? Yes?" Bragg was becoming even more impatient.

"We are in a strong position holding against what I perceive to be the enemy's left flank." Polk continued. "General Cleburne, with General Cheatham supporting, has driven the enemy back across the fields almost to the road, but was unable to continue the assault because of the darkness."

It was obvious to General Bragg that there was little to be gained by any continued questioning of his senior general. All that Polk had just relayed to him, he already knew. His couriers had been racing back and forth between the action and his headquarters continuously throughout the day. He stood, clasped his hands behind his back, and walked to the flap of the tent, looked out for a moment, then turned again and walked to the table and the map thereon.

"General Polk," He said, without looking at him. "I have decided much over the past several hours. We are, indeed, in a strong position, not as strong as I would like, but…. Well, I do think we may have a slight advantage in numbers, and we must continue to assault the enemy's left flank. General Longstreet has arrived in Ringgold and should be here momentarily."

Polk looked at him, tilted his head to one side in an unspoken question.

"That being so," Bragg Continued, "I have decided to fight this army in two separate wings. You, General Polk, will command the Right Wing; General Longstreet will command the left…."

"Sir," Polk interrupted. "What of General Hill?"

"What of him?" Bragg asked.

"General Bragg," Polk said. "General Hill is the equal in rank of both General Longstreet and myself. What position do you propose for him? Would it not be better to fight with three corps positioned to the right, center, and left? This would provide General Hill with a situation worthy of his rank."

"You seem to forget, General," Bragg said, "Hill is newly appointed, and thus the junior lieutenant general; also, I fear he cannot be relied upon to diligently carry out my orders. He will therefore be acting under your orders; his divisions will be part of your Right Wing, along with those of General Walker, General Cheatham, and General Forrest."

Polk looked at Bragg, opened his mouth as if to speak, but remained silent, obviously not happy with the situation.

"You, General Polk, will begin your attack at five-thirty in the morning. At precisely that time, General Walker's corps will advance against the enemy's left flank. The rest of the army will then advance in succession: General Hill will follow Walker; and he will be followed by General Longstreet. General Longstreet's divisions also in succession will advance against the enemy's right flank. Do you have questions, General Polk?"

Polk, looked at Bragg, but merely shook his head.

"In that case, General, I will leave it to you to issue the necessary orders to your corps and division commanders. Please, be certain that each commander is fully aware of what is required of him. And…" he paused and looked Polk directly in the eye, "you, too, must understand that it is imperative that you launch your attack on time, at precisely five-thirty. I will brook no delays. Do you understand, General Polk? At five-thirty precisely!"

"General, I understand."

"Then I bid you good night, and good fortune." And with that, Bragg turned away; Polk rose from the stool, turned, ducked out of the tent and walked to his horse, shaking his head as he went. He mounted, and then rode back to his own field headquarters at Alexander's Bridge, meeting along the way General Breckinridge, one of Hill's division commanders, and two of Hill's staff officers. Polk informed Breckinridge of the new command structure, and they parted ways. Polk continued on to his headquarters where he wrote orders for Generals Hill, Walker, and Cheatham, informing them of the new order of battle and giving them their orders for the following morning. These were then dispatched by courier, and General Polk retired to bed, a somewhat unhappy man.

Walker and Cheatham received their dispatches within the hour; General Hill did not. In fact, General Hill could not be found: he was lost in the forest.

It was just after eleven o'clock when General James Longstreet, along with colonels Sorrel and Manning, arrived at Bragg's headquarters. Bragg was asleep in one of the wagons.

Without hesitation, General Longstreet hammered with his clenched fist on the side of the wagon, and then stepped back; General Bragg awoke with a start.

"What is it?" he shouted, scrambling to his feet inside the wagon. He was still dressed, all but his uniform frock coat.

"General Longstreet, Sir," said Moxley Sorrel.

Bragg scrambled down from the wagon, returned Longstreet's salute, ran his fingers through his tousled hair, adjusted his suspenders and the seat of his pants, and then stormed off toward his tent.

On reaching the tent, Bragg threw back the flap and strode inside; Longstreet followed.

"Where, in the name of God, have you been, General? Bragg said, indicating for Longstreet to sit on the stool not long ago vacated by General Polk. "I expected you on the field long before now."

"And so I would have been, had you thought to send an escort to meet me at Catoosa. Instead, we had to wait more than two hours for the horses; an intolerable situation, if I may be so bold."

Bragg glowered at his exalted guest. He did not like Longstreet, and was barely able to tolerate his presence within the tent.

Longstreet, too, had little respect for his new commanding general, considering him a weak and ineffectual battlefield commander. Nevertheless, he was tied to this man for better or for worse, and would obey him to the letter.

"My apologies, General," Bragg said, little meaning it. "We have been heavily engaged for the greater part of the day. I assumed," he continued, "that your horses would travel with you and that you would have little trouble reaching the field."

"Apology accepted, General," Longstreet said, his steely gaze never leaving Bragg's face. "Now, if you wouldn't mind, General," he continued. "Please tell me the situation, and what part you require me to play in tomorrow's proceedings."

Bragg nodded his head, and looked down at the map on the table, at the same time motioning for Longstreet to rise and join him.

Over the next several minutes, Bragg described the action that had taken place throughout the day, pointing out his own positions, and those of the enemy on the map.

"It is my plan, General, Bragg said, turning his head to look at Longstreet, "to fight the army in two wings. The Right Wing under the command of General Polk will be comprised of his own corps, plus those of Generals Hill, Walker, and Forrest; General Cheatham will also fight his division under the command of General Polk.

"You, General," Bragg continued, "will command the Left Wing which will include your own and General Buckner's Corps, you have also been assigned the divisions of Generals Bushrod Johnson and Thomas Hindman; General Wheeler's cavalry will support your left flank."

Bragg paused for a moment and gazed at the map laid out on the table. Longstreet said nothing; he just continued to stare at General Bragg.

After a long moment, Bragg continued, "General Polk is to advance against the enemy's left flank at precisely five-thirty in the morning. You, General, must wait for General Polk to commence his attack before you commence yours.

"As soon as General Polk does so, so you will move your wing forward against the enemy line across the Lafayette Road, here," Bragg pointed out the position on the map.

"General," Bragg said, "it is imperative that both wings attack in concert, one division after the other from north to south; any delay; any delay at all, on either flank will give the enemy time to prepare their defenses. General, we have the advantage both in numbers and position.

There is no reason, that I can see, why we should not defeat General Rosecrans and drive him from the field. Do you agree, Sir?"

Longstreet stared for a moment at the map, then looked at Bragg and nodded his head. "I do, General. If... if everything goes as you have described. If not..."

Bragg stood upright and lifted his arm in salute. "Enough, General," he said impatiently. "I suggest you get some sleep. It is less than six hours until sun-up."

Longstreet returned the salute and, without saying another word, spun on his heel, and ducked out through the flap of the tent.

Sometime after midnight, deep within the dense woodland, General Hill, who with several of his staff officers, was trying to find General Bragg, ran into Major Anderson, also one of his own staff officers and one of those who had been at the meeting between Generals Polk and Breckinridge. Anderson informed Hill of the new command structure, and that General Polk wished to see him. Now Hill, too, was not a happy man. He was also exhausted, and he needed to think. Thus, he dismounted, set himself down with his back against a tree, and took a nap. It was not until three in the morning that he resumed his search for General Polk, with much the same result as his earlier search for General Bragg, not knowing that General Polk's courier was also searching for him. That courier returned with the orders undelivered; General Polk was by now sound asleep and the courier did not disturb him.

Chapter 51

Meanwhile, just a little more than a mile away at the Widow Glenn's house on the hill overlooking the Lafayette Road, General Rosecrans was conducting a council of war of his own. Unlike General Bragg, however, he had gathered together all of his battlefield commanders, some dozen or so high-ranking generals, including his three corps commanders, Generals Thomas, Crittenden, and McCook. Also present were General Garfield, his chief of staff, and one most unwelcome guest, the Assistant Secretary of War, Charles Dana.

Dana, first and foremost a journalist, had been sent to Chattanooga by Edwin Stanton, Secretary of War, for no other reason than to spy on Rosecrans. This, the good general was well aware of, but there was little he could do about it, other than suffer in silence.

The small room was overcrowded, and very warm; a huge log fire was burning. General Thomas was standing with his back to the fire, legs akimbo, hands clasped behind his back. General Rosecrans was at his map table.

"So gentlemen," he began. "Not the best of days, I fear, but certainly not the worst. And, I think, we are well situated and should be quite able to hold the line along the Lafayette Road." He looked around the room; most of the assembled generals were nodding their heads in agreement.

"We used the enemy harshly today," Rosecrans continued. "General Bragg has suffered a great many casualties...."

"So have we," Thomas growled. "At least I have. General, if I am to hold the left tomorrow, you must give me more reinforcements."

"What exactly is your situation, General Thomas?"

"According to reports from the field, I am facing no less than three full corps – perhaps seven divisions – plus Forrest's cavalry corps. I have less than half that number and a battlefront more than a mile wide. We are building breastworks and abatis but... we need reinforcements, and many of them.

General Rosecrans looked at Thomas and said, thoughtfully, "I agree, General. We must secure the left flank but... if General Bragg plays his usual game, by morning we may find ourselves in control of the field. I would not be surprised if he were to retreat back across the Chickamauga."

"With respect, General," Thomas said. "That, I think, is not likely. With Longstreet now in the field, Bragg holds a decided advantage in numbers. Were I in his position, I would throw everything I had at my left flank, and I would do it before the sun was up."

Rosecrans nodded his head. "Perhaps you are right, General" he agreed; "perhaps you are right. In any event, we cannot afford to be wrong."

Rosecrans looked down at the map table and motioned to Garfield to bring pen and paper. Then he said, "General McCook, you will move your two divisions northward to join General Thomas's right flank. General Crittenden, you will position your divisions to the rear and center of the line, here and here," He indicated the positions on the map and then continued, "You will hold them in reserve, but ready to move immediately, should they be needed."

Garfield wrote the orders and Rosecrans signed them. It was eleven-thirty.

Chapter 52

Saturday September 19th, 11p.m. - The End of the Day

By nine o'clock, the fighting was essentially, over for the day. The battlefield now covered almost twelve square miles.

As the fighting ended, and darkness descended over Chickamauga Creek, the Confederate line, now some five to six hundred yards to the east of the Lafayette Road, extended almost five miles from Reed's Bridge Road in the north to the Alexander Road south of Hazelwood: General Polk's corps was to the right; General Hood was to the left. General Breckinridge's division, having marched northward all day, had crossed the Chickamauga at Alexander's Bridge and was in position at the extreme north end of the Confederate line, on Polk's right flank. General Forrest was guarding Breckinridge's right flank.

Brigadier General William Preston's division was some five miles to the south on the Confederate left. General Bragg, finally, had his entire army on the field, more than sixty five thousand men in eleven divisions, with four cavalry divisions under the commands of Generals Forrest and Wheeler.

The Federal line of battle extended southward for about three quarters of a mile from the Kelly farm, crossed the Lafayette Road, then extended southward more than three miles to a point some two hundred yards south of the Glenn Kelly Road and two hundred yards to the west of the Lafayette Road, almost to Hazelwood. Three quarters of a mile to the west, the line continued south beyond General Rosecrans' headquarters at the Widow Glenn's house where John Wilder's Brigade, on top of the hill on the west side of the Dry Valley Road, was holding the extreme right flank of the army.

Rosecrans, with the exception of General Grainger's Reserve Corps, also had all of his army on the field; General Negley on the left; General Phillip Sheridan on the right, slightly more than sixty thousand men in ten divisions, with two cavalry divisions under the command of Brigadier General Robert Mitchell.

In the camps on both sides, men were cold, many were freezing, trying to find some comfort by wrapping themselves in blankets worn too thin to merit the name.

Despite general orders to the contrary, many of the soldiers lit small campfires to ward against the continuing drop in temperature, only to draw enemy fire from one side of the road or the other. Fires lit were quickly extinguished. Even a match lit to fire up a cigarette drew a quick response from an enemy rifle. Thus, they sat or lay, trying in vain to sleep as the axes of the Federals beat relentlessly on through the night, and with the beat of the axes, the great log breastworks and abatis continued to grow. General Thomas was consolidating his position, and the soldiers in the Confederate lines less than a quarter mile away were filled with trepidation.

On the hill, Colonel Wilder's brigade was also settling in for the night. Blake Winter, just returned from Hazelwood, Eli Lilly, and Wilder were huddled down behind breastworks of their own. They, too, lay and listened to the incessant beat of the axes away to the north. Sleep did not come easily to any of them, but eventually it did, fitful though it might be.

At Hazelwood, things were also quietening down, although everyone was still busy with the wounded, it was too dark for the ambulances to operate. By eleven o'clock, the last of the wounded soldiers had been transferred from the kitchen to the tent village, and the doctors, along with the Bradleys, had retired for the night. They were fortunate, if such a thing could be considered, to have a roof over their heads.

The three doctors stripped off their blood-soaked pants and shirts and washed away the blood from their faces, hands and arms before falling into beds Sarah had prepared for them. But sleep did not come easily to them either, nor did it come easily for Sarah as she lay with the covers pulled up to her chin, and stared up into the shadows of the darkened rafters, and listened to the relentless beat of the axes.

Far away to the north, Jesse Dixon and Patrick McCann were still on the move. Keeping the light from what few campfires were visible to their left, they were working their way eastward toward what they hoped were their own lines.

By ten o'clock, they were on a narrow dirt track roughly fifty yards to the left of where Nathan Bedford Forrest's cavalry was camped. Quietly and slowly, they picked their way northward along the track. By eleven o'clock, they were within earshot of the axes beating in the Federal line, but they had no idea of what they meant; on they continued westward until, at last, they saw two men with rifles standing on the dirt road.

They stopped, and stood quietly, unseen, for a moment, then ducked into the bushes at the side of the road and peered out at the two soldiers less than fifty yards away.

"What do you think, Pat?" Jesse whispered.

"I don't know. I don't know," he said, already a little panicky.

"Stay here. Don't move. I'll go take a look. They gotta be ours; I just know it."

Pat did not say anything.

Jesse took a deep breath and stepped out onto the track. "Hey there," he shouted.

The two men spun around and lowered their rifles to the point. "Who goes there?"

"Friend," Jesse shouted.

"What friend?"

"Jesse Dixon, Sergeant, 10th Indiana," he shouted, and then he closed his eyes and waited. If he were wrong, well, he would be wrong, and dead.

"Advance, Friend, and be recognized."

"Come on, Pat," he called back. "They're ours."

Part 3
Chapter 53
Sunday September 20th – 12:25am Federal Headquarters
It was a little after midnight when General George Thomas finally left the meeting with General Rosecrans at the Widow Glenn's cabin. He did not, however, go immediately back to his divisions. Instead, he wandered in the darkness a few yards to the crest of the hill, found a convenient spot, and sat down. He gazed out into the darkness, over the battlefield laid out under the light of the quarter moon, and pondered the day ahead.

All across the valley, he could feel the shadowy presence of the two great armies. He watched the flaring points of light in the distance – campfires lit for a moment or two, only to be quickly extinguished as the flickering flames drew sporadic outbursts of small arms fire from one side or the other. It was cold, bitterly cold, especially in the bottoms among the mist.

Thomas shuddered, the heavy field coat doing little to keep out the icy breeze.

"Are you all right, General?"

Startled, Thomas looked round and said, "Yes, Colonel Wilder. Just taking a little time for myself. And you, Colonel? Why are you not sleeping?"

"I am well, Sir. Couldn't sleep. I'm sorry I disturbed you, Sir." Wilder replied, taking a step backwards as if to leave.

"Oh... stay for a moment, if you will, Colonel." Thomas sat quietly in the darkness, staring out into space, and then said, "Please, Colonel, sit down."

Wilder sat down on the grassy slope beside him and, together, they looked out into the night.

"Have you ever seen anything quite like it?" Thomas said, nodding his head in the direction of the sleeping giant that was the battlefield.

"I have not, General."

"Why do we do it? Why must we kill each other like this? Surely there must be a better way."

"It is the nature of things, General," Wilder said, staring off into space. "We have been killing each other ever since Cain killed Able. The human animal is the ultimate predator."

"It's barbaric, Colonel. There are perhaps one hundred forty thousand men, human beings, out there and, in less than six hours they will be at each other's throats, each side trying to slaughter as many of the other as possible. Slaughter, Colonel, slaughter on a grand scale, and for what?"

"It's not our doing, General."

"I know that, Colonel, but we are supposed to be civilized. We should be better than this. And tomorrow, Colonel? How many tomorrow? How many lives will be changed forever? How many men will lose their lives, limbs? How many children will lose their fathers? How many wives will lose their husbands and, perhaps even worse, how many men will survive this conflict too severely maimed ever to be able to provide for themselves, or their loved ones?"

Wilder looked at Thomas, but his face was a mask, unreadable in the dark, and then said, "A great many, I am sure, General," and then he changed the subject. "How are things on the left flank?"

"Better than they were.," Thomas said. "The enemy assault this evening was determined, and we had to concede ground, but the new line is strong and we are strengthening it still. It will hold, of that I'm sure, but...." Thomas shook his head, and then said. "Tomorrow morning, all will be in God's hands. I pray that he will be gentle with us."

Together, for several moments, the two men sat and stared out over the darkened battlefield. Far away in the sky to the east, a shooting star burned brightly as it streaked across the sky, and then faded away into nothing.

"How are your men doing, Colonel?"

"They are well, General. On edge, sleepless, but in good spirits."

"That's good; very good. Well, Colonel, I must go and see to my men. There will be no sleep for them." Thomas listened for a moment. The steady, hollow beat of the axes to the north echoed among the darkened trees. "As you can tell, they are hard at work."

Thomas rose wearily to his feet. Wilder also rose. The two men faced each other and saluted.

"May God be with you tomorrow, General."

"It is already tomorrow, Colonel. Good luck, and may God be with you too."

Thomas spun on his heel and walked quickly away into the darkness. Wilder stood for a moment, staring out across the moonlit battlefield, then he, too, went his own way.

On his return to his own positions, just a hundred yards or so to the south, he found that most of his brigade was awake, up and about, unable to sleep; many were sitting together in small groups, talking.

Wilder sat down on a stump with Winter, Smith Atkins and Eli Lilly, and listened; the conversation was not a happy one.

"We are, indeed, fortunate to be up here," Atkins said. "I would not wish to be on the line tomorrow morning."

"It matters little, I think," Winter said. "We will be well within range of the enemy artillery. And, I think, Eli's guns, not to mention our Spencer's, will be a priority target when the enemy attacks."

"True," Wilder said. "But we must not dwell upon such things. Our priority must be the defense of this position and that of General Rosecrans. We have an open field of fire, and our breastworks are strong. Therefore, gentlemen, I suggest we take advantage of what little time is left until daylight and try to get some rest. I fear we are going to need it."

It was close to two o'clock in the morning when General Thomas arrived back at the Kelly farmhouse where he found General Absalom Baird waiting for him. Baird was extremely concerned that the left flank of the army was vulnerable, that his division would not be able adequately to cover the entire length of the line assigned to him, just north of the Kelly farm to Reed's Bridge Road. Thomas agreed, and sent a courier to General Rosecrans with a report explaining the situation and requesting reinforcements. He did in fact request that Rosecrans send the Second Division, one of the four divisions that comprised his own XIV Corps. The Second was under the command of General James Negley, and they had only lately arrived from Crawfish Springs; they were, in fact, fresh troops.

Rosecrans replied that he would indeed send Negley's division and he sent orders to General Negley that he was immediately to move his division northward and into position on Thomas's extreme left flank; General Wood's division would fill the gap left in the line by Negley.

Meanwhile, down in the bottoms, among the trees in the thickening mist, some sixty yards behind the Confederate lines, Billy Cobb and Jimmy Morrisey were huddled together beneath a fallen tree trunk, wrapped in thin blankets, not asleep, but dozing, and shivering in the cold and damp.

A little father to the east, General Longstreet lay, fully clothed, but for his uniform coat, on a canvas cot in his tent; his eyes were closed, but he was not asleep.

And it was a little after midnight when Jesse Dixon and Pat McCann finally found their way to where the 10th Indiana was fully involved in the frenzied preparations for the coming battle. Some six hundred yards to the west, beyond the Lafayette Road, they were felling and trimming trees to be used to build the Federal defensive line. There would be no sleep for them, or even rest.

As soon as they arrived, they were assigned to a team of horses and put to work dragging the hundreds of huge logs into line, constructing a great crescent-shaped line of breastworks just to the east of the road. Some of the logs were positioned as abatis, their branches shortened and trimmed and sharpened to points and then laid in front of the fortifications, end on, the stumps set against the breastworks, with the sharpened ends, and branches, facing the direction from which the enemy was expected to come. It was a fearsome and daunting defense – the masses of sharpened points crammed together looked like a giant briar patch, ten or fifteen feet high, a tangle that the defenders hoped would be impenetrable. And the work continued into the night.

Chapter 54

The sun rose around five-forty-five that morning, a blood red disc watered by the mists in the hollows of the battlefield. Could it be an omen of what was to come? Perhaps. In any event, the commanders on both sides were pleased to see it; the day was dawning clear and crisp. The commanding generals of both armies were already up and about and preparing for the day.

But, as they say, *the best laid plans....*

At six o'clock, General Rosecrans, accompanied by half-dozen staff officers, including General Garfield, and Assistant Secretary Dana, set off on horseback to inspect the army. As much as he disliked Dana, regarding him as little more than Secretary Stanton's spy, he was in an optimistic mood. Incoming reports from the field informed him that the defenses along the Lafayette Road were all but complete, and that his positions were virtually impregnable. Thus he rode with a slight smile upon his face, at a smart clip, from Widow Glenn's cabin, northward along the Dry Valley Road. Along the way, he took time to bid a cheery good morning ad a few well-chosen words of encouragement to Generals Crittenden, Palmer, Davis and Van Cleve before turning east along the Glenn Kelly Road where he encountered non-other than... General Negley, who was talking animatedly with General McCook.

"General Negley. General McCook," Rosecrans said, staring intently at Negley. "Good morning to you both. Might I ask, however, what, General Negley, you are doing here? Did I not ask that you move your division into line in support of General Thomas?

"You did indeed, Sir. But preparations had to be made, and it was not possible to move the division in the darkness, what with the undergrowth...."

"Yes, yes," Rosecrans said, impatiently, "but you must move now, Sir. Immediately. Get your division on the move and then report to General Thomas for further orders."

Negley saluted, spun smartly on his heel, and walked quickly away.

"And you, General McCook," Rosecrans continued. "You will move your divisions to the left, and close up on General Thomas's right.

"General Garfield?" Rosecrans turned in the saddle and gestured for Garfield to come forward, at the same time casting a withering glance at Secretary Dana, who was seated comfortably in the saddle, both hands, reins between his fingers, resting on the pommel, and smiling mockingly.

"General Garfield," Rosecrans said when his chief of staff came alongside. "Please write the following to General Crittenden...."

Garfield nodded and wrote the order for Crittenden to also move his divisions to the left and close up on General McCook's divisions and then for him to join General Rosecrans. That done, he called for a courier and sent him off at a fast clip to deliver the order.

General Rosecrans, his once amiable mood deteriorating quickly, along with his retinue continued on along the Glenn Kelly Road, stopping along the way to offer a word of greeting here, a word of encouragement there, and all the time asking questions of his battlefield commanders: moral, the situation, etc., until finally he arrived in the vicinity of the Snodgrass house just to the east of the Lafayette Road, the Kelly farm, and the center of General Thomas's defensive line. It was just after seven o'clock in the morning.

General Thomas was waiting for him; he was on foot. General Rosecrans dismounted and handed the reins to one of his aids.

"Good morning, General Thomas," Rosecrans said, affably, and returning his corps commander's salute continued, "I trust you managed to get some rest."

"Thank you, General. I did not get any rest at all, but no matter, I am well and I am awake."

"So I see, General. And what of your situation?"

"Well, Sir, the enemy appears to be moving up toward our left flank, where I have placed General Baird's division. General Johnson holds the center; General Palmer, the right flank. The breastworks are strong enough to hold and, if the events of yesterday are to be considered prophetic, we will win the day." Thomas paused for a moment then continued, "Even so, General, I am concerned that our left flank could be our weakness. The line there is dangerously thin, and needs to be strengthened. I was, so I understood, to receive General Negley's division. Is that not so, General?"

"I gave orders for General Negley to move his division and, in fact, less than an hour ago, I reaffirmed those orders. He is on his way."

"Thank you, General." Thomas said. "Would you care to review the left flank?

Rosecrans nodded his head in agreement. "I would, General. Please lead the way."

Thomas mounted his horse and, together, they all rode to the Lafayette Road and turned north. By eight-fifteen, they were at the extreme left flank of the army, where they were met by Generals Absalom Baird and Richard Johnson.

"Good morning, gentlemen," Rosecrans greeted them, returning their salute. "All is well, I presume."

"Indeed it is, General," Baird said. "If you would like to follow me, sir, you will see for yourself."

"Lead on, General."

For the next several minutes, the gaggle of Federal Generals road slowly along the high ground just to the rear of the breastworks, greeting one brigade commander after another.

Here and there, through openings and clearings in the trees and scrublands to the east, Rosecrans could see the massive build-up of Confederate troops some half-mile to the east. Through his field glasses, he could see the banners and guidons of what appeared to be a half-dozen divisions, not to mention the massed batteries of artillery just beyond.

The further they rode, the more concerned Rosecrans became. Finally, shaking his head in frustration, he ordered the small column to a halt

General Thomas," He said, in a tight voice. "You are right, Sir. This position is quite weak. General Negley should be here by now. It is imperative that we strengthen this flank. I will go myself to see what is detaining General Negley. Please keep me informed of your situation, by the minute, General." And with that, he spun his horse, clapped his spurs into its rump, and galloped quickly away down south along the Lafayette Road followed by his staff and... Assistant Secretary Dana. It was almost eight o'clock.

Rosecrans found General Negley exactly where he had left him, and he was not at all happy.

"General Negley, Sir. Why are you still here? And where is General McCook?"

"As you say, General: where is General McCook? I did not feel, sir, that it was right and proper for me to move until General McCook relieved me. To leave now would be to leave this section open to the enemy."

General Rosecrans was beyond frustrated. He was not used to having his specific orders ignored, nor would he tolerate such. Even his horse could feel the rage building inside him, and restlessly stamped and wheeled beneath him.

"General Crittenden," Rosecrans snapped, fighting to control his high-stung ride. "Go at once and bring General Wood's division here and into line. General Negley," he continued. "As soon as General Wood arrives, you will move your division with all haste to reinforce General Thomas's left flank. And I do mean haste, sir. An enemy attack on that quarter is expected imminently, and we are not ready for it; not ready, Sir. Do you understand, General Negley?"

Negley assured him that he did, and Rosecrans rode off at the gallop along the Lafayette Road to find McCook. And find him he did, but finding also along the way that the defensive line to the west of the Glenn Kelly Road was far too extended and thus, in several places, thin and over-exposed.

Quickly, he explained his findings to General McCook, issued orders to tighten up the line by moving all units slightly to the left onto Wood's right flank, and then he rode back again to the center of the line and Wood's section of it, only to find Negley still there; General Wood had not yet arrived. Rosecrans was dumbfounded.

"General Negley. Why are you not yet on the move?"

"Sir, as you can see, General Wood has not yet arrived. My orders were that he was to replace me in this position. He has not yet done so."

"So I see, General. So I see, and so I *shall* see, by God. In the meantime, General, move your division forthwith to General Thomas's left flank. NOW"

He looked around the field and, spotting Brigadier General John Beatty, one of Negley's brigade commanders, rode to him and he himself ordered Beatty to move his brigade northward to Thomas's left flank. Beatty looked over at Negley, who merely nodded his head; Beatty saluted Rosecrans and immediately began issuing orders for his men to move.

General Rosecrans returned Beatty's salute, glared once more at Negley, then turned again and galloped off to the west to look for General Wood, followed closely by his staff and, of course, a widely grinning Assistant Secretary of War.

Rosecrans found General Wood with his division just to the south of Negley's position and, as far as Rosecrans could tell, he had not yet even begun to prepare to move his brigades into the gap soon to be left by Negley's departure. Which was unfortunate for Wood, because Rosecrans was by now spitting and spluttering with rage, and all of his frustrations with Negley and McCook were about to fall upon him.

"WHAT is the meaning of this, General?" Rosecrans shouted at Wood.

Wood, surrounded by his own staff officers was, to say the least, taken aback. The said staff officers stared at Rosecrans in surprise, some with mouths wide open, but Rosecrans continued his rebuke unabashed.

"Sir," he spluttered. "You have disobeyed my direct and specific orders and, in so doing, you have endangered the safety of this entire army and, by God, I will not tolerate it." He paused for a moment, breathing hard. Wood said nothing; he just stood and stared at his commanding general.

"You will move your division at once, as I have instructed, immediately or the consequences for you, General, will not be pleasant." Rosecrans snapped a salute, wheeled his horse, and galloped away in the direction of the Widow Glenn's cabin. General Wood did not return the salute, nor did he say a word other than to begin issuing orders to his staff to begin the move. They all were too shocked at the spectacle they had just witnessed to do anything other than to comply without question.

It was now almost nine o'clock

Chapter 55

Sunday September 20th, 5:45a.m. - Hazelwood

Sarah Bradley, her father, the three doctors and their staff were all up and bustling about well before dawn. Breakfast had been cooked and eaten by the light of a single oil lamp, the inhabitants of the house unwilling to risk drawing the attention of snipers or artillery on either side.

By sun-up, the kitchen and all of the downstairs rooms had been cleared for action. Makeshift tables had been constructed, great kettles of water were already bubbling over the kitchen fire, and all were waiting, for what... well, no one was quite sure of what to expect, but all had a somber feeling that what was to come would not be pleasant.

By nine o'clock, the doctors had visited all of the wounded soldiers in the tent village to the rear of the house, providing what little comfort they could, and encouragement where it was needed, each doctor knowing there was little enough to be done for them until the battle was over and the wounded transferred to more permanent and better equipped facilities. And they knew, that by the end of the day, the size of the tent village would have doubled, at least.

From outside of the kitchen door at the rear of the house, Sarah looked out over the field to the top of the hill where she knew Blake Winter and his regiment were already behind their breastworks. All she could see were the logs piled high, and the blue uniforms of the Federal officers on the porch of the Widow Glenn's house. Sadly, she returned to the kitchen and poured herself another cup of strong black coffee; it was her fifth of the morning.

George Bradley was upstairs looking out of a window on the north side of the house. From this vantage point, he could see almost the full length of the Federal line as far as the Brotherton House, almost a mile. He looked down on the massed Federal divisions and shook his head in despair. To the east, he could see activity in the Confederate lines beyond the Lafayette Road; much of what was going on was obscured by trees and scrubland, but he could see enough to know that the Confederate forces were gathering in vast numbers.

High on the hill to the rear of Hazelwood, behind the log breastwork, Colonel Wilder's brigade was on the extreme right flank of the army with General Philip Sheridan's division now on his left. Between them, more than four thousand soldiers were in line along the top of the rise all the way to the Widow Glenn's house.

Wilder, Blake Winter, Smith Atkins and several more officers were looking out across the battlefield to the east, trying to assess the strength of the enemy, most of which was concealed by the woods and forests to the east of the road. Eli Lilly was making some last minute adjustments to the positioning of his six Parrott guns. Winter turned his head a little and, through his field glasses, managed to catch a glimpse of Sarah Bradley as she turned and walked back into the house.

"More coffee, anyone?" Wilder said.

Chapter 56

Sunday September 20th, 5:45a.m. - General Bragg's Field Headquarters

Confederate General Bragg also rose before sunrise, though he could not see it from where he was headquartered at Thedford's Ford. Nevertheless, he was up and breakfasted well before dawn. By five-thirty, he was in the saddle, surrounded by a small army of staff officers and aids, waiting anxiously to hear the sounds of battle that would tell him that General Polk had commenced his attack. As the minutes turned into an hour, Bragg grew more and more agitated. Soon agitation turned into anger, and anger into rage.

"MAJOR LEE," Bragg shouted over his shoulder. "Go to General Polk and enquire as to why the attack is delayed, and urge him to commence immediately.

Lee was not gone for long. On his return, he reported to General Bragg that he had found the general eating breakfast at a farmhouse some three miles from the battle line. He also reported that not only had General Hill not received his orders, he was also nowhere to be found.

"DAMN, DAMN, DAMN," Bragg shouted. "Damn Polk and damn Hill." Bragg was apoplectic with rage.

"Major Lee," Bragg said, angrily. "You, Sir, will immediately ride the line of battle and order each and every brigade commander to engage the enemy immediately." Bragg paused for a moment while Lee looked at him in horror, then he reached into his coat front and pulled a cotton square from within and wiped away the spittle from his beard. Then he calmed down a little and continued, "I will write the order myself."

Bragg called for paper and pen and then quickly scribbled a line or two, signed it with a flourish, and then had copies made for each of his division commanders. That done, handed them to the waiting Major Lee.

"Now, Major. Go now!" And with that, General Bragg rode out in search of General Polk.

Chapter 57

Confederate General Polk rose from his bed just before sunrise. To him had fallen the most important assignment of the Confederate order of battle. He was to strike the opening blow against the Federal right flank; the rest of the Confederate army would follow his lead, each opening the action, one after the other, from right to left. And all was to begin at sunrise.

Thus, as the sun rose, General Polk was already late for his appointment with destiny, and matters only became worse when, much to his dismay, he learned that his orders to General Hill had not been delivered, and that no one knew where Hill was.

Polk realized that he now had a serious problem on his hands. General Bragg's orders were specific, and not up for interpretation: General Polk's primary responsibility was to ensure that each of his battlefield commanders, especially General Hill whose division was to lead the attack at daybreak, received specific orders: exactly what they must do, and when they must do it.

Unfortunately, Polk did not have a lot of respect for his commanding general and, for the most part, the relationship between the two generals was strained, to say the least. General Polk did not fear General Bragg, and his attitude toward him was at best, indifferent. Thus, upon learning that Hill could not be found and so had not received his orders, he had shrugged his shoulders and gone to bed, assuming that General Bragg had sent out duplicate orders, and that Hill must be in receipt of those. But that was not the case.

Polk, still not knowing Hill's whereabouts, was now in something of a panic. His first priority was to issue fresh orders to Generals Cheatham, Breckinridge, and Cleburne to commence the attack immediately. These he handed to one of his aides, Captain Joseph Wheeless, with instructions to place them directly into the hands of the generals themselves.

His second priority was... to eat breakfast, and so he did. Major Lee had arrived from General Bragg just moments after Polk had sat down to eat.

Chapter 58

Sunday September 20th, 6:15am – Confederate Battle Line

Captain Wheeless found General Cheatham almost at once and delivered Polk's orders into his hands. Some ten minutes later, he found Generals Breckinridge and Cleburne sitting, along with the erstwhile General Hill, around a campfire drinking coffee, surrounded by the men of their divisions, and this Wheeless certainly did not expect. He was, in fact, in a somewhat embarrassing situation.

"Generals, good morning," Wheeless said, dismounting and approaching the campfire. "I come with orders from General Polk."

General Hill, the senior general present, held out his hand to receive them.

"Uh...." Wheeless exclaimed, not a little flustered. "These orders are for Generals Breckinridge and Cleburne," he said as he gave them each their copy.

"Sir," he said to General Hill. "General Polk sent orders to you late last evening and only this morning learned that you had not received them. That being so, he has sent orders for the attack to each division commander directly."

"Captain," General Hill replied, leaping to his feet. "I have spent most of the night scouring the battlefield, looking for someone who might be able to tell me the part I am to play in today's conflict. I could find neither General Polk nor General Bragg. I left messages for both in several places, and have received replies to none of them.

"I learned only during my encounter with General Breckinridge, here, that I am to consider myself under General Polk's orders. As yet, however, I have not received official confirmation from anyone. Am I, then, to assume that those are, indeed, General Bragg's orders?"

"As far as I have been informed, sir, those are indeed General Bragg's orders."

Hill, stared at Wheeless, but said nothing more. He sat down again, and then looked in turn at Breckinridge and Cleburne, and then again from one to the other as they read their orders; his brow creased in a frown, the corners of his mouth turned down, his eyes half-closed.

"Captain," Breckinridge said, handing his copy to Hill. "I cannot commence an attack at this time. My men have not yet had breakfast, and it will be at least two more hours before the rations can be distributed and consumed. General Hill?"

Hill looked up at Wheeless and said in a very quiet voice, "I agree, the men must eat before they can be expected to fight."

Wheeless, by now more than a little uncomfortable, asked General Hill if he had anything he wanted to convey to General Polk. Hill replied that indeed he did, and that the captain was to wait while he wrote a message to the general.

As he waited, Captain Wheeless walked a short distance away from the campfire to afford the general some privacy. There were thousands of men encamped around him, some still huddled under blankets, some in a state of semi-undress, some drinking coffee, some writing letters; none were even remotely ready for what was soon to come.

"Captain," Hill, still seated, gestured for Wheeless to return to the campfire. "Hand this note to General Polk, if you please, and thank you."

Some fifteen minutes later, Wheeless handed Hill's note to General Polk. It was almost seven o'clock.

Polk read Hill's note and, on learning of the proposed delay, told Wheeless to have his horse prepared and that he was riding to the lines himself to find out exactly what the situation might be.

Ten minutes later, Polk was in the saddle and, followed by a retinue of staff officers and aides, rode out into the woods. And, not another ten minutes later, Wheeless was receiving General Bragg himself.

"Captain Wheeless," Bragg said. "Where in the name of all that is holy is General Polk, and why has he not commenced the attack?"

"General Bragg, Sir. General Polk did, but minutes ago, leave to ascertain exactly why the attack is not yet under way.

"General Hill did not receive his orders last night, and I have just returned from delivering General Polk's attack orders to each of the division commanders, but I fear it will be at least two hours before any such attack can be mounted." Then Wheeless gave General Bragg a full account of his visit to the lines, and his meetings there, including the content of General Hill's note to General Polk and the proposed delay for breakfast, and then he added:

"General Bragg, Sir. General Cleburne was very concerned that the enemy had been felling trees along his front all through the night, and that he was still doing so."

"It would seem to me, then," Bragg stated, with no little ire, "that it would be even more desirable to commence the attack sooner rather than later. Would you not agree, Captain?"

"Indeed, Sir, but General Hill did not seem to be concerned about the enemy's works."

"Then I suggest we go to the line and see for ourselves," Bragg said, angrily. "Lead the way, if you please, Captain."

They arrived at the campfire vacated by Generals Hill, Breckinridge, and Cleburne at around eight o'clock. The campfire was, in fact, at the center of Cleburne's division; Major Person, one of Cleburne's staff officers, was standing at the fire with a cup of coffee in his hand.

Bragg, followed by some twenty staff officers, walked his horse slowly forward into the clearing and approached the campfire. Person, on hearing the approaching horses, turned, looked, and recognized the commanding general, stood to attention and saluted, the coffee cup still in his other hand.

Bragg reined in his horse, sat for a moment, looked around the crowded encampment, returned the salute, and then said, "Major Person," can you tell me why you are not engaged here?"

"No, Sir. I cannot." He replied, still at attention.

Bragg nodded his head, and then said, icily, "Where is General Cleburne?"

Person looked around, spotted Cleburne some distance away in the woods talking to members of his staff, pointed the way and said. "There he is, sir."

When Bragg arrived at the gathering of officers inside the line of trees, he found not only General Cleburne, but General Hill as well.

For a moment, the two generals, observed by General Cleburne, who had taken two steps back, stared at each other: General Hill defiant, General Bragg shaking with rage, barely holding himself in control.

General Hill," he said, in a tight voice. "What in God's name is going on here? My instructions were for you to attack at daybreak. Why, sir, have you not done so?"

"General Bragg," Hill replied, a little too loudly; men all around were, by now, standing, watching and listening. "This is the first I have heard of your orders for the attack. I learned less than an hour ago that you had placed me under the command of General Polk. No attack orders have been relayed to me, to Generals Cleburne and Breckinridge, yes, and those only moments ago; to me, personally, no, General."

"General Hill, this is intolerable," Bragg was barely able to control himself. "The attack was supposed to begin at daybreak, more than two hours ago. Instead, I find General Polk eating breakfast and you drinking coffee. INTOLLERABLE, I say!" He looked around the now bustling encampment, and then continued, "It is obvious, General Hill, obvious I say, that your divisions are not ready to mount an assault, nor will they be for some time to come."

Hill, too, looked around the encampment, then at Cleburne and the rest of his staff, then back at General Bragg, looked him squarely in the eye and said, "Indeed, sir. I will look to my divisions and ready them for the assault."

Bragg shook his head in frustration, did not reply, and spun his horse around and rode back through his own staff, almost at a gallop, leaving Hill standing looking after him, a sardonic half-smile upon his face. It was almost eight-thirty.

Chapter 59
Sunday September 20th, - The Situation at 9:30a.m.

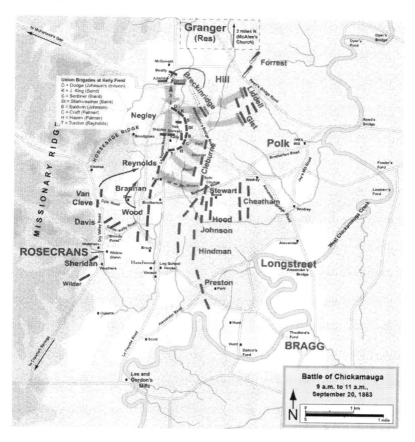

As General Polk was rising from his bed, Confederate General Longstreet's divisions had already been assembled and had been in line of battle awaiting the order to advance. By nine-thirty, the men of Longstreet's Left Wing had, for almost four hours, been standing in a line of battle more than a mile wide facing the Lafayette Road; most of them were hidden by stands of tall trees and thick scrublands. The seventeen veteran brigades under the command of General James Longstreet, one of the ablest generals in the entire Confederacy, totaled more than twenty three thousand men.

General Bushrod Johnson's division was stationed at the center of the Confederate line: the brigades of General Evander McNair and Colonel John Fulton in line abreast with General John Gregg's brigade, now commanded by Colonel Cyrus Sugg, were stationed to the rear and right of the two leading brigades. Privates Cobb and Morrisey and the 30th Tennessee Regiment were at the front and right of Gregg's brigade, straddling the Brotherton Road. General Hindman's division of three brigades was on Longstreet's left, General Buckner's Corps was to his rear; General Stewart's division was on his right, and General Cleburne's division of Polk's Right Wing was stationed on Stewart's right flank.

Confederate Right Wing

Extending from General Cleburne's left flank northward to a point some quarter mile beyond Reed's Bridge Road, where General Forrest's cavalry corps held the extreme right flank of General Polk's Right Wing, the Confederate line of battle stretched almost a mile and a half.

Generals Breckinridge, Walker, and Liddell with eight brigades held the right flank of General Polk's Right Wing. To their left, General Cleburne held the left flank with General Cheatham's division just to the rear. In all, Polk's Right Wing was comprised of five divisions, including sixteen brigades.

General Breckinridge's division was at the head of the column with his three brigades in line facing west: Major General Daniel Adams was on the right, Brigadier General Marcellus Stovall was in the center, and Brigadier Benjamin Helm was on the left.

General Walker's Division was behind Breckinridge in reserve, and General Liddell's division was behind Walker's.

From the extreme left flank of Buckner's Corps on the Left Wing, to General Breckinridge's extreme right flank, the Right Wing of the Confederate line of battle stretched more than two and a half miles.

Federal Line of Battle

General Thomas had made good use of the time allotted to him. At nine-thirty, he called a halt to the construction, which had been going on throughout the night. The great, crescent-shaped fortification stretched along a front from the Poe farm one hundred yards west of the Lafayette Road circling east and northward almost to Alexander's Bridge Road to finish just short of the Lafayette Road. The fortifications were manned by the four Federal divisions commanded by Generals Palmer, Baird, Richard Johnson, and Reynolds. Thomas had effectively turned his battle line into a single, giant crescent-shaped fortress that stretched north and south for more than a mile.

From Thomas's right flank, the Federal line now stretched from the Poe farm some one hundred yard to the east of the Lafayette Road for a little more than a mile, stopping just short of Hazelwood. The line was comprised of General Crittenden's corps to the left with his left flank – General Brannan's division - joining General Thomas's right flank; Colonel Croxton's brigade was on Brannan's left – with the 10th Indiana and Jesse Dixon and Pat McCann on Croxton's extreme left.

General McCook's corps completed the line to the right of, and adjoining, General Crittenden's right flank, with General Wood's division to the right of Brannan's division, and extended south of the Brotherton house, to a point less than one hundred yards from Hazelwood.

Chapter 60

Sunday September 20th, 9:45am – It Begins

It was around nine forty-five when the Confederate Right Wing finally surged forward. Federal General George Thomas was ready behind his breastworks with four divisions in line, waiting. General Negley was... well, only General Beatty's brigade had reached Thomas's left flank, and that only because General Rosecrans had, himself, taken a direct hand in his movements. Beatty would, however, be joined shortly by a second of Negley's brigades: Colonel Stanley's, Stanley also having finally complied with Rosecrans direct orders.

By eight-thirty Beatty was moving toward Reed's Bridge Road at the extreme left flank of Rosecrans army. Negley and his remaining two brigades were not yet on the battlefield. Having taken a circuitous route, he had strayed too far to the east, and was enjoying a somewhat leisurely march in the quiet of the early morning some quarter mile away to the west and rear of Thomas's line of battle. General Grainger's division was about two miles away at McAfee's church, acting in reserve.

General Thomas was, however, better prepared to receive the initial Confederate assault than even he realized. True, he was sure that his breastworks would hold, but how well they would hold would surprise even him.

The church bells in Chattanooga away to the north could faintly be heard ringing in the crisp morning air. The sun was shining in an almost cloudless sky; birds were singing in the treetops; it was an idyllic, September Sunday morning.

All along the Federal line of battle, General Thomas's divisions were poised, lookouts on top of the fortifications, scanning the trees for any sort of movement that might predict the beginning of the onslaught they knew they soon would face... nothing.

And then... six tremendous bangs, first one, then one after the other in close succession, shattered the uneasy silence as the first of the four Confederate batteries on General Breckinridge's right flank opened fire on General Thomas's Federal positions.

9:45am – Confederate General Hill

By nine forty five, General Hill's forces were finally in position and ready for action. General Hill, himself, was at his field headquarters just to the rear and center of General Polk's Right Wing, discussing the coming attack with his division commanders, Generals Cleburne and Breckinridge, and he was in a foul mood. Still smarting from his encounter with General Bragg, he was anything but enthusiastic about carrying out his attack orders.

According to Bragg's battle orders issued to Polk and Longstreet the previous evening, General Breckinridge was to initiate the attack with the rest of the army joining in successively, division by division, southward until the entire Confederate army was involved. This, of course, would depend entirely upon how those orders were interpreted, and then carried out by the commanders in the field. Then, of course, all had been changed when Bragg sent Major Lee down the line issuing new orders to each division commander, individually. Therefore, the interpretation and implementation of the orders became subjective, and it did not go well.

While General Longstreet was the consummate general officer, General Polk was more clergyman than battlefield commander and he did not see eye-to-eye with Bragg, about anything, and he certainly did not agree with Bragg's battle plan.

There was quite a gathering in the small clearing just to the rear and center of the Confederate Right Wing. General Polk, some dozen members of his staff, along with Generals Breckinridge, Cleburne and Cheatham, plus a large retinue of their staff officers, were in serious conversation.

"Gentlemen" Polk looked around at the gathered officers and said. "It is time." He pulled his pocket watch from the inside of his uniform coat, opened it, glanced briefly at it, nodded his head, then snapped it shut and returned it to its pocket.

"The enemy has taken full advantage of our delay; he is ready for us!" Polk paused and looked again at his senior officers.

"General Forrest has informed me that the enemy's defenses are extensive; ranked in three lines of log breastworks, one behind the other, each larger and more formidable than the previous line; the final line of defense is a solid wall of logs piled six, or more, feet high. This is flanked by natural abatis' at least as high as the wall itself.

"Each line is heavily defended. General Thomas, so our good General Forrest, reports, has as many as four divisions at his disposal, plus at least a couple of detached brigades, perhaps more." Polk paused for a moment, then continued, "Thomas's divisions are supported by at least eight batteries of artillery on the breastworks and six more in elevated positions to the rear. It is, gentlemen, a formidable task that we face.

"General Bragg is most concerned about the attack; I, too am concerned, but for very different reasons. Be that as it may, gentlemen.

The time has come for us to do our duty. General Breckinridge?" It was spoken more as a question as to Breckinridge's readiness, than to get his attention. He already had it.

"General?" Breckinridge sat upright in the saddle and saluted.

"Please commence your assault as we have discussed at some length.

"Yes, sir." Breckinridge turned in the saddle and called for his chief of artillery, then turned again to his brigade commanders. "General Adams, General Helm, General Stovall." He looked at each in turn. "You may go to your brigades."

When General Breckinridge returned to the head of his division, Generals Adams, Stovall, and Helm, along with his chief of artillery, Major Rice Graves, were already waiting, it was almost nine forty-five.

"Well, gentlemen," he said, dismounting. "It appears we are to get this thing started. Are you ready, sirs? Good, then, on my mark, we will move out.

"Major Graves. Go to your batteries, sir and immediately engage the enemy."

Graves rode off at the gallop.

Breckinridge took up a position a few paces forward in front of Stovall's brigade, with Stovall just behind him, Adams to the right, and Helm to the left.

For a long moment, the entire division stood silent and still, not a cough to be heard, not a click, not a word. Breckenridge drew his sword and raised it above his head, looked left, then right, then shouted:

"READY?"

To his left right and rear, his regimental commanders raised their swords aloft in answer. The long lines of gray-clad soldiers were silent.

"ADVANCE THE COLORS,"

To the left and right the regimental color guards stepped forward, red and white guidons; blue and gold regimental banners; red, white and blue battle flags unfurling, flapping and snapping in the morning breeze. Then, to the rear, the drums began to roll.

"GUIDE CENTER! FORWAAARD!"

General Breckinridge lowered his sword to point the way and stepped forward. As he did so, there was a tremendous, loud bang as the first of Graves' six guns hurled its deadly load toward the Federal fortifications; and then, BAM.... BAM, BAM, BAM, BAM.... BAM,BAM,BAM; almost instantly, the rest of Graves' battery, and another to just to his right, opened fire together.

The earth shook and great clouds of blue-white smoke billowed and swirled out over the field.

The advance was slow at first, a slow walk toward the bristling breastworks almost six hundred yards away to the west. As the three Confederate brigades advanced in line, a line of battle almost a half-mile wide, Stovall's and Adams' Brigade extended far to the north of the Federal positions, and so they wheeled slowly to the left with Helm's brigade anchoring the turn. The maneuver would bring Adams onto Thomas's left flank and, perhaps, even his rear. Stovall and Helm would, within minutes, arrive directly in front of the great, crescent-shaped Federal breastwork.

9:45am – The 10th Indiana

At about the same time as Confederate General Breckinridge was returning to his division, Jesse Dixon, Pat McCann, the 10th Indiana and the other four regiments of Colonel Croxton's brigade, had settled down behind a sturdy section of breastworks at the center of the Federal battle line. Three great logs, one set on top of two together, formed a solid wall some three feet high. It was a good position, a strong position, both Jesse and Pat knew it, but both men were filled with trepidation at what they knew was about to fall upon them. Jesse, unafraid, but nervous; Pat was both nervous and afraid; his hands were shaking, his teeth chattering, perhaps from the chill of the morning, perhaps from fear. Either way, it was something that Jesse knew he had to watch carefully.

The two of them were kneeling, shoulder-to-shoulder, in line, rifles resting on the topmost log, waiting. They would not have to wait much longer, or so Jesse thought.

"You doin' all right?" Jesse said to Pat, in a low voice, not looking at him.

Pat said nothing. He glanced to his left and looked at Jesse, who looked back at him. Then he gave a single nod of his head and turned again to gaze out over his rifle barrel to the road beyond, and the trees away in the distance.

"Pat." Jesse said. No reply.

"Pat." He said again, a little more loudly.

"What, Jesse?" He said in a low voice. He sounded tired, no, resolved.

"Pat, it's going to be all right. Just keep your head down; we'll get through this. Understand?"

Again, Pat nodded his head but said nothing, and continued to stare out into space.

"Pat, talk to me!" Jesse said, sharply.

"Pat rolled over onto his back, his head resting against the lower log, and said, "What the hell do you want me to say, Jesse? That I'm all right? Well, I'm not all right. That I'm not scared? Well I am scared; I'm scared shitless and if I could run, I would, and I'd not stop until I was back in Indiana. You understand, Jesse? I messed up; I messed up bad, and I don't know what to do. I'm gonna get kilt, Jesse. I just know I am, and… and I don't want to die." His eyes were watering, and his hands were shaking.

"I know, Pat, but you ain't gonna die." Jesse shook his head, his own eyes watering as he looked at his friend. "We'll be fine, I promise." He gripped Pat's upper arm and squeezed it. "You hear, Pat?"

Pat nodded his head, then shook it, wiped his eyes on the sleeve of his jacket, rolled back onto his stomach and stared once more out over the top of the breastwork and the Lafayette Road.

Away to the north, a single cannon roared, BAM, and then another, and another, and….

9:45am – 30th Tennessee

A little more than three hundred yards away to the east, beyond the Lafayette Road, behind the line of trees and scrubland, as yet unseen by the defenders behind the Federal breastworks, the Confederate divisions of General Longstreet's Left Wing waited in line. At the center of the line was Bushrod Johnson's division, which included the 30th Tennessee and privates Billy Cobb and Jimmy Morrisey.

"I prayed last night, Billy, Morrisey said, quietly. "First time in many a long year. I ain't been a terrible bad person, but I figured it was time to make amends. The good Lord, I think, will forgive me my transgressions, though I can't really recall a whole lot I need forgiving for; that encounter back in Bell Buckle, maybe, but there warn't a whole lot of harm in that. She seemed happy, anyways." He thought for a moment, then continued, "Then there was that old boy back in 58, but hell… that warn't nothing either."

Jeeze, Jim. You are ramblin'," Billy said.

Jimmy Morrisey was standing upright, his head down, looking at his hands which were grasping the barrel of his Springfield rifle, the butt of which was resting on the ground between his feet.

The two men were standing in line, had been for more than four hours. The air was still chilly, but the sun was shining, the birds were singing, and the two of them had been reminiscing about times gone by.

Morrisey lifted his head and stood up straight and tall. As he did so, a breath of early morning breeze ruffled the wisps of hair that hung over the collar of his jacket. Then he looked sideways at his friend and said, "You know, Billy boy, I want you to have my watch, right?" He reached inside his coat and pulled it out by the chain. He held it up, and swung it back and forth. Then he flipped it up into the air, caught it and, with a dirty fingernail, pried it open, and looked fondly at it. It was nine forty-five.

"It's a real nice watch, Billy. Shame to let some Yank blue belly walk away with it. You'll take it; you promise?"

"Awe, Jim. You'll be lookin' at that old watch when I'm long in my box and six feet under. I knows it and you knows it."

"You promise, Billy"

"Yeah, I promise."

"And just one other thing I'd like you to do for me, Billy. Will you do it?"

Billy sighed a deep and heavy sigh and said, "What, Jim? What do you want me to do?"

Morrisey returned the watch to his jacket and took out a small, folded piece of paper.

"I want you to look in, just once in a while, and see that Sissy is all right, her and the kids. An' I got this note for her, too. You'll take it to her for me, Billy, please?"

"Yeah, that too," Billy said, as he took the note from him. "But I ain't gonna need to. After this, we are going home. I cain't stand it anymore'n you can. This one is the last. I told you before, you stick by me an' I'll get you through it."

"So you say, Billy boy; so you say." Jimmy smiled sideways at him, winked, and then continued, "But I've told you, Billy. Today's the day. And it's all right; it's all right. I told you, I prayed to the Lord last night, and I am at peace, Billy. Whatever happens today, I am at peace."

As if to punctuate the words, the sound of a single cannon shot in the distance startled both of them, and signaled the beginning of....

9:45am – Wilder's Brigade
On the rise above Hazelwood, Blake Winter sat alone on top of the breastworks, his hands wrapped around a tin cup still three-parts full of coffee, his elbows resting on his knees. His uniform jacket was open, revealing his white shirt and blue suspenders. From his vantage point, he could see the hustle and bustle going on around the farmhouse and the

tents at its rear. Now and again, he caught a glimpse, a flash of blue dress, going in or out of the house, or between the tents, and his thoughts returned to the short few minutes he had spent with her the night before.

He smiled as he remembered the mess that she was, blood smears on her face, the once beautiful fair hair matted with sweat and stuck to her face, her cheeks wet with tears. And he remembered how she had clung to him, and whispered nonsensically into his chest. It had been a fleeting moment, just a minute or two, and then she had looked up, told him she needed to go back to work, and turned away from him. Then he, too, had turned and walked out of the kitchen door and back up the hill.

Now, as he looked down upon the house, he wished he'd stayed longer, said more, but....

He took a sip of coffee and gazed out over the battlefield. There was still some mist hanging in the hollows, even a few wisps of smoke rising from the ashes of the burned out sections of scrub. Away in the distance, he could see movement among the trees, but it was too far away to make out any details. A little closer, just below him and to the left of Hazelwood, he could see the long lines of blue-clad soldiers, the men of General Woods' divisions were moving into defensive positions along the Lafayette Road: too many to count, or even estimate. Regiment after regiment filed down the hill and into line. It was an impressive sight, and one that afforded him at least a little confidence. He looked again at Hazelwood; no signs of the blue dress, just dozens of soldiers moving in and out of the tents, carrying... what, he could not tell.

To the east, the sun was climbing higher; it was going to be a beautiful day. His face twisted in an ironic grin at the thought. *Beautiful day?*

"Are you all right, Colonel?" He twisted round to find John Wilder standing behind him.

"Whew, you startled me. Yes, I'm all right. Just taking a moment to clear my head, and I was thinking: It's going to be a beautiful day."

Wilder looked at him quizzically, "You think?" He said.

"Well, I was being facetious, of course, but the sun is shining and all is quiet, at least for now."

But his words were premature, for just as they were out of his mouth the noise of cannon fire to the north split the air.

Winter stood, pitched what was left of his coffee onto the ground, handed the cup to Wilder, and buttoned his jacket. Then he took back the cup and said, "Well, it would seem I spoke too soon.

"John, if you don't mind, I need a favor."

"If I can."

"I'd like to run down to the Bradley place for a couple of minutes; just to say goodbye. I'll be gone no more than that, I swear."

Wilder nodded, "No more than a couple of minutes. I have a feeling all is about to explode, and I need you here. Together, the two men walked quickly away toward the rear, Wilder to consult with his staff, Winter to get his horse.

9:45am Hazelwood

In the kitchen at Hazelwood, everything stopped at the sounds of the cannon fire to the north. For a moment all was quiet in the room; they stood still and listened, and the thunder in the distance slowly intensified.

Sarah Bradley, her gingham apron clasped tightly in both hands, raised it to her lips and bit down on it.

The three doctors looked at each other, but said nothing; they all knew what was coming and, unfortunately, were well used to it.

Doc Marshall shook his bowed head and began to arrange his instruments on the great kitchen table. The two Confederate doctors turned to their own tables and did the same. Charity looked to the water bubbling over the fire. George Bradley stared out of the window of the next room; smoke was already rising over the trees away to the north.

Blake Winter's horse clattered onto the brick paving at the rear of the house. He swung his right leg up and over the animal's ears, dropped to the ground, and strode quickly to the half-open door. Pushing it aside, he entered the kitchen and looked around.

Everyone present turned and stared at the Federal officer. Winter saluted Doc Marshall, acknowledged the two Confederate doctors, all of this without taking his eyes off of Sarah Bradley. He twitched his head in the direction of the rear door, indicating that he wanted to speak to her outside.

She nodded her head, took off the apron, and walked quickly out through the back door, followed by Winter. Once outside, she turned to face him, threw her arms around his neck, and buried her face in his chest.

Winter held her for a moment then pushed her gently away, put a finger under her chin, and tilted her head upward until she had no choice but to look into his eyes. He kissed her lightly on the lips then said, "Sarah, this has to be quick. I am needed with my regiment and, as you can hear, the enemy, no, sorry, your people are already on the move, and I fear that the situation is about to turn very nasty.

"I just wanted to... well, I wanted to say goodbye, at least for now. There's no telling what the outcome of this day may be. If we lose today, your home will be back among friends and I will be... God only knows where; that is if I make it out alive."

Sarah was devastated.

"Oh Blake," she said, what is to become of us? I fear I will not see you ever again."

"No, no," He said, pulling her in close. "I will be back. I promise. When, I don't know. Tonight, I hope, but.... If your people win the day, I will be long away from here, but I will come back. If it takes a month, a year, or even longer, I will be back, and somehow I will get word to you that I am all right."

She held him tight for just a moment, and then pushed him away, stood on tiptoe and kissed him fiercely. "Goodbye, Blake Winter. I will be waiting for you."

She kissed him again and, before he could say another word, turned and ran back into the house.

Winter stood for a moment, staring after her, bemused, and then turned away, grabbed the reigns of his horse, swung quickly up into the saddle and away up the hill at full gallop.

9:45 General Longstreet

General Longstreet had arrived early on the battlefield and, as was his practice, made his way quickly to seek out his subordinate commanders.

He went first to General Hood, who commanded one of his, Longstreet's, divisions of five brigades that had lately arrived fresh on the field from Virginia. Hood was already arranging his columns in battle order, to the rear of General Bushrod Johnson's division of three brigades. He had lined up the eight brigades in a deep column to assault the enemy on what he perceived would be a narrow front,

"General Hood! Good morning to you, sir," Longstreet said, affably. "How are we proceeding? In good order, I presume."

Hood turned in the saddle and saluted, a slight smile on his dour face.

"Indeed we are, General Longstreet, and, if I may say so, sir, it's good to see you."

Longstreet nodded his head, stood up in the stirrups and looked around, taking in the vast numbers of soldiers milling around, but very much in order, and very much under orders.

"Thank you, General. It's good to see you too." He paused for a moment and then asked, "And the men, sir? How are their spirits?"

"Oh very good sir; very good indeed." Hood said. "In fact, General, I don't think I have ever seen them in better spirits.

"We had a good day yesterday, sir; a very good day indeed."

"Good, good." Longstreet smiled, and then said, "And we will do even better today. We will drive them entirely from the field, sir."

Hood nodded his head enthusiastically. "I am glad to hear you say so, General. I would wish, however, that more of these southern commanders were as confident.... Never once have I heard talk of victory, not even from.... I tell you, sir, we drove the enemy back significantly yesterday, more than a mile. The men performed admirably, but...."

"Well, General Hood?" Longstreet could tell that there was obviously something on Hood's mind. "What is it, sir, what do you have to say?"

Hood would not normally have continued his thread, but he had known Longstreet a long time, and had served with him through countless campaigns over the past two years, including Gettysburg, and so he took a deep breath and said:

"As I said, General, we drove the enemy back more than a mile. General Stewart's division broke through the enemy line and advanced quickly, perhaps too quickly, deep into enemy territory. He soon found himself outnumbered and under severe pressure, but he continued his assault. He called for reinforcements but, even though General Bragg had men enough to spare, he would not commit them. Had he done so, we might well have not been here today. General Stewart was forced to withdraw, much to his dismay, sir"

"I see," Longstreet said. "And where is General Stewart now?"

"He is with his division, General. That way," Hood replied, pointing to the right.

Longstreet saluted Hood, Hood returned it, and Longstreet rode off in search of General Stewart. He found him not two hundred yards away from Hood's position.

Stewart was on foot, conversing with several of his staff officers. Stewart spotted him as he approached, and grinned broadly at the prospect of meeting with his old friend. The two had been roommates at West Point, along with their now mortal enemy, General Rosecrans. He turned back to his officers, said something Longstreet couldn't hear, saluted them, then turned and walked to meet him.

Longstreet dismounted, clapped his hands on each of Stewart's shoulders, shook him gently, and said, "How are you my old friend? It's so good to see you again."

"I am well, General, very well indeed. I am honored to see you, sir."

The honor is all mine, I can assure you." Longstreet let go of Stewart's shoulders and took a step backwards.

The two old friends talked for a while, discussing times gone by, old and well-remembered friends, including General Rosecrans. It was a pleasant few moments, for both of them. Then Longstreet became serious, and said:

"I hear you did very well yesterday, General. Would you like to tell me about it?"

And he did. By the time he had finished his narration, Longstreet's face was dark red, his mouth a thin red line among his heavy beard. Never had he had much respect for General Bragg, believing his high rank had been achieved more through his, Bragg's, friendship with Jefferson Davis than through ability, and now he had even less respect for his commanding General.

"Well, General," He said to Stewart. "There is little we can do about the situation. We must do our best work today and, if the Lord is willing, we will drive our erstwhile friend from the field in disarray.

At that point, both Generals started, then turned to face the north from which the sounds of cannon fire could be heard.

"And so it begins, General." Longstreet turned to face Stewart and the two men saluted each other. "I wish you good fortune." And Longstreet remounted his horse and rode away into the woods.

9:45am – General Bragg's Field Headquarters

General Bragg had been in the saddle since sun-up. He had gone chasing after General Polk, then General Hill. He had changed his battle orders, placing the responsibility for the attack under the direct control of the individual division commanders, and was now back at his field headquarters at Thedford's Ford, still in the saddle, still agitated, and still waiting.

Throughout the morning, he had drunk copious amounts of strong coffee. He was, to all intents and purposes, strung out, anxious, even panicky, all at the same time. And, as time relentlessly passed, his demeanor did not change for the better.

Thus it was, that at nine forty-five that morning, when the first gun of General Breckinridge's 5th Washington battery opened fire on the enemy positions, General Bragg almost jumped out of the saddle, so startled was he. He stood in the saddle, straining to see over the treetops, looking northward for any signs that Polk was indeed commencing his attack.

As one cannon roared after another, plumes of blue-white smoke rose lazily above the trees. Bragg clapped his hands, looked skyward and muttered something that none around him could hear. Then he began issuing orders to his couriers to ride out to the lines to gather intelligence.

9:45am – General Rosecrans' Field Headquarters

High on the hill overlooking the battlefield that stretched away to the north and east, from the front porch of the Widow Glenn's house, General Rosecrans, surrounded by his senior staff officers, including General Garfield and Assistant Secretary Dana, also turned toward the sounds of gunfire.

"So, gentlemen," He said, rubbing his gloved hands together, "it begins."

Rosecrans raised his field glasses to his eyes and tried to see… something, anything, of the action, but it was all too far away, and hidden by the forest. He turned and looked eastward, first at his own lines of massed infantry less than a half-mile away to the northeast on the western side of the Lafayette Road. Beyond that, he could see little of the Confederate battle line to the east. They were not yet moving and were still hidden by the trees and scrubland a mile away to the east.

"General Garfield, if you please…."

Chapter 61

Sunday September 20th, 9:45am – Confederate Line of Battle

General Breckinridge's three Confederate brigades advanced in line-a-breast: General Helm heading for a full frontal attack on the extreme left of the Union line, with Stovall and Adams advancing along the Alexander's Bridge Road, wheeling slowly to the left as they went, a maneuver designed to bring them around the end of, and onto, the Federal left flank. General Forrest's cavalry was guarding Breckinridge's right.

General Polk and his three division commanders watched as Breckinridge's division moved out. General Cleburne was fidgeting in the saddle, anxious to be a part of the action himself.

"General Polk, sir, "Cleburne said. "Am I not also to attack?"

"Indeed you are, General, but not just now. Let us bide our time a while; see what transpires for General Breckinridge's division."

"But sir." Cleburne replied, somewhat testily, "General Bragg's orders are quite specific. We are required to attack in concert. In fact, he gave those same specific orders to each of the division commanders in the field."

"General Cleburne," Polk said, quite at ease. "Am I not commanding General Bragg's Right Wing?"

"Indeed you are, sir."

"Then please allow me to decide when and if you are to become engaged. In the meantime, as I have already stated, we will bide here for a short while."

Cleburne gritted his teeth but said nothing. General Cheatham smirked behind Polk's back, then grinned at Cleburne and shook his head, a suggestion that Cleburne might be wise to keep his mouth shut. Cleburne nodded his agreement.

Adam's and Stovall's Confederate brigades made easy going along Alexander's Bridge Road; they made it all the way to the Lafayette Road, then wheeled again to the left, across the open field behind Thomas's flank and his fortifications. Had it not been for the timely arrival of Federal General Beatty's brigade, now joined by that of Colonel Timothy Stanley, Thomas may well have lost the day in those early moments of the Confederate attack.

As it was, Adams and Stovall ran slap into the newly arrived Federal reinforcements. For a short while, they prevailed, and pushed forward along the rear of Thomas's fortifications, almost a quarter mile; it seemed as if Breckinridge was to achieve a quick and easy victory. But Thomas was quick to respond, and sent in two more brigades to aid the now beleaguered, but stubborn, General Beatty.

Beatty and Breckinridge's brigades stood virtually toe-to-toe across the open ground behind Thomas's left flank. Both sides were supported by artillery and both sides were blasting each other with double-loaded canister – a nightmarish curtain of death and destruction that howled across the body-strewn field in both directions. Thomas continued to send in fresh Federal soldiers. Breckinridge's assault stalled.

Confederate General Helm's frontal assault fared no better. His brigade ran into the bristling defenses that Thomas's men had been building throughout the night: long rows of almost impregnable, deadly spiked abatis flanked by logs piled man-high. It was a futile effort. From behind the defenses, the Federals opened a withering storm of rifle and cannon fire. It was an untenable position for Helm. Thomas's breastworks were impervious to any frontal attack. Helm had no option but to wheel to the right in support of Breckinridge's other two brigades.

The high watermark for Breckinridge's attack came at around noon when Stovall's brigade, having made it almost a quarter mile behind Thomas's line, was finally turned back. Stovall and Adams retreated to a more tenable position where they took what cover they could, and opened a sustained rate of fire on Thomas's positions.

Breckinridge's artillery slowly chopped away at the log breastworks, but the overall effect was too little, and the Federal line held.

Back in the clearing, Generals Polk, Breckinridge, Cheatham, and Cleburne were watching as Breckinridge's sorely used brigades were returning. Even from where he was sitting, Polk could see that casualties had been very heavy, and so could the rest of the assembled officers.

At that moment, a rider from General Helm's brigade rode up at the gallop, slewed his horse to a stop, saluted the gathered officers, then turned to General Polk and said, "General, sir. General Helm is shot; he is dead.

Polk heaved a heavy sigh and shook his head. Cleburne's Irish temper was up; he was seething.

"General Polk," Cleburne said, through tight lips. "I must protest, sir. I am astounded; indeed, I am thunderstruck that you had us sit here and watch as General Breckinridge's division was so roughly used. Had you allowed me to coordinate my advance with that of General Breckinridge, Thomas would have been unable to send reinforcements to face him, and the outcome might have been... it might have been... well, sir, General Helm might still be with us. And furthermore, General Polk....

"Enough, General Cleburne!" Polk interrupted him angrily. "You forget your place, sir." Polk, an Anglican bishop, rarely raised his voice in anger, but he was indeed angry, and he was extremely upset, not just that Cleburne had the temerity to question him, to criticize him, but also to do it front of his, Polk's, staff.

For a moment, it seemed that General Polk might lose his temper completely, but then he took a deep breath, gave a loud sigh, smiled condescendingly, and said in a very quiet voice, "Now, General Cleburne. You may give the order for your division to advance. And do so quickly, if you please."

Without a word or a salute, Cleburne, on horseback, side by side with, and facing Polk, wrenched his horse's head to the right, and dug his spurs into its flanks. The horse reared, spun on its back legs, and leaped away at full gallop, leaving Polk and the assembled Confederate officers staring after him.

It took Cleburne just a couple of minutes to reach his three brigade commanders who were already waiting impatiently for his arrival. Without a pause, he shouted orders, for them to join their brigades and commence the attack.

General Cleburne's division entered the fray on the left of Breckinridge's division, which was regrouping and turning to face the Federal positions once more. Cleburne hurled all three of his brigades in line against the Federal breastworks. Again, the withering fire from behind the defenses decimated Cleburne's division, but they did not falter; they drove through the Federal pickets like a herd of raging bulls through a cornfield. They carried the first line of log defenses, then the next, and then they were in front of the main defensive wall and bristling rows of abatis.

And there the attack stalled. The main Federal defensive line was all but impregnable.

The firestorm from the Federal lines was beyond reality: rifle fire from the infantry, virtually unseen by the advancing Confederate columns, was continuous, each soldier firing more than two rounds per minute. The Federal gun crews were also maintaining a similar rate of fire, each gun firing double-shotted canister at point-blank range into the faces of the advancing Confederate brigades. The result was devastating, the noise a constant, unbroken roar that shook the ground and the trees: a nerve-shattering cacophony.

General Cleburne's brigades were halted; men in the front ranks were blown away as if in a windstorm; and it did not take long for the erstwhile Irishman to decide that to continue in like fashion would be a futile exercise, and a total waste of manpower. And, without sending word to General Polk, he ordered his brigade commanders to withdraw to a defensible position, and from there to maintain a steady rate of fire, rifle and artillery, on the enemy breastworks. The time was eleven-thirty.

Chapter 62

"Can't see the enemy, Jess," Pat McCann said, "They're there, though. Every once in a while you can catch a flash of light through the trees; reflections, I guess."

He looked sideways, first to the left, and then to the right. Then he twisted and looked behind him. Everywhere, as far as he could see in any direction, thousands of blue-clad soldiers were sitting, standing, lying in long lines behind the log walls. To the rear, more than a dozen batteries of artillery were lined up along the crest of the rise, gun crews at the ready.

McCann tilted his head and listened. All was quiet, even the birds had stopped singing; all he could hear was a soft rustling of leaves as a gentle breeze wafted through the trees.

Then…. BAM!

To the north, a tremendous explosion echoed and reverberated over the woodland, shattering the quiet of the early morning. It was quickly followed by another, then another, and then a dozen more. Seconds later, the sounds of the Confederate artillery fire were joined by an unbroken howl of small arms fire as thousands upon thousands of soldiers on both sides opened fire, one side against the other.

For a moment, no one moved; then Jesse threw himself forward behind the log wall where Pat McCann was crouched, his back to the logs, head down between his hands, his elbows on his knees, his rifle lay unheeded by his side. He was shaking violently.

"It's all right, Pat. It's way over there, not here." Jesse yelled in Pat's ear as he grabbed his friend's forearms and pulled them down. Jesse looked wildly around, fearful that someone might have seen his friend's lapse in composure; no one had noticed; if they had, they gave no indication of it, much to Jesse's relief.

"Get ahold of yourself, Pat," he yelled, trying to make himself heard. "There ain't nothin' happnin' here."

McCann took a deep breath, nodded, and shouted, "Sorry, Jesse. I was startled, is all. I'll be all right." He turned, rose onto his knees, and looked east over the top of the logs: nothing. To the north, the sounds of battle slowly increased in intensity. By eleven-thirty, it had become a single unceasing roar, and was growing ever louder as the combat expanded and crept slowly southward and toward them.

Chapter 63

When the first shots were fired by General Breckinridge's artillery, Billy Cobb and Jimmy Morrisey had been standing in line for more than four hours. Major General Bushrod Johnson's brigade was at the right forefront of Longstreet's Left Wing; Major General Thomas Hindman's division of three brigades was in line to Johnson's left. In the front line of Johnson's division were the brigades of Colonel John Fulton and Brigadier General Evander McNair. Immediately behind them was Brigadier General John Gregg's brigade, now commanded by Colonel Cyrus Sugg.

Behind the two leading Confederate divisions came three more: those of Brigadier General William Preston, Major General John Bell Hood, and Brigadier General Joseph Kershaw. Finally, Major General A.P. Stewart's division of three more brigades was in position on Hood's right flank. In all, Longstreet's grand column included slightly more than twenty three thousand men. It was a column that stretched back from the front line for more than three quarters of a mile: a tightly packed sea of death waiting to be unleashed upon the enemy.

The 30th Tennessee Regiment, including Privates Cobb and Morrisey, was in the front line of Sugg's brigade, and on its right flank. As was typical, Billy Cobb had picked out a spot as far away from the colors as he could get. Just to his right, four three-inch rifled guns of Bledsoe's Missouri Battery were ranged, in line, to fire over the trees at the Federal positions beyond the Lafayette Road; *not the best spot I could've picked*, Cobb thought, looking all around him, *but probably makes no never mind anyway*.

Cobb listened to the battle raging to the north, and he was depressed. "Whooo eee, Jim. It's gonna to be a big one, I reckon."

Jimmy Morrisey, nodded his head in agreement, but said nothing. He just stood stolidly, holding the barrel of his rifle, its butt on the ground between his feet. He looked neither up nor down, nor sideways; he stared, eyes blinking only every ten seconds or so, over the tops of the heads of the brigades lined up in front of him.

What's he thinkin' of? Cobb wondered, as he looked sideways at his friend. *Daydreamin', I shouldn't wonder.*

Chapter 64
Sunday September 20th, 10:30am – General Thomas

By ten-thirty, General Thomas had already sent to General Rosecrans five times for more reinforcements. General Rosecrans had complied all five times and General Thomas now had under his command more than three fifths of the entire Army of the Cumberland, but it still was not enough. With General Breckinridge pressing him on three sides, he was still not confident that he had the manpower to maintain a protracted defense of his positions. Realizing his position was precarious, he sent his aid, Captain Kellogg with orders to General Brannan. Brannan was to withdraw his division from the fortified line and move to the rear, then to the north in support of Brigadier General John Beatty who was taking the brunt of Breckenridge's assault

Brannan was able only to send Colonel Van Derveer's brigade; the rest of his division couldn't follow, could not leave the battle line, without being relieved.

When Thomas heard that Brannan was unable to make the maneuver, he sent Captain Kellogg posthaste to General Rosecrans with a request for more reinforcements.

As Kellogg galloped away from the Kelly farm, along the Glenn Kelly Road, he could see the massed Federal divisions that were manning the battle line. As he passed by the rear of the position where General Brannan's division was supposed to be deployed, he noticed what he thought was a gap in the Federal line. In fact, he supposed that Brannan had, after all, moved to the rear in compliance with Thomas's orders, thus leaving a gap some three hundred yards wide in the line of battle. What Kellogg did not know was that Brannan was indeed in his proper place, still in the line of battle, but hidden by thick scrub and dense woodland.

Chapter 64

Sunday September 20th, 10:45am – General Rosecrans Field Headquarters

"General Rosecrans, sir," Captain Kellogg said, leaping down from his horse in front of the commanding general who was on the front porch of the house watching the action as it unfolded..

"Yes, what is it this time, Captain?" Rosecrans sounded impatient.

"Sir, General Thomas requests more reinforcements to secure his left flank." Kellogg handed the written request to Rosecrans, who tore it open and quickly scanned its contents.

"General Garfield." Rosecrans said, without turning. Please write an order for General Sheridan. He is to move his division as quickly as possible north to strengthen General Thomas's left flank."

The order was written and then dispatched to General Sheridan, who was with his division just to the east and south of the Glenn house.

"Yes, Captain Kellogg. What is it now," Rosecrans could see that Kellogg was somewhat agitated.

"General, Sir," he began. "As I rode by the rear of the line of battle, I noticed what appeared to be a large gap where General Brannan's division is supposed to be. I think he must, after all, have complied with General Thomas's orders and moved his division to support General Beatty and his left flank. If that is indeed the case, our line is wide open to the enemy."

Rosecrans took his field glasses and scoured as much of the line as he could see from the porch. He shook his head, frustrated.

"Are you sure, Captain?"

Kellogg nodded his head, then shook it, then nodded again, obviously quite unsure as to what to tell the commanding general who was, by now, quite angry.

"If there is a gap," Rosecrans muttered, almost to himself. "We are in trouble." He moved to the map table and studied it for a moment, then made up his mind and said:

"Major Bond." Rosecrans turned to his Aid-de-Camp and continued, "Write to General Wood. He is to move his division and close up on General Reynolds right flank as quickly as possible.

"Captain Kellogg, you will take the order to General Wood and place it in his hand. Do you understand, Captain?"

"Yes, sir." Kellogg took the written order from Bond, stuffed it inside his tunic, mounted his horse, and rode away at the gallop. General

Rosecrans stared after him; little did he know that Kellogg was on his way to deliver orders to fill a gap that wasn't there.

Chapter 65

Sunday September 20th, 10:45am – General Wood

General Wood was not in the best of moods. Still smarting after the rebuke he had received earlier from General Rosecrans, and harboring no little resentment for it, when Kellogg arrived he snatched the order from him, tore it open and read as follows:

"The general commanding directs that you close up on Reynolds as fast as possible and support him. Respectfully, etc. Frank S. Bond, Major and Aid-de-Camp."

Wood stared at the order, totally bewildered by its ambiguity.

To Wood, the order required that he must do two things: first that he was to close up on Reynolds. To do that he would have to move his entire division to the left so that his own left flank would make contact with, and touch, Reynolds' right flank. Second, that to "support him" meant that he was to form his division behind Reynolds in column of brigade.

It was therefore obvious to Wood that he could not do both: he could not both form his division to the right of Reynolds' division and behind it at the same time. But there was more. Wood knew that Brannan's division was still on the battle line, between himself and Reynolds.

Fortunately, or perhaps unfortunately, for Wood, General Alexander McCook, commander of the XX Corps, was just to the rear of his, Wood's, division, on horseback, watching the action; his own corps commander, General Crittenden, was nowhere in sight.

Now thoroughly beset with indecision, Wood rode the few yards to where McCook was sitting and handed him the written order from General Rosecrans. McCook quickly scanned it and handed it back to Wood who folded it and inserted it inside his tunic.

"What am I to do, General?" Wood asked of McCook

For McCook, it was not his concern, so he shrugged, stared over Wood's head, and said, "You must, sir, do as the commanding general has ordered. Move your division as quickly as possible."

Wood, now totally frustrated said, "Yes, General, I will certainly move it, but move it where? I cannot move on Reynolds' right; General Brannan is holding that position, and if I move it behind Reynolds in support, I will leave a gap in the line here."

Again, McCook simply shrugged his shoulders, then said, "You must do as you think best, General, but were I you, I would move to the rear in support of General Reynolds. I will see to the gap."

Wood, now in no mood to argue with anybody, especially after the drubbing he had received from Rosecrans earlier that morning, saluted the corps commander, wheeled his horse and, without another word, galloped back to his division and gave the orders to his brigade commanders to move to the rear, and then to the left. As his brigades moved out, they left a gap in the Federal line of battle where none had been before. It was eleven o'clock.

Chapter 66

Sunday September 20th, 10:30am — Confederate Left Wing

General Longstreet, with a staff of more than a dozen officers, was conversing with five of his six division commanders - only General Stewart was absent - and he, Longstreet, was tired of waiting.

"I don't understand," Longstreet said, to no one in particular. "Why is General Cleburne not engaged? General Bragg's orders were clear, and specific. General Breckinridge, I assume it's General Breckinridge, has been engaged now for more than an hour, but there is still no movement to our right." He shook his head; he looked somewhat bemused. Then, as if in answer to his question, some five hundred yards to the north, he heard the ripple of gunfire as Cleburne's batteries opened fire: it was just after ten-thirty.

A little to the south of Cleburne's attack, General A.P. Stewart was at the head of his own division in deep conversation with his brigade commanders. Only moments after Cleburne opened fire, General Bragg's courier, Major Lee, arrived at the gallop.

"General Stewart, sir," He shouted, in order to be heard over the roar of gunfire. "I am from General Bragg. He is very distressed, sir, that the attack is delayed, and orders that all field commanders must immediately move upon the enemy."

"You may tell General Bragg that I will commence my attack at once," Stewart shouted. "And that I will be very pleased to do so." He saluted Lee, spun his horse to face his brigade commanders, and shouted:

"Well, gentlemen. It seems we need wait no more. To your brigades. We move on my guide."

Five minutes later, on Longstreet's right flank, Stewart's batteries opened up a firestorm of canister and shell that ripped through the trees and cleared a great swath in front of them.

"ADVANCE THE COLORS," Stewart shouted. Raising both of his arms, his sword in his right hand, his pistol in his left, he looked first to his left, down the line of General Brown's brigade, then to the right, and General Bate's brigade.

Other than the artillery fire to the rear, there was not a sound among the men in the long lines; it was as if every man had stopped breathing at the same time.

"GUIDE CENTER! Forward!" Stewart shouted, as he stepped off through the trees. Stewart's brigade was on the move, slowly at first, then gathering speed as they approached the green fields to the west. Then they were through, out into the open, out into a firestorm of canister and rifle fire.

Stewart broke into a run, heading for the log breastworks; so did Generals Brown and Bate. The had gone only a few yards when Stewart's third brigade, commanded by General Clayton, also burst from the trees and followed the two leading brigades into the open field.

Now, Stewart turned to face his charging division, running backwards, his back facing the enemy, yelling and shouting and waving pistol and sword in the air.

Four hundred yards away, in the log breastworks, three Federal batteries, eighteen guns, were hurling load after load of canister into the charging Confederate division. On the top of the rise, eight hundred yards away to the northeast, four more Federal batteries were firing case shot.

The effect of the canister on the Confederate division was devastating; fortunately, they were moving too fast for the batteries on the rise to do much damage, but Brown's brigade, now leading the other two, was coming under heavy flanking fire from Colonel King's Federal positions to the north. The Federal battle line was holding and Brown was forced to fall back, General Stewart along with him. General Bate and Clayton did not even make it to the Lafayette Road before they, too, were forced to fall back into the trees. It was eleven fifteen.

Three hundred yards to the south, Longstreet heard Stewart's artillery barrage begin, and he knew exactly what it must be.

"What in God's name?" He yelled. "Is that Stewart I hear?"

As if in answer to the question, Major Lee came galloping into the clearing where the Confederate officers were gathered. He pulled his horse violently to a stop and, breathless, he shouted the same message to Longstreet he had just relayed to General Stewart.

"Very well, Major. You may tell General Bragg that I hear and understand. And that I will move against the enemy directly."

Lee nodded his head, saluted, put spurs to horse and rode away out of the clearing.

Longstreet looked around at his division commanders, his horse stamping and rearing nervously.

"General Johnson, General Hindman, you may advance at will. General Hood, General Preston, General Kershaw," He saluted each general in turn as he shouted their names, "please ready your divisions. It is, at last, time we made our presence on the field felt"

General Johnson was but minutes away from his lead brigades. The mood among the men was charged, tense; everyone knew something was about to happen.

At the far right of the third rank of the third brigade, the 30th Tennessee, Billy Cobb and Jimmy Morrisey, after more than five hours of standing, sitting or lying down, were already on their feet and making ready to move. To their right, they could see Captain Culpepper readying his six guns; to the left, Bledsoe's Battery of four more guns was doing the same. The two brigades in line in front of them were all on their feet and straightening the lines. Brigadier General McNair and Colonels Fulton and Sugg were standing together in front of the two leading brigades, waiting for Johnson to arrive.

Morrisey took a small package from his tunic pocket, opened it, took out what was left of the small lump of black and very nasty looking tobacco, tore off a small piece and stuffed it into his mouth. Without looking, he passed what was left to his right, offering it to his friend. Billy refused, pushing it back and away. Morrisey returned what remained of the chewing tobacco to its wrapping, and then to his pocket.

It was exactly eleven o'clock when Johnson arrived at the head of his division. By then, Stewart's leading brigade was already across the Lafayette Road and had come under withering rifle and cannon fire from the front, left, and right of the Federal positions, now no more than a hundred yards away.

"Here we go," Morrisey shouted. "Good luck to you, Billy boy." As he said it, Johnson, having already sent orders to his battery commanders, dismounted, turned his horse over to an aid, faced his brigades, raised his sword, and signaled to each of the batteries to open fire.

Immediately, all three of Johnson's batteries, along with eight more all along the Confederate battle line opened fire, almost as one.

To Billy Cobb's right, all six guns of Captain Culpepper's battery roared together:

BAM, BAM, BAM, BAM, BAM, BAM. The noise was ear-shattering. Cobb and Morrisey watched as the six Hotchkiss shells arched over the trees and disappeared beyond them. Before they exploded among the Federals some six hundred yards away, the gun crews were already in action, it took them less than thirty seconds to reload and fire again. To their left, the batteries of Bledsoe and York were already maintaining a rate of fire of more than two rounds per minute.

To the front, at the head and center of the two leading Confederate brigades, General Johnson, unable to be heard over the crash of gunfire, signaled the charge. Johnson's division moved out at the double-quick, burst out through the trees. Screaming and yelling, they charged across the field toward the Lafayette Road.

To the left of Johnson's division, General Hindman also gave the order for his division to move forward.

Billy Cobb and Jimmy Morrisey followed Johnson's two leading brigades out of the trees at the quick march, and they watched as the two brigades charged across the fields toward the Lafayette Road.

The two leading Confederate brigades in line stretched north and south for a front almost four hundred yards wide. To their left, they could just see the right flank of General Hindman's division, also advancing in line with Johnson. Both divisions were now under heavy artillery and small arms fire from the ridge – Wilder's Spencers were creating havoc in the front lines.

Double- loaded canister from Lilly's guns on the rise was tearing great swaths in the front ranks of the advancing brigades. Often ten, even as many as fifteen, or sixteen soldiers at a time were literally blown off their feet by the firestorm of one-inch iron balls that hissed as they hurtled toward them. Limbs, hands, even heads were torn away by the iron clusters.

The two Confederate privates watched in awe at the carnage as they advanced slowly across the field.

"Oh, my God, Jim," Cobb yelled above the noise. "This is gonna be bad."

Morrisey said nothing; he just looked sideways at his friend, nodded his head quickly, just once, and chewed fiercely at the quid of tobacco.

Soon, they too were in range of the enemy's fire. To Jimmy's left, a canister ball slammed into the head of the man next to him, completely obliterating his face and spattering Jimmy with blood and brains. In front of them, two men went down, almost as one, but they moved on, stepping over them. All around them, men were staggering, falling, tripping; their heads down, one arm raised in front of their faces in a vain attempt to ward off the incoming hail of lead and iron.

And then the two leading brigades were at the breastworks, and the incoming cannon fire slowed almost to nothing, the Federal gun crews not wanting to kill their own troops.

The Federal defenders in front of General McNair's brigade put up a stubborn, but short, fight before being slowly pushed back. General Fulton's brigade, to the left of McNair, hit the gap left by the recent departure of General Wood's Federal division, and blasted on through with little to no resistance.

As General Johnson's division moved forward across the Lafayette Road, a little more than six hundred yards away to the north, the 10th Indiana was at the front and center of Brigadier General John Brannan's Federal division facing General Stewart's charge.

Just to the north of Johnson's charging troops, General Stewart's leading brigade commanded by Brigadier General Brown had made it all the way to the Federal breastworks where they slammed into two Federal brigades in line: Connell's and Croxton's. The three Confederate regiments on Stewart's left drove Connell's brigade back from the breastworks in heavy hand-to-hand fighting. But Connell's men rallied and counter attacked, driving the Confederates back and retaking the breastworks, the Federal positions were holding, barely.

To Connell's left, Croxton's brigade, including the 10th Indiana, was also holding steady and, slowly, Confederate General Bate's brigade, under shattering artillery and small arms fire, from all sides and the ridges to the east, was driven back across the Lafayette Road and into the trees. The Federal line of battle was seemingly invulnerable....

Chapter 67
Sunday September 20th, 11am Federal Line of Battle

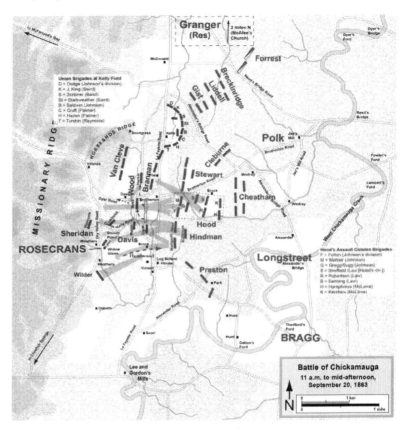

Jesse Dixon and Pat McCann were hunkered down behind the log breastworks on the right flank of the 10th Indiana when the first shots from General Stewart's artillery came screeching in over the trees. One after another, six Hotchkiss shells arched overhead, and then down to explode in the air some fifty yards to the rear. They did little physical damage, just a few shrapnel wounds among the soldiers lying prone at the rear of the defenses.

Jesse Dixon looked over the top of the logs and, to his dismay, he saw the first fluttering Confederate banners emerge from the trees some four hundred yards away to the east beyond the Lafayette Road. As he watched, the banners were followed by rank upon rank of gray-clad soldiers of General Stewart's division.

"Get ready, Pat," he shouted. "They're coming."

Patrick McCann was seated with his back against the logs; he looked up at Jesse, nodded his head, and raised himself up and turned so that he too could see over the top of the logs. What he saw filled him with dread and an overbearing fear, but this time he didn't panic. He rested his already loaded Springfield rifle on the topmost log and sighted on the oncoming gray line.

"Wait for it, Pat," Jesse yelled. "Wait for Taylor."

McCann merely nodded in reply. He felt his gorge rising. He shook his head, clamped his teeth together and his cheeks bulged as the bile rose in his throat. He tried to force himself to relax, to think of something else, but he could think of nothing but the oncoming wave of gray. The noise was unbearable; the continuous crash of the cannons, a self-sustaining ripple of earsplitting explosions that shook the ground beneath him. His teeth were bared, his fingers rigid on the rifle, and he watched as the advancing Confederate line drew ever closer.

Only a few yards away to their right, Lieutenant Marco Gray was pacing back and forth to the rear of the six Parrott rifles of his 1st Ohio Battery C. From somewhere to the rear, they heard a shout, but could not make out the words; Marco Gray, however, could. He stopped pacing and turned to face his guns.

"READY," He shouted.

Each of the six gun Chiefs signaled that they were.

"COMMENCE FIRING!"

And six gunners pulled their lanyards in unison.

BAMBAMBAMBAMBAMBAM: six deafening explosions shook the ground, the logs, and the defenders as the great guns went into action. Six double loads of canister hurtled across the Lafayette Road and the field beyond and tore into the Confederate front rank, stripping away the clothing, flesh, and limbs of forty, or more, men in the front rank. The front rank did not falter in the slightest; men from the rear ranks quickly moved forward and filled the gaps in the line; and on they came, now at the run.

The gap between the charging Confederate brigades and the Federal breastworks was closing. Confederate General Brown's brigade charged across the Lafayette Road; the distance between the two opposing sides was down to less than two hundred yards, then one hundred and fifty.

At one hundred yards, Lieutenant Colonel Marsh Taylor stepped forward and shouted the order,

"FIRE BY FILE!"

All along the Federal line of battle, regimental commanders also gave the order for their ranks to commence firing.

Jesse Dixon and Patrick McCann looked sideways at each other, nodded their heads, looked forward again, pulled back the hammers of their Springfields, aimed, and fired. Immediately they both rolled over onto their backs and went into action reloading their weapons.

"Slow down, Pat." Jesse yelled. "Take it nice and slow."

But McCann didn't look up. He completed the loading sequence, rose up, sited the weapon over the logs, fired, and then dropped back down to load again.

To their right, the six guns of Battery C were keeping up a steady rate of fire. They were not working as fast as they might, but every shot was taking its toll.

The massed ranks of General Brown's Confederate brigade were slowing. Men were dropping to one knee, reloading and firing, moving forward a few yards, then dropping down and firing again.

The virtual hurricane of shot, shell, canister, and Minnie balls was decimating Brown's brigade. At a distance of fifty yards, point-blank range, his men were making little to no impression upon the defenders behind the breastworks; those same defenders were, however, taking a heavy toll on his brigade; already he had lost more than thirty percent of his force. He had no other option but to call for his men to fall back. This they did, at first in good order, and then they ran for the trees, falling and stumbling over General Clayton's advancing brigade as they went.

All along the Federal line, cheering, yelling, shouting, and laughing broke out as the defenders watched the retreating Confederate division.

Together, Jesse Dixon and Pat McCann, backs to the logs, slid down until they were sitting side by side on the hard-packed earth. They looked at each other, then laughed aloud and punched each other's arms.

Chapter 68

Sunday September 20th, 11:05am – Bushrod Johnson's Division

Confederate General McNair's brigade hit the barricades hard, but they were too strong. Colonel John Connell's Federal brigade was holding the position at the extreme left flank of General Brannan's division just to the left of the gap left by Wood's departure. Connell's men put up a stubborn and very bloody fight. Firing by file, they kept up a non-stop hail of Minnie bullets that decimated McNair's leading ranks.

McNair's brigade faltered, and then stopped altogether, only yards in front of the log barricades. They fell back and regrouped, then pressed forward again. This time they went through the gap in the Federal line, wheeled to the right, making room for Sugg's brigade to pass through the gap on their, McNair's, left, and slammed into Connell's flank. This time, there was no stopping McNair's Confederates. They charged forward at the run, firing as they went, and scrambled over the logs, fighting hand-to-hand with bayonet and gun butt.

The 82nd Indiana, took the brunt of the attack, and was overwhelmed; the 14th and 31st Ohio regiments, to the left of the 82nd, collapsed, turned, and retreated. Almost at once, Connell's brigade was on the run. McNair's brigade had the breastworks. Dozens of his men braved the incoming hail of lead and iron and jumped on top of the logs, banners waving, yelling, and cheering. It was a grand sight, but one that had cost McNair dearly: he had lost more than forty percent of his brigade.

In the meantime, Sugg's Confederate brigade had inserted itself between the two leading Confederate brigades, and was already pushing on through the gap in the Federal line to McNair's left, screaming, and howling as they went.

Connell's Federal brigade, now vastly outnumbered and in complete disarray, was streaming away, up the hill to the northwest. For them, the battle of Chickamauga was over. And they were not on their own.

Confederate General Fulton's brigade, now to the left of Sugg, had found Colonel George Buell's Federal brigade, the remnants of Wood's division still trying to comply with Rosecrans' orders to fill the gap that wasn't there. Buell's brigade was still on the move, marching northward in column, but lagging behind Wood's two leading brigades.

Fulton's brigade slammed into the flank of Buell taking them completely by surprise; the effect was devastating: Buell's soldiers had no chance to respond. They were mown down where they stood. They started to fall back, but the hailstorm of rifle and canister fire from the advancing Confederate brigades was too much. They panicked, and what started as a hasty withdrawal turned into a rout as they turned and ran for their lives, away from the battlefield in complete disarray.

And it was the same all across the southern end of the battlefield. General Davis' division, along with that of General Sheridan, was hit by elements of Fulton's brigade, and by General Hindman's entire division. General Davis could do no more than watch as his division disintegrated under the overwhelming Confederate onslaught. Within minutes, Davis' entire division was streaming westward away from the battlefield, closely followed by that of General Sheridan.

General Fulton's brigade, in line with and to the left of General McNair's brigade, hit the gap in the Federal line created by the recent and rapid departure of General Wood's Federal division, and blasted straight on through, General Johnson leading the charge with Fulton at his side.

Johnson was so excited he was rushing forward with little regard for his own safety; Colonel Fulton, trying to keep up with him, was yelling for him to take care, but Johnson was having little of it. On he ran, sword waving over his head, yelling for his men to keep up, "give them hell, boys."

Then he stumbled, almost fell, but managed to regain his balance. He stopped running, put his head down, his hands on his knees, and gasped for breath. Fulton also stopped, and so did the long lines of Fulton's brigade, most of them dropping to their knees to reload their rifles. They were in the open fields just to the west of the Brotherton house.

It was to be a short-lived respite. Lilly's battery on the rise to the south of the Widow Glenn's house already was turning and ranging his guns to bear on Johnson's brigade.

Johnson stood upright, gazed around him, caring little for the hissing of the bullets as they passed close to him. As he looked back over the ground he had just covered, to his far left, he could just see Tom Hindman's Confederate division. Hindman, too, was across the Lafayette Road and moving quickly to engage the two Federal divisions of Jefferson C. Davis and Philip Sheridan.

Behind him, he could see his own third brigade, Sugg's, now moving into position between Fulton and McNair; McNair's advance having stalled when it hit the right flank of Connell's brigade. To the rear, just to the east of the Lafayette Road, General Hood, at the head of his own division, was on horseback, urging his brigades forward in support of Sugg and Fulton.

Johnson was in awe. Never in his life had he seen anything like it. Thousands upon thousands of Confederate soldiers were moving like a great, flowing tidal wave; hundreds of red, blue, white, and gold banners fluttered in the breeze and, even above the incessant roar of gunfire, he could hear the beating of the drums and the call of the bugles sounding the charge. It was a heroic site, one he would never forget, but he had no time to dwell upon this glorious vision; all hell was breaking out around him.

He dropped to one knee and turned to Fulton, "We must keep going." He shouted, pointing toward Lilly's Federal battery. "If we stay here, they will tear us apart." He was breathing heavily. "Colonel," he shouted, pointing in the direction of two more Federal batteries that he knew were just beyond the top of the rise in front of them, but could no longer see, "we must take those batteries.

"Corporal," he shouted over his shoulder to a man on both knees just behind him. "Go to Lieutenant Everett; tell him to bring forward his battery and place it in the field, there." He indicated a spot just to the south of the Brotherton house. "He will know what to do, but you must tell him to engage that battery, just to the left of the house on the hill, and make it hot for them, or they will do for us all." Again, he indicated the position where Lilly was about to open fire.

Then, with a great yell, Johnson was on his feet and running forward, up the rise toward the two Federal batteries. "Come on, boys. Those guns are ours."

At that same moment, the first of Lilly's guns opened fire, with devastating results, but there was time only to get off one barrage; General Hindman's brigade was already at the bottom of the rise and moving fast toward them. Wilder and Lilly could do no more than defend themselves against the gray, screaming hoard that was flowing across the fields below them.

Finding themselves now right at the front of Sugg's charging brigade, and only yards behind General Johnson himself, Billy Cobb and Jimmy Morrisey threw all caution to the winds.

The two men were oblivious of the carnage that was being created around them. Solid cannon shot, shells, and canister were tearing great gaps in the ranks on either side of them, but they, too, seemed to be invincible; not a single projectile came even close to them. On and on they ran, hurdling over fallen bodies, firing and screaming as they went, voices cracking, choking as they ran through seemingly solid banks of gun smoke, stopping every dozen yards or so to reload their now smoking

Springfields. The noise was intolerable, an incessant, never-ending crackling ripple of rifle fire, hissing canister balls, exploding shells and thousands of screaming, charging men.

Three men to Cobb's right took a double load of canister head on; their bodies were ripped and shredded by dozens of one-inch-iron balls. One man's arm was ripped clean off at the shoulder, another ball struck him in the chest, two more smashed his right leg; he spun in the air, blood from his shoulder spraying out in all directions; he was dead before he hit the ground. Another man was struck twice in the face; he was hurled backwards, landed flat on his back and lay still. The third man took a single ball low in his groin; it passed clean through, shattering his pelvis and pulverizing his innards, and tearing a huge exit wound in his lower back as it went through. He stopped running, a surprised expression on his face, looked down at the small hole in his pants, dropped his rifle, grabbed his groin and sank slowly to his knees, then pitched over sideways.

Cobb and Morrisey had no time for words, not that they could be heard if there was; barely was there time enough to reload.

All around them, men were falling as the never-ending barrage from the Federal positions ripped and tore into the Confederate ranks but, by some miracle, the two of them continued on unscathed. Leaping over one body after another, dodging this way and that, they charged on up the hill, always keeping an eye on General Johnson, who seemed to be living a charmed life.

Johnson seemed to be in another world, to have taken on some wild and crazy new identity. Screaming like a demon, his eyes wild and popping, his hat hanging by its cord behind him, his hair flying loose, a wild and wooly nest, his frock coat torn and rent in several places by the passage of bullet and shrapnel, but not a single a scratch did Johnson receive.

Then they crested the hill and slammed into the two Federal batteries. If the fighting had been desperate before, it now became frantic as the two sides fought hand-to-hand. But it was a one-sided battle. Armed only with broadswords, he artillerists were not equipped for such close quarters combat. As the screaming Confederates charged up the hill, they threw solid shot and canister balls down upon them. Then, as the fighting continued among the guns, they hacked at the enemy with their swords. But it was to no avail; in less than two minutes the Federal gun crews were running from the field, leaving the victorious attackers in control of twelve three-inch guns, more than sixty men either dead or wounded, and almost as many horses; most of those dead, or close to it.

And then, all was quiet, at least for the moment.

General Johnson stood just forward of the captured guns and surveyed the battlefield to the east. Hardened veteran that he was, he was not prepared for what he now saw. The open fields spread out before him were littered with dead and wounded soldiers.

Johnson was now more than a mile beyond his starting point, and he was on his own with the remains of his division. It was a glorious victory for him, but the costs were high. He had lost more than thirty-five percent of his division. General McNair himself was seriously wounded, and he had lost more than forty percent of his brigade.

Billy Cobb and Jimmy Morrisey were no less devastated by the awesome sight than was General Johnson. Still with nary a scratch between them, they leaned over the barrel of one of the captured guns and gazed out over the battlefield in silence. Stones River had been devastating for both of them, but they had had no idea of the big picture. Here at Chickamauga, the battlefield lay before them like a vast tapestry. As far as the eye could see, the ground seemed to be moving as the wounded lay like ants, twitching, squirming, waving their arms. Dead soldiers lay everywhere. In the distance, to the south, they could see General Hindman's division still engaged, but moving steadily up the rise toward the Widow Glenn's house.

General Johnson, realizing his now over-exposed position, sent his aide-de-camp, Captain Blakemore, to deliver his report to General Longstreet, and to request reinforcements. It took less than five minutes to write the report and send Blakemore on his way. Johnson and his brigades then turned again to the task in hand, and it was onward once again toward Snodgrass Hill more than a mile away to the north.

Meanwhile, all was not well with General Thomas. He was now under heavy pressure from the three Confederate divisions advancing from the east, those of Generals Walker, Liddell, and Breckinridge, with General Cleburne's division moving swiftly northward to support them.

Chapter 69

Sunday September 20th, 11am – Wilder's Positions at the Widow
Glenn's Cabin

At eleven o'clock, up on the rise, just to the east of the Dry Valley
Road, and south of the Widow Glenn's house, John Wilder's brigade was
hunkered down behind their log breastworks. Behind them, a small group
of officers, including Wilder, Blake Winter, Colonels Atkins, Funkhouser,
Monroe, and Major Jones, were standing together talking and smoking
cigars.

For several hours, they had been listening to the sounds of the battle
raging away to the north, but slowly, surly moving southward toward
them. They had been listening to it, but could see little, just the great
clouds of blue-gray smoke rising above the trees.

"Look," Colonel Monroe said, pointing to the east. "I think I see
something; just there, at the edge of the trees. Do you see?"

All six officers had their field glasses to their eyes.

All along the line of trees, which stretched for almost a mile from north
to south, three hundred yards to the east of the Lafayette Road, it seemed
as if the trees had come to life. At a distance of more than one thousand
yards, it seemed if they were moving, rippling, heaving, much like an
anthill.

As they watched, small swatches of color, flags, banners, guidons, men
on horseback, on foot, then long lines of gray-clad soldiers emerged from
the undergrowth marching slowly forward, row after row, rank after rank,
they moved steadily across the fields toward the Lafayette Road. Within
minutes, the fields were covered in an unbroken sea of gray and
thousands of bayonets glittering in the sunshine.

Way off in the distance, even over the din from the north, they could
hear the rolling drums and the sweet, echoing sounds of bugles. Then
they heard what at first seemed to be thunder rolling over the treetops as
more than thirty Confederate cannon opened fire. And then they heard
the yelling and screaming of the charging soldiers, and the shrieks of the
incoming Hotchkiss shells.

To the rear of the charging Confederate brigades, beyond the trees to
the east, a huge pall of blue-gray smoke rose into the sky. From the ridge,
the view was both terrible and awesome to behold.

"My God," Wilder said, "have you ever seen anything like it?"

No one had, and they continued to watch as the seething, gray sea
continued to grow.

Finally, with a shake of his head, Wilder said, "Well, gentlemen. It would seem we have a little work to do.

"Captain Lilly, please see to your guns. Load Hotchkiss and aim for the front ranks; you may fire at will, sir."

Lilly saluted, spun on his heel, and ran to his guns, shouting orders as he ran.

"Gentlemen, go to your regiments, but do not fire until I give the word. Then keep those Spencers hot."

No sooner had he spoken, than the first of Lilly's Parrotts opened fire. Together, the six officers watched as the lone Hotchkiss shell arched up, and then over the Brotherton house and the Lafayette Road and exploded more than fifty feet above the advancing Confederate divisions. A second, and then a third followed the first shot; within a matter of seconds, all of Lilly's six guns were in action. The assembled Federal officers watched in awe at the carnage Lilly's guns were inflicting upon the enemy. Carnage or not, the barrage did little to slow, much less stop, the Confederate advance.

Soon the leading brigades were across the Lafayette Road, and moving on past the Brotherton house, and still wave after wave of Confederate soldiers continued to emerge from the trees. Behind the breastworks, Wilder's Spencers remained silent.

Then, as they watched, the leading Confederate brigade, in the fields now several hundred yards to the west of the Brotherton house, slowed and then stopped.

Through their glasses, Wilder's officers could see the figures at the front, one a general officer and several lower ranks, were conversing.

"Lieutenant Roy," Wilder shouted.

"Sir," The lieutenant jumped to his feet and ran to Wilder.

"Mr. Roy, please go to Captain Lilly as ask him if he might be able to do something about those officers down there," he said pointing toward the small group in the field below.

"Yes, sir." Roy turned and ran to where Lilly was directing his guns.

Wilder watched as Lilly bent his head to listen to Roy as he shouted in his ear, then nodded and turned back to his guns. Lilly walked quickly to the rear of the two Parrotts at the left side of his battery. The two guns were quickly turned and Lilly put himself to estimating the range. He looked through his glasses at the Confederate officers, and was surprised to see the general looking right back at him, and pointing. It unnerved him not a little. And, even as he calculated the range, the Confederates were moving forward again, and at the run; fast as they were running, Lilly could not keep a bead on them.

Chapter 70

Sunday September 20th, 11:30am – Federal Line of Battle

At eleven-thirty, General Hood's division, following General Johnson, crossed the Lafayette Road and wheeled to the right

In the Federal defensive line, with Connell's brigade now gone from the field, Colonel Croxton's brigade was next in line, facing the Confederate advance, with Brigadier General John King's brigade supporting his left flank.

Brigadier General Henry Benning's Confederate brigade moved across the Lafayette Road and on through the gap in the Federal line, then wheeled to the right and charged northward toward Croxton's line.

Croxton realized he was in deep trouble and immediately gave orders to his regimental commanders to pull their units back into the trees at the northern edge of the Poe field. Croxton's new line in the trees was facing south and, ready or not, he prepared to meet Hood's advancing Confederate division.

The 10th Indian was on Croxton's left flank, end on to the Lafayette Road, and the situation there was critical. Hood's Confederate division, led by General Benning's brigade, was now moving quickly toward the newly and hastily erected Federal line of battle, to the front of which Jesse Dixon and Pat McCann were now standing in line, rifles at the ready.

"You all right, Pat? Jesse yelled.

His friend did not answer; he seemed not to have heard. He seemed riveted to the floor, every muscle in his body was rigid. The crotch of his blue pants was wet. Patrick McCann was already in shock, and had retreated into some quiet world of his own.

Two hundred yards away to the south, Jesse could see the front rank of the advancing Confederate division. Just to the front and right, Croxton's Battery C opened fire on the advancing gray-clad hoard:

BAM… BAM… BAM… BAM… BAM… BAM… six rounds of double-shotted canister screamed through the trees toward Benning's troops. The effect was devastating, but before the Federal battery could reload, the enemy was upon them.

Croxton's brigade began to fall apart. The three regiments to the right took the brunt of the Confederate charge and were quickly overwhelmed by sheer force of numbers. The crews of the six guns of Battery C were desperately trying to hold onto their pieces; the fighting around them was hand-to-hand. One by one, the three Federal regiments gave way and tried to retreat; the retreat quickly turned into a rout with men streaming away through the trees toward Snodgrass Hill.

Seeing that his brigade was being crushed, Colonel Croxton ordered his two remaining regiments to pull back through the trees and reform. The 10th Indiana, along with the 74th Indiana, pulled back as ordered, but somehow managed to separate themselves from the rest of the brigade and retreated slowly northward along the west side of the Lafayette Road.

Jesse grabbed his friend by the arm and wrenched him round, almost pulling him off his feet.

"C'mon, Pat. We gotta get outa here," he yelled in McCann's ear.

McCann responded; he seemed to come out of his trance-like state. He stood for a moment, stared wildly around him, then at Jesse, nodded his head, several times, very quickly and, together they ran after the retreating 10th Indiana.

General Brannan's division had been completely shattered; his brigades were decimated and running northward.

Connell's brigade had been completely routed and was in full flight. Remnants of the brigade were scattered all across the western edge of the battlefield, beyond the Dry Valley Road, and were heading toward Missionary Ridge, taking some of Croxton's men along with them.

Croxton's brigade had been decimated; it had lost more than forty percent of its numbers. Croxton had no idea of what had become of his regiments; they were scattered and streaming away to the north. But no matter, Croxton himself was not yet finished, and he was determined to continue the fight. By two o'clock in the afternoon, he had managed to gather together all he could of what was left of his brigade, and he gave orders for them to pull back and reform on the heights of the hill just to the north.

From their vantage point on Snodgrass Hill, Jesse Dixon and Patrick McCann looked down upon the battlefield that stretched for miles, in almost every direction. And everywhere, they could see blue-clad soldiers running from the field, some of them were heading toward them and would, eventually, join them on Snodgrass Hill. Exhausted, the two men dropped to the ground....

Chapter 71

Sunday September 20th, 11:15am — Rosecrans' Retreat

As General Longstreet's divisions swept across the Lafayette Road, General Rosecrans, accompanied by his staff and Assistant Secretary Dana, was on horseback just to the west and rear of General Davis's division on the slopes of the hill north of the Widow Glenn's house. He was watching the action on the Lafayette Road and conferring with members of his staff, General Crittenden, and two of his division commanders, General Sheridan and Davis. The small group watched from above, Rosecrans with a slight smile on his face, as Connell and Croxton held their ground, and Brown's Confederates retreated into the woods. Rosecrans was a happy man.

With his field glasses to his eyes, he scoured the line of trees east of the Lafayette Road, nodding his head in approval as Brown's brigade reached the trees, turned and dropped to the ground, seeking whatever cover they could find. Slowly, he scanned the tree line south of Brown's positions, then stopped and stared. What he saw took his breath away. The trees themselves seemed to be alive. It was an illusion; the edge of the woods was a solid mass of humanity; thousands of Confederate soldiers were advancing toward the road, rank upon rank, brigade after brigade: the line stretched north and south for almost a mile.

At the bottom of the ridge, the long lines of Federal soldiers in the breastworks were now taking heavy fire from eight batteries of Confederate artillery: shell after shell slammed into the Federal breastworks, or burst in the air above them; either way the carnage was devastating, casualties were too numerous even to estimate.

Even as Rosecrans watched, the leading elements of General Hindman's division smashed into those of Generals Davis and Sheridan. Sheridan's division was moving to the north and was completely surprised by the sudden and devastating onslaught. Those two generals, now supposedly conferring with their commanding general, watched with him as the front lines of their divisions began to give, and then break.

General Davis' division was the first to fold, and then General Manigault's Confederate brigade slammed into Davis' front rank with such ferocity that the Federals had no other alternative than to run or die, and run they did. Slowly, the rest of Davis' division collapsed before him; both he, Sheridan, Rosecrans, Dana and the entire Federal staff watched open-mouthed and in abject horror as the entire Right Wing of the Army of the Cumberland began to collapse.

Within only a matter of minutes, Davis' division was in full flight and streaming westward toward the Widow Glenn's cabin, and General Rosecrans' assemblage on the hilltop.

Next to fall was General Sheridan's Second Brigade under the command of Colonel Bernard Laiboldt; his resistance lasted no longer than that of General Davis' leading element only moments before: General Zach Deas' brigade of Hindman's division simply ran right over them, and they too ran from the field in panic.

Soon, both divisions were in full flight and streaming westward. Rosecrans and his gathering were slap bang in the middle of the rushing tide. All three generals tried in vain to rally the routed brigades but it was to no avail. The tide of panicking Federal soldiers was unstoppable; General Lytle of Sheridan's division was killed in the exodus.

Now it was Rosecrans' turn to panic, and he did, though he did it with some dignity. As the blue-clad hoard rushed on by, he turned in the saddle and, waving one hand in the air while trying to control his surging horse with the other, he shouted to the gathered officers and observers, "We have to get out of here. If not, we will be killed or taken."

And so it began. Still trying to rally the troops as they ran past them, Generals Rosecrans, Crittenden, Sheridan, and Davis allowed themselves to be swept along by the surging tide of retreating Federals, first westward through McFarland's Gap, then on into Rossville and finally Chattanooga. The Federal Army of the Cumberland was, with one exception, leaderless. Only General Thomas continued his tenuous hold on the breastworks he had defended for so long, but all that was about to change.

In the meantime, only Colonel Wilder's brigade, in position on the rise just to the south of the Widow Glenn's house, was standing between Rosecrans and death or capture. His brigade was hurling a hailstorm of bullets and artillery fire at the advancing Confederate brigades. Finally, even Wilder could not see any good resolution to the deteriorating situation, and he began making plans to move north and join his brigade with General Thomas.

Chapter 72

Sunday September 20th, 12:30p.m. – General Thomas Field headquarters

By twelve thirty in the early afternoon, General Thomas was beginning to feel the pressure from the now almost encircling Confederate forces. His own divisions had been engaged almost non-stop since nine-thirty in the morning; it had been a very long three hours. While the front of his breastworks, facing east, were still holding strong, his left and right flanks were slowly yielding to the determined Confederate attackers. The left flank had been pushed back and was now facing north, while the right flank, at the southern end of the breastworks had also been pushed back and was now facing due south.

By one o'clock, General Stewart's Confederate division was pressing Thomas's right flank hard, while General Liddell's division was doing the same to the north; what once was a crescent-shaped defensive line was now a giant inverted "C" with its tips growing ever closer.

Major General Gordon Grainger, commanding the Federal Reserve Corps at McAfee's Church some two and a half miles away to the north of the Snodgrass Farm, was impatiently awaiting orders to move his divisions to join with General Thomas.

All morning long, Grainger, together with Brigadier General James Steedman, and Colonel Daniel McCook, commanding the First and Second Divisions of the Reserve Corps, had been listening to the faraway sounds of the battle. Grainger, an aggressive battlefield commander, was not happy to be so far away from the action, and Steedman and McCook were of a like mind.

Far away to the south, the thunder of heavy guns could be heard rolling across the fields like a distant thunderstorm.

Grainger and his commanders discussed their options, of which there were not many.

Well aware of the close proximity of the Confederate Cavalry, and lacking specific orders from the commanding general, Grainger was reluctant to commit the Reserve Corps in its entirety. After some little discussion, now knowing that Thomas was alone on the battlefield, the three men agreed that he, Thomas, must receive help. Grainger ordered Steedman to move his division of two brigades south in support of Thomas, and to move as quickly as possible. Steedman's division was under way by eleven-thirty; the march to Snodgrass Hill would take more than two hours.

261

Chapter 73
Sunday September 20th, 1p.m. – Wilder's Brigade

Colonel John Wilder, his face grimy from the sweat and dust, was hunkered down behind the log breastworks on the top of the hill just to the southwest of the Widow Glenn's cabin. For almost three hours, his brigade had tried to help the fortunes of the Federal divisions in the fields below. The rate of fire from the Spencer repeating rifles had effectively turned his single brigade into five. But, try as they might, the outcome of the battle was in no doubt. Now, Wilder and his staff could only watch as the entire right flank of the Federal army collapsed and streamed westward off the battlefield in disarray.

The view from the top of the hill was mind boggling. For more than a mile in every direction the battlefield was littered with thousands of dead, dying and wounded soldiers of both sides; they lay like a gaudy, multicolored carpet, the blue and gray uniforms blending with the green of the grass. Hundreds of horses lay dead; many more were on their sides struggling, twisting, and trying to regain their feet. The noise of gunfire was, by now, somewhat abated; only the muted roar of battle to the north where General Thomas still held tenuously onto what was left of the army's right flank could be heard.

Down the hill to the southeast, Hazelwood was a hive of activity. Blake Winter could see Confederate officers coming and going in every direction. The tent village that housed the wounded had grown to immense proportions. Hazelwood itself was unscathed. He wondered at the luck, or whatever guardian angel, that had protected the house through the maelstrom. He took a deep breath, and then slowly shook his head as he pulled his field glasses from their pouch and tried to get a glimpse of Sarah, but there was none.

Wilder called together his officers and staff; there were decisions to be made.

"Well, gentlemen, I have received word from General Sheridan. It would seem that our commanding general and all of his staff have left the field. General Sheridan says that we are to get out while we can, and that leaves us with something of a predicament: what are we to do? If we stay here, we will be overrun, and that I do not want to happen. Nor do I wish to follow General Rosecrans into oblivion. From the noise," he pointed toward the rising clouds of smoke away to the north, "General Thomas appears to still be engaged. I am of a mind to join him. Gentlemen?"

The assembled officers looked at each other and, one by one, they nodded in agreement.

"Good," Wilder said, "then I suggest we move quickly. Captain Lilly, please limber your guns and prepare to move out on my command. The rest of you, please prepare your regiments. We will move out on foot as soon as Captain Lilly is ready; the horses will follow on behind."

Less than twenty minutes later, Wilder's column was on the move north across the field that so lately General Bushrod Johnson had crossed in the other direction.

They had not been on the move very many minutes when a single rider came over the crest of the hill. He stopped, put glasses to his eyes, and then came on at the full gallop.

On reaching Wilder at the front of the column, he pulled his horse to a skidding halt, and shouted excitedly, "Who are you, sir? What unit?"

"I am Colonel John Wilder commanding the First Brigade, 4th Division of the XIV Corps. And who might you be, sir?"

"I, sir," the red-headed, somewhat bedraggled man said, "am Charles A. Dana, Assistant Secretary of War, and I have become detached from General Rosecrans' party. I need assistance, Colonel Wilder."

"Mr. Dana. I am going to join with General Thomas. Do you know where General Rosecrans is? Do you know the state of the battle elsewhere?

"Dana, breathing heavily, ran his fingers through his hair, shook his head, and glared at Wilder.

"Colonel Wilder," he said, agitatedly, "I repeat, I am Charles A. Dana, Assistant Secretary of War. I was with the commanding general and his staff when the enemy overran us. As to General Rosecrans, I have no idea, sir, of his whereabouts or disposition. I became separated from him. He is either killed or captured I am sure. The army is routed, routed, Sir. You, Colonel," Dana continued, "have the only intact unit left on the entire battlefield. It is imperative, sir, that you escort me at once to Chattanooga; I must telegraph the news of this defeat to Washington."

"Mr. Dana, sir. I suggest you calm down. You were heading away from Chattanooga, not toward it. Had you not ran into us, you would soon have been a guest of General Bragg.

"The firing to the north, Mr. Dana, has not changed position in more than an hour, and the heavy fighting there suggests a major battle is being fought and, sir, that I do not have the only brigade left on the field."

But Dana was not convinced and seemed to Wilder to be in a state bordering on panic.

"No, sir," Dana insisted. "What is happening over there is that the enemy is pursuing and killing General Thomas's men. Again, Colonel

Wilder, I am Charles A. Dana, Assistant Secretary of War, and I order you to move your command and escort me to Chattanooga as I requested."

"That, Mr. Dana, I cannot do. I can, however, provide you with a scout and a small escort. They will be able to get you quickly to Chattanooga. Do you accept to my offer, Mr. Dana?"

Dana reluctantly nodded his agreement, then said, "I will accept your scouts, Sir, but my orders for you are to fall back to Chattanooga and place your command on Lookout Mountain and hold it at all hazards. Chattanooga must not fall into enemy hands."

Wilder was nonplussed. Never before had he heard of a civilian giving orders to a military unit, even in time of war. But Dana was indeed a very high-ranking civilian, and a member of the War Cabinet to boot, albeit an assistant secretary. And who was he, a mere colonel, to question such a man? Therefore, with a shrug of his shoulders, he did as Dana ordered. He regrouped his brigade and turned west toward McFarland's Gap and Chattanooga.

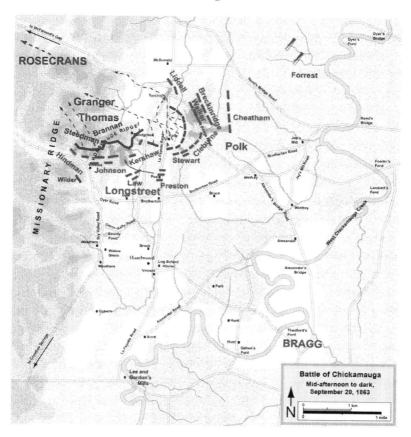

By one o'clock, the collapse of the Federal right flank was complete. The Confederate forces under the command of General Longstreet held most of the entire battlefield south and west of the Kelly farm, and south of Snodgrass Hill and Horseshoe Ridge.

The commanding general of the Army of the Cumberland, William Rosecrans, and two Federal corps, the XX, and the XXI, along with their commanding generals, Crittenden and McCook, had been routed and driven from the field in disarray. Only General George Thomas remained in the field and that only by virtue of his strong defensive positions at the

265

Kelly farm and Snodgrass Hill. His positions were, however, in imminent danger of being flanked, both left and right, and being overrun.

To the east of the Federal positions at the Kelly farm, Confederate General Leonidas Polk commanding the Confederate Right Wing of the Army of Tennessee was still assaulting, though piecemeal, the Federal positions there with six divisions. Polk had assaulted Thomas's breastworks more than a dozen times; each attack was repulsed with the Confederate brigades suffering heavy casualties. Polk's Right Wing had, by two o'clock, settled down, under whatever cover they could find and were keeping up a steady rate of fire against the log defensive barricades.

To the south, General Longstreet, his Left Wing of the army having broken through the Federal line of battle and swept the field clean, was positioning his divisions to assault the Federal right flank, Snodgrass Hill and Horseshoe Ridge. General Hood had been severely wounded, having been hit in the upper right thigh by a Minnie bullet and knocked from his horse; it was a wound that would cost him is leg.

The scope of the breakthrough by the Confederate Left Wing was all-encompassing. Longstreet's entire force was stretched from just to the west of the Dry Valley Road to a point some five hundred yards east of the Lafayette Road, a distance of almost a mile and a half, and they were now facing north toward the Federal right flank, Snodgrass Hill and Horseshoe Ridge, and they were driving the remaining Federal brigades before them.

There was little order among the Federal troops as they retreated before Longstreet's onslaught. Here and there, small groups would gather together, rally, and then turn and face the enemy in a valiant, but futile, attempt to stem the onrushing tide of gray-clad soldiers. Time and again, small pockets of Federal resistance were dealt with and either swept away or sent streaming back across the fields toward Horseshoe Ridge.

One such pocket of resistance consisted of the remnants of Connell's brigade of General Brannan's division. This band of stalwarts, consisting mostly of the 82nd Indiana had conducted a running battle all the way from the Brotherton farm to Horseshoe Ridge, a distance of more than half a mile, stopping every fifty yards, or so, to turn and fire at the pursuing Confederate brigades.

The 82nd Indiana was commanded by Colonel Morton C. Hunter of Bloomington, Indiana. Hunter was something of an enigma: on the one side a tough and unforgiving commander, on the other a man with a soft heart and an inordinate concern for the well-being of his troops, a trait that had led him to face a courts martial only months before the battle.

The good colonel had taken it upon himself to give a sick lieutenant a pass to leave the brigade and go to hospital for treatment. It was a pass he did not have the authority to give; thus, he was charged with conduct prejudicial to good order and military discipline. Hunter was ultimately acquitted of all charges, but there's no doubt that the experience left him a bitter man, determined to reestablish his good name and reputation.

On reaching the ridge, after enduring more than a dozen standing/running fights, Hunter looked around and, finding that he was on his own with what was left of his brigade, decided that enough was enough: he would retreat no more. He would establish a new position on the ridge and make a stand.

Horseshoe Ridge was a wild and desolate place, a land of forested ridges, gullies, ravines, and escarpments to the west of and adjoining Snodgrass Hill that spread across the high ground and south-facing slopes like fingers of a half-dozen hands. The ridges, natural trenches, stretched for almost a mile from east to west from the Dry Valley Road to the eastern slopes of Snodgrass hill; that they were ranged one above the other in ascending order up a steep slope, along with the excellent cover they provided, made the ridge and hill almost impregnable.

The face of Horseshoe Ridge looked south over the battlefield, at least it would if the battlefield could be seen through the trees, shrubs and dense undergrowth. Horseshoe Ridge was a natural fortress, and the ideal place to make a stand, and an absolute nightmare to assault.

As soon as he arrived on the ridge, Hunter set about placing his men to take best advantage of the terrain. No sooner had he begun than he was joined by the 9th Ohio regiment of Colonel Van Deever's brigade, also of Brannan's division, and then by Colonel George Buell with what was left of the 58th Indiana.

General Brannan himself arrived shortly after and, after having assessed the situation building on the ridge, sent out a call all across Federal held territory for any and all remaining elements of his division to assemble with him on the ridge. By mid-afternoon, he was back in command of his division; more than two thousand soldiers from various regiments, brigades, divisions and corps, but his command now totaled less than forty percent of its original numbers.

Still, it was the beginning of big things yet to come. Throughout the afternoon, more and more disconnected Federal units including the 10th Indiana, joined Brannan on Horseshoe Ridge, and on Snodgrass Hill.

Only the top of the ridge to the northeast of the Snodgrass cabin had been cleared of the dense undergrowth and forest and on the north side, the ridge sloped gently down to the Snodgrass meadows and farmland. And it was here on the southeastern slope of Snodgrass Hill, almost at the same time as Hunter was establishing his position on Horseshoe Ridge, that Colonel Charles Harker of Wood's division began to assemble his brigade.

General Thomas himself arrived on Snodgrass Hill shortly after one o'clock in the afternoon. He was now in command of what was left of the Army of the Cumberland, effectively seven divisions, including those of Generals John Palmer, Richard Johnson, Joseph Reynolds, and Absalom Baird, all still holding firm behind the log breastworks at the Kelly farm. As he rode the crest of the ridge, he soon realized the potential strength of his positions and quickly established a new field headquarters just to the northeast of the Snodgrass cabin, a minimal, somewhat utilitarian log structure.

Thomas's small army consisted of the four divisions still holding the fortified line east of the Lafayette Road, and the gathering remains of a half-dozen scattered divisions, including that of General Brannan who was taking the leading role in organizing the defense of Horseshoe Ridge.

So, from west to east, the defenses steadily built; first General Brannan's division took the central position on Horseshoe Ridge. To his left was a somewhat lightly defended area adjoining Snodgrass Hill where General Wood was organizing the defenses there: Brigadier General William Hazen and Colonels Charles Harker and William Stoughton, now commanding Stanley's brigade, Stanly having been wounded and taken from the field. Those stalwarts would take the brunt of the Confederate attacks on the Hill. To Brannan's right, the ridge stretched westward and would eventually be defended by General Steedman's division of General Grainger's Reserve Corps; as it was, at two-thirty, that section of the ridge was manned by a scattering of assorted brigades and regiments from seven divisions. In all, more than thirty thousand Federal troops were defending the line from the Kelly farm to the western reaches of Horseshoe Ridge.

General Thomas was a big man, not more than five feet ten inches tall, but heavy set; he weighed in at over two hundred and twenty pounds. His presence was one of stolid reliability. Not much given to show, he preferred instead to keep a low profile; his private life he guarded jealously. On the battlefield, however, he was aggressive and tenacious, totally unwilling to give even an inch of territory, and totally committed to his cause and to his men. And so it was that he rode out from his field headquarters some four hundred yards to the rear of the Snodgrass cabin, to inspect his lines of defense. As he slowly navigated the crest of the hill and the ridge, he watched as the milling thousands of his men manned the natural trenches and made ready to receive the enemy. In the distance, to the south, through the gaps in the trees, he could see the long, gray-clad lines moving slowly into position.

Thomas nodded his head and thought, *soon, soon it will be mayhem. Thousands more will join the thousands already gone to meet their maker. Look at them, all eager to die, mine, and theirs. Almighty God, protect us all this day and, if it should please you, provide us with the means to hold until nightfall and then safe passage away from this place.* He looked skyward and muttered, "Amen."

He walked his horse slowly westward, hailing this brigade commander and then that one, taking time out to offer a word of encouragement to the men in line along the way. The moral among the men was good, even though most of them had been sent running from the field in disarray; they were glad to have the chance to fight again and perhaps remove the stain of defeat.

"Enthusiastic, so they are," he said to General Wood who was at his side. "If the mood holds, General, we can hold this place until nightfall. The natural defenses off these positions are more than we could hope for; it will be a good day."

"So you say, General," Wood replied. "But most of these men have taken a beating. It would only be natural for them to turn and run yet again, but maybe not," Wood was more thinking aloud than trying to converse. "Can they really hold, do you think?"

"That, General, is something only God knows for sure," Thomas replied. "If they don't hold, then this army is destroyed, and that, General, must not happen. We will hold these positions, not because we can, but because we must, and we will hold them against all hazards. How goes the preparations south of the cabin?"

"All goes well, General. Harker, Stoughton and Hazen are consolidating their positions, and we are moving three batteries onto the crest of the hill here, and two more onto the crest of the ridge. It's not enough, but it's all we have; it will have to do, unless you can spare more from the Kelly farm."

"No. Not now, at least," Thomas replied. "What we have is needed there. That line is holding, but the artillery is a large part of the reason why."

Thomas quiet for a moment, seemingly staring out at nothing. Wood looked at him in askance, and then said, "What is it, Sir? What do you see?"

"It's what I don't see that I'm worried about," Thomas said, as he opened a leather pouch strapped to his saddle and took out a pair of brass binoculars. They were on the crest of Snodgrass hill, just to the south of the cabin.

Thomas put the glasses to his eyes and looked intently through them, then he handed them to Wood, pointed and said, "Look down there. What do you see?"

"I see nothing, General," Wood looked puzzled.

"Precisely. Nothing! And it's quiet, too quiet. Something is up, General, and I think we may soon know what." He took his glasses from Wood and looked again at the dense undergrowth some quarter mile away beyond the lower slope of the hill. Then, "Look. Down there," Thomas handed the glasses to Wood and pointed down the slope toward the Poe farm and the Lafayette Road. "It's hard to see," he continued, "but there. Do you see them?"

Wood stared in the direction Thomas was pointing. "No, Sir. I see nothing but brush and undergrowth."

"There. Look. Now. Do you see it?"

And then Wood saw at what Thomas was pointing. Although due to the distance, maybe a half-mile, maybe a little more, it was hard to make them out, but he could see thousands of gray-clad soldiers moving out of the trees and slowly toward them, toward the lower slopes of Snodgrass Hill.

Wood drew a sharp breath, and then said, "I see them, General. There are thousands of them."

Thomas grinned, and showed his famous Welsh sense of humor. "Uh huh, but there's not as many of them as there was this morning, I vow."

"What do you make of it, General?" Thomas asked Wood.

"A large force, Sir; at least a division, perhaps more."

"I agree," Thomas said, turning in the saddle and beckoning for one of his staff officers to join them.

The lieutenant rode up, joined the two Generals, saluted each in turn, and said, "Sir, Lieutenant Dickinson at your service."

Thomas smiled at him and said, "I know who you are, son, and thank you. Now then, I need you to ride to General Hazen and Colonels Harker and Stoughton. They are with their brigades somewhere down there on the slopes. Tell them to make haste and join me here as quickly as possible."

"Yes, sir." Dickinson saluted, wheeled his horse, and rode off through the brush at the canter. In less than five minutes, he was back with all three officers following.

"Good afternoon, gentlemen," Thomas said, returning their salutes. "It would seem we are about to have company," he continued, nodding his head in the direction of the advancing Confederate lines, and pointing. "And you, sirs, will be receiving the enemy quite soon. Are you ready for them?

All three officers answered in the affirmative; they were indeed ready.

"How many are there, do you think, General Thomas?" Hazen asked.

"It's hard to tell at this point, but one has to assume that it's the spearhead of Longstreet's corps, probably General Hood's division. If so, Sirs, we are in for a rare test. Those men are battle hardened veterans that arrived here only hours ago from General Lee's army in Virginia.

"Well, gentlemen," Thomas continued. "It begins again. This time the stakes are indeed high. We have to hold this hill and the ridge to the west at least until nightfall. If we can hold until dusk, we will be able to withdraw toward Chattanooga. That being so, I suggest you rejoin your brigades and prepare to defend every inch of ground. We cannot retreat from here. If we do, they will be upon us and we, and the rest of the army, will be destroyed. Good day to you, sirs, and may God be with you and protect you."

All six officers, including Lieutenant Dickinson, saluted each other and then the four of them rode away, each in a different direction, leaving Thomas and Wood alone on the crest of the hill.

"Now, General Wood," Thomas said, wheeling his horse to the right, "let us look to our artillery."

Less than fifty yards away, the gun crews of Battery I of the 4th United States Artillery had anticipated the need and were readying their six guns.

"Good work, Lieutenant Smith," Thomas said to the battery commander. "What do you estimate the range?"

"I estimate the leading regiments to be close to nine hundred yards distance, General."

Thomas nodded. *Let's see what you men from Virginia are made of*, he thought. "Make ready to fire, Lieutenant Smith. Case shot, then canister when they come within effective range; fire when you're ready."

"Yes, sir." Smith stood to attention, saluted, then turned smartly to his right to face the line of six guns.

"By detail, LOAD CASE SHOT. EIGHT HUNDRED YARDS." Smith watched as the gun crews swung into action loading and priming the guns. Then he walked quickly down the line, from one gun to the next, checking the direction and elevation of each piece. Finally, he returned and stood to the left of the gun nearest to General Thomas. For a moment, he watched the advancing gray lines and then, judging the distance with a practiced eye, "FIRE."

BAM, BAM, BAM, BAM, BAM, BAM.

Thomas, Wood and Smith, and every member of Thomas's staff watched the six case shots take a low trajectory out over the slope and explode over the heads of the advancing Confederate soldiers. Smith was good at his job and Thomas watched through his glasses and smiled with satisfaction as dozens of men in gray fell under the rain of iron projectiles.

"By detail, LOAD CASE SHOT. SEVEN HUNRED AND FIFTY YARDS." And so it went on until, at three hundred and fifty yards, Smith changed the ammunition to canister, double-loaded. By now, however, all three Federal brigades on the upper slopes were pouring a devastating hail of rifle fire down on the advancing Confederate lines.

At first, things went well for the advancing Confederates. Colonel Harker's Federal brigade, on the left of the Federal line of battle, was soon put under heavy pressure by Kershaw's Confederate division, and he began to fall back, but not for long. Finding a deep divide in the hillside, he rallied his troops and stood firm. Meanwhile, as Kershaw came under heavy small arms fire from the now consolidated Harker, they also came under heavy artillery fire from the crest of the hill.

It did not take Kershaw very long to realize that he was in big trouble, and that the ridges were better defended than anyone, including Longstreet, had thought. Kershaw was not a general to give up easily, but a quick look around at the carnage told him that his division was facing insurmountable odds, and he gave orders to sound the recall and retreat.

As quickly as they had come, the long lines of gray melted away among the trees leaving several hundred dead and wounded men behind.

Thomas tuned to Wood and said, "It will not go so easily next time, General. That was but a small force; testing the waters, I think. Expensive, at least for Longstreet. He should know better.

All through the early afternoon, General Thomas had been receiving couriers bearing bad news, but not the worst of it. The latest to arrive was Major Gates Thruston of General McCook's staff of the XXI Corps. At this point, General McCook, along with Generals Rosecrans, Crittenden, Davis, Sheridan, Garfield, and a whole gaggle of staff officers, were already gone from the battlefield and heading for McFarland's Gap,

Rossville and Chattanooga. From the noise of battle away to the east, these officers knew that General Thomas was still in the field and fighting hard. McCook, wondering if Thomas was even aware of the disintegration of the Federal left flank, took it upon himself to send Major Thruston to appraise him of the situation.

Major Thruston was a resourceful man, not for him the long and winding trail from McFarland's Gap to Thomas's positions. Instead, with a small escort, he galloped cross-country, heading directly toward the sounds of the battle still raging away to the east. His route took him directly behind the Federal positions that were now building all along the crest of Horseshoe Ridge. He found Thomas at the rear of the Federal defensive line at the Kelly farm, not far from Snodgrass Hill.

"General Thomas, Sir," Thruston said, as he reigned in his horse in front of the general. "I am from General McCook. I bring news of the battle, sir...."

Major General George Thomas was tired, impatient, and stressed, even so, he cut a daunting figure, especially on horseback, as he was. And Thruston, being a mere mortal, and only a major, was more than a little overawed.

"Well, go on man," Thomas said, irritably. "What about it?"

"Sir," Thruston replied, warily. "General Rosecrans and his staff have left the field. The right flank is collapsed, gone, sir. General McCook and General Crittenden are with General Rosecrans. The divisions of Generals Sheridan and Davis have been defeated and are retreating to Chattanooga."

Thomas stared at him. Although he didn't show it, he was astounded. He knew that things had not been going well for the army, but this was the first he'd heard of the true state of the right flank.

"What of Generals Sheridan and Davis' divisions, Major? Are they destroyed?"

"No, General. They are retreating in good order with General Rosecrans toward Chattanooga."

"How far away are they?" Thomas asked, quietly.

"Not more than three miles sir, less than two hour's march."

Thomas stroked his beard, deep in thought.

"Major," he said. "Go to Generals Sheridan and Davis and tell them they are to return immediately to the field. They must bring up their divisions to support my right flank. Go, Major, and go quickly, sir."

Thruston saluted, wheeled his horse, and together with his escort, galloped back the way he had come, along the crest of Horseshoe Ridge.

Thruston arrived at the Dry Valley Road some thirty minutes later only to find that Sheridan and Davis had already left. Without stopping for even a moment, Thruston and his men turned onto the Dry Valley Road and galloped on toward McFarland's Gap where they caught up with the stragglers at the rear of the two retreating divisions and their commanders. As he worked his way quickly forward, through the mass of soldiers on the road, he continually relayed Thomas's instructions to the officers he encountered along the road; none of them were interested in returning to the battle, referring him instead to the two commanding generals leading the column.

When Thruston finally caught up with Sheridan and Davis and passed on Thomas's orders to them, Sheridan was having none of it; he was determined to press on into Chattanooga. General Davis, however, seemed to be very glad to hear the news that Thomas was still holding his own and, without waiting to clear it with General Rosecrans, he ordered his division to turn around and march back to join Thomas on the battlefield. It would be almost dark before Davis arrived.

And then there was the Federal Reserve Corps commanded by General Gordon Grainger. Thomas had, all morning, been holding out the hope that Grainger would send him reinforcement, but that hope was by now dwindling. One after another, his division commanders had let him down: first Negley, then Van Cleve, and now Sheridan and Davis, although he was unaware that Davis was indeed on his way. How many more disappointments would he have to endure? Only God could answer that question.

Couriers from the Kelly farm had been hurrying back and forth between the farm and the Snodgrass cabin, keeping him informed as to the state of the battle, and his defenses east of the Lafayette Road. He knew that his left flank there was holding, but he also knew that Confederate forces were swinging around the northern flank of those defenses, and that they might well inundate them, or worse still, pass to the rear of the Kelly farm and assault his rear at Snodgrass Hill. And none of this took into account the fact that Nathan Bedford Forrest was roving north and west of the Kelly farm and might, at any time, decide to ride south and assault Thomas in the rear.

Thus, early that afternoon, Thomas was seated astride his horse, with a dozen or more of staff, and General Wood, in attendance, gazing northward across the Snodgrass fields and pastures toward Rossville, and imagining the worst. And then he saw it! Far away, in the distance to the north, a low-lying cloud of what could only be dust.

"General Wood," Thomas said. "What do you make of that?" He asked, gesturing with his glasses.

"Wood already had his own glasses to his eyes and, for a moment, he said nothing, then, "It's a column, General. It can't be anything else."

Thomas nodded his head and continued to stare through his glasses at the dust cloud shimmering in the sunshine. Slowly, the dust cloud grew larger, the more so, the more Thomas became alarmed.

"Ours or the enemy, General Wood? What do you make of it?"

"I can't tell, General. It's too far away, and obscured by the dust."

Thomas turned in the saddle and shouted to the assembled officers, "One of you, with a steady horse, to me. Now." He held out his glasses.

A captain rode forward and took the glasses from Thomas. "There, tell me what you see. I need to know if they are infantry or cavalry. If they are cavalry, it can only be Forrest, and there will be the devil to pay. Quickly, now. What do you see?"

"General, I cannot see who they are, but they seem to be infantry."

Thomas nodded his head and said, "I agree, but whose infantry?"

"General, Sir," another officer said, "It must be General Grainger and the Reserve Corps. Who else could it be?"

"Any one of a dozen enemy brigades that could have slipped past General Baird's left flank. That's who it could be."

It was at that moment that a captain of cavalry came charging into the clearing at full gallop, slowed, spotted the assembled officers, kicked his horse toward then, and then slid to a stop just in front of Thomas.

"General Thomas, sir," he shouted as he saluted. Captain Gilbert Johnson, 2nd Indiana Cavalry reporting for duty."

"Welcome, Captain. It's good to see you. I thought you were with General Negley."

"I was, sir," Johnson said, looking at Thomas warily. "I became separated from General Negley's division, sir, and I now have no idea where they might be. Can I be of service to you, General?"

"Indeed you can, Captain. Here, take these glasses," Thomas said, handing them over. "Tell me, what do you see, over there?" He pointed toward the cloud of dust, still more than a mile away.

"It's hard to tell, General. Infantry, for sure, but...."

"Captain Johnson, ride over there and find out. Then report back to me, and make haste, Captain; make haste."

Johnson saluted, wheeled his horse, and galloped away across the field toward the growing cloud of dust.

Thomas and his staff watched, and waited, but not for long. Johnson disappeared over a rise and came under fire from a Confederate cavalry patrol; one of General Forrest's, but the captain wheeled and dodged and then all went quiet. Back on Snodgrass Hill, General Thomas and his staff watched and waited, and they waited, and then they saw him, heading back over the rise at full gallop, whipping his horse, side to side with his reigns, and he was not alone. Alongside him was another rider; this one was carrying high a fluttering banner, and the two riders were whooping and hollering as they came.

Through his glasses, Thomas could see the flag, and he heaved a sigh of relief; it was red, white, blue, and emblazoned with a white crescent. It was the battle flag of General Grainger's Reserve Corps. General Steedman and his staff arrived a few minutes later and he was heartily greeted by General Thomas.

"General Steedman," Thomas said, grasping his hand. "Never before have I been so glad to greet anyone. Welcome, sir. How many men do you have with you?"

"It's good to see you, too, General. I have two brigades, sir, seventy-five hundred men in all."

"Good, good. Come with me, General. I will show you where you are most needed."

Together, the two generals, followed by Thomas's staff, rode west along the top of Snodgrass Hill and onto the crest of Horseshoe Ridge. There, Thomas directed Steedman to insert his two fresh brigades, into line to the west of General Brannan's positions. The Federal defensive line now stretched for more than a mile westward from the Snodgrass cabin and along the crests of the hill and the ridge. And it was not a moment too soon.

As Steedman's two brigades crested the ridge, the situation was easily assessed. From this vantage point, they could see down the south face of the ridge, now virtually cleared of trees and undergrowth, to the long lines of the two Confederate divisions of Generals Johnson and Hindman storming onto the lower slopes. Steedman's men, bayonets fixed, at his command, charged over the top and down the hill toward them, yelling and screaming loud enough to rival even the Rebel yell.

The two forces clashed midway on the slope and the fighting soon became desperate, hand-to-hand; there was no time to reload. Empty rifles were used as lances or clubs. The fighting rolled first one way and then the other, surging up and down the slopes as first one side rallied, then the other.

Slowly Steedman's fresh troops began to prevail, and Hindman's men were driven back down the slope.

Just to the east, at the center of the Confederate line, Bushrod Johnson's Confederate division was in an equally deadly conflict with General Brannan's rag-tag force. The fight lasted more than half an hour until finally Johnson, too, was driven back down the hill.

Both Confederate divisions retired to the fields to the south of the hill and the ridge, to rest for a moment, and regroup.

On the ridge, Brannan and Steedman were ecstatic, slapping each other on the back and reliving the moment, almost blow-by-blow. But it had been a costly win; Steedman had suffered more than a thousand casualties, Brannan almost as many. On the Confederate side, Longstreet's three divisions had lost almost two thousand men, and there was more to come, much more.

Chapter 75

Sunday September 20th, 1:30p.m. – Confederate Line of Battle

It was just after one-thirty when the two Confederate privates flopped down under the shade of a tall, old growth oak tree on the southern approaches to Horseshoe Ridge. Somehow, the giant tree had survived the devastation of the past several hours almost unscathed. True, the trunk, more than five feet across, had been pierced by a half-a-hundred Minnie bullets, and several pieces of shrapnel, and below ten feet little was left of its bark, but most of its branches were intact and they now offered refuge from the sun for some twenty exhausted Confederate soldiers.

It had been a long morning, and one they were sure they would never forget. The carnage they had witnessed, and had been a part of, over the past four hours was beyond description. After two days of fighting, the 30th Tennessee had lost more than fifty percent of its number. Of the one hundred and eighty-seven officers and men that had arrived on the battlefield just two days earlier, only ninety remained fit and able to fight; Billy Cobb and Jimmy Morrisey were two of them, and they were tired, very tired.

"Don't know how much more of this I can take, Jimmy," Cobb said.

Morrisey said nothing. He just looked at his friend with a slight smile on his face.

"What? What you smilin' at?"

"Nothin, just thinkin'." Morrisey said.

"I dunno, Jim. We lost a lot of men today, and more to lose yet, I think. Cain't be more than a hundred of us left."

The two men were quiet for a moment, contemplating. Then Cobb continued, "We need to get out of this mess, Jim; get away; go home. We cain't keep on bein' this lucky. Sooner or later one of us, maybe both of us, is gonna get it."

"You changed your tune," Morrisey said, again he smiled.

"Nah, just facin' facts. Jimmy. We was, what? There was more than nine hundred of us when the regiment was formed back in sixty one; now look at us. Almost all of 'em are gone. We must have lost the best part of a hundred today. It cain't go on Jim. We gotta go. I gotta go; go home."

"Hey, listen," Morrisey said. Far off in the distance to the east the sounds of the Rebel yell from a thousand throats came drifting in on the gentle breeze. It grew louder, and then, BAM, BAM, BAM, BAM, BAM, BAM as all six guns of Battery I of the 4th United States Artillery on Snodgrass Hill opened fire.

"On your feet, men."

They both looked up at Sergeant Hawks, then at each other. Then, with an effort, they scrambled to their feet and gathered what little was left of their belongings. It was one-thirty, and time once again to move out. Minutes later the two Confederate divisions were moving north onto the lower slopes of Horseshoe Ridge, and were already coming under heavy fire from General Steedman's two Federal batteries on the crest of the ridge.

Chapter 76

Sunday September 20th, 1:30p.m. – Confederate Positions Horseshoe Ridge

By one-thirty that afternoon, the Confederate Army of Tennessee was in control of three-quarters of the battlefield. General Longstreet's Left Wing, with six divisions engaged had crossed the Lafayette Road, wheeled to the right, and was quickly approaching the lower slopes of Horseshoe Ridge.

General Longstreet was of the opinion that the Federal positions on the ridge were disorganized and vulnerable and, knowing that General Johnson and Hindman were already assaulting Horseshoe Ridge, he gave orders to General Kershaw to try the southeastern slope of Snodgrass hill, thus Longstreet's entire wing was engaged over a mile wide front.

At around two o'clock, Longstreet, flushed with thoughts of an impending victory, took time off for lunch. Sweet potatoes, one of his favorite dishes, was served in the shade of the trees. Although he had been keeping General Bragg appraised of the fast moving, fluid situation on the Left Wing, he had heard nothing from him, Bragg, since he had launched his attack across the Lafayette Road.

Then, at around two-thirty, while Kershaw's assault on Snodgrass Hill was still underway, Longstreet received orders to report to Bragg's headquarters; the general wished to see him.

Longstreet took to his horse and with a small party of staff officers rode east to meet with the general. General Bragg was not in the best of moods, and not pleased to see him.

"Good afternoon, General," Longstreet said, as he dismounted and flipped Bragg a somewhat casual salute.

"Good afternoon, General Longstreet. I would like to know the disposition of your troops, and the state of the battle in your department

"Well, General," Longstreet replied. "It would appear that we are on the verge of a great victory."

"How so, General?"

The southern reaches of the battlefield are in our hands. The enemy is driven from the field in disorder. We have captured some sixty guns and it would appear that General Rosecrans has deserted the field, with his entire staff. I would say that that is a victory, at least in part. Would you not agree, General?

"No, sir, I would not," Bragg snapped. "In fact I would say that just the opposite is so, and it is we that are on the verge of defeat. General Polk has made no headway whatever, and General Hood is sorely wounded and has been removed from the field. And you, sir, should be pressing your perceived advantage. Again, I ask you, what is the disposition of your troops, General Longstreet?"

"My troops are in excellent spirits, General Bragg, but you, sir? I do not understand how you can be of the opinion that we are defeated. It makes no sense, sir, none at all."

"General Longstreet," Bragg said, quietly but forcefully. "The Right Wing of this army has been assaulting the enemy positions since early morning and not a yard has General Polk won. Reports indicate that this army over the two days has already suffered in excess of fourteen thousand casualties, more than eight thousand today alone; and it is not yet over. This army is widely disorganized, tired, and unresponsive." Bragg took out his pocket watch, looked at it, noted the time, and returned it to its pocket.

"It is now past three o'clock," Bragg continued, "and the enemy appears to be holding positions of great strength, not only on their left flank where they are holding General Polk's forces at bay, but now, so General Forrest informs me, on the heights of the ridges to the west. There, sir, General Thomas is forming a new and formidable line of battle where, so you tell me, General Longstreet, the enemy has been driven from the field. I don't think so, sir."

"That is true, at least in part, General Bragg," Longstreet said, the frustration in his voice now apparent for all around them to hear. "But the new enemy positions on the ridge, so General Wheeler informs me," - his voice was harsh, and dripped with sarcasm and contempt - "are minimal, insecure and can easily be overrun, and so they will be, and in very short order. In the meantime, General, I formally request that you provide me with reinforcements in order for me to hold the ground already gained, assault the new enemy positions on the ridges, and pursue the enemy to McFarland's Gap where I intend to take and hold the Dry Valley Road and thus cut off General Thomas's retreat, for retreat he must. If not, his forces will be destroyed in total."

"General Longstreet, that will not be possible. What troops I have remaining have little fight left in them. I will not commit any of them to the left. We must continue to assault Thomas's left; it is there that victory will be won or lost."

Longstreet was dumbfounded, and said loudly for all to hear, "I cannot agree, sir. We have already broken the enemy's right flank. Surely the best course of action would be to continue to destroy what remains and then to assault Thomas's rear. That would put him under attack from both front and rear; he could not hold, sir."

"No, General Longstreet. You will return to your divisions and assault the ridges. I have already sent orders to General Polk to renew his attack. That he has not yet done so is an aberration. If I do not hear something from him soon, I will go myself to Reed's Bridge. General Polk must renew and redouble his efforts against the enemy's left flank."

Longstreet looked at Bragg for a long moment, then shook his head in frustration, remounted his horse, saluted the commanding general and, with his staff officers trailing behind, rode west toward the Lafayette Road at full gallop. It was almost three-thirty when he arrived back at his own field headquarters. By which time, all three of his divisions had been driven off the slopes of the hill and the ridge.

Chapter 77

Sunday September 20th, 3p.m. – McFarland's Gap

In the meantime, General Rosecrans too had received word that Thomas was holding firm, and he immediately gave orders to General Garfield that he was to carry on into Chattanooga without him and prepare for the defense of the city, should Thomas be defeated. In the meantime, he, Rosecrans, would return and join with Thomas.

General Garfield was having none of this. He was not, so he informed the commanding general, sure of his ability to handle such a great responsibility.

Rosecrans looked quizzically at Garfield, and was silent for a moment, then he nodded his head and said, "Very well, General. One of us has to go to Thomas and find out how he fares, and one of us has to ensure that the commissary train gets to Chattanooga, and also to give the orders for the defense of this road and the preparations for the defense of the city."

"Sir," Garfield said, "I think it would be best if I went to General Thomas, and that it would also be best if the orders for the defense of this road and the city, be given by the commanding general, you, sir."

Rosecrans looked at Garfield, nodded his head, and then said, "You are, of course, correct, General Garfield. I will go myself to Chattanooga and see to its defenses. You go to Thomas, and...."

Rosecrans paused and thought for a moment, then continued, "He will, undoubtedly, try to hold his position until nightfall. You will tell General Thomas that I have given orders for General Sheridan to hold the Dry Valley Road, here, and that he, General Thomas, is to keep me abreast of his situation to me as it unfolds. He is also to use his discretion as to whether or not to continue the fight until darkness, or to retire immediately from the field and move to Rossville."

"Sir, Garfield said, "it is my considered opinion that it would indeed be best if General Thomas would immediately withdraw to Rossville. A defensive line there would aid our withdrawal and secure the route into Chattanooga."

Rosecrans looked up at the sky, shook his head, once, then turned again to Garfield, and said, "Perhaps that would indeed be the best course of action. Unfortunately, however, we do not know General Thomas's situation; we must know how the battle is going for him and we must know intentions. Please ride to him at once, General, and then report back to me"

Garfield was not a stupid man, far from it, and he took Rosecrans' final words as script; he took it that General Rosecrans meant for Thomas to retire from the field at once.

Garfield saluted Rosecrans and, with a small staff of two orderlies and three officers, he rode out along the Dry Valley Road back toward the battlefield and Snodgrass Hill; it was three-thirty in the afternoon.

Chapter 78

Sunday September 20th, 3:30p.m. – Confederate Positions South of Snodgrass Hill

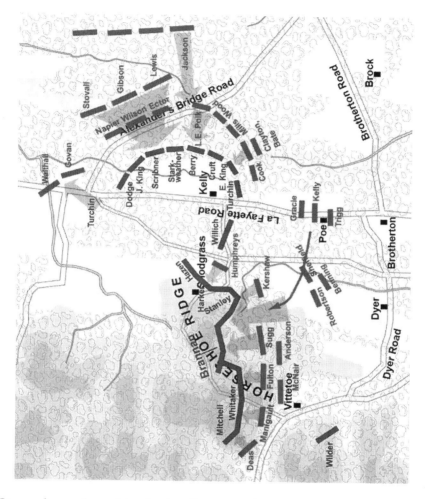

It was almost three-thirty in the afternoon when Longstreet rejoined his field commanders to the south of Horseshoe Ridge after his confrontational meeting with General Bragg. He was frustrated and angry, bordering on loss of temper.

No sooner did he arrive, even before dismounting, than he was calling for his division commanders. General Bushrod Johnson was the first to arrive, quickly followed by General Kershaw. General's Hindman, Preston, and Law, now commanding Hood's division, arrived just a few moments later.

Well, gentlemen," Longstreet began. "It seems we have a little work to do." He looked northward, toward Horseshoe Ridge and Snodgrass Hill.

"General Bragg has tasked us with the taking of the high ground, there," he nodded his head in the direction of the ridge. "It will not be easy. The heights form almost a perfect rampart, similar to that of a medieval castle. We must attack in force, and the going will be difficult. The cost will be high, as it always is."

Longstreet looked pensive for a moment. Then he turned to General Joseph Kershaw and said, "General, I hear it did not go well for you. How are your men? I understand they took quite a beating."

"All is well, General Longstreet," Kershaw replied. "The men are in good spirits."

"Good, good. Well, General Kershaw, there will be no rest for your division. We, you, have to take that hill, and quickly.

General Johnson, General Hindman," Longstreet turned to face the two generals and continued, "I understand that things have not gone well for you either. The hill, there to the right, so I am told, now represents Thomas's right flank, and as such is well defended, better in fact than I would have expected. The ridge, I think, is not so well defended and I am of the opinion that a concentrated and sustained assault there will crush the enemy, leaving the way clear to move to the right in support of General Kershaw. If we can do that, gentlemen, this battle will be over in less than an hour. General Bragg has ordered a general assault against the enemy's left, so he will have two fronts to defend. Both are heavily fortified but, what troops remain with Thomas are all that is left of that army."

Longstreet looked hard and his three division commanders, then continued, "We can do this, gentlemen. We can destroy his army in its entirety. We can set the Federal cause back at least a year, maybe more. Can you take that ridge, General Johnson, General Hindman?"

"We can, General," Johnson said, with enthusiasm.

"That we can, sir," This from General Hindman.

"And you, General Kershaw, can you take the hill?"

"I can, General, and I will."

"Then please do so. Go to your divisions and move out as soon as you are ready.

"General Preston, your division has not yet arrived on the field, but they should be here within the half-hour. You will then follow General Kershaw and support his assault on the hill." Longstreet saluted his four generals and watched as they rode away at the canter.

When General Kershaw rejoined his division, he found Colonel Oates of Hood's division waiting for him with his regiment, the 15th Alabama. Oates apparently had become separated from his division and requested that he join Kershaw. Kershaw, knowing he would now need every soldier he could get his hands on, agreed, and immediately gave orders for his brigades once again to assault the hill.

To the west, Generals Johnson and Hindman were preparing to advance toward the ridge; to the east, General Preston was hurrying his division westward toward the southern slopes of Snodgrass Hill.

Chapter 79
Sunday September 20th, 3:30p.m. – Federal Positions on Snodgrass Hill

By mid-afternoon, General Thomas was in rare high spirits, although he didn't show it. The repulse of the early Confederate attacks against the southern slopes of Snodgrass Hill and Horseshoe Ridge had bolstered his confidence. And, as the afternoon wore on, he had received more and more reinforcements, stragglers from a dozen or more shattered brigades had found their way onto the crest of the hill and were quickly deployed among the commanders now awaiting Longstreet's next move.

To the east, in the heavily defended line of battle at the Kelly farm, things were, for the most part, quiet, and he felt that he had little to worry about there on his left flank. What he was worried about was the massed Confederate divisions he could now clearly see in the fields to the south, the trees that once had obscured the view had been ravaged by cannon fire from both directions and stripped bare of leaves and branches.

"I think we will soon have company," Thomas said to General Wood, his field glasses to his eyes. The two general officers were on horseback on the crest of Snodgrass Hill.

Wood did not reply, but Thomas continued, "Four, perhaps five divisions, General, close to twenty thousand men, I think." He ranged his glasses back and forth, from east to west, then again, and again, trying to estimate the numbers and their objectives.

"General Wood, please send couriers to the field commanders and have them all report here to me at once." He took the glasses from his eyes, but his gaze never left the gathering hoard in the fields to the south. Thoughtfully, he tapped his chin with the rim of his glasses, *Is there no end to them? He thought. We will be lucky to survive this day. Twenty thousand, at least, and more joining them.* Thomas shook his head. The confidence he had enjoyed only moments ago had quickly dissipated, leaving in its place a feeling of impending doom. He looked at his pocket watch; it was almost three-forty-five. He looked up at the sky; the sun had barely dipped toward the west. It would be more than four hours before darkness fell.

"*We do not have the numbers. They are too many. Artillery, too - one... two... three, four... seven batteries.* He looked around, to the west and rear. All was quiet, but retreat was not an option, so he thought.

At the sound of approaching horses, he look again toward the south. Generals Brannan and Steedman were approaching along the crest of the ridge from the west at full gallop; Hazen, Harker, and Stoughton were fast approaching from the slope to the south.

Thomas waited until the officers were all assembled; Wood was at his side, his staff within earshot just to the rear.

"Upon these next several hours," he began, "depends the fate of this entire army. Look you to the south. Within the next hour, they will be here, on the hillside, and this time they will be supported by artillery, a great many artillery. I count seven batteries so far. We have to hold this hill and the ridge until nightfall."

Thomas paused for a moment, made eye contact with each of his field commanders in turn, and then continued, "This, gentlemen, will not be a test of strength. Were it to be so, we would lose quickly, for they outnumber us here by at least three to one. This will be a test of wills. General Longstreet, and that is whom we face, is a man of great will, and he will not give an inch; that I can promise you. But we also are strong willed, and neither will we give an inch; we *cannot* give an inch. If we do.... Well, gentlemen, I will leave it up to you." He looked at his pocket watch, and then continued, "If the line at the Kelly farm holds, and if we can hold here until sundown, we can make a fighting withdrawal toward Rossville. If not, we will go down here, fighting. Agreed?"

The officers, field commanders and staff, all raised their hats and cheered.

Thomas nodded his head in thanks and continued. "We must fortify this position as best we can. As long as this quiet time holds, have the men make best use of fallen trees and branches, anything that will provide cover; form whatever breastworks you can. General Steedman, put your batteries into line on the ridge to support the breastworks. To your commands, then, gentlemen, and prepare to receive the enemy."

The enemy was already approaching the southern slopes of both Snodgrass Hill and the ridge.

While General Thomas was rallying his field commanders on the crest of the hill, Jesse Dixon and Pat McCann had found cover in a deep, natural trench about a third of the way down the south face of Horseshoe Ridge. It was a strong defensive position, some four feet deep with a steep face to the south and an even steeper rise behind them. They were waiting with the rest of what remained of the 10th Indiana for the inevitable Confederate attack. Behind them, on the crest of the ridge, they could see General Brannan, on horseback, surrounded by a dozen, or more, officers and staff. He was surveying the view to the south of the ridge through a battered, but still serviceable, pair of field glasses.

Jesse looked sideways at Patrick; he was quiet, but appeared to be in good spirits; there was a slight smile on his face and the ever-present tremble of his hands seemed to have abated. They were lying on the bellies, against the face of the defile, rifles loaded and at the ready.

"You all right?" Jesse asked, for the umpteenth time.

Pat smiled at him and nodded.

Jesse looked at him, doubtful. "You sure?".

Still smiling, Patrick McCann merely nodded his head and pulled himself up to look over the edge of the trench, and down upon the long lines already moving toward the lower slopes of the ridge.

BAM, BAM, BAM, BAM, BAM, BAM. The ground shook as the 4th U.S Battery opened fire behind them. Almost at once, the ground not more than 20 feet in front of them seemed to bulge upward and then explode in a fountain of dirt and rocks as a Confederate Hotchkiss shell slammed into the open face of the ridge. By instinct alone they, and some fifty others, to their right and left ducked their heads and dropped down into the trench.

Again, Jesse looked at his friend, now seated on the floor of the trench with his back against the wall. "You sure you're all right," he shouted over the din of battle now building exponentially.

"Oh yeah," McCann replied. "I finally figured it out. We been through hell these last two and a half days, and we ain't gotten a scratch. I don't figure we ever will, coz someone up there is lookin' after you and me. We're gonna get out of this mess, Jess, and I have no doubts about it. So let's you and me just get busy and give them Johnny Rebs hell. Yeah?" he asked, with a broad grin on his face.

"Hah, you betcha," Dixon replied. "But for God's sake don't get cocky. Just keep your head down, and think about every move you make, before you make it."

McCann nodded his head, a grin on his face, then he jumped to his feet, stuck his head up over the top of the trench, and what he saw immediately wiped that grin off his face. Even so, still seemingly undeterred by the terrifying sight of thousands upon thousands of men in gray heading resolutely toward them, he wriggled in the dirt and grass, trying to get more comfortable, and readied his rifle.

Jesse watched open mouthed, amazed at the transformation his friend seemed to have undergone. Then, with a shrug and a shake of his head, he joined him and looked over the top of the trench at the advancing enemy.

Chapter 80

It was just after three-thirty when Johnson and Hindman ordered their divisions forward once again to assault Horseshoe Ridge, having been driven back more than an hour ago by General Steedman.

The Confederate lines, in order of brigades in line, stretched from east to west for almost three-quarters of a mile. To the east, Kershaw's line of battle stretched another half-mile, and to Kershaw's rear, General Preston's division was moving quickly to his support. Although Hindman ranked Johnson, Longstreet had placed him, Johnson, in overall command of the two divisions. So, when the brigades stepped forward, it was his order that started them on their way, and they soon came under concentrated artillery fire from the two Federal batteries on Horseshoe Ridge; the batteries on Snodgrass Hill were concentrated on Kershaw and Preston's divisions, already advancing toward the lower slopes of the hill.

In the meantime, Johnson's batteries, some thirty-one guns of various calibers, were doing their best to ease the way for the advancing gray-clad lines.

Ten minutes earlier, Billy Cobb was doing his usual thing, trying to find out what was going on at command level, listening to what was being said by the junior officers scattered around him. As usual, the 30th Tennessee was at the center of Johnson's division, which was itself positioned on the right side of the Confederate line. Both Cobb and Jimmy Morrisey watched as Johnson returned from his meeting with Longstreet. Johnson conferred briefly with Colonel Sugg and his two other brigade commanders, Colonels McNair and Fulton. The two privates, however, could hear little of what was being said; their position was already receiving fire from the Federal batteries on the crest of the ridge. The explosions overhead from the high-flying case shot were deafening; the rain of iron balls was devastating.

After much animated gesturing, a lot of head nodding, and head shaking, the commanders saluted one another and took up positions at the heads of their brigades.

"Here we go agin," Cobb said to Morrisey.

"Yep, not long now," Jimmy replied. "Soon all will be over."

"What do you mean by that?"

"Hell, Bill. You know what I mean," he grinned at his friend, then turned to face the way forward, chewing energetically on the large wad of tobacco he had only minutes before torn savagely from the wad in now residing in his jacket pocket.

"Hah," was all Cobb could think of to say, and he, too, turned to face the way forward, and then ducked quickly as a Federal shell screamed overhead to explode just beyond one of the Confederate batteries. He looked up the slope ahead. In the distance, he could see the tiny figures of the gun crews on the crest of the ridge working feverishly to reload their pieces. From where they were he could see where each of the pieces were aimed. He grabbed Jimmy by the right sleeve and pulled him sideways, indicating they move to the right. Together, as they advanced toward the slope, they began working their way through the ranks, out of the line of fire. It was little enough, but Cobb believed it might make a difference.

As they advanced at a fast walk, they soon came under small arms fire from the Federal infantry on the upper slopes of the ridge. All around them, men were pitching and falling. The hail of lead did not let up for a second. Just ahead, and to the left, the 30th Tennessee color bearer went down with a devastating wound in his neck. The man behind him snatched it up, only to go down himself within just a couple of steps. A sergeant grabbed the staff of the banner before it could hit the ground and, waving it high in the air and yelling an unintelligible scream, he ran out front, turned, and walking backwards shouted for his men to close up and follow him.

To the far right, General Kershaw's division, slightly father forward than Johnson's and Hindman's divisions, was not only under heavy small arms fire from the Federal positions on the hillside, it was also taking massive artillery fire. But there was nothing else for it; Kershaw's brigades could not effectively return fire because the enemy was, for the most part, still unseen behind its natural defenses.

To the rear of the advancing Confederate brigades all seven batteries were engaged and concentrating their fire either on the Federal batteries or the Federal infantry entrenched in the shallow cuts and divides that provided cover for the enemy defenders.

A dozen bronze, twelve-pound mountain howitzers, operating almost at extreme range, were hurling load after load of case shot into the Federal emplacements on the hillsides, while the rifled guns concentrated on the Federal batteries above.

As the long gray lines moved forward, the ground in front of them began to rise. On up the gentle slope they marched, still more than a third of a mile from the nearest Federal emplacement, but the way ahead was wide open and they were fully exposed to the unseen enemy lurking behind the ridges and mounds on the hillside. The Federal batteries on the heights was now concentrating on the Confederate gun crews to the rear, but the Minnie bullets from above came howling in like thousands of angry, deadly hornets, and they were taking a horrendous toll on the Confederate brigades.

Billy Cobb and Jimmy Morrisey had worked their way to the extreme right of the ninety, or so, remaining members of the 30th Tennessee and, with heads down and rifles held forward with bayonets fixed, they continued, still unscathed, onto the lower slopes of Horseshoe Ridge.

Chapter 81

Sunday September 20th, 3:45p.m. – Federal Positions on Horseshoe Ridge

On the crest of Snodgrass Hill, General Thomas, along with General Wood and a small group of staff officers, was anxiously watching events unfold in the fields to the south. Back and forth, he rode along the crest of the ridge, seemingly oblivious of the Minnie bullets from the lower slopes, and the barrage of solid shot and shells from the Confederate batteries.

Time and again, he came within yards of an exploding shell aimed at one of his own batteries some fifty yards to his rear. General Wood and members of his staff pleaded continuously for him to withdraw to a safer position, but he would not. At one point, much to their consternation, he dismounted and walked the line of batteries to assess their effectiveness for himself and, in so doing, narrowly missed being hit by a Hotchkiss shell that dismounted the next gun in line to the one he was attending. Instead, he was showered with shards of wood from the shattered gun carriage and blood and body parts from two of the gun crew; the shell landing on the left wheel of the carriage by which they were preparing to reload the weapon.

Disoriented, his head was ringing from the concussion of the blast, but it lasted only for a moment, Thomas walked slowly the few feet to his horse and, with some difficulty, managed to heave himself back into the saddle. And there he sat, gathering his wits and reorganizing his thoughts.

It was not long before Thomas had regained control of himself. He twisted in the saddle, called for his staff to follow, and then rode at the gallop, more than a half-mile, to the extreme right flank of his positions on the ridge. There he offered a few words of encouragement to General Steedman and his beleaguered defenders, turned again and rode the more than a mile back to the crest of Snodgrass Hill. Along the way, he stopped to exchange a few words with General Brannan, who was directing the defense at the center of the ridge, now under heavy fire from the Confederate batteries in the fields to the south.

Snodgrass hill was now coming under heavy pressure from General Preston's Confederate division. Longstreet had ordered them to pass through Kershaw's division and they had crossed the gentle rise of the lower slopes of the hill at the run and were already starting the climb toward the entrenched defenders.

On the crest of the hill, Thomas was directing incoming remnants of several assorted, disorganized brigades and regiments to defensive positions on the slopes. Many of them never made it; under heavy Confederate artillery fire, they were either wounded or killed before they could reach cover.

Some one hundred feet down from the crest of the ridge, in the shallow ravines, trenches and troughs, now somewhat fortified by the addition of fallen tree trunks and branches, General Brannan's troops were taking heavy fire from the Confederate howitzers. The effect was devastating.

As they peered over the top of the earthen bank in front of them, Jesse Dixon and Pat McCann could see the batteries in the fields away to the south. At almost a thousand yards, they looked tiny.

One after another, BAM, BAM, BAM... followed a second later by billowing clouds of white smoke erupting from the muzzle of each gun in line; and then the high-pitched whine of the incoming projectiles. and then, KABAM, KABAM, KABAM... as each shell hit the hillside, trench or ravine and exploded, raising a gigantic fountain of dirt, rocks, tree limbs and, in some cases, soldiers thrown high into the air, spinning and showering those below and around with blood and guts.

A private lying alongside Pat McCann jerked, tried to rise, then flopped down again and lay still. A shell splinter had ripped a huge gash in the top of his head, splashing blood and brains over his, McCann's, left cheek, shoulder and arm. McCann looked at his dead compatriot for a moment, reached inside his jacket, took out a colored piece of rag, wiped the mess from his face, then gritted his teeth and turned again to look over the top toward the advancing gray lines, now less than five hundred yards away.

Chapter 82

Sunday September 20th, 4p.m. – Reed's Bridge, General Polk's Field Headquarters.

For more than an hour, General Bragg sat and fumed at his field headquarters at Thedford's Ford. Finally, with a snort of anger, he called for his escort, mounted his horse, rode out of the clearing at full gallop, and onto the dirt road that lead northward toward Reed's Bridge. When he eventually caught up with General Polk, it was almost four o'clock. Polk was in an expansive mood, apparently quite happy with the way things were going with his Right Wing. He did, after all, have General Thomas's left flank almost completely surrounded, and his own divisions had settled in behind defenses of their own and were carrying out a war of attrition against the Federal defenses. His artillery was bombarding the breastworks, from long-range, and his infantry was maintaining a steady rate of small arms fire from behind whatever cover they could find.

Bragg rode into the clearing where General Polk, sitting astride his horse, seemed to be quite at ease, talking quietly to several of his staff officers. On hearing Bragg and his staff entering the clearing at a fast canter, he turned in the saddle and waved at the commanding general, a broad smile on his face.

"Good afternoon, General Bragg," Polk greeted him. "All is well, I trust," he was beaming.

"No, General Polk, all is not well. What in the name of all that's holy are you doing? This is not a picnic, sir. Your wing has not gained an inch in almost a full day of battle. You, sir, are a disgrace," Bragg fumed. "I would have you arrested were it not for the severity of the situation. We sir, are about to be overrun; DESTROYED, sir," Bragg shouted.

Polk was astounded; his staff looked on, open mouthed in dismay.

"General Bragg, sir, I do not understand. We have General Thomas surrounded. It is only a matter of time before he falls. I do not understand what more I could have done."

"DONE? DONE? You don't know what more you could have done? Why, sir, you could have attacked the enemy in force. That is what you could have done; that was my specific order. Instead, you sit here, as far away from the field as you can in all conscience get, and you twiddle your fingers while the enemy consolidates and prepares to annihilate us."

Bragg was beside himself with anger. As he shouted at Polk, spittle flew from his mouth, dribbled down into his beard, and landed on his horse's head.

"It's not good enough, sir," Bragg snarled at the astonished General Polk. "Not good enough at all. What is the disposition of your troops?"

Polk took a deep breath, looked around at his staff; all of them immediately looked away.

General Bragg, sir," he began in a quiet voice. "I deeply resent your berating me in front of my staff. It is unseemly and not a little embarrassing."

"UNSEEMLY! EMBARASSING! I have a good mind to have you arrested on the spot. What you are doing here, and your conduct this morning is not just flagrant disobedience, dereliction of duty, IT BORDERS ON MUTINY, SIR, MUTINY. Now, General Polk. I will ask you once more, and once more only. WHAT IS THE DISPOSITION OF YOUR TROOPS?

Polk looked at Bragg, stared him right in the eye, not in the least bit afraid of his commanding general, and said, "You, General Bragg, must do exactly as you see fit. I have carried out my orders, done my duty, to the best of my ability. Arrest me if you will; I am sure President Davis would have something to say about that. In the meantime, General, the disposition of my troops is as follows," Polk paused, took a deep breath, and continued, providing Bragg with his most up-to-date intelligence from General Forrest, and with the general state of the battle on his front. It took almost ten minutes to relay all the information, and by the time he had finished, Bragg had calmed down, somewhat.

"General Polk," Bragg said. "I hear what you say, but it is not good enough, sir. It is time for you to get off your behind and carry this fight to the enemy. Do you understand, sir?

Polk merely nodded his head.

Bragg continued, "I expect you to attack the enemy in force, sir, drive him from behind those breastworks. You must do it quickly; you must do it now. Do you understand?"

Again, Polk merely nodded his head.

Bragg looked long and hard at his wing commander. "No more of these delays, General Polk; no more, I say. Gather together your division commanders and put them to work, and do it now. I am waiting."

Polk turned to his staff, gave the necessary orders, and sent couriers to each of his field commanders, including Generals Hill and Forrest. Bragg stood back and watched, and waited.

It did not take long for the generals to begin arriving. General Cleburne arrived first, followed by Breckinridge, then Cheatham, Stewart, Walker and Forrest.

There followed a somewhat lengthy speech by the one-time Bishop of New Orleans during which he laid out a new plan of attack on the Federal defenses. The four divisions of Generals Stewart, Cleburne, Breckinridge, and Walker were to attack in line, in concert, all along the entire Federal line of battle. General Cheatham's division was to follow on behind, filling in where necessary. General Hill would stay with General Polk. As all this was happening, General Bragg and his staff had retired a few yards, close to the edge of the clearing, and Bragg listened intently to every work Polk said, and to the questions and answers that followed, but he said not a word.

When Polk's generals left to carry out their orders, it was almost five o'clock, and the all-encompassing attack on Thomas's left flank was soon under way.

Chapter 83

Sunday September 20th, 4p.m. – Federal Positions on Snodgrass Hill

General Garfield arrived at Thomas's field headquarters at a little before four o'clock after a not uneventful and somewhat wild ride. At full gallop, Garfield and his escort rode through open fields, swampland, marshes, rocky defiles, and stands of blackthorn. As he neared the battlefield, he came under heavy Confederate fire. So heavy was it that two of his men were killed in the saddle and another had his horse shot from underneath him; his own horse took a wound during the ride, and yet another just a few moments before he arrived on the northern edge of the battlefield where he found Thomas. Garfield's horse skittered to a stop, took a deep breath, staggered sideways several steps, and then dropped dead.

"General Garfield," Thomas greeted him. "You have had a rough journey, so it seems."

"Indeed, General Thomas. So I have."

"And what would be so urgent that you would risk your neck so to tell me about it?"

"I am from General Rosecrans, sir," Garfield said, breathing hard. "He has asked me to relay to you that he requires that you withdraw immediately from the field and fall back toward Rossville and form a defensive line there; this would aid the withdrawal of the army and secure the route into Chattanooga. General Rosecrans has given orders for General Sheridan to hold the Dry Valley Road and that he, himself, will ensure that the commissary train gets safely to Chattanooga."

Thomas shook his head and said, "You must tell General Rosecrans that it is not possible for me to withdraw from this field at this time. To do so would put this army in dire peril; we would be overwhelmed. No, sir, we must; we will, hold this position until nightfall."

"I understand, General," Garfield said. "I will return to General Rosecrans. He will be pleased to hear of your situation, but he was quite definite, General. You are to retire your force to Rossville and form a new defensive line there. May God be with you, sir." And with that, He saluted, mounted the horse he had been provided with by one of Thomas's staff officers, saluted and rode away northward toward Rossville at full gallop. At Rossville, he stopped at the telegraph office and sent a message to Rosecrans telling him of Thomas's situation and continuing, in part that "Thomas is still holding his positions; the man is a rock."

In the meantime, General Thomas was tirelessly patrolling the perimeter of his defensive line, offering a word or two of encouragement, here and there, as he saw fit. His troops were in fine spirits, and so, for the moment, was he, but things were rapidly coming to a head.

Snodgrass Hill, his left flank, and Horseshoe Ridge to the right, had been under continuous assault by three Confederate divisions for more than an hour. Time and again, his meager force of defenders had beaten back the oncoming hoards, and time and again, the Confederate forces had regrouped and resumed the attack. As he looked out over the battle-torn hillside, now clear of trees, undergrowth and brush, he could see the long lines once again moving slowly, but resolutely up the lower slopes.

Fire from the Confederate batteries was continuous and demoralizing. As he watched, a Hotchkiss shell exploded in front of him, showering him and his horse with dirt, rocks, shards of wood and even whole branches. Thomas didn't flinch, although his horse took several steps backwards, but the animal was well seasoned and remained quiet.

All along the slopes of the hill and ridge, he could see his troops, relatively safe from small arms fire, firing steadily at the oncoming enemy. Fire from the Confederate artillery, however, was a different story. Shell after shell slammed down on the entrenched soldiers, tearing earth and bodies apart with great efficiency. The ground on the upper slopes was littered with dead, wounded and body parts. The scene was horrific, the devastation, total. *How long could it last?* he wondered. *Not long, of that I am sure.*

He pulled his watch from his jacket pocket, looked at it, noted the time, It was almost four-forty-five. Thomas looked up at the sky, and then turned in the saddle to speak to General Wood.

"We can't take much more of this, General, but we must. We are taking more casualties than we can afford. Yes, they are suffering even more, but we are considerably outnumbered and, unless we can delay them, we soon will be overrun, especially the right flank. General Brannan and General Steedman are holding there, but the position is weak, extremely weak. It is almost five o'clock, and perhaps time to consider withdrawing from the field."

General Wood did not reply; there was nothing he could say. General Thomas was right. The Federal right flank was in imminent danger of collapse.

Chapter 84

Sunday September 20th, 4p.m. – Confederate Positions South of Horseshoe Ridge

At the center of the Confederate line of battle, almost half way up the slope of the ridge, Billy Cobb and Jimmy Morrisey and what was left of the 30th Tennessee, had taken cover in a shallow depression and were engaging the Federal positions not more than fifty yards away farther up the ridge. Of the ninety men that had started up the ridge with them, twenty-one had been either killed or wounded. The rest of Johnson and Hindman's divisions were also taking advantage of the ground and cover they had just won, at great cost.

General Johnson, as always, was at the front of his troops, on his knees in a depression, shouting and urging them on. Then he was on his feet, oblivious of the hailstorm of bullets and shrapnel.

"WITH ME, BOYS. TO THE TOP, he shouted and, waving his sword, head down, he started to run up the slope. Behind him, hundreds of gray-clad soldiers leaped to their feet, Cobb and Morrisey included, and stormed up the hill, surrounding and protecting their general, firing their weapons, stopping, reloading, and then surging forward again.

In minutes, the first line of the Federal defense had been overrun; minutes later the second line fell, and then they were at the top, banners waving, voices screaming the Rebel yell, and then they wheeled to the right and prepared to charge along the top of the ridge toward Snodgrass Hill. As they turned however, they stared into the face of a Federal battery, six guns, triple-loaded with canister.

BAMBAMBAMBAMBAMBAM! At almost point-blank range, the effect was devastating; the Confederate ranks were decimated. More than twenty soldiers were cut to pieces; fifty more were severely wounded. Two men took a triple load of canister at point-blank range, less than seventy feet; more than a hundred one-inch iron balls tore into their heads and bodies, disintegrating them, tearing and ripping them apart and scattering blood, flesh and bone over a dozen men and an area of more than fifty square feet.

As the battery worked desperately to reload their pieces, Brannan's troops rose from cover and fired a shattering volley into the now demoralized Confederate ranks.

Then, BAMBAMBAMBAMBAMBAM, and they were hit again, with the same devastating effect. It was too much, and slowly the Confederate ranks began to withdraw the way they had come. As the last man in gray slipped below the line of the ridge, a great cheer went up from the Federal defenders; the line had held, barely.

Thomas rode at the gallop to General Brannan.

"Well done, General," he shouted, even before he reached Brannan who, completely drained, had dropped to the ground and was lying on his back, trying to catch his breath. When Thomas arrived, he jumped to his feet, saluted, and then waved his hat in the air.

"General Thomas," Brannan shouted, almost beside himself with excitement. "Did you see that, sir? They had us; they had us, sir, but we held. We held, sir."

Thomas was almost as excited as Brannan. He swung his right leg over his horse's withers and jumped to the ground, grabbed Brannan's hand and pumped it vigorously.

"Well done, General," he said. "Well done, sir, but we need a little more time. Can you continue to hold, General Brannan?"

"We will hold the ridge, General, or we will go to meet our maker from it," Brannan shouted, and a great cheer went up from his men in the trenches. "We will hold, General. We will hold."

"Good, good." Thomas said, swinging himself back into the saddle. "Just an hour, or two, General. Just an hour, or two," and then he rode away at the gallop, back to the crest of Snodgrass Hill where he ordered the two batteries of artillery forward.

"Canister. Double load. Smash them down," Thomas shouted, pointing down the slope of the hill to where, almost three hundred yards away, General Preston's Confederate division was advancing resolutely toward the crest of the hill.

"Not yet, boys," Sergeant Clark shouted. "Wait..., wait..., wait..., FIRE!"

From the depression on the south face of the ridge, more than six hundred Federal infantrymen loosed a volley of rifle fire down the slope and into the front rank of the advancing Confederate brigades. All along the face of the ridge, white smoke billowed, boiled, and rose into the bright, afternoon sunshine. No sooner had they pulled the trigger than they dropped down and began feverishly reloading their weapons.

"All right, boys," yelled Sergeant Clark, "Give 'em hell. Fire at will."

Patrick McCann popped his head over the top of the natural trench, dragging his rifle up to rest on the dirt. He could see little more than a few yards; the heavy pall of white smoke hung low over the ridge. But he could hear them. He could hear the men in gray, closer now, yelling and screaming their battle cry as they crashed, scrambled, and tumbled up the slope toward him. Aiming, at what he had no idea, just by instinct, down the slope at the howling entity he could not see, he pulled the trigger. The rifle slammed against his shoulder. He dropped, rolled onto his back, and then went through the routine of reloading the weapon. Beside him, to his right, Jesse Dixon was doing the same.

KABAM! They both dropped flat on the ground as a shell exploded in the heart of the depression just a few yards away to Jesse's right, showering them with dirt and rocks, killing a corporal and a private instantly, and wounding several other men.

KABAM, KABAM. Two more shells exploded just a few feet down the slope in front. Again, the troops in the trench were showered with debris, but the cover provided by the natural trench saved the defenders from taking more casualties.

McCann and Dixon, rose to their feet, peered over the top, and aimed their weapons down the slope, but before they could pull the trigger there was an horrendous roar, a rippling, crackling burst of fire from more than a thousand Confederate rifles less than a hundred yards away down the slope. The air was filled with a throbbing whine as a hail of Minnie bullets screeched overhead, slamming into the hillside above and below them, and tearing what little was left of the trees and shrubs into flying splitters that tore clothing and inflicted deep and bloody wounds in faces and hands.

The screaming and yelling on the slopes below had ceased, but the rippling rattle of several thousands of rifles being reloaded less than one hundred yards away could plainly be heard by the Federal soldiers manning the defenses on the upper slopes of the ridge.

"Back at 'em, boys." Sergeant Clark yelled. "Get them rifles over the top and give 'em hell. Them Rebs'll be on us, if we let 'em.

"Get up! You man," he screeched as he jumped down into the trench, his own rifle in hand, and grabbed a man by the collar of his jacket and dragged him up off his knees. "Now get to it, or I'll shoot ya m'self."

Clark turned from the man, then shoved and scrambled and jammed himself into line between Pat McCann and Jesse Dixon and without a second thought raised up and leveled his rifle over the top.

SLAP! A Minnie bullet hit the sergeant in the face, just to the right of his nose, exploding the man's cheek, throwing him backwards and showering Jesse Dixon with blood, flesh and bone; Clark was dead before he hit the ground.

Jesse Dixon dropped his empty weapon, wiped the blood from his face with the sleeve of his jacket, grabbed Clark's left hand and dragged his body out of the way. Then he grabbed his rifle, returned to the top of the trench, cocked the weapon, aimed into the smoke and down the hill, and pulled the trigger... click. The weapon wasn't loaded.

"God damn," he yelled as he dropped below the rim, rolled onto his back, dragged the ramrod out from under the barrel, and went about reloading. It took him less the fifteen seconds and then he was back looking over the top, aiming at the shadowy figures he could now see surging upward through the billowing gun smoke.

"Here they come, Pat," he yelled in his friend's ear.

McCann, white-faced and trembling slightly, nodded his head once, then peered over the rim, aimed his rifle and fired.

Just above them, on the crest of the hill, the crews of the two Federal batteries, twelve guns, were swinging the muzzles of the weapons into line and turning the elevating screws to maximum depression. The guns now in position on a slight downward slope were aimed over the heads of the troops in the line of defense, directly at the advancing Confederate line.

"Get your heads down," the gun captain yelled at the men in the trenches.

"FIRE."

BAM,BAM,BAM,BAM,BAM,BAM! Great clouds of billowing white smoke gushed out from the Federal battery, over the heads of the men in the defenses, filling every clevis and depression on the hillside. For a moment, they just lay there, choking on the acrid, fowl-smelling smoke. Then the smoke lifted, carried upward by the heat of the sun and slight breeze blowing in from the south.

A little less than a thousand yards away to the south, the Confederate gun captains, through the thinning smoke on the hillside, had seen the Federal batteries preparing to fire, and they too made adjustments to range and direction. Three Confederate rifled guns were quickly ranged onto the ridge top.

Then, on the top of the ridge, the federal battery opened fire and, a hundred yards down the slope, the Confederate advance came to a shuddering halt as the front ranks were torn to shreds by a storm of triple-loaded canister, followed by a volley from more than a thousand Federal rifles.

The men in the front lines of the Confederate advance, those that were unharmed by the artillery barrage, dropped to their knees, some rolling around in the debris, trying to find some little cover from the rifle fire from above. Then they were moving back down the slopes, running, slipping and sliding on the loose leaves, dirt and pine needles, faster, then faster, then at the full run. And all to shouting and cheering in the Federal defenses.

But the shouting came to an abrupt end at the howl of incoming shells from the Confederate batteries.

KABAM, KABAM, KABAM, KABAM.... Shell after shell slammed into the trenches and onto the crest of the ridge. Before the Federal gun crews could reload after their initial barrage, dozens of Confederate shells were raining down on and around them. And the Confederate gun crews were quick. They were maintaining a rate of fire of more than two rounds per minute, forcing the Federal gun crews to drop flat on the ground, taking whatever cover they could.

The first incoming Confederate shells hit two of the Federal guns, dismounting them, flipping them over onto their backs like enormous insects. A third gun was put out of action when a 12 pound, solid round shot slammed into the crest of the ridge only yards in front of it. The black ball bounced low under the barrel of the gun and crashed into the carriage, destroying it and sending the gun barrel spinning upward and backwards, taking two of the crew with it, and then smashing into a riderless horse, killing it instantly.

General Thomas immediately ordered the batteries to be moved twenty yards to the rear, out of sight of the Confederate gunners on the plains below. From there, the Federal gun crews commenced firing on them, blind but for directions passed back from the crest of the ridge by a brave, but somewhat foolhardy, young artillery lieutenant. Noisy they were, accurate they were not. The Federal shells and round shot fell in a disorganized pattern in front of, around, and beyond the Confederate batteries, doing little harm, other than keeping the crews ever wary, but slowing them down not even a little.

Now, unable to see the Federal guns on the ridge, they recommenced bombarding the Federal positions on the hillside.

General Longstreet, angry and frustrated, decided that the time had come to finish what he now considered a debacle. Time after time, his Confederate divisions had assaulted the heights of the ridge and the hill, and time after time, they had been repulsed. His casualties now numbered in the thousands; he rode along the line of battle, from one division commander to the next, and ordered each in turn to renew the attack. One last all-out effort would do it, would drive the entrenched enemy off the ridge. It would then be just a matter of mopping up the remains of

Thomas's right flank. One more drive up the slopes and victory would be his.

To the east, he could hear the thunder of guns as General Polk's Left Wing finally reengaged the breastworks at the Kelly farm. It was, Longstreet pondered, now or never.

General Kershaw, now in support of General Preston already on the lower slopes of Snodgrass Hill, ordered his division forward. A quarter mile to the west, Generals Johnson and Hindman also sent their division back into the hell that Horseshoe Ridge had become.

Chapter 85

High on the top of Snodgrass Hill, General Thomas and his assembled officers, including his four division commanders whose troops were holding the line at the Kelly farm, watched as Confederate General Longstreet's all-out assaults on the hill and ridge began to gather momentum. Muttering under his breath, he counted the battle flags of the advancing Confederate divisions, "One, two, three... fourteen, fifteen."

"Fifteen brigades," he said, to no one in particular, although all of his staff was listening. And then he heard it, the sudden explosion of artillery fire to the east, at the Kelly farm.

Thomas pulled his watch from inside his coat, took note of the time, then looked again at the sky, returned the watch to its pocket, swung his horse around so that he was facing his staff.

"It would seem that we have little option but to comply with General Rosecrans' order to withdraw. It's time, gentlemen. Time to go. We cannot hold against such odds." He looked at each officer in turn, and then continued, "We will begin to withdraw immediately and in order. General Reynolds, you have the farthest to go, so you will withdraw your division first. Generals Palmer, Johnson and Baird, you will follow General Reynolds in that order, westward toward McFarland's Gap. General Baird, you will be the last to leave the farm. It will therefore fall to you to hold the enemy until the other divisions are clear. You will then withdraw, leaving skirmishers at the farm to protect your rear."

"General Thomas, I am of the opinion that it's too soon to begin such an early withdrawal," General Richard Johnson said emphatically. "It is still daylight, and will be for some time yet. I fear the enemy will take quick advantage of any weakness in our lines at the farm. Could we not delay, at least until dusk?"

General Palmer nodded in agreement, but Thomas was adamant. "No, General, to wait would be to put the entire army at risk. Look down there," he pointed down the slope of Snodgrass Hill and then continued, "At least fifteen brigades. We have the remnants of but eight. If we wait, we will be overwhelmed. Go to your divisions and begin to withdraw them as I have indicated."

The four generals rode away to the east and Thomas turned in the saddle to address his remaining division commanders. Generals Wood, Brannan, and Steedman had been joined by General Grainger and Colonel Dan McCook, both lately arrived from McAfee's Church; McCook's brigade was now in position on the rise to the northeast of Snodgrass Hill, and ideally located to protect Thomas's left flank once the divisions of Reynolds, Palmer, Johnson, and Baird had withdrawn.

"Colonel McCook," Thomas said, "You will remain in position to the north where your brigade will hold the left flank.

"General Brannan, General Steedman, you must both hold for a little while longer," Thomas continued. All five batteries will support you. As soon as the enemy falls back, you, too, will withdraw toward McFarland Gap. General Grainger, you will stay here and cover the withdrawal of Generals Brannan and Steedman."

Grainger nodded his head in agreement, but looked decidedly ill at ease.

"That is all, gentlemen. We will begin to withdraw on my command. Go to your divisions, and may God be with you all."

Chapter 86

Sunday September 20th, 5p.m. – Confederate Positions South of Horseshoe Ridge

In the confusion, following General Longstreet's order for one last, all-out assault on Horseshoe Ridge and Snodgrass Hill, The Confederate order of battle became fluid and interchanging. The 30th Tennessee Regiment had been reduced to no more than a handful of men with no real place to call their own in the line of battle.

As Longstreet's entire Left Wing moved forward onto the lower slopes of the ridge, Billy Cobb and Jimmy Morrisey had joined the 25th Alabama at the far left of the Confederate advance.

It began slowly. The leading ranks moved forward at the walk; they were more than four hundred yards from the Federal emplacements on the hillside. The walk soon turned into the double-quick, and then into a run as the Confederate ranks hit the lower slopes and charged onward and upward. Cobb and Morrisey, screaming and yelling, were at the extreme left of the 25th Alabama and angling slightly toward the right as they ran; incoming fire was relatively light at this point in the Confederate line. To Cobb and Morrisey's left, the line of trees and the heavy undergrowth beyond were intact, almost undamaged; to their right, more than sixteen thousand men in gray were streaming up onto the lower slopes of the ridge and the hill.

The noise grew, the Federal fire intensified, and men in the Confederate ranks began pitching and falling. The two privates charged onward up the slope, firing their weapons as they went, stopping every now and then to reload. Ahead, heavy white smoke hung over the hillside like a soft white blanket, obscuring all before them. They reached the first of the natural depressions, the Federal first line of defense. It was empty, the defenders were gone; the fire from above continued unabated.

Suddenly, Jimmy staggered, his headlong run faltered, and he pitched forward, hard, onto his face into the soggy mush of rotting wood and leaves, his rifle went spinning forward onto the ground in front of him. Billy stooped, grabbed his arm, and, thinking his friend had tripped, screamed in his ear for him to get up and get moving. But Jimmy Morrisey didn't move.

"Oh, Christ, NO!" Cobb dropped his own rifle, fell to his knees, and rolled Jimmy over onto his back. His eyes were open and he was breathing hard. There was a dazed look in his eyes and a slight smile on his face.

"Told you, didn't I?" He looked up into Billy Cobb's eyes, coughed, coughed again, and a thin trickle of blood appeared at the corner of his mouth.

Billy looked for the wound and, horrified, found it just above Jimmy's belt: a small hole, no bigger than a man's thumb, that oozed blood and was quickly soaking his clothing. As soon as he saw it, he knew it was all over for his friend. Never had he seen a man gut-shot and live to tell of it.

"Bill," Jimmy gasped, and with a great effort reached inside his jacket and pulled out his watch. "It's time," he whispered without looking at it. "You... take... it.

Billy shook his head but, with tears in his eyes, he took the watch from his friend. And he hugged Jimmy's head close to his chest, rocking him and moaning quietly as the last moments of his life ebbed slowly away. Jimmy never said another word. Within minutes of taking the Minnie bullet, he was dead, and Billy Cobb's life had changed forever.

For a long moment, he knelt beside his lifelong friend, cradling his head. Then he lowered him gently to the ground, put the watch into his pants pocket, took off his pack, unrolled his blanket, and covered the body. Then he stood, looked down at all that had been Jimmy Morrisey, and something deep inside him seemed to snap He spun on his heel, screamed out loud, grabbed up his rifle, and started through the trees at a dead run, yelling at the top of his voice.

Chapter 87

Sunday September 20th, 5p.m. – Federal Positions on Horseshoe Ridge

General Thomas looked westward at the setting sun. He shook his head. It was over; time to give the final orders to withdraw. He called for his chief of staff and dictated the order to retreat westward through McFarland's Gap, then sent riders to each of his field commanders to the east, and on the hill and ridge. Regiment by regiment, slowly, what was left of Thomas's small army began to move out.

Jesse Dixon and Pat McCann were at the western end of a natural depression on the southern slope of Horseshoe Ridge when they heard the distant call just to the north of the ridge for the regiment to move out, and were preparing to climb back up the slope to rejoin it.

"Let's go, Jesse," Pat yelled. "And together they turned, and looked up the hill behind them; it was an inferno; Confederate shells were raining down on the upper slopes of the ridge. There was nowhere to go.

Pat looked desperately around, first to the left and then to the right. "This way," he shouted and, heads down; they ran westward along the bottom of the defile they had so lately been defending, and into the trees. Once again they were on their own, separated from the main body of the 10th Indiana by a forest fire that spread westward almost as quickly as they did.

They came to a clearing. They were now beyond the flames, but close to the enemy lines. "Keep quiet, and keep your head down," Jesse said, barely loud enough to be heard. "And go slow."

And slowly they went, through the trees and scrub until they came to a small clearing. Jesse raised his arm, a silent signal for Pat to stop and stay still. Jesse looked around: nothing.

"Come on, this way." Together, they continued on, up the slope, just inside the line of trees, skirting the northern edge of the clearing, taking advantage of what cover was available among the now thinning trees and shrubs. They stopped again, listening.

"Which way, Jess?"

"Dunno. Better keep going this way, I think," Dixon said, turning again toward the west. There," he shouted, pointing up the slope. "Up there; there they are." Just visible through the low-lying scrub, the tail end of a line of blue-clad soldiers was making its way slowly up and over the crest of the ridge.

It was at that moment that a 12 pound round shot fired from almost half a mile, away came crashing through the treetops and severed a huge limb of an oak tree that towered above them, tearing it away from the tree

311

close to the trunk, and it fell, landing right on top of Jesse. He fell to the ground as if he'd been pole-axed, unconscious and imprisoned by the foliage, pinned down by a dozen or more branches.

McCann turned and shouted to the retreating Federal soldiers for help, but the noise of battle was too loud and he watched as the last blue-clad soldier scrambled over the top of the ridge and out of sight.

McCann dropped his rifle and began tearing at the foliage, trying to free his friend.

Suddenly, they heard a man screaming at the top of his lungs and crashing through the trees toward them. Patrick reared back against the trunk of the oak tree and looked wildly around. He spotted his rifle on the ground just a few feet away. He ran to it, stooped and picked it up and, without thinking, raised it, took a firm stance and waited.

He didn't have to wait long before Billy Cobb came crashing out of the woods and into the clearing. Cobb immediately spotted the Yankee soldier, raised his rifle, and snapped off a shot, screaming as he did so. The shot was wild, and missed McCann by almost a foot, but Cobb didn't falter for a second. On he came, running across the clearing, screaming, heading for McCann with his bayonet thrust forward at the ready.

McCann took careful aim at the charging Confederate soldier and prepared to fire. He took a deep breath and pulled the trigger... click; the rifle wasn't loaded, and still Billy Cobb charged on toward the now petrified Patrick McCann.

As the gap between the two men closed, so Cobb could see his enemy through a haze of red mist, and then he was on him. He smashed McCann's weapon to one side with the butt of his rifle sending it spinning out of his hands, took a step back, leveled his bayonet, and started forward again, and then he stopped, the point of the bayonet touching McCann's chest.

Billy Cobb blinked, and McCann's face became less blurred, more defined. And, slowly, the great rage within Billy's chest and brain began to subside, and he stood, staring into the youngster's terrified face.

The image of McCann's face wavered and a new one took its place. For a moment, Billy Cobb was back at Stones River, and the face he saw before him was that of another youngster. He shook his head, the image cleared, and he saw again the terrified face of an unarmed boy, and still Billy almost thrust the weapon home. But he didn't. Instead, he lowered the point of the bayonet and said, "It's all right, son. I ain't never goin' to kill again." And then he turned, and walked slowly back the way he'd came, leaving a bewildered Pat McCann shivering against the tree trunk.

Billy Cobb walked on, southward through the devastated woodlands until he finally emerged onto the fields so expensively won by Longstreet's charge. The fields for more than a mile in every direction were littered with bodies, both blue and gray.

He looked westward. The last rays of what must have been a beautiful sunset silhouetted the Widow Glen's cabin. She was on the porch. He waved at her; she waved back. He reached into his pocket, withdrew the ornate silver pocket watch, flipped it open, and checked the time. The he closed it, looked again at the Widow Glenn, and returned the watch to his pocket and smiled. For the first time in three years, he was at peace.

I'll be home in time for Christmas," he thought, and continued on his way.

Pat McCann looked around, gathered himself together, and ran to the heap of branches under which Jesse was trapped, and he couldn't even see him. Desperately, he grabbed one of the limbs and began to pull, but it was too big, heavier than he could manage by himself.

"Hold on, Jesse," He yelled. "I'm going for help." Nothing, not a sound came from beneath the great tree branch. To his right, higher up the slope, he could hear movement through the undergrowth. Rebel or friend? He had no idea. He ran a few yards up the slope, through the undergrowth and into a company of Federal infantry, moving west, up and away from the ridge.

"Hey, guys," he shouted. "We have a man trapped under a tree. I can't move it. I need some help."

At the head of the group a sergeant, grizzled, unkempt, his uniform jacket torn in several places, his pants stained and dirty, stopped, turned, looked at him and said, "Where is he, son?"

"About twenty yards down that way," McCann pointed the way.

"Griff, Chester, Hart, Sampson, come with me."

Together, McCann and the five soldiers scrambled down the hill and into the small clearing where Jesse, well hidden under the tree branch, was just coming to.

"Jesse, can you hear me?"

He was answered by a low groan, then: "I hear you. I can't move."

"Hold on, Jess."

Together the six men gathered around the huge branch and pulled it up and away, leaving Jesse flat on his face, bruised and shaken, but otherwise unhurt.

What unit are you?" The sergeant asked.

"Tenth Indiana...."

At that moment, less than a hundred yards away, down the slope to the south, they heard a great noise: cracking and rustling undergrowth, the rattling of steel on steel, and the bone chilling Rebel yell.

"We gotta go, and damn quick," the sergeant said. "Can you walk?

"I think so," Jesse nodded, and struggled to his feet.

"This way, and quick about it. The rest of the regiment is already away, and I do not want to spend the rest of this war in a Confederate prison."

Together the seven men ran back up the ridge, through the brush, blackthorn, and poison oak and out into the last beams of the setting sun. Ahead of them stretched the open fields of the Snodgrass farm and, to the west, Missionary Ridge, McFarland's Gap and Rossville.

For as far as they could see, long lines, thousands of retreating Federal soldiers were heading quickly away from the battlefield.

The seven men joined the line and began the long walk to Rossville and Chattanooga. It was over, at least for now.

"We made it," Jesse said, looking sideways at his friend.

Pat McCann nodded his head, looked at Jesse, and then said, "Until the next time, Jesse. Until the next time."

Back on the slopes of Horseshoe Ridge, General Brannan was struggling to hold his position against overwhelming odds. At five-thirty, as the sun was going down, Brannan was joined by elements of Harker and Hazen's brigades. He would hold the ridge against a series of concerted Confederate attacks for more than two and a half hours; Brannan and his sadly depleted division would not leave the ridge until eight-thirty, when quietly, like ghosts in the night, they melted away into the darkness.

General Thomas, General Wood and more than a dozen Federal staff officers, watched from the crest of Snodgrass Hill as the first of Reynolds' brigades at the Kelly farm began to withdraw northward along the Lafayette Road, then west toward McFarland's Gap. By six-thirty, all four divisions were on the road; by seven thirty, Thomas himself had left the crest of Snodgrass Hill, leaving Generals Grainger, Steedman, and Brannan to hold the enemy in check and protect the rear of the withdrawing army.

At seven o'clock, in the gathering darkness, General Steedman ordered his division off the ridge and onto the road to McFarland's Gap; he was quickly followed by Grainger and McCook, leaving only General Brannan to face the Confederate onslaught.

But the gathering darkness was kind to them; the terrain, the debris - fallen trees, thick undergrowth and an ever-increasing inability to see the way ahead, brought the Confederate attacks to a halt. Under cover of darkness, at eight-thirty, General Brannan quietly withdrew what was left of his shattered division. By nine o'clock, with the exception of three of Grainger's regiments, which had been in a forward position on the ridge and were captured, not a single blue-clad soldier was left on the field. The battle of Chickamauga was over, a glorious Confederate victory. But was it?

Author's Note:

The battle of Chickamauga was, indeed, a Confederate victory, but a costly one. Casualties on both sides totaled more than 37,100.

General Bragg's Army of Tennessee's losses included 2,673 killed, 16,274 wounded, and 2,003 missing. General Longstreet alone lost more than 8,600 of the almost 23,000 men he took onto the battlefield, most of them on the slopes of Snodgrass Hill and Horseshoe Ridge.

General Rosecrans' Army of the Cumberland suffered almost 16,200 casualties; Rosecrans himself would never recover from the ignominy of his defeat. On October 19, 1863, he was removed from command of the army and replaced by General Thomas.

This is a novel and, as such, I have taken some creative license, both with characters and dialog. I have tried my best to stick to the historical facts, and the timeline.

Almost all of the officers herein, and the Widow Glenn, actually lived through the Battle of Chickamauga. Most of their words are the figment of my imagination.

As to the conflict between the Confederate generals, it is well known that General Bragg was an irascible martinet, short tempered and with little patience for those he considered fools. For more than a year before the battle of Chickamauga, Generals Polk and Breckinridge had been trying to have him removed from command of the Army of Tennessee, and Bragg was well aware of it. It is also well known that General Polk had no respect for Bragg, and disagreed with most of his tactics and strategies. It is also well known that Polk was less than conscientious in carrying out Bragg's specific orders and was indeed found reading a newspaper and eating breakfast some two hours after the hour when the assaults of the 20th were to begin.

The fictional characters include Billy Cobb, Jimmy Morrisey, Pat McCann, Jesse Dixon, Blake Wilder, Doctors Marshall, Marr and Roark, and Sarah Bradley and the members of her family and household. Any resemblance to actual people, living or dead, is entirely coincidental.

Hazelwood? Another figment of my imagination; It never existed.

So, I thank you for purchasing the book. I hope you enjoyed reading is as much as I did writing it. If so, you will also enjoy my other novel of the Civil War, The Mule Soldiers. You can get your copy here at Amazon: http://www.amazon.com/dp/B00R0AIA1O

If you have questions, or would like make a comment, you can email me at blair@blairhoward.com.

Made in the USA
Middletown, DE
26 March 2018